GUIDE TO THE CAMARILLA™

ROSES WATERED WITH BLOOD

By Richard E. Dansky, with Geoffrey C. Grabowski, Kenneth Hite, Clayton Oliver and Cynthia Summers

CREDITS

Written by: Richard E. Dansky, Geoffrey C. Grabowski, Kenneth Hite, Clayton Oliver and Cynthia Summers

Additional Writing by: James Kiley

Additional Assistance: Justin Achilli, Robert Barrett, Bruce Baugh (statistics), David Bolack, Bryant Durrell, Greg Fountain, Jess Heining, Chris Nasipak, and Alexander Williams

Development by: Richard E. Dansky

Editing by: Cynthia Summers

Art Direction by: Larry Snelly and Richard Thomas

Art by: Gary Amaro, Andy Bennett, Matt Clark, Richard Clark, Guy Davis, Jason Felix, Daren Frydendall, Mike Gaydos, Pia Guerra, Mark Jackson, Vince Locke, Greg Loudon, William O'Connor, Adam Rex, Andrew Ritchie, Steve Sadowski, Alex Shiekman, and Christopher Shy

Cover Art: Bill Sienkiewicz

Front and Back Cover Design: Pauline Benney

Endpapers: Phill Hale

Layout and typesetting by: Pauline Benney

SPECIAL THANKS TO:

Varney the Vampire, Dracula, "The Transfer," *The Case of Charles Dexter Ward, Vampire Junction, Carrion Comfort, Lost Souls, Fevre Dream, Those Who Hunt the Night* and all of the other wonderful stories that have continually re-invented the vampire for us.

735 PARK NORTH BLVD.
SUITE 128
CLARKSTON, GA 30021
USA

This book uses the supernatural for settings, characters and themes. All mystical and supernatural elements are fiction and intended for entertainment purposes only. Reader discretion is advised.

Check out White Wolf online at
http://www.white-wolf.com; alt.games.whitewolf and rec.games.frp.storyteller

PRINTED IN **CANADA**

Guide to the Camarilla

Contents

ROULETTE:
A CAUTIONARY TALE

It had been about two months since the last Sabbat scouting excursion, which meant that we were due for another one. Every so often, one of the bishops hiding in the SoCal sandbox decides the time is right to send another couple of shovelheads into town on some sort of bad Hunter S. Thompson-style info-gathering jaunt, and it's my job to watch out for that sort of thing. Truth be told, it's not so hard to watch out for. This town is neck-deep in anarchs who think they're hardcases but aren't; a real Sabbat badass sticks out like a sore thumb.

So that's my job. His Majesty (Prince Benedic, not that low-rent Giovanni Rothstein who claims to run the town out of Bally's) tells me to watch for Sabbat infiltrators, which I do. When one (or two, or three — they like to travel in groups, I've found) members of the other side show up, I make my report to the prince, and we bang heads and decide what to do. The decision varies from case to case, but usually we have to be delicate about squashing the bastards as soon as they show their faces. I mean, Sabbat spies aren't necessarily stupid; they go to ground with the best of them. That means that if Tzammy Tzimisce tzchows, err, shows up he's going to do it with a safety pin fleshcrafted through his nose so he can claim to be an anarch, not Sabbat. So if I go out there with my squad and take down the impostor, well, let's just say that any real anarchs he'd managed to fool would be up in arms about "being oppressed by the man." At that point the neonates would start throwing things and blowing the Masquerade to hell sideways, and that would mean more work for me and mine.

His Majesty, in case you were wondering, does not like to pay overtime.

No, it makes a lot more sense to play along, and then either stake the spy *en route* to his "private audience" with the prince, or feed the mark false information about our defenses, numbers, disposition and so on. Send back three different

scouting parties with three different reports, and you can almost hear them tearing into each another from here once someone takes the time to compare notes. It's a joy to ponder.

Vegas is a very volatile town, you see. This burg survives on tourism, which means that if tourists start going missing, the visiting traffic goes down and the place goes to hell. But if we control the take, make sure that it's just the lonely and unloved who get taken, well, then, this place is a paradise for our kind. You think the casinos have all-night buffets, you should see what the streets look like. That's why people like me — and I use the term "people" loosely — have to make sure that all of the rules and regulations get followed. If anyone gets greedy, or takes too much, or does anything stupid in public, the entire game could go in the crapper. I like this place, and so does His Majesty, entirely too much to allow that to happen.

The red phone rings. It only rings when there's something about to go down. I sigh as the damn thing keeps jangling, then walk across the room to pick it up. The prince gives me a nice suite in the Mirage as part of my compensation package (it's a running joke that one of these years we're all going to get dental), and I like that just fine. I never could have afforded a place like this when I was alive, and it's nice that Benedic appreciates what I do enough to give me this as a token of his esteem.

I place the phone to my ear and made a noncommittal noise. Duke, the ghoul who works hotel security, answers, "Mr. Montrose?" As if it would be anyone else on my direct connect phone. Good help has *never* been easy to find.

"Yes? I take it we've got visitors?"

"Oh, we've got a live one indeed, sir." A live one. That was Duke's idea of a joke. He'd been using it every time he spotted a Kindred for the past 15 years, and he hadn't quite warmed to the notion that none of the rest of Prince

Benedic's employees found the gag particularly amusing. Still, he's a good man in a fight, and loyal. Plus, he has a good nose for sniffing out infiltrators. Useful talent, that.

"Just one?"

"Two, actually. A man and a woman. He's currently giving the desk help something of a hard time, claiming his name is Tom Cruise. He's too tall by half for the impersonation to take, but it's one of the more clever attempts I've seen in a while."

"Get his room assignment and make sure no one goes in or out once he and his friend settle in. Have one of the specials handle the valet parking on their car, and check the trunk for ordnance. Also run the floorboards to see if they're trying to smuggle anything in, and have your friend at LVPD run the plates to see if the car is hot."

Duke's annoyance is palpable as he responds, "They self-parked, Mr. Montrose. It was part of what tipped me off to their presence. Otherwise, I'll perform the usual functions, as per our SOP. Do you have any other instructions?"

I find myself frowning. Something about this caper feels wrong. "Nothing else. Just be extra careful on this one, OK? I've got a feeling."

"You always have a feeling, Mr. Montrose," Duke says as he hangs up. He's right, though. I always have the same bad feeling in what used to be my gut, and I always give him the same orders once a suspicious character checks in or otherwise appears on the scene. That's one of the strengths of the team, though: routine. Tradition. The knowledge that we're going to do it right this time, because we've done it right a hundred times before.

An hour later, Duke is sitting in the almost-but-not-quite overstuffed beige chair in the corner of my suite, nursing a hideous concoction he calls a Rusty Nail. He claims that the taste of one of those monsters allows him to look forward to the tang of the vitae he receives every month from Prince Benedic, but I think he just has lousy taste.

"Where shall I begin, Mr. Montrose?" he says, as I plant myself in the chair opposite his.

"Start with the basics. As always."

Good old long-suffering Duke. Completely predictable. "The car was our first area of inquiry. It is, much to my surprise, completely legitimate. There's not much else spectacular about it, save that it can probably get up near 200 mph in a pinch, guzzles gas dreadfully and has the sort of solid steel chassis that can serve to knock down telephone poles."

I let out a low whistle. "Impressive. I take it the trunk had equipment for dayproofing?"

Duke coughed embarrassedly. "Delgado didn't get a good enough look to see, Mr. Montrose."

"He didn't? Well, why the hell not?" I fling a coaster — why the hell does housekeeping insist on putting coasters in my room? — in disgust.

"Because of the Kindred in the way, Mr. Montrose."

"The *what?*"

"Apparently there was a recently Embraced Cainite, an African-American youth in his early teens, locked in there.

Delgado opened the trunk, and the unregistered passenger started thrashing about. He shut the trunk and reported to me."

"Where is he now?"

"He's at home. I rotated him off shift, so our visitors don't see his face, match it with any description the childe in the trunk might give, and put two and two together."

"Ah. I'll want to talk to him. Have him give me a call here. How about our happy couple?"

Duke shuffled his papers and flipped to another page in his notes. "They're in Room 1413, and we're reasonably certain they've done some crude lightproofing. By the sounds at the door, they're sleeping in the bathroom, most likely in the tub. The arrangement is nothing we haven't seen before, should we wish to extract our visitors quietly. They haven't even made contact with any local Kindred, so it's not as if they'd be missed."

"Hmm. Let me think. Do we have descriptions on them?"

Without a word, Duke hands me an envelope containing enhanced images of the pair from the lobby's security cameras. Two are close-ups, while the third is a wide-angle pan. "All right, I see the woman's quite attractive, and that cowboy hat looks like it's welded on. She probably dug herself out of the ground with it. The other one — I don't see anything interesting here. What's the deal with the third picture? I can barely see their faces!"

"If you please, Mr. Montrose." Duke takes the picture in question back, grinning that smug little grin that means he thinks he's about to show me up. "If you will observe, this picture was taken from camera four, which takes a long sweep of the lobby and silhouettes those who are checking in—"

"—against the mirrors on those columns."

"Exactly, Mr. Montrose." Duke is nodding, and he still has that smirk on his face. "I believe I suggested we install camera four for precisely that purpose, so that we might see if any of our guests might be—"

"Lasombra. They actually sent in a Lasombra this time. *Beautiful.*"

Duke loses the smirk and looks slightly alarmed as I chortle. "Mr. Montrose, shouldn't we inform Prince Benedic? If there's a Lasombra in the city—"

I cut him off again. It's getting to be a habit. "I will inform the prince in due time. In the meanwhile, I think we're going to run a disinformation job on this guy. I want you to get me, let's see, how about Cantor, and get the team in place, and meet me back here in an hour." I'm up out of the chair now, pacing excitedly. This could be a good break. Duke is rising as well, heading for the door as he mumbles some impeccably polite and semantically empty parting.

Once Duke is gone, I head for the other phone, the one that speed-dials Benedic's private line. We know better than to take our conversations onto cell phones — one particularly sensitive conversation got picked up by a kid who had stumbled across Benedic's frequency with some sort of pirating device, and I had to arrange a very tricky accident on short notice to hide the evidence. These nights, it's all as close to solid state as we can make it.

That doesn't mean that I don't eavesdrop on other Kindred's cell phones. I'm just not dumb enough to use the things myself.

Benedic's phone rings precisely thrice before the prince picks up. "Yes?" His greetings always sound tentative, like he's afraid the receiver's going to bite his ear. Then again, considering how old Benedic is, I'm not surprised he still has vague suspicions about technology.

"Your Majesty? It's Montrose. We have two infiltrators at the Mirage, with a third party hidden in the trunk of their car. One of our two guests is a Lasombra, while his friend is anyone's guess. I'd say Toreador *antitribu* by her looks, but it's only a gut feeling."

"Interesting," Benedic rumbles, and falls silent for a long moment. "What are your plans?"

I launch into my spiel. This plan might take some selling, as it's going to cost Benedic a valuable asset. "Well, the fact that one member of the team's a Keeper changes things. If he disappears, it sets whoever's holding his leash on alert. I'd rather put on a good show for him and send him back with a head full of misinformation than eliminate him. However, this deal's going to require a lot of selling for him to believe it. We had better be prepared to go all the way on this one, or he's going to think that something's up."

Benedic flips through something on the other end of the line, moves some papers and produces some other noises that I can't even begin to identify. "I'm interested in hearing what sort of lies you want to pass off to our visitor, and what you mean by 'all the way.' You worry me when you say such things, Montrose. I am usually the one who foots the bill for your excesses."

"You say that every time, but have I failed you yet?" It's an old, old argument. Benedic loves the idea that I keep his city safe, but wishes I could do it for a bit less. When the job's this important, though, I prefer not to skimp on the details.

I can hear the prince chuckling on the other end. "Not yet, and I'm hoping you don't start now. What will this one cost me?"

I take an unnecessary, but soothing deep breath. "How do you feel about Duke?"

❖   ❖   ❖   ❖   ❖   ❖   ❖

An hour later, I'm in the sub-basement of the Mirage, the hole where they keep the janitorial supplies, the cleaning chemicals and the bodies. Standing with me is a low-level Ventrue flunky by the name of Alexander Cantor, who's dressed in a suit that's entirely inappropriate for this puddled mess. He keeps on stepping back and forth, in hopes of keeping the gunk off his shoes. It's not working.

I've got a headset on, and it's linked to the mike that Duke is wearing. "I'm inside the room and ready to go, Mr. Montrose. Wish me luck," I hear him breathe into his wire, and then the rat-tat-tat of his knuckles on door. "Mr. Cruise? Mr. Cruise?"

Over the wire, I can hear the distant fumbling, and a muted voice complaining. "I'm afraid the matter is of considerable urgency, Mr., err, Cruise." More mumbling, and something about a girl. "No, Mr. Cruise, there's no girl out here."

Duke is playing his part *just* right. The tone of his voice indicates that he knows the "girl" story is bullshit and that he doesn't care if his target knows that he does. Then there's the sound of the door cracking open, and the curtain comes up on Duke's final performance.

"We have rules in this town, Mr. Cruise— I beg your pardon?" There's more indecipherable attitude that comes over the line, and Cantor does this odd little contortion to get as close to the mike as possible without touching me. Meanwhile, Duke isn't breaking stride. "…appears that you care little for the rules in our town, and that your presence is not one of benefice to us." Now there's some shuffling, and what sounds like someone walking off. "…sure you're familiar with our Traditions, and that you have no intention of flouting them. My employer wishes to speak to you, and I am to escort you to his offices." There's nothing for a second, then a wisecrack and assent. They're coming.

The elevator grinds to a halt at the far end of the storeroom. The doors squeak as Duke and Cruise, or whatever his name is, walk out. "Cruise" is tall and thin and good-looking, and he's flicking his eyes from side to side looking for an ambush. He doesn't seem to be surprised, though, that his meeting with "authority" is happening in a crudhole sub-basement, down among the bottles of floor wax and crates of toilet cakes. I swear, that's one of the biggest weaknesses these Sabbat guys have. They think that since their big bosses like to hang out in shitholes, ours do as well. Benedic wouldn't be caught down here if there were a six-pack of Caine's blood sitting in the middle of the floor. Still, their delusions serve my purposes. A meeting that would seem like a transparent scam to any normal vampire makes perfect sense to a shovelhead.

Duke and the Lasombra are talking, saying lots of nothing. I'm suddenly anxious to get this over with, and so I nudge Cantor. He looks at me with disgust for a second because I dared to touch him, then he remembers his lines. "Duke, this isn't Tom Cruise," he says, with precisely zero enthusiasm. Next time I'll get myself a Toreador.

The ghoul and the vampire stop, right on the mark I'd taped for Duke on the floor. Perfect. "We've already been through this," Cruise says petulantly. "Your clerk spelled my name wrong." He puts his hands on his hips and looks around. It's showtime.

I drop the Obfuscate, and mentally give the guy points for not flinching when he sees me. Even the other Nosferatu think I'm unattractive, but he took it in stride. Beside me, Cantor looks his usual impeccable self, radiating unconcern as he picks some imaginary lint from his Versace. Cantor may be a no-talent yutz, but he at least *looks* the part of a player. "Welcome to Vegas," I say, "I am Montrose, and this is my associate, Alexander Cantor. Perhaps you'd care to inform us as to your business here?"

The Keeper sizes us up, decides he might be able to take us both. I can see it in his aura that he's about to do something stupid. "Not business. Pleasure. I'm in from California to do a bit of gambling."

"And the Kindred in the trunk?" I raised what was left of an eyebrow. His move.

"We were driving in shifts." His tone is defensive. Beside me, Cantor shifts ever so slightly, and I know without looking that he's pumping up his blood for a fight. "He had the night before."

I laugh, a signal to Cantor to back down. What's going to happen has to happen, and heroics will just screw things up. "Quite an odd set of circumstances, don't you think, Adam Stiers from the Anarch Free State?" I emphasize each capital letter to make it seem like I'm proud of myself for digging up those choice tidbits. "Perhaps an object lesson in how Prince Benedic keeps the rabble in line would do you some good." That's Duke's cue, and he slams a meaty hand down on Stiers' shoulder.

I grab Cantor's hand and pull him back into a shadow, where I can hide us again. Duke's eyes get wide as he sees us vanish — that wasn't part of his briefing. Stiers turns and nearly rips the ghoul's arm off, then slams him against a rack of paper towels. Duke staggers, then starts screaming as the Keeper does something to the darkness in the room that makes shadow spill out of Duke's mouth and damn near tear him in half. Beside me, I can feel Cantor tensing up like he's going to jump into the fight, and I have to clamp my hand on his wrist to keep him from going off half-cocked.

Duke is down now, the Keeper tearing at his wrists and fumbling in his pockets for the elevator key. Next to me, Cantor is visibly shaking as he restrains himself from going after... what? The blood? The Lasombra? I don't want to know. There's a squelching sound — blood on boot soles — as the vampire heads for the elevator, then I hear the familiar grinding sound of the doors and we're alone.

Duke's almost gone when Cantor and I get to him. He's lost a lot of blood. That's actually a plus, as it will make what comes next easier. I kneel down next to him and lift his head up with my left hand. "Don't worry, Duke. It's going to be OK. I won't let you down. Everything's going to be OK." He looks at me, eyes dulled with pain, uncomprehending. I just hold his head up and mutter soothing nonsense as the blood runs out of him. Beside me, Cantor has his straight razor out and rolls up his cuff so he doesn't get blood on his shirt sleeves when it's finally time to bring Duke across. Everything's going to plan. Everything's going to be all right for Duke. Everything's going to be just fine.

❖   ❖   ❖   ❖   ❖   ❖   ❖

Duke is sitting in his same old chair, riffling the same old papers. It took him a night to get back on his feet after Cantor Embraced him, but considering what he'd been through, it's a remarkably fast recovery. He's looking a trifle pale, even for a Ventrue, but otherwise it's the same old Duke, right down to the same ill-fitting blue suit. He's discussing the fallout from our little misadventure. "We've discovered one body in the garage, and one dead cashier at the parking lot exit."

"Taken care of?"

"Of course. The cashier's family received the normal package, plus some extra flowers. There was also one tourist badly hurt when Stiers apparently clipped him with a tire iron from a moving car, but other than that, I was the only fatality." An untouched Rusty Nail sits in front of Duke on the table, a symbol of the way things were. It's important to him to hang onto that symbol, I think, so I made sure to pour it for him when he walked in. The little things count.

"And is that it?"

"Apart from the traffic violations, yes, Mr. Montrose. We've painted the incident as...," he riffles the papers again until he finds what he wants, "some sort of gang incident with riff-raff from Los Angeles. Fortunately the robbery across town a few months ago makes our story seem credible."

I nod. "Good. Did we get a read on Stiers' lady friend?"

"Yes. She was responsible for the corpse in the garage. Apparently she has some small skill with your favorite parlor trick, as DiFelice says he saw her simply appear next to the car while I was taking Stiers to meet you. Other than that, she did not evince any spectacular abilities. She did, however, seem to have a rather short temper, to the point of near-psychosis. The victim was a passerby headed for his own car, and she simply... snapped when he walked by. DiFelice says it seemed that she was tired of waiting."

"And the kid in the trunk?"

"I believe he is still there."

I wave the detail away as unimportant. "Fine, fine, whatever. So Stiers and his lady friend get away, convinced that we're a bunch of idiots and pushovers, and that Cantor actually has some power in this town. I mean, if we were tough, we *never* would have let him kill one of our prize ghouls, right?" Duke flinches, but it's part of the hardening process. Once you're dead, you can't allow yourself to shudder at the fact. "In the meantime we learned the caliber of scout they're sending in — and that maneuver he pulled with the shadows tells me that Stiers is some fairly heavy artillery. If the other side is using guys who are that powerful for scouting missions, then an offensive is coming. A major one. But if we can keep feeding them false information about how weak we are — by, say, running away the second the big bad Lasombra takes a swing at a ghoul — we can make them overconfident and have them hit too early. Before they're really ready."

Duke nods, comprehending. He still doesn't like what happened to him, not that I blame him one little bit, but he's a pragmatist. He understands the necessity. Meanwhile it's up to Cantor to get him up to speed on his Disciplines before the assault comes, while I have to train his replacement and maybe pick a few reinforcements out of the crowd.

Across from me, Duke flips to a clean page and starts sketching out plans for improving the defenses on the parking garage. That's the way things should be. Loyal service and a promotion, once you earn it. Now it's up to us to make sure things stay that way. Even if we can goad the Sabbat into striking too early, it's still going to be a bloodbath, and I'm going to have to be going triple-shift to keep the Masquerade in one piece. There are going to be bodies and bullets, blood and death *everywhere*. It's going to be a royal bitch to clean up.

Still, it beats working.

INTRODUCTION

Give way - thy God loves blood! - then look to it: -Give
way ere he hath more!
— Lord Byron, *Cain: A Mystery*

Welcome to the end of history.

The edge of the millennium is here (though even among Vampires the question of *when* precisely the millennium is due sparks much debate), and in the face of the 21st century, the Camarilla is undergoing drastic and fundamental changes. For five centuries, it has maintained the Masquerade, provided for balance between the mortal and immortal worlds, and most of all striven to uphold the status quo. For more than five centuries, it has been successful. More than that, since the mid-1400s, the Camarilla has been essentially synonymous with vampiric society.

But now, all of that is changing. The Camarilla is beset by foes, within and without. The Sabbat devours the cities of America's eastern coast, while Cathayans probe for weaknesses in the west. In Europe, the old struggles flare into new prominence, while everywhere the signs foretold in the *Book of Nod* are apparent to those who are looking for them. Even more shocking, one of the seven clans of the Camarilla has left the fold. In the hour of the Camarilla's greatest need, one of its pillars has proven untrustworthy.

It is under such dire circumstances that you are welcomed to **The Guide to the Camarilla**, the complete sourcebook for all things relating to this most august gathering of vampires. Inside this book is everything you might have wished to know about the Camarilla, the vampires who make up its ranks, the way in which the organization functions, the powers its members and officers possess, and perhaps even a few of the secrets the group's elders have been hiding.

WHAT IS THE CAMARILLA?

To understand what the Camarilla is, it is first necessary to understand, on a deep and abiding level, what it is not. Specifically, the Camarilla is most definitely *not* the group that contains the vampiric "good guys." There is nothing intrinsically good, true or nice about the Camarilla or the vampires who comprise it. The Camarilla does not exist to protect humanity from vampiric depredation; rather, its function is to ensure the safest and most profitable existence possible for its members. The care the Camarilla takes not to make too overt a presence is precisely the same effort the wolf makes to disguise his presence among the sheep.

What the Camarilla is, then, is a sect by the vampires, of the vampires and for the vampires. It exists to protect its members from the surging seas of humanity, who by dint of sheer numbers could wipe most of the Kindred off the face of the earth. The Camarilla's single greatest creation, the Masquerade, exists for precisely this purpose. A veil of misdirection and falsehood, the Masquerade hides the very fact of Kindred existence from the mortal world. What humanity can't see, it can't kill, and thus the Kindred are safe. The fact that the necessity of preserving the Masquerade cuts down somewhat on the casualties Camarilla vampires inflict on the mortal population is merely a by-product of the need to preserve the illusion.

What the Camarilla is really about, though, is the status quo, and the preservation thereof. The elder vampires who dictate the Camarilla's policy *like* having power. They *like* having control over hundreds and thousands of younger Kindred. They *like* having wave after wave of subordinates there to protect them. And, most important of all, they want to keep things exactly the way they like them. The Camarilla works, at least for the vampires who make the policy decisions, and thus they direct the sect's policies toward preservation rather than improvement. *Could* the Camarilla work better? Possibly, but then it wouldn't serve the interests of those who control it nearly as well.

Even those vampires lower down in the power structure — primogen and elders, for example — have a vested interest in keeping things as they are. Relics of ages long past, these Kindred have no place in the modern world. By themselves, they'd soon perish. The Camarilla provides them with a buffer against the harsh winds of change, protecting them from an era that has no use for fencers or nobles from the court of the Sun King, but every use for coders and phone phreaks. By keeping the Camarilla the quasi-feudal organization that it is, these Kindred make a comfort zone for themselves. By wrapping the Camarilla up in Traditions and offices, they keep the sect on a level they can operate on. Whether this deliberate retardation of the sect's evolution is ultimately harmful, none can say, but there are any number of younger Kindred who are less than pleased with the current state of affairs.

As for the youngest of these immortals, what does the Camarilla offer them? In a word, security: The sect is protection (stifling though it may be) while the new vampire comes into his powers and learns the customs of his new existence. It is a group of allies against the mortal world and other vampires, a shelter against the new and terrible perils of unlife. While that security can quickly grow oppressive, in the beginning it is worth a great deal to a newly Embraced Kindred, who would otherwise be completely and utterly alone.

The Basics

In theory, the Camarilla is the universal organization of vampires (called Kindred, as a means of cushioning the harsh reality of vampirism) that speaks for and legislates for every vampire in the world. Bound by a series of Traditions regarding the creation, behavior and destruction of Kindred, the Camarilla is open to any vampire, regardless of clan or origin. The sect also strives, in accordance with one of the Traditions, to hide the existence of all vampiric activity from mortal eyes. This deception, called the Masquerade, is the defining detail of the Camarilla's existence; the creation, maintenance and armed struggle to uphold the Masquerade is what drives

much of the sect's overt policy. Regardless of how powerful any individual vampire might be, there are still only a relative handful of Kindred in the world. Should humanity become aware of vampires' existence, the resultant war could only have one possible conclusion: humanity victorious, the Kindred essentially exterminated. The sheer weight of numbers would be too much for even the most potent Kindred to withstand. Fear of the day when that genocidal tide rises is why the Camarilla strives as hard as it does to defend the Masquerade.

In truth, the Camarilla is far from universal. Of the 13 full-fledged clans of vampires, only six pledge their allegiance to the sect. One (the Gangrel) has recently abandoned the Camarilla, two stand in direct opposition to it as the heart of the Sabbat, and four stand aloof, supposedly neutral or at least unaligned. Even the supposedly loyal clans are imperfect in their loyalty; so-called *"antitribu"* abandon the Camarilla's clans to serve the enemy, and more Kindred proclaim themselves to be anarchs, beholden to no sect or group save the ones they themselves create.

So, beset by foes within and without, the Camarilla must be a tiny, crumbling collective, yes? Hardly. Even on the doorstep of the Final Nights, the Camarilla is the largest, strongest and most populous sect of vampires in the world. It still controls much of the Americas, has inroads in the Far East and rules almost all of Europe. While fewer than half the clans belong to the Camarilla, it still boasts more clans than any other sect. And while the ferocity of the sect's foes may give them certain plusses, the Camarilla's unparalleled mastery at working with and through humans offers it a tremendous advantage.

In Practice

In practice, the Camarilla is a sect of cities. The faction as a whole is ruled by the Inner Circle, though few outside that body's ranks can tell you who, what or how large that Circle might be. The most popular rumor is that the Inner Circle consists of either the quasi-legendary Founders or their childer, but no one seems to know for certain. The Inner Circle meets once every 13 years to appoint new justicars, who then serve as the ruling council's agents in the field for the next decade-plus. Each justicar in turn appoints and blood bonds archons to assist in her work, and thus the internal policing of the sect is assured.

The vast majority of the Kindred, however, are not archons, justicars or members of the Inner Circle. They dwell in the cities, and are frankly more concerned with the nightly business of whatever metropolis they call home than they are with the sect's sweeping policies. Cities under the Camarilla aegis are ruled by a prince, who is advised (or sometimes dominated) by a council of elders called the primogen. Beneath the prince is a whole array of appointed and self-appointed officers who keep order, uphold the Traditions, and squabble amongst themselves seeking more power. Those Kindred who don't hold titles seek them, those in power seek more power, and at the top of the pyramid the prince seeks to maintain his authority while still keeping his domain strong enough to repel attacks from all comers.

For the average vampire on the street, the Camarilla exists as a series of laws to follow, powers-that-be to avoid or impress and peers to maneuver against. His concerns are keeping his haven safe against mortal and immortal intruders, finding a way to advance in the city's hierarchy (or at least to keep himself from being ground underfoot by the machinery of rule), and keeping himself fed without drawing the ire of a more powerful Kindred. It's as far from the grand and glorious war against the Sabbat or the high intrigue of the elders as one can imagine, but this, too, is an essential element of the Camarilla.

Age

Many of the movers and shakers of the Camarilla are old — centuries or even millennia old. They have seen empires rise and fall, philosophies and utopias crumble and have moved, unchanged, through all the tumult. Theirs is the stabilizing — some would say, ossifying — presence that anchors the Camarilla firmly in its Traditions and history.

At the same time, there are more young Kindred in the sect than ever before. As the mortal population has exploded, so too has the capacity of the cities to support the Kindred. That means more and more young vampires, all of whom look at their staid, stable and terrifyingly powerful elders with a combination of fear and resentment. Even as age defines the Camarilla, it divides the sect as well.

Imagine This

Imagine working for a normal, mortal corporation. You're brought on fresh out of college, work your way up the ranks, and, as those ahead of you retire or seek employment elsewhere, you make your steady way to the top. The process is time-consuming, yes, but inevitable. Everyone grows old and dies, even CEOs.

Now imagine that same corporation, but with no competitors for employees to flee to and no chance of the executives growing old and dying. There is no opening above you, and there will never be — unless you make it. Either you force your way into the power structure by any means necessary, or you spend eternity as entry-level. You have no authority, no hope of advancement and no protection against the whims of your superiors.

That, in a nutshell, is the dilemma of the young vampire.

Power

Power is the currency of the Camarilla. Power over one's childer, power over one's domain and power over one's foes — all these are the coin the vampires behind the Masquerade trade in. Alliances are formed and broken, childer and ghouls created and destroyed, and murders carried out in the shadows of night, all for the sake of power. In truth, what else is there for the sect's vampires to acquire? Money is worthless, sex pointless and love easily compelled. Power, then, becomes the only thing worth pursuing.

That is not to say that the only struggles for power take place within the sect itself. The Camarilla wrestles with its foes for dominion in the wider world; individual Kindred face the Sabbat, the Lupines and other enemies on a nightly basis. Regardless of whether the conflict is over a prized city office, control of a nightclub or the rule of an entire city, the struggle for power is one that envelops all Camarilla Kindred, willing or no.

Intrigue

The prime benefit of the vampiric condition is immortality. The Kindred need not worry about aging, becoming decrepit and finally succumbing to death. They have literally all eternity before them.

With that in mind, the average vampire becomes very, very cautious about exposing herself to risk. Consider all that she has to lose by placing herself in the line of fire: not years or decades, but centuries and millennia. As a result, no sane vampire wants to risk her boundless future any more often than is absolutely necessary.

That means that the vampires of the Camarilla don't go in for gun battles, brawls in the street or sword duels atop abandoned factories. They're just too *dangerous*. As a result, the predatory instinct for dominance and control innate to all Kindred needs to be sublimated, redirected and channeled into less risky pursuits.

And so the Kindred weave intrigues and plots the likes of which would have amazed the di Medicis, often for prizes so small as to make the whole affair pointless. Sometimes the machinations reach across centuries and continents, with the authors of the schemes watching patiently as the events they planned so carefully unfold. Other times the intrigues are the creation of a moment, a contest between two jaded Toreador to see who can seduce or destroy a mortal more quickly.

The plots serve their purpose, ultimately. They provide the predators with distance from one another and give them something with which to while away the never-ending nights. In the end, though, the games of intrigue are inescapable. Those who don't initiate them inevitably are caught in them. Since it is better to be the puppetmaster than the puppet, Kindred caught such begin intriguing on their own, and so the chain continues unto the very weakest.

How To Use This Book

This book serves as the overview to all things Camarilla. It's not a be-all end-all of everything affiliated with the sect, but rather an overview of everything you need to run or play in a chronicle centered on the Camarilla. Most of the book is information for both players and Storytellers; only a few chapters are Storyteller-specific. If you look in here for the answers to questions like "Who was the Ventrue primogen in Poitiers in 1762?", you're going to be disappointed, but that's the nature of the beast. If we put in that sort of detail, the book would simply drown in a sea of names and dates, and not be very useful to anyone. On the other hand, if you're trying to find information on how to build a city, what high-level Disciplines are available to Camarilla characters, how the sect was founded and how it functions from night to night, all that you need is in here. **The Guide to the Camarilla** is not intended to dictate to you how to run your Camarilla chronicle. Rather, it's a tool to help you understand the options available for playing Camarilla characters or running Camarilla chronicles.

Breakdown

Chapter One: (The Basics in Blood: The Sect Defined) is an overview of the Camarilla — what it is, where it came from, and where it's putatively going. Included are breakdowns of the various offices, rights, privileges and Traditions of the sect, as well as places where those customs are starting to break down.

Chapter Two: (Thin Traceries of Blood: The Clans) contains information on the clans, bloodlines and associated lineages of the Camarilla. In addition to the six basic clans (along with the remaining Gangrel), smaller groups such as Lasombra *antitribu* and Gargoyles are covered. Finally, there's information on Caitiff.

Chapter Three: (From the Beginning: Character Creation) is a guide to Camarilla character creation, including additional Archetypes, Abilities, Backgrounds, Merits and Flaws.

Chapter Four: (Powers Beyond Understanding: Advanced Disciplines) details the advanced Disciplines of the Camarilla clans, including new Thaumaturgical paths and rituals.

Chapter Five: (The Rhythm of Immortality: Tactics and Systems) is a night-to-night guide to how the Camarilla does everything from trials to blood hunts.

Chapter Six: (The City By Night: Building Your Setting) is the complete guide to building a Camarilla city — what you will and won't find, what sort of mortals and immortals are likely denizens of the town, how the Camarilla influences the mortal politics of the city and more. Also included is a sampling of standard characters to populate your city with — everyone from Caitiffs and ghouls to princes and archons.

Chapter Seven: (Tales of Imagination and Mystery: Storytelling) is the Storytelling chapter, with ideas for running all flavors of Camarilla-based chronicles. The emphasis is on what makes a chronicle Camarilla-specific, and on using the unique features of the Camarilla to help create stories.

Chapter Eight: (Allies, Enemies and Others) wraps up the book, with information on anarchs, elders and ghouls (human and less than human), enemies and allies of the Camarilla.

Lexicon

A different existence calls for a different vocabulary. There are titles, experiences and whatnot that are common matters to the Kindred that have no equivalent elsewhere — and such things demand their own phraseology. Below is a listing of some of the more common terms used exclusively by the Camarilla to explain and define their nightly existence. Not every Camarilla vampire knows or uses all of these terms; many cling to humanity by refusing to adopt a vampiric vocabulary. In the end, though, the phrases below are what the Camarilla uses to help define the experience of its members, and thus itself.

Note: Many vampiric terms that are not Camarilla-specific can be found in **Vampire: The Masquerade**.

Allthing: A gathering of Gangrel, often called by the eldest clan member in a particular region. A smaller gathering is called a *thing*.

Anarch: A vampire who has rejected the Camarilla to exist as an independent. The vast majority of anarchs are under a century old.

Archon: A vampire in the service of a justicar. Archons are rarely of the same clan as the justicar they serve so as to avoid the appearance of favoritism, and are deputized with a wide array of powers. Most archons are blood bound to the justicar they serve.

Ball: A gathering of Toreador and invited guests.

Barrens: The areas outside a city proper that are uninhabitable by Kindred. Generally the Barrens start in the near suburbs and extend outward from a city.

Blood Bond: The supernatural love created by the act of ingesting a Kindred's vitae three times. Bonds can rarely be broken, especially if they are periodically reinforced with more vitae.

Blood Hunt: The process by which a prince declares another vampire to be outlawed, and the prosecution (in the form of an actual hunt) that follows.

Breach: A violation of the Masquerade, usually punishable by death.

Camarilla: The sect of vampires, theoretically universal, that defines itself by the Traditions and the Masquerade.

Chantry: A communal haven-cum-workshop for a city's Tremere.

Conclave: A gathering of the entire sect, usually called by a justicar.

Convention of Thorns: The treaty that ended the Anarch Revolt.

Coterie: A group of Kindred who work more or less in concert. Most coteries are made up of members of multiple clans, and few endure for more than a few decades.

Court: The formal audience granted by the prince to his subjects, often given at Elysium. When a prince holds court, in theory any of the city's Kindred may approach him to present themselves, request boons or otherwise make requests for favor or action.

Domain: A territory assigned to a single vampire, who then has primary rights to feeding, industry and whatnot within her domain.

Destruction: The power of life and death over other Kindred. Possessed by a city's prince and occasionally bestowed on others within his dominion.

Embrace: The act of turning a mortal into a vampire.

Elysium: A haven of art and culture within a Camarilla city. Elysiums are, by long tradition, zones wherein combat or the use of Disciplines is strictly forbidden. Much of the harpies' work is done in Elysium.

Final Death: The ultimate destruction of a vampire.

Founders: The legendary group of Kindred who established the Camarilla.

Ghoul: 1. A mortal (usually, but not always a human) who has been fed vitae and acquired a hint of vampiric power as a result. 2. The act of making someone a ghoul.

Harpy: A *de facto* title given to the Kindred who sit in judgment on the rest of a city's social status. The harpies mandate the social pecking order through innuendo, rumors, favoritism and other such tools.

Inner Circle: The council of elders that controls the Camarilla and its policies. No one knows how many Kindred sit on the Inner Circle, let alone the clans and names of those who do so.

Justicar: A roving representative of the Inner Circle charged with upholding the Traditions and laws of the Camarilla. There is one justicar from each clan, elected to a 13-year term by the Inner Circle and subject to replacement at the end of that term. Justicars have sweeping powers, including the right of destruction, to enforce the laws and Traditions.

Keeper of Elysium: The vampire charged with upholding the sanctity and quality of a city's Elysium.

Malkavian Madness Network: The poorly understood connection that links all Malkavians by means of their shared altered perceptions. Outside theorists postulate that the network has developed some sort of link to the Net, but details are understandably hard to come by.

Masquerade: The Camarilla's strict policy of concealing the existence of vampires from the mortal world.

Ordeal: A form of trial among the Kindred, wherein the accused undergoes some sort of test (combat, sunlight, etc.) in order to prove her innocence.

Pioneer: The first Kindred into a city or area. Pioneers often set themselves up as princes, and call for reinforcements to help them maintain their holdings. Few pioneer princes last long; once they've stabilized their domains, most are rudely shoved aside by usurpers less inclined to take risks.

Primogen: A member of the council of elders who putatively advise the prince of a city. The primogen council's actual power varies from city to city.

Prince: The ruler of a city or its equivalent in the Camarilla; the supreme authority in local Camarilla affairs. The title applies to both male and female Kindred.

Pyramid: Slang term for the formal structure of Clan Tremere.

Rack: The prime feeding grounds in a given city. Often composed of clubs, bars and shopping districts.

Rant: A formal (in some sense of the word) gathering of Brujah.

Red List: The listing of those Kindred whom the Camarilla most ardently desires to see purged from the face of the earth. Vampires on the Red List are considered under continual blood hunt.

Retainer: A mortal or ghoul who serves a Cainite directly.

Scourge: Title given to a Kindred charged by the prince with cleansing the city of unwanted, unauthorized vampiric rabble.

Seneschal: A prince's right-hand vampire. The seneschal handles many of the night-to-night operations of a city.

Sheriff: Kindred charged by a prince with the duty of upholding the laws and Traditions of the city.

Spawning Pools: Breeding chambers for ghouls used by the Nosferatu. The water of the pool is tainted with Nosferatu vitae, making ghouls of any and every living thing therein. Over centuries, these creatures can grow to monstrous size and power.

Traditions: The most sacred and basic laws of the Camarilla, established at the same time as the sect.

Vitae: Blood. More specifically, Kindred blood, but the definition is not an absolute one.

VULGAR ARGOT

Just because there's a word for something doesn't mean that everyone wants to agree on that particular terminology. The younger Kindred of the Camarilla have their own phraseology, which they use to establish their own identities and to confound their elders. Most of the following terms are Camarilla-specific in their usage, but as slang knows no borders, many of these have cropped up in unlikely places.

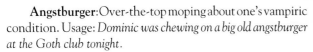

Angstburger: Over-the-top moping about one's vampiric condition. Usage: *Dominic was chewing on a big old angstburger at the Goth club tonight.*

Apeshit: Frenzy.

Ash: A vampire who's been destroyed. Usage: *Tomasino pissed off the sheriff; now he's ash.* Sometimes used as a verb, meaning "to kill."

Bloat: Taking more blood than one needs, resulting in reddened eyes, a ruddy complexion and the continual shedding of tears of blood.

Blooded: A vampire.

Boojum: Any other supernatural creature, usually non-vampiric.

'Bot: Someone clearly acting under the influence of Dominate. Often reserved for mortals reduced to automaton status.

Brightening Sunsets: Another term for a destroyed Kindred. It refers to the way in which excess dust and ash produce particularly brilliant coloration. Usage: *Lisette crossed the Nosferatu elder, so now she's brightening sunsets.*

Cannibal: A vampire who indulges in diablerie.

Cleanup: Repairing an *Oops,* or otherwise working to protect the Masquerade.

Clockwatcher: A vampire who worries excessively about the approach of dawn.

Collar: Blood Bond. The term has a distinctly sadomasochistic inference attached to it.

Cub Scouts: Archons.

Dessert: Feeding for pleasure, not need.

Doornail: As in, "dead as a." Used to refer to a corpse left behind. Usage: *We went out for supper and dropped a couple of doornails in the river.*

Do Over: The process of erasing memories from a mortal's mind. Often used to cover up evidence of feeding.

Fossil: Derisive term for a vampire who is stuck, stylistically, in an anachronistic mode of behavior. Often used to refer to elders.

Futon: A coffin.

Fuzzy: A Lupine.

Grandpa: A member of a vampire's lineage more distant than her sire.

Half-Breed: A ghoul. Sometimes phrased as "Half-Blood."

Happy Meal: The process of drinking from a mortal who is intoxicated or otherwise under the influence of some sort of controlled substance.

Inky: A hunter, specifically a member of the Inquisition.

John Law: The sheriff; less frequently, the scourge.

Juice: Vitae.

Leftovers: Blood taken from a corpse.

Laid: Fed.

Lunch: Vitae, or the mortal from whom the vitae is obtained. Usage: *I met lunch at the coffeehouse tonight.*

Lupine Alley: Travel arteries that run through Lupine territory, and are notoriously dangerous for vampires to traverse.

Monster: A vampire who terrorizes younger, weaker Kindred. Sometimes spelled *Monsta,* usually by poseurs.

Munchies: Hunger for vitae after heavy use of Disciplines.

Nibs: The prince or any other important vampire. Not intended as a compliment.

Oops: A breach of the Masquerade. Usage: *We had a little Oops tonight, but it's taken care of.*

Perv: A vampire who insists on indulging in mortal sexuality to mask the process of feeding.

PF: Short for "pity fuck." A Kindred who receives the Embrace because of guilt or pity on the part of his sire.

Prefrosh: A mortal who is a candidate for the Embrace.

Princeling: A derisive term for the leader of a coterie.

Rabbit: A vampire who only feeds on animals. Animal blood is sometimes also known as *rabbit food.*

Rag: The weakest vampire in a coterie.

Recruiting: Breaking the Masquerade so as to prepare a mortal for the Embrace.

Renfield: A long-time ghoul, usually one who has far exceeded normal mortal lifespan.

Rug: A dead Lupine. Alternately, a dead Gangrel.

Sabbot: A derisive term for the Sabbat. Pronounced "SAA-bet," usually in some form of ridiculous accent.

Sand Castle: An unsafe haven or vulnerable domain.

Scoutmaster: A justicar.

Shovelhead: Sabbat vampire.

Snap: A broken *collar.*

Soy: Vitae taken from an animal; a less-filling and tasteless substitute for the real thing.

Speed Bumps: Mortals or inexperienced ghouls pressed into combat against vampires.

Starfucker: A vampire who makes a habit of feeding from the rich and famous.

Suntanning: Being staked out for the sun. A common punishment used by princes on rebellious Kindred.

Teardrop: A Kindred who kills mortals on a regular basis. Possibly derived from certain mortal gangs' custom of tattooing teardrops on the cheek of gang members who have committed murder.

Tentacle: A hideously deformed vampire, usually a Tzimisce.

TFBS: *Bela Lugosi's Dead,* by Bauhaus. Nearly universally loathed by all Kindred, who have simply heard it too damn many times for the joke to be funny anymore.

Trashman: A vampire who feeds on the homeless and other human detritus. The term derives from such Kindred's tendency to pick up supper from alleyways or curbsides.

Uncle: An elder who takes an interest in or who patronizes a younger Kindred. Sort of a vampiric sugar daddy.

Valentine: 1. A Kindred who uses his powers to achieve mortal celebrity, often in violation of the Masquerade. 2. The mortal lover of a Kindred, usually the source of much angst.

Vector: Vampire who spreads mortal diseases; so called because the CDC has taken an interest in the way in which blood-based diseases have been spreading.

Vlad: A Kindred who acts in stereotypically "vampiric" fashion. Vlads usually wear capes, flaunt their powers and speak in strained Eastern European accents. Few last very long.

Whack Job: Malkavian, or a victim of Dementation.

Wolfie: A vampire, often a Gangrel, who prefers spending time in a non-human shape.

Yawp: The claims of a prince or other Kindred who can't hold his territory.

Old Form

The Camarilla is a sect of tradition and heritage, and many of its older members refuse to learn new terms to replace ones they've been comfortable with for hundreds of years. While old-form terminology is incomprehensible to many young Kindred — few freshly Embraced Brujah have any idea what a *cauchemar* is, for example — the elders insist on using it as a way of maintaining the dignity of the sect.

Of course, the fact that the use of such archaisms also renders conversations between elders unintelligible to many inexperienced Kindred has nothing to do with the matter.

Autarkis: An anarch or other lawless vampire. Specifically used by elders to refer to those rebels who took part in the Anarch Revolt.

Becoming, the: The Embrace.

Blood: Not vitae, but rather a Kindred's lineage and heritage. Many Kindred refer to themselves as being "of the Blood" of a particularly notable ancestor. For example, some of the most prominent Ventrue proudly declare themselves to be "of the Blood of Hardestadt."

Carthagos: Archaic form of Carthage. Any city that a vampire considers to be an exalted or special place.

Diaspora: The dispersal of elders from their lands in Europe, remembered bitterly by many American elders. Also used to describe the exile of vampires from the Second City.

Fall, the: The Anarch Revolt, considered by many elders to be the first step on the road to Gehenna.

Fealty: Another name for the blood bond.

Jus Noctis: Literally, "the law of the night." In practice, the authority a Kindred has over her childer until she grants them their freedom as responsible members of the Camarilla. Under the Jus Noctis, a sire is totally responsible for her childer's actions until she releases them.

Jyhad: The great game played by the Antediluvians amongst themselves, in which all younger Kindred fear they are merely pawns to be moved about the board.

Kiss, the: The act of taking blood from a mortal. In some cases the term has also grown to mean the Embrace.

Labyrinth: A particularly well-fortified or ancient haven.

Nemesis: The Sabbat. More generically, a vampire with whom another Kindred has had a rivalry extending across centuries.

Noddist: Of or relating to vampiric legend. Also, a vampire who studies such lore.

Pax: A formal truce between two elders or clans. Often the name of the Kindred who brokered the peace is attached to the term.

Praxis: The right of a prince to rule. Often extended to mean legitimate authority.

Pueri: A derisive term for childer.

Promethean: A thief or other undesirable. Often used to refer to elders of the Sabbat, as opposed to the street-level rabble.

Siren: A vampire who seduces mortals in order to feed on them, but who does not kill his prey.

Somnus: Antediluvian. More generally, any ancient and powerful Kindred rumored to be asleep beneath a city.

Vessel: A mortal, often one intended for feeding.

Whelp: A neonate or young vampire. In practice, any Kindred younger than the speaker.

THE BASICS IN BLOOD: THE SECT DEFINED

Society is a madhouse whose wardens are officials and police.
— August Strindberg

The Camarilla is many things, but it is not easily defined. Is it the universal organization of Kindred, sheltering them beneath the cloak of the Masquerade? Is it a tool of the Antediluvians, used to keep the vampiric masses docile in preparation for the night of their slaughter? There's no set answer, but everyone initiated into the world of the Kindred has an opinion.

ORGANIZATION AND DEFINITION

The Camarilla is, at best, a loose affiliation of Kindred. There are few laws among the Kindred, only Traditions. There are no policies on immigration or borders, only customs. Indeed, for a sect that places such heavy reliance on tradition and history, the Camarilla has precious few mandated behaviors. Most of those are covered by the Six Traditions; the rest are common sense. Otherwise, the Kindred of the Camarilla act as they please, within the boundaries established by local princes.

Almost all Camarilla vampires are urban. They are social creatures, and few who are not seeking Golconda have the slightest use for solitude. Even the relatively spacious suburbs are too sparsely populated for most Kindred to feel at home, so the vast majority crowd into urban hives. The basic population ratio is one vampire for every 100,000 mortals; in some neighborhoods that can drop by 75 percent, while in others, there are no vampires to be found at all.

The rule of the Camarilla is theoretically the rule of princes. While the sect claims the entire world as its purview, there are regions (the American Northeast, for example, and Central America) wherein the Sabbat holds near-absolute sway. Furthermore, as the Camarilla has no true centralized government, only an Inner Circle that meets infrequently and a roving enforcement squad of justicars, the attitude of the sect toward its territories can best be described as *laissez-faire*. As long as there aren't obvious problems, each prince is free to run her domain as she sees fit. Clan ties are often stronger than sect ties, and this also makes it difficult to impose central authority on the Camarilla's membership. In truth, though, many elders say in private that the lack of central authority in the Camarilla is a good thing; any attempt to impose more regulation on a bunch of ancient and powerful Kindred would only meet with disaster. As is, the Camarilla rules with a light touch and an eye toward preventing disaster, not creating policy.

Commerce and travel between Camarilla cities is brisk, though the former is usually carried out by mortal catspaws. Travel through Lupine- or Sabbat-infested regions is difficult and unsafe, so many vampires spend centuries at a time in a single metropolis. Those who rove either learn survival skills very quickly or meet Final Death within a few short years. There are no legal restrictions on traveling, other than the Tradition of Hospitality (see page 23), so those Kindred who dare to wander can do so with equanimity — so long as they are polite.

The Camarilla has no standing military, other than the cadres of justicars, archons and alastors whose work more closely resembles espionage or special ops. Each city is responsible for its own defense, drawing from its own population to guard its borders and territories. Occasionally one city will "lend" support to another, but such maneuvers are rare; too many times the city offering help has found itself under attack immediately after detaching part of its strength to assist a neighbor.

Socially, the Camarilla is an exceedingly polite society. With bloodshed outlawed and carefully watched for, it has to be. Salons, Elysiums, meetings and deal-cutting — all of these are part and parcel of nightly social life for the sect's Kindred. Even the Nosferatu occasionally indulge, climbing out of the sewers to sell secrets or shock the Toreador with their presence. Insults and damning praise, left-handed compliments and shocks to vampiric composure — the art of delivering such is one of the highest to which the Kindred of the Camarilla can aspire.

A Very Brief History

The Kindred of the Camarilla trace their sect's path from its roots in the Renaissance through the birth of the modern democracies in the 18th century to the present night. Though some elders speak longingly of the days before the Masquerade, modern Kindred are most affected by events in the last five centuries. The study of vampiric history is a most curious one; while human history relies on dusty records and shattered relics, in many cases the Kindred witnesses to important events are able and willing to describe those events directly to a modern listener.

While this fact has its benefits (as any mortal historian could tell you), it carries with it the disadvantage of perspective. Vampiric minds, like human ones, unconsciously edit their memories in light of personal wishes and agendas. Elders who misrepresent the past may not be lying about historical events; the Toreador who was on the fence during the French Revolution but who profited from a democratic France is likely to forget the reasons he ever had doubts about the uprising's success. From there it is a short step to forgetting that he had such doubts at all. Human memories can be wildly inaccurate within hours of an event; can it be any wonder that vampires' memories lose their fine edge after a century or two?

Nearly all Kindred, however, agree upon certain historical events and forces. The history of the Camarilla has been shaped by three constant conflicts: the struggle of the elders to retain their power and relevance in the face of younger Kindred fighting for power and respect; the eternal risk of rediscovery by the kine; and the war between the Camarilla and Sabbat. These core conflicts shaped the three most important eras in the history of the Kindred: the formation of the Camarilla, the expansion into the New World, and the modern day.

The Founding

The Camarilla's roots date back to a crucial event in 1381 — revolt by mortal peasants in England against the local

The Gangrel Depart

The Gangrel have been part of the Camarilla since its inception. As such, their sudden and unexpected departure from the sect was a tremendous shock, not only to the rest of the Camarilla but to the other clans and sects as well. Kindred of all generations and affiliations are scrambling to adjust to the new balance of power — whatever that might be.

Both the circumstances and causes of the Gangrel's departure are hazy to outside observers, even those close to the clan. Rumor has it that the former justicar Xaviar, rather than stand for re-election before the Inner Circle, merely walked into their presence, uttered a single sentence, and then turned his back on both the council and the sect. What that sentence was remains a topic of much debate among Kindred who consider themselves to be "in the know," but it's unlikely anyone other than Xaviar and the Inner Circle know the truth. There was no formal resignation of allegiance, no ceremony of departure; one night the elders of the clan decided that belonging to the Camarilla was not in their best interest. Word was passed through the usual channels, and within a month, the bulk of the clan had simply stepped away from the sect. Any attempts made by Camarilla (or other) Kindred to ask separatist Gangrel about the move get two-word answers if they're lucky, rough treatment if they're not. The Gangrel simply don't want to discuss it. They left, and their reason for doing so was good enough for them, so that ends the discussion. Pressing the issue is a certain way to get oneself seriously hurt.

nobility. These mortals were aided in this cause by freedom-loving Cainites (the term "Kindred" was not yet in vogue) of many clans. Though the humans' revolt was soon put down, the spark of revolution spread among disenchanted young vampires throughout western Europe. Oppressed childer began attacking one another's sires in a bid for freedom from eternal servitude; opportunistic childer took advantage of a chance to increase their own power through diablerie. Kindred historians will later point to this rebellion — more specifically, to an attack on the Ventrue Hardestadt by the Brujah anarch Tyler — as the true beginning of the Anarch Revolt.

The early 15th century saw a number of setbacks for the elders of Europe. The anarchs, emboldened by Tyler's success, staged a terrifying coup and destroyed the Lasombra Antediluvian. They attacked the Tzimisce Antediluvian as well, and claimed his destruction. The rebels even discovered a means of breaking blood bonds, and coordinated their attacks with Assamites, who were only too happy for the chance to commit diablerie on European elders.

In 1435, Hardestadt called a convocation of elders to deal with the anarch problem. He proposed that a league of vampires be formed to address problems that crossed territorial or clan lines. Though most elders were suspicious of the idea and rejected it, a small group joined Hardestadt. Over the next decade this group pushed the idea of the Camarilla more subtly, in small councils and one-on-one meetings.

By 1450, the Founders of the Camarilla had enough support from European elders that they began to assert their authority, directing cross-clan coteries in attacks on anarch strongholds. At the same time, the Founders encouraged a few coteries to search out the Assamites' hidden fortress of Alamut.

The centralized power of the Camarilla seems to have been the key to the anarchs' defeat. In 1493, leaders of the Anarch Movement acquiesced to the Camarilla's demand for a convention to discuss the terms of the anarchs' surrender. The Convention of Thorns brought most of the anarchs back into the Camarilla proper and arranged for the punishment of Clan Assamite for its role in the fighting. It also saw the Toreador Rafael de Corazon's first public speech demanding the enforcement of the Traditions with the Masquerade. Those anarchs who rejected the terms of the Convention of Thorns fled, later to form the Sabbat.

The New World

Though some elders had heard rumors of a land across the Atlantic Ocean, none were prepared for the impact the opening of the Americas had upon the new society of the Kindred. Though the newly formed Sabbat waged war on the Camarilla in Europe through the 16th century, the New World would become the real chessboard for the war between the sects.

The elders of the Camarilla saw the Americas as a place to send troublesome childer. To the ancillae of the Camarilla, the Americas were a place to carve out a fief without having to wait for the death of one's immortal master. Thus blessed with a rare unity of vision, the Camarilla sent many of its most promising ancillae to the New World. These Kindred staked out their territories in English, Dutch or French colonies, as the Sabbat influenced Spain, Portugal and their transoceanic assets.

This arrangement settled into a sort of stalemate. While Camarilla vampires had interests on both sides of the Thirty Years' War, and may have helped to encourage the French and American Revolutions, there was little movement in the struggle between sects. Allegiances solidified, rhetoric was tossed back and forth, and skirmishes were fought to little effect, but mostly the 17th and 18th centuries were a time of retrenchment and reinforcement for the Camarilla. Burgeoning industrialization moved more and more mortals to the cities and opened new avenues of power; the clans of the Camarilla were more interested in pursuing those than in fighting off war packs.

The War of 1812 between the young United States and the British Empire concealed an all-out war for control of the Atlantic seaboard between the Sabbat and Camarilla. Pincered by Sabbat territory in Quebec and Florida, the American Camarilla lost the East Coast a city at a time over the next 50 years. The Camarilla managed to retain control of a few key

cities after the onslaught, but the fighting in the nighttime streets has never truly ended. If truth be told, these nights the Camarilla is losing ground faster than ever.

The next decisive battle between the Sabbat and Camarilla would not occur until the mid 1800s, as the two sects fought for control of the newly opened frontiers. Both saw opportunity in the wide expanses of land, room to grow and entrench themselves so thoroughly as to be impossible to dislodge. The Camarilla came extremely close to losing this (and, according some scholars, America itself), but several sudden losses on the Sabbat side granted the staggered sect a reprieve, allowing them to force the Sabbat's hand back. Some claim to this night that only these losses allowed the Camarilla to maintain itself in America; such claims, however, usually bring chilly silences to the rooms where they are mentioned.

The 20th Century

When empires grow calcified, stuck straining against one another, force applied to precisely the right point can trigger a huge reaction. Mortal revolutions against the old royalty and staid governments combined with new social theory made for a volatile mix that encouraged Sabbat incursions into cities in turmoil and left the Camarilla occasionally scrambling to muster defense.

Numerous forces conspired to take control of Europe during the devastating depression left in the wake of the Great War, but none of the vampiric sects involved were able to exert enough influence to do much more than nudge European society one way or the other before the rise of Adolf Hitler in Germany. Wise Kindred without access to the halls of power in Europe got out of the way and let the kine fight their war. Foolish Kindred tried to direct the tides of battle, and were usually crushed by them.

The postwar boom was good for the United States, and by extension, it was good for the American Kindred. American anarchs had taken advantage of the war's chaos by overthrowing the princes of many West Coast cities; firm action by princes such as Lodin in Chicago quelled the tide of anarch expansion by the late 1960s. Chicago came to prominence as America's First Kindred City soon thereafter. All across the continent, however, the Kindred presence expanded. Cities boomed with waves of immigration and the decline of the rural communities, and more mortals meant more food for the Kindred.

Public fascination with vampires surged in the late '80s, providing an unexpected (but not entirely unwelcome) boost to the Masquerade; many mistakes could be written off as misguided mortals trying to be trendy. However, it also meant that when breaches happened, they were more unforgettable and difficult to cover up. New markets and industries became new opportunities for younger Kindred to advance when older vampires blocked the traditional routes to power. The new generations of vampires bore exceedingly thin blood, sometimes such that they could not create progeny, and these tides of youth found themselves searching for routes to the

same rights and power as their elders. Still, the ranks of the Camarilla increased, and within those borders proscribed by enemies too strong to dislodge, it prospered.

Today things are changing too quickly for the jaundiced elder eye to follow. The return of Hong Kong to China means the loss of the only Camarilla toehold in East Asia, and rumors abound that the Cathayan vampires may be making a move on the American Pacific Coast. Quiet war rages along the American East Coast, as the Camarilla tries to retake long-contested territory or at least prevent the Sabbat from gaining further ground. Only in Europe do things remain relatively static for the Kindred; the elders there have long since learned how best to keep control no matter the changes to kine society.

The Traditions

The Traditions are the laws of the Kindred, but especially those of the Camarilla. The customs codified in the six Traditions have been in place in some form long before the formation of the sect; some Noddist scholars believe that Caine himself handed them down to his childer. Others dispute this claim, making all sorts of arguments about linguistic structure and the like. In the end, though, it doesn't matter. The Traditions exist, and have the weight of centuries behind them. These six laws are the universal legislation of the Camarilla. All the rest is just commentary and addenda.

All Camarilla neonates are expected to learn and understand the Traditions. Ignorance is no excuse when it comes to a violation of one of these precepts. These laws are absolute; any violation of them is met with swift and severe retribution.

Unless, of course, it isn't — and it is those lapses in enforcement that can make unlife in the Camarilla so interesting.

The First Tradition: The Masquerade

The Masquerade is at the heart of the Camarilla's very existence. The fact that vampires are real must be hidden from mortal eyes. Violations of this Tradition are usually punishable by death, if not worse. Every Camarilla vampire is supposed to be on watch for violations of the Masquerade, and to stop any breach he might come across. Failure to halt a violation of the Masquerade, or to report such to the appropriate authorities, is almost as bad as breaking the Tradition itself; the Camarilla takes the Masquerade *very* seriously. As a result, sheriffs and their deputies constantly scan the Rack and the barrens for even the slightest errors in upholding the Tradition. While the other laws of the Camarilla are occasionally subject to looser interpretation, the First Tradition remains inviolable.

The Second Tradition: The Domain

The meaning of this Tradition has changed in the modern era. Once Domain meant territory, pure and simple. That was all well and good in nights when the Kindred were scarce and each could claim a city as her own, but things have changed. Now cities host, in extreme cases, up to a hundred Kindred. Modern metropolises have sprawled beyond the capability of any individual vampire to control directly. And so, the meaning of domain has been forced to change to meet the challenges the modern Camarilla faces.

In theory, the prince still holds domain over his entire city. He then has the option of parceling out areas of control — from city blocks to whole neighborhoods or boroughs — to be held by the Kindred of his choice. While the prince still holds ultimate authority, these smaller areas are a combination of fiefdom and controlled hunting preserve for the vampires lucky enough to receive them. Of course, those Kindred are also responsible for enforcing the city's laws within their domains, so domain comes with responsibility as well authority.

The concept of domain, however, is one of the most misunderstood in the Camarilla. Old and powerful vampires often stake out their own claims of domain, and unless the prince is willing to risk war to dislodge them, such claims are often allowed to stand in exchange for token favors. Neonates and anarchs claim their havens and the areas around them as domain, when really they just have squatter's rights. Usually a prince is content to let these petty claims pass and ignore the matter. It's not worth her time and energy, after all, to persecute every piss-ant anarch for misusing the term. So the prince still holds domain over the city, grants lesser domain to trusted servants or potential allies, and accepts claims by those strong enough to hold them or too weak to worry about.

Recently, the concept of domain has undergone something of an alteration. The term used to refer strictly to real estate, but within the past hundred years the word "domain" has been applied to industries as well. Hundreds of Kindred claim local software, steel, heavy manufacturing, export and other businesses as domain, setting themselves up to rule both the physical plants appropriate companies possess and their business dealings as well. A similar concept saw experimentation during the nights of the Italian merchant states, but ultimately failed. Since the beginnings of the '90s, the idea has been resurrected and seems to be gaining momentum. Now, an ambitious young Ventrue lobbies the prince for domain over the local software or telecomm industries, not a dozen-block holding on the north side of town. Most elders are content to let the childer chase such ephemera, but a few worry as to what sort of power the younger Kindred are actually accruing for themselves.

The Third Tradition: The Progeny

One of the most difficult problems facing the Camarilla is that of numbers. Vampires beget more vampires, and population control is a far more serious matter than among mortals. Having too many vampires in a city threatens the Masquerade and makes hunting difficult. On the other hand, having too few Kindred leaves the city open to attack. As a result, princes naturally want to know how many Kindred are in their cities, and to whom they putatively owe allegiance. Hence, the rise of the Third Tradition.

In the Camarilla, the right to create progeny is one of the most fiercely sought-after boons a prince can offer. So long as he controls the right to bring mortals into the blood, the prince has a never-ending stream of Kindred currying for his favor. The dispensation to create is one of the most powerful tools a prince has in his arsenal for buying the loyalty of his subjects.

Wise princes enforce the Third Tradition ruthlessly. Strict adherence to the custom means that the prince knows how many Kindred are in his city, who sired them and what clan they belong to. Not only does this give the prince an accurate assessment of the resources available to him, but also gives him a picture of city demographics (and if things are becoming too unbalanced in someone's favor).

In recent years, the Third Tradition has been advanced by some princes to cover the creation of ghouls as well, primarily in America (European princes still see ghouls as not worth worrying about in this fashion). While unofficial tabs have always been kept on precisely how many retainers a given Kindred might have, the Camarilla's increasing reliance on its mortal servants has sparked a more serious interest in ghoul demographics as well. The debate still rages as to whether ghouls can and should be included under the Third Tradition, but in cities where princes choose to do so, the penalties for unauthorized ghoul creation are as great as those for unauthorized Embraces.

The Fourth Tradition: The Accounting

Bringing a mortal into the world of the Camarilla is a tremendous risk. Any neonate has the potential to blunder spectacularly, and thus to bring down the Masquerade. As a result, a new vampire's sire is held responsible for that childe's actions — all of them. Any penalty the childe's behavior earns, the sire faces in full. Older princes in particular take this Tradition seriously, feeling that the Accounting forces young Kindred to take the Embrace seriously and choose their progeny carefully.

A sire is responsible for her childe's actions until such time as the neonate is presented, that is to say, officially introduced to the prince as a fully fledged member of the Kindred community. After that presentation (and assuming the prince accepts the neonate as being worthy of dwelling in his city), the new vampire is treated as an adult in Camarilla society. He is responsible for his own actions, and his sire no longer has to worry about being staked because of his errors.

Because of the risk attendant in siring a childe, some Kindred try to rush the presentation process as much as possible. To counter that ploy, many princes have resorted to giving a sort of oral examination of the neonate, making certain he is well-versed enough to take his place properly in Camarilla society. If the neonate fails, the consequences for both him and his sire are severe; exile is the most common punishment.

In rare cases, a neonate who has been presented to the prince and turned loose proves to be a work in progress. If the neonate's incompetence can be laid at the feet of a sire who didn't train him properly, princely wrath is apt to fall on all the concerned parties.

The Fifth Tradition: Hospitality

Predators are always very polite with one another. Social graces keep them from tearing into one another on sight, and allow them to establish relationships other than kill-or-be-killed. The Fifth Tradition is a perfect example of this sort of social buffering, as it allows Kindred to move in one another's territory without immediately coming into conflict.

At its simplest level, the Fifth Tradition is simply a mandate for all strangers entering a city to present themselves to the prince. The presentation can take many forms, from a simple greeting to a recitation of one's lineage (British and Dutch princes often insist on the latter, much to the annoyance of their visitors, who frequently attempt to insert spurious ancestors into their lineages to see if someone's napping) to a demand for service while in the city. Princes who demand the latter generally don't last long, though it is technically within their rights to do so.

By accepting a vampire who presents himself, a prince grants that Kindred permission to stay, dwell and hunt within his city. By presenting himself, the vampire acknowledges the prince's authority and ensures that he is isn't immediately brought down by a scourge who doesn't know him on sight.

More and more vampires are circumventing or ignoring the Fifth Tradition these nights. Some feel that any sort of mandatory appearance at the prince's behest might be a trap or a sell-out. Others simply don't wish to recognize princely authority in any way, shape or form (elder Kindred — particularly if the prince in question is younger than they — many anarchs and some independents see things thusly). However, by refusing to present herself, a vampire becomes an outlaw, and she moves from the prince's jurisdiction to the sheriff's — or the scourge's.

The Sixth Tradition: Destruction

According to the oldest known readings of this Tradition, the Sixth grants a sire the right to destroy any and all of his progeny. Under the Camarilla's auspices, that right has been usurped by the prince, who now holds the right of life and death over all of his subjects. He cannot exercise that right too cavalierly, lest he risk a coup to deprive him of this power, but through the office of the blood hunt, a prince can sentence any Kindred in his domain to death.

Part and parcel with this princely power is the restriction of that power to the prince, and only the prince. Sires are still allowed to destroy their childer before presentation, but otherwise kin-slaying is strictly outlawed in Camarilla do-

In theory, the Masquerade extends to all vampires, which means that the members of the sect spend a fair bit of time cleaning up after breaches made by independent or Sabbat vampires. Oddly enough, though, even those vampires who profess to hate the Masquerade and all it stands for rarely make that much noise among mortals, either. Curiouser and curiouser…

mains. Any Kindred who seek to usurp the prince's privilege and end another vampire's unlife more often than not find themselves on the receiving end of a blood hunt. Even sires attempting to reclaim what was once their birthright find their ancient right denied them; once a neonate has been presented, he is the city's and not the sire's. Creation and destruction are the two most potent weapons in a prince's arsenal, and he guards them jealously.

The Masquerade

The Masquerade is the *sine qua non* of the Camarilla, the single binding thread that holds the sect's fabric together. In so many words, the Masquerade is the policy of hiding vampiric existence from mortals. Such a drastic policy demands draconian enforcement, meaning that the Camarilla takes no chances with potential breaches of the Masquerade. All it takes is one heartfelt confession from a lovelorn neonate or one interview granted by a vampire desperate for the spotlight to blow the entire matter wide open, so the Camarilla refuses to allow risks. Neonates are instructed in the preservation of the Masquerade from the moment of their Embrace, all vampires are charged with preserving it, and sheriffs and scourges are granted the power to kill in order to preserve it.

Why the Masquerade?

One might think that the Kindred, with manifold supernatural powers at their disposal, would have no need to hide from humanity. Instead, by dint of sheer power, the Kindred should rule, and do so openly. Why should vampires, the ultimate predators, hide from the human kine?

The answer to that question is simple: Because there are an awful lot of human kine out there. The best estimates currently available to the Camarilla peg the human-to-vampire ratio at 100,000 humans for every Kindred. That's a lot of humans, and not many Kindred are up to taking out a hundred thousand mortals if push comes to shove.

As a result, concealment really is the best policy for the Kindred. Initiated in the days when the Inquisition demonstrated a marked talent for flushing out and exterminating vampires, the Masquerade serves to keep humanity ignorant. The resources of the kine are vast, and should they be turned to destroying the Kindred, few vampires would survive the purge. It is infinitely safer for the Kindred to rule from the shadows, to direct subtly rather than rule openly. Otherwise they run the risk of a war with the herds on whom they depend, a war they cannot possibly win.

Methods

There is a basic etiquette that each and every Kindred should follow in order to preserve the Masquerade. In a nutshell, the policy is "No witnesses." Don't flash your fangs or your claws in front of mortals, don't let anyone see you feeding or disposing of a corpse, don't take a clip full of bullets to the gut and then let the gunman get away to sell his story to the tabloids, don't let your vessel live without doing something to

conceal his memories of your feeding — in other words, don't be stupid. Remembering these admonitions, however, is harder than one might think, especially for younger Kindred. They tend to get excited or flustered, or to lose control during feeding, and thus make messes. Ancillae and older vampires almost never make accidental breaches of the Masquerade, and when they do so, they take care of their own affairs.

However, slips and accidents do occur. Witnesses do spot feedings and uses of Disciplines, sometimes even reputable witnesses. Fortunately for the Camarilla, the other half of the sect's policy for preservation of the Masquerade has been in place for a very long time.

The sect, in addition to trying to prevent active breaches, also maintains a massive disinformation campaign designed to make mortals think that vampires couldn't possibly be real. Assisted by Polidori, le Fanu and Stoker, the Camarilla has used narratives and images to cement the notion of the vampire in the popular consciousness as a fiction. Every straight-to-video fangfest, every trashy novel with a vampire plunging his fangs into a nubile woman on the cover, every patently absurd "documentary" with investigative fallacies apparent to a child — all of these reinforce the notion that vampirism is just a convenient cultural trope, good for an infinite number of fictional variations but nothing more.

So when the formerly reputable citizen comes screeching to his local news station with videotape he has shot of a vampire feeding at a nightclub, the video is dismissed as a home movie. The puncture wounds left in a young woman by a sloppy feeder are from a "copycat" killer with a "vampiric *modus operandi.*" Blood-drained corpses are the work of Satanic cults — as seen on tabloid television. Western civilization no longer wants to believe. Any mortals who do are mocked as naive or deluded, even in the face of hard evidence left behind by careless Kindred.

And thus is the Masquerade maintained.

Breaches

Regardless of the Camarilla's best efforts, breaches in the Masquerade do occur. When catastrophe strikes, the sect's cleanup efforts are intense and immediate. Kindred with influence in the media lean on their allies and ghouls to kill or bury any incriminating stories. Witnesses have their memories wiped — or simply disappear. Physical evidence is tampered with or stolen; undeveloped film is particularly easy to corrupt. The credibility of anyone coming forward to testify about vampires comes under immediate attack; wise princes have a finger on "expert witnesses" and psychiatrists who can be used to demolish a witness' credibility in minutes. Alternate explanations for incontrovertible evidence — drained corpses being one example — are put forward and pushed by media outlets. In short, everything possible is done to confuse the issue. The efforts of the city's Kindred are bent toward this goal, momentarily unifying them in a desperate defense of the Masquerade. After all, squabbles about who gets to be Ventrue whip won't mean much if a city of 12 million people suddenly transforms itself into a torch-wielding mob.

And the instigators of all of this effort? The poor souls who breached the Masquerade and triggered the entire cover-up? If they are lucky, they'll be staked. If not, things can get ugly. Princes have been known to expose particularly egregious offenders to sunlight, an inch at a time, over a period of months or years. The torments of the Kindred can last a very long time indeed, for those who warrant them.

WHO'S WHO IN THE CAMARILLA

THE INNER CIRCLE

The Inner Circle is the ideal cabal; it is the unobserved model for the "Secret Masters" so many conspiracy theorists speak of. The Kindred of the Inner Circle are those who pull the strings of the entire sect, creating justicars and casting them down with equal equanimity. No one knows who the vampires of the Inner Circle are, but none can deny that the Inner Circle is the true hub around which the Camarilla revolves.

Once every 13 years, the very eldest elders of the Camarilla's clans meet to discuss the sect's future direction and current business. Other vampires may be brought in to speak, but only the elders may cast their clans' votes. The lesser clans and bloodlines have no represenation here, and the presence of others is at the Circle members' sufferance.

During this time, the members of the cabal appoint justicars (replete with wrangling, threats, bargaining and other such talk), consider and determine the Camarilla's direction for the next 13 years, and rule upon Camarilla-wide issues. Many believe that the members of the Inner Circle continue to correspond through the years, directing the justicars as necessary and meeting if circumstances demand it. None are certain how the members of the Inner Circle achieve their position, except simply by surviving to be a ripe old age and ascending to monstrous power.

Who comprises the Inner Circle manages to remain one of the Camarilla's best-kept secrets. It is known that they are supposedly "the eldest" of their clans, but that definition is open to debate. Some believe that the Inner Circle's composition has changed over the centuries as one clan representative or another met Final Death, went into torpor or simply went missing. Others believe that the members of the Inner Circle serve other factions in their clans' unlives; the Tremere, for example, suspect that a member of their Council of Seven sits with the Inner Circle, but as none have ever tested the theory, it remains speculation. Such secrecy is largely a matter of tradition, but in these nights it has become a matter of grave security. With the assassination of Justicar Petrodon, the vampires of the Inner Circle realize anew that they are the ultimate prize, and take no chances with their unlives.

Few Kindred, even the justicars, quite know what the Inner Circle does with most of its time. Many believe that they remain in touch with the elders of their clans, keeping their fingers on the changes within the rank and file and

A CLASH OF TITANS

A justicar's actions may only be challenged by another justicar, which can lead to some high-level quarrels. If things grow too heated, a conclave may be called by the parties or another justicar to resolve the matter before it gets too out of hand. As a number of bitter Kindred can attest, when justicars decide to start duking it out, few are safe from being used and abused at a whim. Fighting justicars have even been known to use cities as pawns, and a prince who dares to object may find herself hosting archons as a result of trumped-up charges. Such tactics often ensure that the objector is thrown out and someone more pliable is put in place, even if it destabilizes the city. When things escalate to such a level, every Kindred runs for cover or begs for outside help. Because of such abuses, elders and younglings alike resent the influence the justicars wield over Kindred life, but the justicars' power and resources preclude many disgruntled vampires from doing anything more about it than grumbling.

gathering news from their justicars so that they may consider what needs addressing at the next meeting. Optimistic vampires even believe that the Inner Circle Kindred occasionally teach their younger brethren, choosing one particular vampire as a designated successor against that inevitable night when a chair sits empty at the council table.

Those who have aroused the Inner Circle's great collective anger have usually done so in spectacular fashion, resulting in spectacular punishment. The most impressive punishment that can be leveled against an offender is a place on the Red List, essentially guaranteeing the criminal an eternity-long, Camarilla-wide blood hunt. The Inner Circle may call upon the justicars to add their strength to the hunt, who in turn call upon their many resources to hound an offender to the ends of the earth.

THE JUSTICARS

These six mighty vampires are appointed by the Inner Circle to be their eyes, ears, hands and occasionally fists. Appointment is a long, drawn-out (and occasionally drown-out) process as each clan fights to place a strong member in perhaps the most powerful position any Kindred can hold. Too often compromise candidates win out, but occasionally the process achieves its stated goal and a truly deserving, powerful and dedicated vampire ascends to the position of justicar.

Sometimes, compromise candidates are ignored, or the Inner Circle attempts to manipulate them. Either action can backfire; those appointed to the position, even those who weren't expecting it, usually take up the mantle with full seriousness. Those who are ignored may quietly amass resources and allies behind the scenes, while those the Inner Circle attempts to misuse may bite the hands that feed them and proceed to demonstrate their grasp of the power that has been given unto them.

Justicars enjoy immense power over Kindred society and the Camarilla across the board, excepting of course the Inner Circle. They alone have the ultimate power to adjudicate matters involving the Traditions, and do so on a grand level. A justicar may call a conclave at any time, either to make a ruling or with a peer to make joint decisions of sect policy. When one of these powerful vampires makes even a polite request, very few Kindred dare refuse.

Justicars do not only serve as grim judges and agents of the Inner Circle. They encourage the social aspects of conclaves, going so far as to host conclaves so that Camarilla Kindred may meet others of their kind, meetings that might otherwise never occur without the opportunities of conclave. With their power, the justicars can ensure that a insane or despotic prince is removed before he does too much damage to the populace, or turn the tide of battle against the enemies of the Camarilla. A right or wrong word at the proper moment from a justicar can be better coin than gold or status for desperate Kindred.

In the end, though, justicars are regarded with awe and fear. Their wrath is terrible, and their power is immense. No Kindred dares to refuse them, even if it aids in that vampire's own destruction. They stride the Camarilla like colossi, and the shadow they cast is long indeed.

The Archons

Archons are the minions of the justicars, set to act in their names for whatever suits their purposes and needs. As no justicar can be everywhere he might want or need to be, an archon can make certain his presence is felt (if not seen). Archons have been part of the Kindred hierarchy for almost as long there have been justicars, although they were not officially named until sometime in the late 1600s, most likely by the Brujah owing to the Greek origin of the word. Archons are typically chosen from the ranks of ancillae and "young" elders, who show some promise by their maneuvers in the halls of power. The tenures of Kindred appointed to the post last for as long as their employers wish to

The Justicars

As of the Inner Council meeting of 1998, the justicars were:

- Brujah: Jaroslav Pascek
- Malkavian: Maris Streck
- Nosferatu: Cock Robin
- Toreador: Madame Guil
- Tremere: Anastasz di Zagreb
- Ventrue: Lucinde

With the exception of Madame Guil, all of the justicars are new. Lucinde is no stranger to the halls of power, but this is the long-time archon's first appointment to the high chair. Xaviar, former Gangrel justicar, was the last of his clan to hold the title, as with the clan's "formal" withdrawal from the sect there is no need for a Gangrel justicar.

retain them, and the employer can become the office, not the person occupying the chair. On the other hand, some justicars select entirely new staff upon their appointments. Recently, the new Nosferatu justicar, in a veritable tantrum of paranoia, threw out all of Petrodon's archons, including Horatius Muir, who had served Petrodon since the latter's first appointment. Horatius has not taken the loss very well, and his fellow archons, both in and out of clan, fear that the former archon will seek gruesome revenge for the insult.

Not every archon strides into Elysium with her mission statement in hand and announces herself to be here on justicar business. Justicars often need watchers or other quiet workers in troubled cities, and the best ones simply appear, do their job and leave with as little fanfare as possible. Archons are not as far removed from typical Kindred unlife as their superiors. Most are able to insert themselves into city business without attracting much attention and gain the trust of others, who rarely suspect that their newfound compatriots are so powerful. Occasionally, justicars choose archons more for their particular insights into a subject, their skills or their political savvy, which does not always walk hand in glove with high profile. Princes have been known to object to such moles, but too much protest brings the notice of a justicar who wants to know what a noisy prince might be hiding.

The Prince

Ostensibly, the prince is the Camarilla's voice in the city she rules. In theory more of a magistrate or overseer than an absolute ruler, it the prince who keeps the peace and makes the laws, whatever is necessary to keep the city orderly and safe from incursion. The prince wears many hats, including diplomat, commander in chief, lawmaker, patron of the arts, judge and Tradition-keeper. The position originally began with the strongest vampire in a given region claiming domain over it. Over time, certain privileges and responsibilities became attached to the position, either at the whim of the ruler or the demands of the ruled. The position reached its familiar modern form during the Renaissance. What exactly the princedom will evolve to in the future is the subject of much hushed speculation, but never when the local prince is within earshot.

There are several ways one can become prince of a city. One is to depose the old prince. This insurrection may take the form of anything from a bloodless, elder-supported coup to a full-scale war with the gutters running with blood. If a prince shows himself incapable of maintaining the safety of the city against incursion, he may be forced to abdicate by the rest of the Kindred. Another way is to become seneschal and hope the prince either dies or is forced from office. Of course there are ways to help that sort of thing along, provided one doesn't mind a few risks that could spell Final Death if one is caught. If one is in a small town or a largely rural area with a scattered population, even a young Kindred may name himself prince. Many times, the elders prefer the relative safety of the cities, and find rural areas both dangerous and boring. Those young vampires who choose to brave the small towns occasionally set themselves up in a

semi-structured organization, with the "prince" being the one who has the biggest gun or has earned the most respect. Such titles (Prince Garrett of the Finger Lakes Region, or Madame Charlotte, prince of the Seven Sisters Hills) sound more grand than they truly are, and rarely carry weight with the elders of nearby cities.

A prince is owed nothing by her "subjects." Indeed, once they follow the protocol of Tradition, most have plenty of other things to keep busy with. A prince rules only so long as she can enforce order, her subjects are sufficiently frightened of her might and the elders support her. If any of those factors disappears, her reign is at an end. On the other hand, if all's in place, then the Kindred of the city can count on being stuck with their prince for a good long while. The elders ensure that a prince's reign is maintained in the name of stability; turmoil in the streets endangers the Masquerade and risks Final Death.

A prince enjoys a great deal of power, one of the major reasons anyone would ever seek the job in the first place. She often gathers great temporal influence in the mortal world to insure that threats to her can be dealt with effectively; few become inclined to do too much to someone who could have their phone lines "accidentally" cut when a gas line is being dug. She may freely create progeny, while other vampires must seek her permission before siring. She may extend her power over those who enter her domain, and may punish her enemies by calling the blood hunt. Whether the perks outweigh the burden of the job is a nightly debate in the halls of Elysium, but enough Kindred seem to think so that there is a never-ending struggle in every city for ascent to the throne.

The Primogen

The primogen is the assembly of elders in a given city. Each clan usually has at least one representative primogen (the title is used to indicate both singular and plural), in addition to any other elders of the clans who wish to sit in on the meeting. No one seems quite certain when the primogen body came into being, but most Kindred scholars interested in such things point to the councils of elders that have been part of mortal communities for milennia. Wherever the organization came from, the primogen councils continue into the present nights as clan leaders, filling seats of remarkable power. As a result, the primogen are either a prince's greatest allies or his worst enemies

Ostensibly, the primogen council is meant to be a legislative body, a representation of the opinions of the various clans with regard to the governance of their city. Such an assessment is correct in very few cities. Some primogen councils are missing one or more clans, their elders forbidden by princely edict to take their seats, or because the clans are composed entirely of younger vampires and the elders will not deign to acknowledge the clan's right to representation. Those primogen who are seated in many cities are less like an assembled body and more like an "old vampires' club," a nest of nepotism, favor-trading, threats and treachery. In some cities, particularly those with small Kindred populations, the prince is often the primogen for his clan. In larger cities, this is not so — those involved claim that the prince should be concerned with balanced governance of the city, and that serving as primogen divides his loyalties. Other Kindred point out that having a second clan member serving as primogen would seem to weigh matters in favor of that clan. Not so, reply those asked. Some of the most vicious disagreements between prince and primogen can be between two members of the same clan who happen to disagree on a particular policy.

The primogen can hold a great deal of power, whether or not it is granted them. Made up of elders who love their unlives with nigh-obsessive fervor, primogen councils can squash pretenders to the throne, weak princes and outspoken youth in the name of stability. It is their support that confirms a vampire as prince or sentences him to be food for the worms. If they wish, the primogen may drive a prince from office with their recalcitrance or votes of no confidence, or ensure a prince's long reign with their powerful support. Some primogen councils can become *the* governing body of a city, with the prince continually engaged in fighting with, cajoling, arguing or threatening them back into line. On the other hand, in cities where the princes are more powerful than most, insane or despotic, the council meets solely at the prince's whim and is often merely a figurehead assembly.

The Whip

Sometimes, even the most organized primogen can be overworked and stretched too thin with demands for his time. Add to this a slow-moving discussion at clan meeting, recalcitrant clan members and general voter lassitude, and the task of primogen can become unmanageable for any lone Kindred. It was for these times that the position of whip was created.

The whip is not an official position within the hierarchy of the Camarilla, but rather a recent phenomenon that seems based almost solely in countries with a democratic legislature. Whips are used in the mortal governments to keep members of a political party informed as to each other's doings, to keep discussions productive and to round up the appropriate members when it is time for voting. In Camarilla cities, a number of clans employ whips for similar purposes. Princedoms within the United Kingdom and United States make the most use of the post.

A primogen may choose not to employ a whip if the situation does not merit it. After all, when the local branch of a clan numbers four, and one is serving as primogen, keeping the rest informed is usually a simple matter. On the other hand, in a large city with eight clan members, a whip can be very useful. Some clans have occasionally pressed their primogen to appoint whips when it became obvious that the primogen was overwhelmed with business. Whip appointments are usually conditional; often the whip is a Kindred who is of some influence within the clan so she will be listened to, but not so much that she potentially overshadows the primogen himself. A whip who begins to outshine his employer is likely to be replaced. Sometimes, a whip position may not be a reward but a warning. Since the whip is required to stay close to the primogen and mind his ways, appointing a troublemaker can

be an effective way to put him on the hot seat and channelling his energies into something more constructive (or put him under the spotlight until he inevitably makes a mistake).

Whips in clan meetings serve to goad discussions along by whatever means necessary. This can include filling in details the primogen has inadvertently forgotten, shouting down more vocal clan members to allow the quiet ones a chance to speak up, insulting someone into blurting out his true opinion or throwing out the occasional inflammatory gambit just to get the ball rolling. Whips may also attend to those reclusive clan members who cannot or will not attend clan meetings for reasons of their own.

In some cities, the whip is viewed as the primogen's second, given authority to sit in primogen meetings if his master is absent, or standing at his right hand during the meetings, ostensibly to serve as "stenographer" for the clan. More often, the whip is taking notes on everything else occurring during the meeting that the primogen may not notice while speaking or dealing with the prince, such as clothing worn by the other primogen, gestures and mannerisms, tone of voice and reactions by those not primarily addressed. Such an observant whip can be worth his weight in gold when it comes time to interpret the meaning behind another primogen's uncharacteristic objection.

The Seneschal

In the mortal world, the seneschal was the keeper of the keys in a noble house, the minder of the affairs, the one who always knew what was happening and who was closest to the master's ear. It was the seneschal who was in charge when the master was away, and who took care of the estate in time of disaster. In the vampiric world, the position hasn't changed much from its original inception. The seneschal is chosen to be the prince's personal assistant, the one who knows what's going on at any given moment, and (according to some wags) the one you really have to deal with to get things done. At any time, he may be asked to step into the prince's place if she leaves town on business, abdicates or is slain.

While a prince may wish to have final authority on the choice, a number of primogen councils have fought to ensure a seneschal candidate to their liking is installed. If the prince is seen as weak or is not well-liked, the fight becomes even fiercer. After all, accidents do happen, the primogen insist, and it were best that the next in line is someone worth having to avoid entanglements at such times. Princes insist that the choice is theirs to make, particularly when the seneschal is in such a sensitive position. They point to certain disasters in Kindred history regarding the seneschal, most often the Nuremberg Incident of 1836, when a Sabbat spy managed to achieve the post and the city narrowly avoided being completely overrun after he handed over the secrets he had learned to his cohorts.

For most seneschals, the job can be a completely thankless one. It may be seen as a stepping-stone up the ladder to greater things, but the rewards aren't always commensurate with the tedium and danger. A seneschal can be called on to be a secretary, clearinghouse of information, prince *pro tem*, advisor, sounding-board, recepient of vitriol, ambassador or point of contact for any new Kindred entering the city. Some princes may have other uses for their seneschals, such as sitting in on certain meetings as the prince's voice when the prince must be absent, or even to deal with certain matters which princes deem not worthy of their attention. For a prince busy with other concerns (such as hunters, Setites or Sabbat), a capable seneschal who can take care of all the nitpicky details of running a city can be a godsend. If the seneschal is incompetent, however, he can be a nightmare. A seneschal unaware of the movements of new Kindred in the city may be in fact inadvertently holding the door for Sabbat troops, or one who has closed down a church on suspicion of harboring hunters may have just alienated the Nosferatu who made use of the place as well.

A number of seneschals have taken advantage of their positions, using them to become often the most well-informed Kindred in the city, even outstripping the harpies. Some, as clearinghouses of information, may selectively edit what their prince does and does not know (on a strictly need-to-know basis, with the seneschal of course deciding who needs to know what). Others may block items on the night's agenda if it suits their purpose, most often when the Kindred bringing the business has offended the seneschal in some way. As the seneschal is frequently closest to the prince's ear, he may inform the prince as he wishes regarding matters of business or policy — lies of omission are a seneschal's stock in trade. If someone is offended with the way the seneschal handles business, the humble vampire may claim that he is merely the prince's voice, and shift the blame upward to an undeserving prince. A wily seneschal with ambition on his mind and a prince burdened with the cares of a large domain can be a lethal combination.

The selection of a seneschal has any number of criteria, varying from prince to prince, and from primogen to primogen. Some prefer tractability over trust, while others see some independence and common sense as ideal qualities. Few primogen have ever permitted a seneschal to be of the same clan as the prince, seeing it as invitation to disaster in the form of clan favoritism.

The Harpy

The harpies are the gossip-mongers, the rumor mills, the status-givers. They are the word in the wrong ear, the ones who can make a vampire's unlife miserable for the sin of wearing an ugly tie or returning an insult. Many of the best (the most observant, the sharpest tongued, the wittiest) harpies are elder age, although not a few talented ancillae hold their own in these halls of hidden power. Neonates are rarely anything more than assistants and apprentices to established harpies, simply because they are too new to the nuances of unlife's etiquette to understand what's happening. A neonate who attempts to ascend to full harpy status too soon finds her betters turning on her mercilessly; most have the ambition verbally flayed right out of them by this treatment. If she's lucky, they'll simply let her embarrass herself.

Harpies are rarely appointed outright. Those with the necessary skills were often part of the elite social scene in life, spending their lives as famous gossips, dilettantes and socialites. As in life, these social butterflies hover where the beautiful people can be found, and simply fall in doing what they did before. They are unimpressed with preening, demonstrate remarkable insight into both vampiric and human nature, and can boast an unerring ability to see through pretense and pose.

A leading harpy may choose to name an assistant or two, particularly in a city with a sizable Kindred population. After all, even the best harpy can hardly hope to keep up with things when there are Elysiums occuring at both the Academy of Fine Arts and at the local Hard Rock Cafe. A major metropolitan city, such as Vienna or London, may contain at least six Kindred who are considered to be the main harpies, in addition to the 20-plus others who serve as additional eyes, ears and sources of material. In a smaller city, as few as two may hold the position, although the question of who is actually in charge is another matter (which no doubt is fought over incessantly). In smaller towns and rural areas, harpies are often completely dispensed with, but here and there one may find a vampire who presides over the diminished social scene like an undead Hedda Hopper. Most harpies tend to be of "social" clans, such as the Toreador and Ventrue, but not a few elder Brujah or slightly more lucid Malkavians have been known to occupy the seat as well.

Not only concerned with who said what to whom, harpies are also interested in the intricacies of Kindred etiquette. There is a right way to do things and a wrong way to do things, and the harpies make sure things are done right. Someone on the harpies' hit list often finds himself banned from all the premiere social gatherings, and it is not all that difficult to incur this sort of ostracism. Rudeness, crudeness, speaking out of turn, showing disrespect or blatant stupidity — all of these can place a vampire squarely in the harpies' crosshairs.

While some might sneer that the disapproval of a few "old biddies" doesn't mean much in the grand scheme of things, the harpies (and their victims) beg to differ. In an era where the most recent news can be passed nigh instantaneously between harpies along a web of gossip that staggers the imagination, the harpies in one city can assure an offender that he receives a less-than-cordial welcome in any city he visits. It is the harpies who assist with the brokering of and recording of prestation deals. Harpies are often called on to assist their princes when dignitaries visit. In these modern nights, the harpies are busy indeed, dealing with the ramifications of email as a proper method of correspondence, the propriety of requesting an elder to step through a metal detector or the polite way to suggest that a potential disease-carrier hie himself to the lab for testing.

The Keeper of Elysium

The job title is self-descriptive — this Kindred is responsible for everything that occurs in Elysium and usually its environs as well. A Toreador wishing to schedule a recital, a Tremere giving a lecture on medieval alchemy or two Brujah who are hosting a debate regarding current Kindred involve-

Harpy Tactics

When the harpies cut loose, they do so with razored tongues honed sharp enough to glisten. While insults may not seem like they would matter much to a vampire, in an arena where wit is the only weapon (such as Elysium), a vampire who relies on brute strength is helpless before the harpies' assault. A particularly cunning insult will be picked up and repeated by dozens of other Kindred, humiliating the target wherever he goes. Just as bad is the snub, a cold shoulder turned by the harpies and those currying their favor *en masse*. A vampire ostracized thus is in an impossible position — he can't walk out without making more of a laughingstock of himself, while staying invites more frustration and barely audible titters from those in on the snub.

While these techniques seem mild compared to, say, ripping someone's throat out with Wolf's Claws and a healthy dose of Potence, one must remember the context. The Kindred dwell in a society wherein internecine violence is strictly proscribed; one cannot respond to an insult by hauling off and slugging one's tormentor unless one is very, very careful about it. A vampire targeted by the harpies literally cannot strike back without incurring the wrath of the prince, the sheriff and the harpies' clan elders — a host of enemies who are capable of turning any lone offender rapidly into ash. Social warfare becomes the only acceptable warfare, and the harpies have everyone else outnumbered and outgunned.

ment with the police — all must speak first with the keeper. The keeper may cancel an event at any time, even minutes before it is to begin, on the grounds that it threatens security and the Masquerade. (Whether or not the claim is accurate is irrelevant; the keeper has that authority to use as she sees fit.) Such power, while not as impressive as the scourge's right of destruction, can be used to great effect; the vampire who has spent months puffing himself up over a recital at Elysium only to have it blithely cancelled stands to lose a great deal of status.

Keepers may be of any clan; most are at least of ancillae status, which gives them the pull they need to hire or create sufficient security for Elysium. Contrary to popular thought, the majority of keepers are not Toreador. Such Kindred tend to get distracted from their duties too easily in Elysium's environs.

The job comes with heavy responsibility and very few perks. A keeper is responsible for *everything* that occurs within Elysium's walls on his watch (and occasionally off it too). While the position is a prestigious appointment, and it can garner a Kindred a great deal of status and recognition, it puts that Kindred under a microscope almost as intense as the prince's. Because the position requires the keeper to interact with mortals on a fairly regular basis, monstrous Kindred (whether in mien or demeanor) are never considered for the job, unless they have some

way to disguise themselves. The appointment is also usually a conditional one — the keeper can expect to be scrutinized for the several gatherings regarding his policies on the Masquerade, mortals, security and Elysium in general. The harpies are not kind to a failed keeper, if he's still around to accept their scorn.

On a nightly basis, the keeper must be certain Elysium abides by the major rules regarding the established Traditions and the Masquerade. He may be responsible for stopping weapons at the door, a job he often requests the sheriff perform. On occasion, he may need to play host, circulating among his visitors and making sure things are going smoothly. If the prince requests that refreshments be provided, it's the keeper's job to procure them. When several Kindred want to make use of Elysium to stage some event (such as dancing lessons, a debate or even a music recital), the keeper needs to juggle the social calendar to ensure that everyone gets a turn and that the Brujah's often-noisy debates will not be trampling the Malkavian performance artist's exhibit of silence. If curious mortals peek in the windows, or a hapless mortal security guard wanders into a Kindred gathering by accident, the keeper must see about removing the intruders neatly. If an incident occurs that attracts the wrong kind of mortal attention, the keeper needs to clean it up, and he may call on any necessary resources to do so. Relying on this sort of fiat too often, however, is a good way to draw a prince's ire, and the best keepers are often those who are noticed least.

"As is the keeper, so goes Elysium," is a familiar saying around the halls of power, and it is quite true. A keeper who is continually paranoid about infiltrators runs Elysium with a grip that can approach a stranglehold, and presents gatherings that are reminiscent of a prison yard's rec time. A keeper who has a great interest in the arts may favor salon-style gatherings that welcome any with something to contribute, while one more interested with social interaction would encourage elder-supported meetings suggestive of the Algonquin Round Table.

Of all the positions in a city, this one is the most likely to change hands frequently. The position is very much a political football, kicked back and forth between prince and primogen. Furthermore, the role offers a Kindred tremendous opportunities to fail; sooner or later every keeper manages to offend somebody. A wise keeper knows when to resign; foolish ones hang in until the bitter end. If a vampire plays her cards right, she may hold the position of keeper three or four times within a few decades; talented keepers are often elevated into the role again and again.

The Sheriff

While the sheriff's job description may vary from city to city, his primary function is to be the prince's "enforcer." He generally assists with the "muscle" aspects of ruling, doing everything from hauling offenders into court to keeping order on the streets and occasionally bouncing fools from Elysium. During wartime, the sheriff is often called on to be the war-chief, leading charges and coordinating the martial side of the fight. A sheriff may select deputies to assist him, who often act fully in his authority, but such appointments usually require the prince's approval.

Far and away, the Brujah and the remaining Gangrel provide the most sheriffs, although anyone with something of a martial bent may be selected. Since part of the sheriff's duties include watching for breaches of the Masquerade, a sheriff is also required to show a little brains in addition to brawn. Straight-ahead brawlers are becoming less common; operators who are precise in their applications of force have become the norm.

Keepers of Elysium and sheriffs can be each other's best friends or worst enemies. A keeper who insists on dealing with security herself at Elysium risks stepping on the toes of the sheriff, who believes that such an action indicates to the harpies he's incompetent. A sheriff who muscles into Elysium and conclave security without asking about existing plans may alienate the keeper, depriving him of much-needed support when it comes time to press for tighter security measures (such as heat sensors). On the other hand, when the two offices work hand in hand, particularly during conclaves, they can weave a web that could hold back the sea. Keepers and sheriffs often have a great deal to say regarding the selection of the other, and it is not unknown for a particularly tightly knit pair of Kindred to hold both offices jointly.

The Scourge

Some claim the position of scource is a relic of medieval times, an older form of the sheriff, while others believe that the post was created only within the last decade (with an equally new-minted pedigree). However the scourge came to be, the office is now part of the landscape of many Camarilla cities. From Bern to Portland, scourges take their mandate to scour the borderlands and barrens of the major metropolises. Their targets are fledgling vampires created without permission, anarchs and those thin-blooded mules of the 14th and 15th Generations.

Proceedings regarding the scourge vary from city to city. Some princes grant their scourges the right of destruction to speed the process of purging along, while other princes demand that the scourge bring the night's "catch" to Elysium for judgment. This last comes in light of some recent tales of over-enthusiastic scourges attacking and killing vampires who had followed protocol and were known in the city, but happened to be in the wrong place at the wrong time. The story currently circulating through Elysium describes a feral Gangrel scourge who encountered three Kindred in a derelict building in the barrens of Milwaukee. As he had been given full authority to destroy any Kindred he did not recognize, the scourge made quick work of the trio, who were unable to give much resistance. He brought back trophies of his work, to the consternation of the Tremere primogen, who recognized the personal effects of three recently acknowledged neonates; apparently they had gone looking for a private place to perform a ritual. The prince initially refused to disbar the scourge, but the outrage of the primogen council and the wrath of the united Tremere clan forced him to reconsider.

Not every prince makes use of the scourge — indeed, a number of princes (usually of smaller or less "prestigious"

TEMPTING FATE

Most of the Kindred who deal with humanity do so with a very careful eye toward the Masquerade. Such vampires understand the risk they run every instant, and take great care not to threaten the veil that protects them from mortal wrath.

Then there are the daredevils. Vampires of this sort, for whatever reason — boredom, usually, though "latent Sabbat sympathies" are often blamed — like to see how close they can come to shattering the Masquerade without actually doing so. This sort of game can go on for years before the players eventually slip, with each player coming closer and closer to the edge. If the participants are lucky, their shenanigans come to the attention of the sheriff, who puts the clamps on before any serious damage is done. If not, the Masquerade suffers what is colloquially known as an "Oops" situation, and all hell breaks loose.

Needless to say, the vampires responsible for the breach never, ever survive the cleanup.

cities) see it as a dangerous and unnecessary office. The legality of the scourge is still under debate in a number of circles, particularly with regard to granting these gendarmes the right of destruction. Many sheriffs see the scourge as chipping away at their power, and as a result they can be the greatest obstacles to a prince or primogen who wishes to introduce the scourge to a city. On the other hand, some sheriffs see the scourge as taking care of a problem that occupies too much of their time when they could be dealing with an infinite number of other matters, such as Sabbat incursions or persistent hunters. A number of vampires, largely those who occupy the barrens on a regular basis and a surprising number of "salon" vampires, also see the scourge as a potential threat; a scourge gone bad or working for the enemy could be deadly, especially if the prince gives the scourge a lot of leeway in her dealings with the thin-blooded.

Scourges in general are not the most popular vampires around. Most are loners, and if they are not initially, the demands of the position soon ensure that they are. Few Kindred are comfortable around the local scourge, and even princes hold their hired exterminators at arm's length. Embittered and isolated, most scourges soon grow disdainful of Kindred company, shunning Elysiums in favor of "work." A few far-sighted Kindred (usually those who have some psychological work in their backgrounds) continually attempt to draw their local scourges into Kindred social life, fearing that without social contact scourges will become automatons, killing machines unable to tell the difference between friend or foe. Such efforts have met with mostly poor results. Some scourges scorn such "do-gooder" attempts as muddling with their thinking, while others find the forced jollity only emphasizes the gulf between them and their fellow Kindred.

THE HUDDLED MASSES

Not every Camarilla vampire holds title; far from it, in fact. The vast majority of the sect's members attend to their own business. Some do have ambitions to achieve power within the sect. These vampires pay careful attention to matters political and may spend decades or even centuries plotting their ascents to power. Others avoid the matter entirely, presenting themselves to each prince in turn, then vanishing back down into the sewers or thaumaturgical labs.

The fact of the matter is that each vampire has eternity stretching before him, and he had best find himself something to do before the crushing ennui of the ages drives him mad. Active participation in politics is an option for only some of the Kindred; there are only so many titles to go around, after all, and promotion is a slow and bloody process. That means that the Kindred need to find other interests and outlets, all the while adhering to the Traditions and preserving the Masquerade.

The most common diversion for the Kindred involves dabbling with mortals. This interaction can take many forms, from indulging in the arts (all-vampire bands are surprisingly common) to meddling with corporations. Other Kindred try to resume or assume mortal lives, living among mortals in an attempt to further their agendas or stave off boredom. Most often, though, a vampire who decides to spend his nights interfering with mortals picks a particular field or institution — one often mandated by the prince, who has no interest in seeing her subjects squabble over a particularly juicy industry — and then sets about working with his plaything. Kindred grow protective of their mortal connections, tending them with the same care and passion that a gardener expends on a prized bonsai. It is often not a matter of the vampire actually caring for the specific area he has domain over (though there are exceptions) as it is a question of possession. Such vampires often take a great deal of interest in the night-to-night concerns of their connections, diving into the details as a means of distraction. Sometimes Kindred carry on mortal crusades beyond the grave, but sooner or later those concerns fade. The form of the vendetta remains, but the motivation shifts; sooner or later, the chase is what matters more than the goal. It is not uncommon for vampires who achieve goals they've been pursuing centuries to slip into torpor shortly thereafter; there's nothing left to interest them anymore.

On the other hand, there are those Camarilla vampires who have no interest in dealing with humans. The Masquerade is a convenient excuse to avoid interacting with humanity save at feeding time. These recluses are more interested in matters vampirical: thaumaturgical research, vampiric philosophy or artistic expression, or other endeavors only possible for those with unending lifespans. Like those Kindred who throw themselves into the Masquerade, though, vampires who stick to immortal concerns have an overriding passion for what they do. In the end, what matters is not so much what each Kindred does, but rather that they do so emphatically, to keep them from drifting aimlessly into madness and eternity.

Thin Traceries of Blood: The Clans

Not even those who lived long ago before us and were sons of our lords, the gods, themselves half divine, came to an old age and the end of thier days without hardship or danger, nor did they live forever.
— Simónides of Ceos, "The Comments of Simónides," Richard Lattimore, trans.

The core of the Camarilla, the heart of its strength, is the collection of vampiric clans who banded together in the 15th century to drape the Masquerade over Kindred existence. It is the interactions of those core clans, the compromises and adjustments they have made in order to deal with one another, that have given the Camarilla much of its shape, definition and flavor. To understand the Camarilla at all, it is first necessary to know the clans — and the bloodlines, stragglers, refugees and hangers-on — that comprise it.

Six...

As things stand, six clans serve as the core of the Camarilla. The Brujah, Malkavians, Toreador, Tremere, Ventrue and Nosferatu are firmly committed to the Camarilla and what it stands for. The *antitribu* of these clans are a distinct minority; numerically, the vast body of each of these lineages supports the Camarilla. The clans do so, not out of any sense of altruism or innate goodness, but rather because the elders of those clans believe that the sect and its attendant customs offer the best hope of survival. Of course, the question of whose survival always hangs, unspoken, but the distance between elders and neonates is great enough that what filters down from generation to generation loses the patently self-serving edge that one might attribute to the elders' pronouncements. For so many new Kindred, the Camarilla is simply The Way Things Are Done, and theirs is not to question — at least not at first.

Even those who grow restless and start to question, however, usually return to the fold.

Clan Prestige

Clan Prestige is an additional Background Trait used to keep track of a vampire's standing within her clan. Clan Prestige bears absolutely no relation to a Kindred's regular Status; a vampire can be highly respected by other Nosferatu but despised by the Camarilla as a whole, or a Brujah prince might be well-respected by his peers, but loathed by his clanmates as a sell-out. Normally a vampire can only acquire Clan Prestige for her own clan, but on rare occasions one of the Kindred has done enough service for one of the other lineages to earn Clan Prestige from them as well. Examples of this would be a Toreador who, despite his sensibilities, regularly feeds gossip from Elysium and the salons to the Nosferatu, or a Gangrel archon who, in the course of performing her duties, foiled a Sabbat plot to assassinate a Ventrue prince.

Clan Prestige normally runs up to a rating of 5, though elders and legendary figures (such as those found in the appendices of clanbooks) can have Clan Prestige up to 10. Clan Prestige cannot be bought with experience. It can only be bestowed through roleplaying by the elders and other members of the clan in question. Furthermore, infamous or stupid acts, or the influence of the harpies, can strip a vampire of Clan Prestige easily. Respect within one's clan is hard to earn and easy to lose, and the way in which Clan Prestige is handed out should reflect that.

BRUJAH

Lo, how the mighty have fallen. Such is the perspective the elders of other clans have on the Brujah. Younger Kindred, who do not remember the clan's nights of philosophy and glory, see the Brujah as a disorganized, anarchic rabble. Then again, in these degraded times entirely too many members of the clan fit that description, or at least enough that the stereotype has become widely accepted.

With hallowed Carthage just a fading memory, the Brujah have become the angry young men (and women) of the Camarilla. Constrained by the Camarilla's traditions and kept in their place by ruthless elders, the street-level Rabble take out their frustrations by moving in packs, indulging in Rants and generally adopting a bad attitude at odds with the enforced gentility of Elysium and the Ventrue.

These nights, the Brujah shun the halls of power. The clan's younger members have little interest in playing the Ventrue's games or exposing themselves to Toreador ridicule. Instead, they stand as the (mostly) loyal opposition to the sect, essentially for the Camarilla but with little interest in its rules and regulations. Elders may take a more philosophical bent in line with the clan's direction at the time of their Embrace, but the common image of the Brujah now is that of the leather-jacketed rebel.

STRENGTH AND INFLUENCE

Within the Camarilla, the Brujah have relatively little pull among princes. With the clan's penchant for getting into trouble (the legendary Brujah temper can produce equally legendary breaches of the Masquerade or other Traditions), few princes are willing to give them much beyond the time of night. Brujah princes are rare, though a surprising number of sheriffs and scourges are members of the clan. As many of the quote-unquote "rabble" that these officers must deal with are Brujah as well, the conflict can make for interesting infra-clan politics.

In truth, the Brujah have their strongest influence on the streets and in the ivory towers. Of all the clans, they have the strongest hold on mortal academia, a relic of the clan's nights as would-be philosopher-kings. Elders still work hard to pull from that base of potential Embracees, but these nights, the clan's primary interests lie elsewhere.

Once ruling from fortresses and training halls, now the Brujah rule the streets, primarily through sheer numbers. Many Brujah came from or were familiar with a rough-and-tumble lifestyle, and chose to continue it beyond the grave. Like calls to like, and vampires who came from the street have made a habit of Embracing those from the street as well. The clan has the widest variety of membership of any of the Camarilla clans; in many cases a flash of attitude or a demonstrated unwillingness to take crap is all that it takes to earn someone the Embrace. All the rest, the Brujah reason, can be taught.

ORGANIZATION

The usual response one gets when asking the Brujah about their clan structure is either laughter or a punch to the gut. The Brujah are the most disorganized of the clans, shunning formal

meetings in favor of informal Rants (often held after concerts or particularly energetic parties). There are no "Boards of Directors" or formal awards of status among the Rabble; instead like-minded Brujah get together to swap news and brag, or to argue about damn near anything. Somehow, news manages to get disseminated by this haphazard fashion, but anyone hoping to catch all of the local Brujah at a sit-down meeting is in for a world of disappointment.

The only organization the Brujah have is a rough breakdown along philosophical lines. Younger, more anarchic Brujah are sometimes called Iconoclasts (though their response to the term isn't printable), and it is from these vampires that the stereotypical image of the clan derives. Older members of the clan, called Idealists (though they prefer something in Greek most of the time) are more interested in the ideals of the clan and reclaiming the scholarship and philosophy that was once theirs; many are of an age to recall Carthage. Idealists look down on the Iconoclasts as unruly children, while the Iconoclasts sneer at the Idealists as do-nothing fossils. Caught in the middle are the Individualists, who straddle both camps in age and temperament. Needless to say, they catch flak from both sides.

CONCERNS

There are almost as many concerns among the Brujah as there are Brujah. As the clan falls short of a unified policy on pretty much anything, it's hard for a single issue or concern to rouse the clan's ire. The anger over Carthage still burns hot for the ancients, but few Brujah created in the last millennium care much for the issue. Iconoclasts raise howls about selective law enforcement and oppression by the Ventrue, but such cries often fall on deaf elder ears.

The only concern that draws members of the clan together across party lines is the encroachment by the Sabbat. The street is where the Sabbat operates, and that means that the Brujah take the brunt of any initial Sabbat assault. As a result, the Brujah feel (rightly or wrongly) that they are being used as a buffer by the other clans against the Sabbat ("Willing to fight to the last Brujah" is a common joke). A few loudmouths have even gone on record as saying that if they don't get any help, next time the Brujah should just let the *antitribu* through, but such sentiments are not yet common throughout the clan.

PRACTICES AND CUSTOMS

Brujah customs are a hodgepodge of half-remembered mortal rites, dusty traditions passed down absently from sire

HUMANITY

The Ventrue may have their fingers in the mortal world up to the elbow and claim they have the most interaction, the Brujah run an extremely close second. The difference between the clans' interactions lies in their approaches. The Ventrue seek out mortal institutions, but the Brujah seek out individuals. As a result, the Brujah might not pull the strings on a mayoral candidate, but may well have connections to people that candidate stepped on during his climb to the top—and the information gathered from such contacts can be as useful as anything garnered by a multi-million dollar Ventrue campaign.

CLAN PRESTIGE

Brujah clan prestige is bestowed more for attitude than specifics. The clan has at least a rough allegiance toward weakening authority and promoting anarchy, and acts which accomplish both or either win their performers status within the clan. Telling off a prince, disrupting a Ventrue deal (and living to tell about it), tweaking the Tremere or exposing a corrupt mortal politician for the fraud he is—all of these can win a Brujah points with her elders and peers. Unfortunately, the Brujah penchant for going after the high and mighty often turns the youngsters of the clan on their elders, which means that matters of prestige can get touchy. Rewarding a neonate for acts which subvert a Brujah elder is asking for trouble, but is also true to the spirit of the clan. Younger Brujah also have a habit of ignoring their elders' pronouncements and setting their own pecking order. Such arrangements are usually based on questions of strength or numbers of adherents; Brujah tend to move in packs and follow charismatic leaders.

to childe and whatever else comes to mind. Most are improvised from city to city, as the Brujah figure it's the meaning of what they're doing that's really important. Besides, it's not as if the Iconoclasts and the Idealists could agree to do anything in unison in any case. Instead, customs among the Brujah are more a matter of aligning along the clan's primary axis of sentiment and acting in accordance with it.

Brujah gatherings, called Rants, are not regularly scheduled. Instead, they just happen when something else interesting does—concerts, exhibitions, festivals, conferences and so on—and often the mortals responsible for triggering the Rant get drafted into it as well. Rants are essentially open to members of any clan, though any Tremere who attends is in for a rough time. The Brujah make no secret of their distaste for the Warlocks, and delight in introducing Tremere spies to new and exciting definitions of pain.

MALKAVIAN

Kooks. Fools. Madmen. Such are the descriptions the other clans have for the childer of Malkav, who frankly don't give a damn what anyone else thinks of them. The Malkavians are insane, but not in the way that others imagine. Each Malkavian sees the world through her own cracked lens of perception, a highly personal distortion that outsiders dismiss as mere insanity. But that distortion is the key to enlightenment, the Malkavians insist — at least those philosophically inclined — and often the Lunatics seem to know more about what's really going on than their so-called sane brethren.

What exactly the Malkavians are doing in the Camarilla is a subject of some debate. While the clan's allegiance to the sect has never wavered, it is nevertheless true that the sect's interests only seem to intersect with the clan's peripherally. As a result, the Malkavians view the Camarilla with a sort of bemused affection, while their counterparts in other clans can't help feeling vague and disquieting suspicion about the Lunatics' real motives.

INSANITY

It is a common misconception among the other clans to regard the Malkavians as cute or childlike, wacky little pranksters who, in the end, are harmless. Nothing could be further from the truth. Malkav's childer sport a wide range of dysfunctions, ranging from relatively mild cases of regression to full-blown psychoses and homicidal manias, but as a rule they are *not* cute. A Malkavian is far more likely to be toting a much-used straight razor than he is to carry a teddy bear; bloody rags are infinitely more common than bunny slippers. While there are some Malkavians who do regress to childish behavior, they do so with all the strengths and powers of a full-grown vampire. Tantrums thrown with the weight of Dementation or a frenzy behind them should not be thought of as adorable, and neither should the Kindred throwing them.

Recently, the entirety of the clan was somehow infected with the Dementation Discipline by the *antitribu* of the Sabbat. The deed was done over the Malkavian Madness Network, though even the Malkavians themselves seem at a loss to explain how exactly that happened. The new Discipline doesn't seem to have affected clan members' behavior overmuch, but with the Malkavians, one never knows.

STRENGTH AND INFLUENCE

Malkavian strength and influence varies from city to city, depending on the individual quirks of the local Malkavian population. In some places the Lunatics are nearly incapacitated by their manias, and thus are a non-factor in city politics. In others, the famed clan dementia is a non-issue or actually feeds an individual's drive to power. A power-hungry Malkavian with an obsessive personality can be a frightening thing for friends and foes alike.

To no one's surprise, the Malkavians find the mental health care system to be a hospitable environment; many set up little fiefdoms in managed care facilities. However, the Lunatics aren't limited to mental hospitals — it's more a question of what an individual Malkavian is driven to experiment with. In some cases that's nothing at all, in others it's art that the Toreador envy or business dealings that give the Ventrue pause. A very few dabble in magic, and the thought of what those Malkavians might be up to gives many powerful Tremere nightmares.

ORGANIZATION

Defining Malkavian organization is like trying to empty the oceans with a sieve. The task is simply pointless, as the Lunatics' ways of arranging themselves mutate and change with blinding speed. The clan's irregular meetings are open to all comers, primarily because the Malkavians don't care about keeping anyone out, but observers often returned chilled by what they saw. At times the Malkavians have mounted eerily accurate pastiches of Ventrue or Tremere clan gatherings; at others they mimic the Sabbat, or engage in behaviors utterly incomprehensible to anyone not sharing the communal cup of madness.

CLAN PRESTIGE

There's no telling what might set a Malkavian above her fellows. Clan standing varies wildly from night to night, and the Malkavian everyone follows one night might be shunned the next. It only makes sense to the Malkavians, and not even to all of them, it seems. An approximate guideline is that anyone who does exceptional work to break down a shared perception of reality (say, by getting a prince to speak in tongues or a keeper of Elysium to hang a finger painting) often wins kudos from her peers, but otherwise the Malkavian system of prestige just seems to be a parody of the other clans' approaches.

There is no local, national or global organization of Malkavians. The clan simply *is*. Trying to force it into the framework of "normal" behavior, as the Ventrue and others have been trying to do for centuries, is utterly fruitless. The Malkavians meet whenever they choose, do whatever they choose and revel in the thread of insanity which binds them all together.

CONCERNS

Do the Malkavians have unifying concerns? No one knows. There is speculation that the infection perpetrated by the *antitribu* has sparked at least some discussion among the Malkavians, but if anyone knows the truth, they're not talking. The more socially adept Malkavians routinely steer conversation away from clan matters, while the less functional ones don't seem to be worth asking.

If the clan can be said to have a core issue, it is the matter of enlightenment through new perception (or what the unenlightened mistakenly call insanity). By removing the scales of "normal" behavior from their eyes, the Malkavians claim to be able to see true reality more clearly than ever before. Not a few clan members want to share that renewed vision with the rest of the Camarilla and then the world. Such vampires are almost universally feared, as their conversion efforts amount to driving their victims insane.

PRACTICES AND CUSTOMS

The Malkavian custom that has the highest profile is the art of pranking, playing "jokes" on other Kindred so as to expand their perceptions. Of course, these jokes can take any form and are usually only funny to the Malkavian playing them; the targets find them to be anything from annoying to fatal. Malkavian pranking doesn't involve whoopee cushions and buckets of water balanced on doors; rather, it is an inspired attempt to kick the crutch of consensual reality out from under other Kindred. Pranks can range from continually rearranging all of the furniture in a vampire's haven to careful use of Dementation to siccing a hunter on an unfortunate target, and a vampire who becomes the subject of a Malkavian's interest rapidly finds his friends abandoning him for fear of being caught in the blast radius.

Malkavian targets for the Embrace tend to be outside the mainstream of society. While not all are clinically insane before the Embrace, none are paragons of stability, and many just need the horror of the Embrace to push them over the edge. Malkavian sires don't seem to be particularly attentive to their childer, but somehow the neonates end up knowing everything they need to know. Outsiders speculate that the Madness Network must somehow be involved, but since outsiders blame the Malkavian Madness Network for everything since the murder of Abel, such theories are often yawned off.

NOSFERATU

Nosferatu are not monsters, at least not in the sense that others might think they are. Yes, they dwell in sewers and filth, have visages that send mortals screaming, and breed strange monstrosities as guardians for their underground domains, but the Nosferatu deal in secrets, not carnage. Hiding their faces behind illusions, they (or their servants) seek out any tidbit that appears worth having, then sell their spoils to those less observant (who would seem to be quite a few judging from their clientele). The Nosferatu's willingness to go places other Kindred disdain serves them well on many occasions, and their reputations as monstrosities ensures that the curious don't attempt to turn the tables on them.

Nosferatu often dwell in the city's sewers, but aren't restricted to them. After all, all the action (and the information that comes with it) are above ground. The sewers are merely a convenient and concealed means of accessing the world above, and an excellent place to hide what's been found. Most Nosferatu turn the sewers around their havens into deathtraps, and the older the vampire, the more complicated and intricate the traps. Nosferatu are *very* fond of their privacy, and intruders had best be prepared to pay the price of trespassing.

What the Nosferatu ultimately deal in is information. Often the coin of exchange is more information, which just makes the clan richer. The Nosferatu aren't afraid to use their knowledge, either, much to the chagrin of other Kindred who have found themselves humiliated, blackmailed or even killed after letting the wrong word fall into Nosferatu hands.

STRENGTH AND INFLUENCE

It is rare for a Sewer Rat to hold a position in city government. Other Kindred are uncomfortable with having a smelly, repulsive monstrosity in a position of authority, and find ways to keep the Nosferatu out of power. Occasionally a prince tosses a position to the clan, either to demonstrate how open-minded he is or in an attempt to secure the Nosferatu's friendship, but most just play it safe and exclude the clan from power as much as possible. A Nosferatu prince is almost unheard of. In truth, the Nosferatu don't seem to care much. Time spent attending to the duties of an office is time not spent gathering information and putting that information to use.

As information-brokers without peer, however, the Nosferatu can easily make up for any loss of "temporal" power. Vast webs of shared information result in being able to acquire dirt on just about anyone, and the Nosferatu make certain that everyone knows it. As a result, other clans wanting what the Nosferatu have are forced to come and deal, and the Sewer Rats drive a hard bargain. Favors owed and gossip shared results in a remarkable amount of influence for the clan, which is valid currency above and below ground.

ORGANIZATION

The Nosferatu organization is loose, but not non-existent. Regional collections of Nosferatu, called Broods, meet on a semi-regular basis, usually to swap information. It's common for Broods to send representatives to one another, either as delegates at meetings or to carry certain precious pieces of news too valuable to trust to letters or email. Such exchanges help disseminate information across the clan with lightning speed.

Meetings of Broods are called Hostings (which leads to all sorts of jokes about parasitism), which operate on no set schedule. Instead, a Hosting happens when a Nosferatu decides that a Hosting needs to happen. The self-proclaimed host of the Hosting must arrange a meeting space and accommodations, but beyond that, the meetings are remarkably informal. Nosferatu treat each other with a great deal of respect; the shared horror of their appearance does much to promote clan unity.

In more recent years, the Nosferatu have invested heavily in the SchreckNET, wiring Brood to Brood in cyberspace and allowing for faster exchanges of data. The SchreckNET is now intercontinental, and its keepers expect to have upward of 90 percent of all Nosferatu burrows connected within the next three years.

CONCERNS

The Nosferatu know too much not to be concerned. They know why the Gangrel left the Camarilla, entirely too much of what goes on between Malkavians, and what's really going on in the corridors of Ventrue power. The Nosferatu are less than sanguine about the Camarilla's future, and have debated leaving the sect themselves at times. If there's a problem with the Camarilla, the Nosferatu know about it and are debating the matter worriedly.

One concern that the Nosferatu have that no others are privy to is the Nicktuku. According to clan lore, the Nicktuku are the clan founder's other children, so monstrously twisted as to make the Nosferatu look normal by comparison. Enormously powerful and utterly hateful, these monstrosities hunt their less deformed brethren across the globe. Reports of the Nicktuku have increased in recent years, and an alarming number of Nosferatu burrows have gone silent as well. Alarmist clan members are taking this intelligence as a sign that the Nicktuku are on the move, and as such they are readying their defenses for what they perceive as the final assault.

PRACTICES AND CUSTOMS

There are few practices common to the Nosferatu that have become known to others. One of the most spectacular and fearsome (which is perhaps why the Nosferatu let news of it leak) is the custom of creating breeding pools in order to manufacture guardian ghouls. Such pools are bodies of water that Nosferatu regularly infuse with their vitae. The results are literally hordes of twisted, massive and utterly loyal ghouled animals which serve as natural warning systems and defenses. Nosferatu also farm fungi and subterranean plants, creating gardens worthy of the finest apothecaries — or the deadliest poisoners.

Standing among the Nosferatu is based on utility and merit. Those who do exceptional work for the clan or who uncover particularly juicy tidbits of information (that can be later put to use; there's not much use for theoretical knowledge down in the storm drains) get acclaim. Furthermore, since the Nosferatu are in continuous communication, a well-regarded vampire's good press gets spread far and wide. Of course, the opposite is also true. A Nosferatu who fumbles an information exchange, gets a burrow violated or assaulted or who passes on false information to the rest of the clan finds his name turned to mud across the entire ShreckNET in a matter of hours.

In the end, all Nosferatu custom among each other breaks down to respect and politeness. The Nosferatu seem genuinely to respect one another and their elders (the Sewer Rats are the only vampires who don't regularly grumble about what evil deeds their elders are really up to), and that makes their dealings fluid, easy and fast. What matters to the Nosferatu is not the order of precedence, but rather actually getting things done, and their dearth of formalized customs reflects this desire.

There is one hobby which the Nosferatu seem to enjoy, and that's pushing the other Kindred. Every Nosferatu knows that the other clans prefer to deal with them as little as possible, and that they only do so when under great duress. Consequently, the Nosferatu take great pains to play up the worst aspects of their existence when the other clans come calling, testing to see just how far their prospective clients are willing to go. When the Toreador are willing to descend into the sewers, or the Ventrue to meet in a soup kitchen, not only do the Nosferatu get ghoulish pleasure out of seeing their visitors so discomfited, but the entire meeting becomes a gauge of exactly how desperate for help the high and mighty are.

TOREADOR

To the Toreador, or at least to any worthy of the name, beauty is as important as blood. The ultimate aesthetes, these Kindred are devoted to the exploration, creation and preservation of art in all its forms, whether that art wants to be preserved or not. Easily transfixed by an image of beauty, the Toreador can also be coldly vicious in destroying what displeases them. And as the same creation — or mortal — can please and displease equal numbers of Toreador, dealing with this clan at all can be a dangerous thing.

Contrary to their image as fops and poseurs, the Toreador are among the most effective manipulators the Camarilla possesses. Masters of intrigue for its own sake (just another art form to some Toreador), these Kindred can give words a sharper edge than a Gangrel's claws. The superhuman senses that let a Toreador bask in the presence of a Van Gogh also give her a clue as to her enemies' moods and anticipated actions. As for the study of art, an immortal sculptor's knowledge of anatomy can be applied with equal facility to a slab of marble or an opponent's throat.

Call it expression, call it art or call it beauty, the Toreador are after something that no other clan is. Excellence and artistry in all things call to the Toreador (those deserving of the Embrace, in any case), and it is the quest to achieve and preserve that sort of achievement that drives the clan. With all eternity before them, the Toreador have all the time they need to seek perfection. They just don't always seek it in ways or places that the other Kindred expect.

STRENGTH AND INFLUENCE

Apart from the Ventrue, no other clan has so thoroughly adapted to the Camarilla as have the Toreador. If the Ventrue are the sect's backbone, the Toreador are its heart. As a result, there are more than a fair share of Toreador princes, sheriffs, seneschals and the like. Even if a city's prince is of another clan, odds are good that there's a Toreador at his elbow advising him. The field of politics is as much a canvas as anything else for the Toreador, and many clan members have gotten very skilled in the medium.

Oddly enough, fewer keepers of Elysium than one might expect hail from Toreador ranks. Popular theory holds that this is because too many Toreador keepers were entranced by the exhibits assorted Elysiums held to do their jobs properly; the Toreador refuse to dignify this rumor with a response and instead flock to join the ranks of the harpies.

It is through the harpies that the Toreador truly exercise their clout. The final arbiters of status in a city, the harpies can make or break a vampire's reputation in a matter of seconds. They can drive him to acts of desperation to reclaim his good name, or exalt him to dizzying heights on the basis of a single deed. Princes can be brought low or created through the harpies' efforts, and as much as other Kindred might want to discount the Toreador's influence, there is too much evidence of their power to allow it.

ORGANIZATION

Toreador organization is a collection of free-floating cliques and artists' collectives. Like so many of the other clans, the Toreador have no formal international organization. Instead, individual Kindred drift from group to group, which can be as formal or informal as the temperaments of their members demand. Deference is showed to Toreador of demonstrable age, knowledge or talent, but for every neonate eager to pay homage to an elder whose work he admires, there's a former exotic dancer claiming that his physical beauty makes him a walking work of art. Such schisms break the clan down into two rough groups: the Artistes and the Poseurs. In truth neither faction is formalized enough to have a name; these are just the insults that each side flings at the others. Artistes are the truly creative among the Toreador, the ones who produce works of true inspiration and beauty. Their opposite numbers are those who are… less talented. The ranks of the Poseurs include critics, agents, substandard creators who were Embraced through lapses in judgment and those who claim their lifestyles or their anatomies make them works of art incarnate. There's no love lost between the two rough factions, and a great deal of time and energy gets devoted to petty squabbles for supremacy on the local level.

Concerns

Most of the clan's concerns are internal. The schism between talents and no-talents, the debates over what makes art, the endless urge to dabble in the mortal world to nurture art and creativity — all of these enfold the Toreador in endless debate. The concerns of the Camarilla are merely political and transient, you see, while the Toreador concern themselves with eternal verities and questions.

On the other hand, that's not to say that all Toreador deal strictly with the ethereal. Prime breeding grounds for culture on the East and West Coasts are being swamped, denying the Toreador access to those pools of talent. The Tremere seem to be making a play for supremacy in the sect, and should they dethrone the Ventrue, it seems likely they will be far less generous patrons of the arts than the Blue Bloods.

Practices and Customs

Of utmost importance to the Toreador is the appreciation of art and beauty. They do this in a variety of fashions: patronizing mortal and immortal artists, purchasing works of art, instigating new artistic movements, acting as "muses" to mortals and so on. However, Toreador patronage can rapidly turn sour; a promising artist who doesn't live up to expectations may find his patron fatally disappointed. Even less lucky are those throwaways the Toreador let live; they are sentenced to a lifetime of broken dreams and desperate longing for what was shown to them once, then snatched away.

Unlike the other clans, the Toreador love gathering. There's an informal clan meeting practically every week (if not every night), when the Toreador get together to swap gossip, compare trends and generally bask in one another's presences. Gatherings of this sort are called Affairs of the Clan, and attendance is strictly voluntary. However, since these Affairs are vital for gaining prestige within the clan, they're always heavily attended.

The clan (local groupings are called Guilds, much to the amusement of those who actually remember what artisans' guilds were like) also has a formal meeting each month on the night of the full moon. Such meetings are called Balls, and they are open to all Toreador. Outsiders can attend only by prior invitation; such invitations are highly sought-after, as the Toreador throw one hell of a party.

The Grand Ball is a once a year event set for Halloween, a Ball put on collectively by several Guilds. The site for the Grand Ball changes from year to year, and competition for the honor of hosting it is fierce. Most of the business discussed at

Clan Prestige

Toreador gain standing within the clan for creating or discovering works of art. Particularly successful Balls, manipulations of other vampires or cutting remarks at Elysium also win a Toreador points with her peers. Substandard discoveries or performances, embarrassing moments and demonstrated failures in social settings, however, can earn a Toreador her clan's unrelenting and eternal scorn.

Grand Balls is Toreador-specific and of utterly no interest to anyone outside of the clan.

Once every 23 years (the significance of the number is still unknown) the Toreador gather for an event called Carnivale, a week-long festival of the Toreador's true nature. Mortal and immortal artists attend, demonstrations of great beauty and savagery are given, everyone (who survives) has legendary stories to tell, and, at the end of the festivities, the mortal whom the Toreador acclaim as the greatest artist of her generation receives the Embrace and much acclaim. The debate over just who receives that gift is subject to much politicking and intrigue, and more often than not a compromise candidate ends up serving as the selection.

TREMERE

Born in stolen blood and awash in it ever since, the Tremere are regarded with suspicion by their allies and hatred by their enemies. A siege mentality has prevailed within the clan of thaumaturges ever since the night Tremere and his associates crossed the barrier between life and unlife, and nothing the Tremere have seen since then has convinced them it's time to let their guard down. Instead, as the centuries have passed the clan has grown steadily more insular and self-sufficient. Today, the other clans know less about what the Tremere actually do than they ever have, and the Warlocks like it that way.

Based out of their chantry in Vienna, the Tremere have always held to a process of slow expansion and consolidation. Once the Tremere acquire a chantry, they fortify and reinforce it before attempting to expand again. Each chantry is a minia-ture replica (in function, if not form) of the home base in Vienna, with laboratories, libraries, residence quarters for Kindred and retainers and other materials necessary for thaumaturgical research. The effort expended in creating each chantry, therefore, ensures that the chantry is not given up easily nor casually invaded by outsiders.

The Tremere are also past masters at the game of prestation. The wide range of possibilities that the Thaumaturgy Discipline makes available to them means that they can render a great many favors to a great many vampires. Handing out a lot of favors means piling up a lot of favors owed, and the Tremere excel at using those debts to advance their aims.

STRENGTH AND INFLUENCE

Strongest in central Europe, the Tremere rarely rise to the position of prince. That's not because individual Warlocks are incapable of holding the position or have no ambition for it, but rather because a Tremere prince would have divided allegiance to city and clan. Clan always comes first. As a result, many princes have Tremere advisors, or even scourges, but duty to clan supersedes duty to city or even to sect.

The real power the Tremere have comes from the unified front they present. Take on one Tremere, and you take on them all. That's not to say there's no bickering or backstabbing within the clan, but once an external threat manifests, all of the Warlocks lock step. (Mind you, there are Tremere hoping that other clan members get conveniently annihilated, but they won't so much as think that loudly for fear of a reprimand.)

The Cup

It's more than good indoctrination policies that keep the Tremere so unified. Each neonate, at the time of her creation, drinks a chalice's worth of the mixed blood of the Council of Seven. Grail imagery and similarities to the Sabbat Vaulderie aside, putting each new Tremere one step closer to being bound to the clan elders is simply good politics. Most neonates stay in line thereafter for fear of having the full bond enforced, while troublemakers are that much easier to Dominate or bond fully. Woe betide a Tremere who gets himself blood bound to someone outside the clan and is discovered, for by doing so he has destroyed his elders' most effective leverage on him. If the error is uncovered, the bound Tremere can expect an unpleasant time, and the vampire he is bound to will probably be marked for death.

Organization

Without a doubt, the Tremere are the most highly structured of the clans. Arranged in a pyramidal hierarchy (Tremere himself at the top, the Council of Seven beneath him, each with control over a different geographic region, and so on), the Tremere all know their exact place in the order of things. Each Tremere can trace the path of power from where she stands up through her superiors to Tremere himself, and can take comfort in having a well-established place.

Underneath the Council of Seven (which is comprised of all fourth-generation Tremere) sits the Order of Pontifices, seven of whom are assigned to each Councilor. Each Pontifex has a domain to oversee; such domains have only the vaguest relation to actual geography, and frequently overlap.

Each Pontifex has direct authority over a group of seven Lords (the aggregate is called the Order of Lords), each of whom oversees a smaller geographic region (a small country, for example, or a few particularly populous states). Each Lord also has seven Regents reporting to him, and each Regent has control over Tremere affairs at a particular chantry.

Neonates receive, along with the Embrace, initiation as Apprentices of the First Circle. As a young Tremere progresses in her studies, she ascends through the ranks to the title of Apprentice of the Seventh Circle. Such lofty "apprentices" help rule the chantry with the Regent; at any given time a chantry can boast a range of apprentices running from First Circle to Seventh. Interestingly enough, there are seven Circles of Mysteries for Regents, Lords and Pontifices as well; the Tremere never cease their studies, nor do they ever stop advancing in their knowledge of the Mysteries.

The Tremere's strict formality of hierarchy begins with the Embrace and never lets up. Each Apprentice of the First Circle must meet with her Regent once a week, and along with thaumaturgical instruction she receives an indoctrination in Tremere organizational thought. Each vampire is part of the clan as a whole and serves a function in the clan as a whole; a single vampire who shirks her duty weakens the clan as a whole, and so on. It is impressed on

Clan Prestige

The Tremere grant prestige within the clan in slow, carefully measured doses. Following orders to successful conclusions, triumphs of thaumaturgical research, eliminations of the clan's enemies and efforts that advance the clan's agenda are all rewarded, albeit in small increments. Tremere who disobey orders, engage in failed experimentation or who weaken the clan drop in prestige dramatically. Considering the rigidly hierarchical nature of the Tremere and the intense competition for advancement within the clan structure, a single misstep can set a Tremere's ambitions back literally centuries.

neonates early that they are exactly where they are supposed to be for a reason, and that the good of the whole comes first.

The Tremere do have a policy of rapid and multiple transfers of Kindred from chantry to chantry. This is done to keep any single Regent from acquiring too strong a power base. The constant turnover breaks up groups that have grown too tightly knit, as well as making it easier for high-ranking Tremere to sneak spies into a given chantry. On the other hand, the constant scattering of Tremere now means that a Regent who won his apprentices' loyalty can have agents in a dozen chantries across the globe.

Concerns

Extinction and power — those are the two concerns of Clan Tremere. The Warlocks never have quite recovered from the terror of their first nights as Kindred and the horrific war waged against them by the Tzimisce. Kindred too young to remember the nights in the Carpathians are fed endless stories of the battles against Tzimisce war ghouls and the nights when every hand was against them. That fear has never gone away. The Tremere are still convinced — perhaps with good reason — that their enemies still wait, and simply seek an opportunity, a moment of relaxed vigilance before striking once again. The Tzimisce are the featured players in such paranoid fantasies, but the Ventrue, the Toreador and even the escaped Gargoyles also play roles.

And what of the Salubri? Ever since Tremere's diablerization of Saulot, his childer have been haunted by the fear of Salubri vengeance. Such fears are ludicrous, of course — the Salubri are a hated, hunted remnant, driven underground by relentless Tremere persecution and propaganda. Surely there is no way they could ever mount a threat. But the oldest of the Tremere remember the strange events that led the clan to abandon its Wallachian stronghold of Ceoris, and wonder.

Practices and Customs

Thaumaturgy demands great attention to detail, and Tremere social practices mirror this. Position in the pyramid is of utmost importance at all times; proper deference to one's superiors must be maintained.

The Tremere follow a highly regimented meeting schedule. Just as every Apprentice of the First Circle meets with the local Regent once a week, each Regent meets with his peers and Lord once a year. Above them, each Lord meets with her associates and Pontifex once every three years, and the Pontifices meet with their peers and their superior once every seven years. (Note: Only the given Pontifices, Lords, Regents etc. under a single superior meet. Cross-pollination is strictly forbidden.) The Council of Seven meets once a decade in Vienna, and occasionally as a result of crises at other times. However, such irregular meetings are extremely rare; the Tremere have a schedule and they like keeping to it, exactly. Variation invites chaos, chaos disrupts control, and the Tremere like having control very, very much.

Beyond these organizational meetings, the Tremere gather frequently for mystical purposes. An entire chantry comes together for a Convocation every Tuesday, with each Convocation serving as equal parts rite and board meeting. Convocations are conducted telepathically, so as to frustrate any eavesdroppers. A city's Tremere also host open meetings the third night of every third month; such meetings are open to outsiders, and are conducted via speech, not mindspeech.

Finally, at the end of each October, the clan joins for two nights in a mystical communion. A sort of hive-mind is formed by a chant in which each Tremere takes part. Knowledge and wisdom can be exchanged (though deep probes of individual minds are impossible), and each Warlock is reminded of his place in the greater whole.

Ventrue

The Ventrue are the backbone of the Camarilla, the clan most firmly committed to the ideal of the sect. Perhaps this is because one of their own is given credit for first envisioning the Camarilla, perhaps it is because they honestly believe in the sect's ultimate good, but the fact remains that the Ventrue are the clan whose identity is most firmly tied to the Camarilla's. The Ventrue boast more princes than any other clan, and seem to take a special pleasure in organizing conclaves. Indeed, the Ventrue see participation in the Camarilla as a duty, and they are capable of going on at great lengths about it to other vampires whom they feel aren't pulling their weight. Such Kindred usually retort with comments about the clan's martyr complex, but the Ventrue take such slanders in stride. They know it is the lot of the noble to be unappreciated.

Always a clan of the aristocracy, the Ventrue these days are transitioning from Embracing the hereditary elite to enfolding the financial elite instead. The clan has always flocked to power, and in these modern nights the power is in the board room instead of the court. As a result, the Ventrue have become firmly enmeshed in speculative markets, industry and other financial arenas. They are well-aware of the power money has, and through their multitudinous mortal pawns they use that power exceedingly well. None of the other Camarilla clans can match the Ventrue in this field; few even try anymore.

The Ventrue do admire breeding, and are among the most urbane, sophisticated and formal of the Kindred. The clan has a plethora of traditions and customs, most of which are utterly nonsensical to other Kindred, but which the Ventrue follow doggedly. Young Ventrue who question the wisdom of doing such tend to have the lessons beaten into them by their sires, who value directed initiative rather than independence.

Despite the guise of gentility the clan adopts, the Ventrue capacity for cruelty and rapacity is boundless. They may be polite, but they are nonetheless vampires — vampires at the top of the power pyramid of the Kindred, no less. Kindness and other admirable qualities had nothing to do with getting them there; ruthless efficiency, burning ambition and tireless dedication did.

Strength and Influence

The Ventrue remain the most powerful clan in the Camarilla. Part of this derives from the fact that they are so much more intensely interested in the sect than their peers are, but part of it also derives from the drive to power that seems to be the clan's unifying trait. In most Camarilla cities, the local power structure is riddled with Ventrue. Even those who don't hold official titles have their fingers in some important mortal pie or other; stock exchanges, financial institutions, city hall and the like are common areas of Ventrue interest.

One of the products of this Ventrue stranglehold on the local hierarchy is that there is often little room for young Ventrue to ascend. They are kept in what amount to eternal apprenticeships to undying masters, and many grow restive under the yoke. As a result, there is a curious dichotomy in Ventrue behavior patterns; normally the most conservative and urban of vampires, the Ventrue also have a habit of seeing their younger clanmates flock into recently opened territories (physical, such as a city retaken from the Sabbat, or financial, *a la* a new industry rising to prominence) in hopes of staking new claims.

Organization

The Ventrue have an exceedingly formal clan organization, but that formality has a surprising degree of flexibility of response built into it. The leadership of the clan, sometimes referred to as the "Board of Directors," has approximately 30 members from all over the globe, though the most important are in New York, London and Paris. Meetings of the Board are irregular but attendance is nigh mandatory; with the power that the directors have at their command there's little excuse for not being able to jet to a convocation of the Board from anywhere.

Less exalted Ventrue make due with a clan structure that seems equal part corporate entity and club. Each city with a Ventrue population hosts a clan headquarters, called a Board and frequently run out of either a gentlemen's club or expensive office space. The Board also doubles as a corporation, and is the tool which the Ventrue exercise much of their financial control on the local level.

One of the Ventrue's self-described strengths is the fact that everyone knows his place within the clan; all roles and chains of command are clearly and formally demarcated. Progress through the ranks is slow for younger Ventrue except in unusual circumstances; too much ambition or initiative is frowned upon by the clan elders.

Concerns

The Ventrue's primary concern is the Camarilla, namely, how to keep it going in the wake of the defection by the Gangrel. While the Ventrue never had much use for the Gangrel,

CLAN PRESTIGE

Clan prestige is acquired by the Ventrue as a by-product of success. Successful acquisitions, business maneuvers, political coups or other activities that benefit the clan or the sect are rewarded with prestige, though it is common practice for as many Ventrue as possible to try to grab some of the credit for any activity that goes well. Activities that circumvent the bounds of normal clan behavior are regarded cautiously; if they succeed without denting the fortunes of other Ventrue, the instigators are lavishly rewarded, but if they fail or hurt the clan, the punishment is severe. Ventrue who don't behave them-selves properly also risk losing standing in the clan, as do their sires and childer. Blood and breeding will tell, after all.

common opinion held that they were extremely useful in defending against the Sabbat. With them gone, the Camarilla stands weakened, and the Ventrue feel they must shoulder even more of the burden of supporting the sect. There is also worry over the successful Sabbat incursions on the east coast of North America, which the clan is trying to spread to the rest of the sect.

Within the Camarilla, the clan's greatest concern is the growing power of the Tremere, who seem poised within a few short decades to attempt to wrest command of the sect from the Ventrue. There's also the usual fretting about increasing anarch activity, but most Ventrue tune this out as white noise. They've heard it all before, seen it come to naught and have no interest in hearing it now.

PRACTICES AND CUSTOMS

The formal practices of the Ventrue are too numerous (and in many cases, too nitpicky) to go into here; suffice it to say that they have a great many. There are customs for who gets to drink first, who speaks in which order at the Board, what sorts of clubs (gentlemen's only; if there are none such, then often the alumni clubs of prestigious universities are chosen as substitutes) can be used to house the Board, parties to celebrate Embrace dates and so on. Every move is circumscribed by tradition and precedent; innovation is smiled upon only so long as it doesn't disrupt existing practice.

The most essential custom of the Ventrue, however, is that of assistance. In all things, the clan comes first, and any Ventrue can come to the Board or to a clanmate for assistance. By long tradition, those Ventrue thus petitioned are obligated to come to their clanmate's aid, regardless of personal risk or preference. A Ventrue who fails in this obligation loses face within the clan, and can expect no help from any of his clanmates should he request it.

When it comes to the Embrace, the Ventrue are exceedingly selective. Only the creme de la creme will do for the Blue Bloods, the best of the mortal best in business, politics, the military and so on. Ventrue take care to instruct their childer in the ways of the Camarilla, seeing as someday it will be those neonates' duty to uphold the sect. Ventrue never really step too far away from their childer unless compelled by

The Mortal World

Of the Ventrue's greatest strengths is the depth of their interaction with the mortal world. They dabble in mortal political and financial institutions as reflexively as mortals breathe, and as a result have more influence among the living than do any of the other clans. While doing such occasionally puts the Masquerade at risk, it also gives the clan admirable resources. The Ventrue also have the most skilled, most highly placed and in general the most numerous ghouls of all the clans, and their expertise at using the mortal tools is one of the keys to the sect's continued survival.

Within the clan itself, there is growing resentment against a perceived "old boys' network" of elders whom younger Ventrue see as denying them opportunities for advancement. The younger Ventrue also feel that the clan's structure is inefficient, while the elders shake their heads over the impetuousness of youth and claim that their experience gives them the mandate to keep things just as they are.

society or distance; the strong bonds between sire and child are part of what helps unify the clan.

The Ventrue meet on the first Tuesday of every month at the Board; attendance is mandatory, and those playing hooky find themselves fetched by the retainers of the "Chairman" (the local elder and head of the board, usually also a member of the primogen council). The meetings are called Directorate Assemblies, though older Ventrue insist on calling them by older names in French, Latin and Greek. Directorate Assemblies resemble nothing so much as mortal board meetings, with financial and political data providing the bulk of the conversation. The meetings are also used to regulate clan standing, with "promotions" and "demotions" coming in the form of public praise or scorn from the Chairman or membership on select committees.

...And One

Gangrel

The Gangrel, as a clan, have formally seceded from the Camarilla. That is not to say that every single Gangrel has turned in her membership card and turned her back on the organization as a whole, as there are plenty of Gangrel who consider themselves part of the sect. Rather, it is the clan as a whole that has withdrawn its support from the governing body, abandoning its right to have equal say and equal power in the sect's councils. The clan's elders attach no stigma to those individuals who choose to remain with the Camarilla—it's the individual's right to choose, after all. However, one must now make the distinction between saying that there are Gangrel of the Camarilla (true) and that the Gangrel are of the Camarilla (false).

Those Gangrel who have remained with the sect occupy a slightly reduced place in the sect's hierarchy. Without the presence of a clan justicar to defend Gangrel interests, members of other clans (particularly the Ventrue and Brujah) are making subtle encroachments on Gangrel territories and domains. The end result of this process may be to drive the remaining Camarilla Gangrel off as well, but long-term planning isn't every Kindred's strong suit.

Even Camarilla Gangrel are generally taciturn and solitary by nature, albeit perhaps less so than their newly non-affiliated brethren. It is rare for a Gangrel to take much interest in a city's government; most prefer moving from place to place, or develop a concern for a specific part of a city's landscape (a zoo, a central park system, an arboretum etc.) and make a crusade out of protecting that one spot. Anything that affects a Gangrel's chosen territory is fought tooth and nail, while the rest of the city can generally go hang.

Contrary to popular belief, Gangrel don't necessarily enjoy running carefree through the woods or spending time with werewolves, as in most cases Lupines regard Gangrel as being just as bad as the rest of the bloodsucking lot. Rumors of cooperation between the two groups are greatly exaggerated, to say the least. While the vast majority of Gangrel do prefer to get the hell out of the cities when they can, they take to the countryside with an eye to self-preservation rather than bucolic splendor.

Strength and Influence

While stronger than the splinter groups within the Camarilla, such as the Samedi or Lasombra *antitribu*, sectarian Gangrel now lag well behind the six major clans in strength. In any given city or region, there are likely to be enough Gangrel to keep anyone from pushing the clan around too much, but when it comes to overall policy decisions, the Gangrel just don't have the muscle anymore. Having given up representation on the Inner Council and the right to present a justicar, the Gangrel are now without voice at the highest levels of power, and are feeling the consequences of that change nightly.

In terms of geography, the Gangrel form a sort of perimeter on Camarilla territory. They prefer small cities or very large ones (which usually house extensive parks, zoological gardens and so on); mid-range urban environments don't do much to tickle the Gangrel fancy.

Organization

The Gangrel who remain with the Camarilla are not so much organized as they are stable. An unofficial hierarchy of respect has emerged among the stragglers, who prefer to keep out of sect business as much as possible. If two Gangrel come into conflict in a situation where one does not have clear-cut dominance over the other, the result is a bloody brawl. Such impromptu duels rarely result in fatalities, but there is considerable loss of face involved for the loser. Some Gangrel would seem almost to prefer dying to admitting defeat. Of late, certain princes have encouraged contentious Gangrel in their domains to settle matters in less violent fashion, or to agree to limits to the carnage, but the notion hasn't taken hold.

In the meanwhile, Gangrel exist as floaters and neoindependents, shunning the need for organization above the

local level. Gangrel gatherings are called by whoever sees a need for one; the informal prestige of the individual making the invitation determines how many guests are likely to attend.

A Gangrel prince is an extremely rare thing; odds are that any such vampire has been forced into her position by circumstance rather than ambition. If a Gangrel takes a position within a city government, it's most likely to be one without rigid responsibilities, such as sheriff. A higher than expected number of Gangrel take up the mantle of archon, possibly because the job's nomadic nature and mandate to circumvent politics appeal to Gangrel sensibilities.

CONCERNS

The primary concern that most Camarilla Gangrel have, unsurprisingly, is the worry that the whole thing is going to come crashing down any night now. While the clan as a whole might not have had any problems with Gangrel remaining behind with the sect, there were any number of hard words and harder blows between individual clan members over the issue. If the whole thing collapses, the survivors are going to have a serious loss of prestige within the clan. Throw in other concerns like, say, survival, and suddenly the durability of the Camarilla becomes of more than academic interest to even the seemingly apathetic Gangrel.

A lesser problem, but still an important one, is the way in which the post-schism Gangrel are being squeezed by their sectmates. With territory growing more and more scarce as broods of childer grow larger and larger, it is often the Gangrel who find themselves being shoved aside to make room for favored neonates descended from primogen members or those whom elders owed favors. The situation has not yet reached a boiling point, but sooner or later someone's going to start comparing notes and then the shit is likely to hit the fan in a hurry.

PRACTICES AND CUSTOMS

While not formal in the sense that a Ventrue or Toreador would understand, Gangrel customs have a strict ritualization to them that the Tremere would be hard-pressed to emulate. Much of what has survived as modern Gangrel culture had come from the clan's concentration in Scandinavia during the past two millennia. Gatherings of Gangrel are called *althings* (or *things*, if they're on a smaller scale), and the recounting of deeds and tales that occurs at such gatherings is reminiscent of the Viking *brag*. *Althings* occur on the equinoxes, while May 8th often hosts smaller gatherings.

Precedence at a gathering of Gangrel is determined by a series of individual contests of dominance. Most such challenges are just staredowns, but a few graduate to brawl status. Such combats are vicious but rarely fatal; there aren't enough

CLAN PRESTIGE

Gangrel gain prestige from one another through the *allthings*, and by having word of their deeds and actions spread by other Gangrel. Prestige bestowed by members of other clans is generally worthless to the Gangrel, unless the outsider in question has done something to earn Gangrel respect.

Gangrel for them to go around killing each other at meetings. Such duels for primacy occur whenever Gangrel meet on their own and for the first time, even if it's just two clanmates coming across each other in the woods. Once precedence is established, the pecking order is fixed and there's no need to repeat the process every time the same Gangrel meet. The only exceptions come when someone on the losing end of a prior encounter decides he's in line for a promotion, and tries again. The winners of such combats gain prestige within the clan, while the losers are reduced in standing (and usually beaten to a pulp as well), which does keep the number of frivolous challenges down.

Once precedence has been established, the leader begins the recitation of names and deeds, plus whatever other information she feels needs to be passed along. If there's no discussion, the floor is then yielded to the second in command, and so on. All in attendance, regardless of whether it's a full *allthing* or just two clan members, are expected to remember what they are told, and to pass on the important and particularly interesting tales to other Gangrel not in attendance. Thus heroes are made of some Gangrel and laughingstocks of others, but the news that needs to travel somehow gets spread.

Gangrel rarely reveal themselves to their progeny at the time of the Embrace. Instead, they watch prospective childer for an extended period of time before dooming another mortal to vampiric existence, then strike without warning. The new childe is abandoned to his own devices (though the sire and usually a few other Gangrel keep an eye on him) and must learn to survive on his own. If he does so well enough, eventually his sire will come forward and induct him into the ways of the clan. If not, incompetent neonates tend to take care of themselves in fatal fashion. A sire whose neonate fails can suffer a loss of prestige, depending upon how fast and how emphatic the failure was.

THE PROUD FEW

The Camarilla, by its own definition, speaks for and includes all Cainites. Needless to say, this claim is either ignored

THE ROM CONNECTION

Regardless of sect affiliation, Gangrel hold the mortal Rom (colloquially known as "Gypsies") in particular regard. Interfering with a Rom *kumpania*, particularly one a Gangrel may have some blood relation to, is a sure-fire way to get the local Gangrel very angry very quickly. Gangrel normally shun human company as much as possible, but it is not too unusual to find a Gangrel moving in and out of a Rom camp, or even sharing time by the fire and companionship with the members of the *kumpania*.

On the other hand, the Ravnos, disparagingly referred to as "Gypsies" by the other clans, have the Gangrel's undying enmity. The various explanations as for why exactly this is the case range from a Gangrel dislike of the Ravnos' playing to stereotype to something to do with the clans' Antediluvians (or Antediluvian, if you believe the tales)

or mocked by the vampires who comprise the Sabbat and the independent clans. More importantly, the assessment is derided by the organizations that stand outside or in opposition to the Camarilla and who, in some part, define themselves by the fact that they're not part of it. The whole setup is a convenient fiction for all concerned: The Camarilla clings to its supposed catholicity as justification for its existence, while the outsiders twit the presumption involved in making such a claim.

In other words, the arrangement works nicely for all of the groups involved. But what of the individuals who fall between the cracks, vampires whose allegiances would seem to lie elsewhere but who, for one reason or another, have gathered under the Camarilla's banner. From the haughty Lasombra *antitribu* to the horrifyingly fascinating Samedi, these stragglers and defectors occupy a place in Camarilla society that is, at best, ambiguous. While the very charter of the Camarilla mandates that these individual vampires be granted the same treatment as any other Kindred, their origins inevitably provide cause for (sometimes justifiable) suspicion and ill treatment. As a result, defectors to the Camarilla side are not always greeted warmly, which makes it that much more difficult to convince other members of the "opposition" to cross the fence.

This is not to say that every Camarilla vampire whose blood doesn't trace back to one of the organization's original clans is automatically treated poorly — more than a few have risen in power and status, to the point where they are feared and respected throughout the Camarilla. No one dares tweak the estimable Montano, for example, about his sire. The vast majority of the so-called "clanless," however, find themselves on the fringes and in between the cracks of night-to-night Camarilla society. No one inside the Camarilla quite knows what to do with them and, cast free from their former associations, they aren't exactly sure what to do with the Camarilla.

Or, for that matter, with themselves.

FOLLOWERS OF SET

To say that the Setites of the Camarilla are regarded as odd is to indulge in gross understatement. Nevertheless, the handful of Serpents who did heed the initial call of the Camarilla (there have been precious few to come over since) seem entirely sincere in their attachment to the sect. Even more bizarre is the fact that the unaffiliated Followers of Set don't seem to be taking any particular steps to wipe out these few aberrations. (The Serpents of the Light are another matter, but then again, the Sabbat always is.)

In reality, the motivation behind the trickle of Camarilla Setites is a simple one. Say what you like about it, but the Camarilla is the most efficient thing the Cainite race has ever put together. It has managed, with very few slips, to conceal the presence of vampires from the masses of humanity despite the best efforts of its enemies to destroy it, and to keep some vague semblance of order over a large portion of the map.

Now what, ask the Camarilla Setites of themselves, if that organization and occasional efficiency could be turned to their ends?

It's a disturbing possibility, which is why these Serpents keep a very low profile.

• Dealings With Others

Camarilla Setites cluster themselves on the fringes of Elysium; the usual crowd there is more likely to discuss matters and less likely to haul out the old "A Setite is a Setite" rationalization before opening fire. Furthermore, those Kindred with passions for art and diplomacy are likely to have passions for other things, things that the Serpents can provide. Still, the Setites of the Camarilla take great care to avoid behavior that is too stereotypical, for the simple reason that none of them want to be mistaken in a dark alley — or a well-lit board room — for a non-sectarian member of the clan.

Followers of Set who have joined the Camarilla have not abandoned their clan's ultimate goal, nor are they necessarily regarded as traitors by their clanmates. The true glory of Set will be made manifest in the subversion or destruction of all of the other clans, but nowhere is written that all of the other clans need to be humbled at the same time. Using the Camarilla to humble the Sabbat, then the independents to humble the Camarilla makes perfect sense from the Setite perspective. In the meantime, Camarilla Setites do their utmost for the sect as a method of working toward that final aspiration.

Oddly enough, it is the Toreador and the Brujah that Camarilla Setites deal with most frequently, and whom they turn to for protection in the face of adversity from other Camarilla Kindred. Both clans are prey to strong passions and desires of the sorts that the Setites can assuage, while Nosferatu, Tremere and Ventrue tend to be cautious in their dealings with any Setites, regardless of sect. As a rule, Camarilla Setites avoid Malkavians whenever possible, reportedly out of the fear that the Lunatics can see right through their schemes. More rational Kindred say that it's because the Setites just don't have anything that Malkavians actually *want*, but to date, it's all hearsay and speculation.

• Roleplaying

Playing a Setite bound by the laws of the Camarilla takes even more delicacy and subtlety than portraying an unfettered member of the clan. Camarilla Setites take great pains to put their sectmates at ease — they voluntarily tone down the serpent imagery and decor, just to accentuate the putative distance between themselves and the "normal" members of the clan. Some sect-aligned Setites go so far as to eschew "traditional" Setite activities like dabbling in a city's drug trade, though they're more likely to make a logical case as to how their connections make them best suited to run the market to the Camarilla's benefit. How much of a charade the performance actually is depends on the individual Serpent, but all Camarilla Setites recognize the necessity of earning their sectmates' trust by any means possible.

In social situations, Camarilla Setites are unfailingly polite and proper, with every action calculated to make those who would rail against them for their origins look bad, boorish and untrustworthy. That's not to say that Camarilla Setites are ineffectual or limited, but rather that they get their hands dirty in private. A Setite strolling into Elysium may have under-the-

table deals going with half the Toreador in attendance, but won't hint at any of them in public. Appearances must be preserved, after all — appearances and a reputation for discretion, so that future deals aren't jeopardized.

DAUGHTERS OF CACOPHONY

It is only the modern nights that the Daughters of Cacophony have truly earned their name, culling the men, *castrati* and boys from their ranks for reasons unknown. The remaining Daughters have no inclination to talk about the topic, and instead seem to be wholly enthralled by the process of creating and performing music. Politics and warfare, it seems, mean nothing to these Kindred. Only music, of all the arts, holds any attraction for them at all.

Camarilla Daughters seem to belong to the sect out of convenience, not conviction. If a city is Camarilla, then the local Daughters abide by Camarilla laws and Traditions without so much as a mellifluous grumble. Daughters of Cacophony have no great love for the sect, but no great dislike of it either, and it has been noted that the bloodline tends to follow the Masquerade whether it is enforced locally or not. There is also speculation that the Daughters prefer dealing with the Camarilla clans to dealing with the Tzimisce and Lasombra of the Sabbat, but speculation is all it is. In the meantime, the Kindred of the Camarilla generally agree that it's better to have the Daughters on the inside than the outside, and best of all to have them so

THE GIOVANNI

There are no Giovanni in the Camarilla. Oh, there are certainly members of the Giovanni clan who *claim* membership in the sect, and who follow the forms, figures and functions of Camarilla membership, but they are no more true Camarilla vampires than a lump of pyrite is true gold. Claiming disenchantment with family policies, Giovanni "defectors" seek asylum in the sect and bring with them valuable intelligence about the Giovanni's true aims and actions.

It should come as no surprise that the "intelligence" is a mishmash of self-contradictory lies, the disenchantment is dissembling, and that these so-called Giovanni *antitribu* are nothing more than deep-cover moles inside the Camarilla organization. Some take a high profile; others attempt to pass as Ventrue or Toreador when they can. Regardless of style, however, every single Giovanni who has weaseled himself into the sect is there to subvert, spy and misinform, and does his level best to accomplish those goals. Some wait decades or even centuries before acting, but all ultimately and unquestioningly owe their allegiance to the clan.

Spies of this ilk who are caught usually don't last long enough to talk; the clan's arrangement with ghosts provides for the equivalent of a suicide pill for the imprisoned Giovanni. Better and better precautions are being taken these days, and "defectors" are being questioned more and more thoroughly, but that just means that the spies the Giovanni are sending in have to be better prepared.

completely distracted by their projects that they pay the rest of the world no heed at all.

- **Dealing With Others**

The Camarilla offers an abundance of clans with whose members the Daughters delight in dealing — so to speak. The Ventrue offer patronage, the Malkavians inspiration and the Toreador collaboration, companionship and competition. Among those three clans, there's more than enough to keep a Daughter busy at Elysium. The other clans of the Camarilla don't seem to interest the Daughters — precious little does, after all — but at least there seems to be no active hostility present, either. A Daughter of Cacophony does not recoil in horror from a Nosferatu; she just has nothing to say to him.

Sirens (for so the bloodline is nicknamed) never take positions in a city's government. A few have been known to deign to sit with the harpies on occasion, but a Daughter serving as primogen, sheriff or *deo prohibe* prince is a notion beyond the bounds of possibility. Those Daughters who are in the Camarilla have no interest in shaping it or its policies.

- **Roleplaying**

Daughters of Cacophony are devoted, at least in public, to their art. Whatever the bloodline's hidden agenda might be, individual Daughters' behavior in public always follows the same pattern: devotion to singing and music, a complete apathy toward all things political, and utter disdain for any not so talented as they. Despite their disinterest in all things martial, the Daughters do not hesitate to defend themselves (and some say that the threshold of provocation has been reduced as the bloodline's songs have grown in power) with all the force at their disposal.

On the other hand, Sirens are often inclined to look favorably on those who praise their work *intelligently* — "You sing real purty" isn't likely to win a Daughter's favor. The Daughters are also likely to haunt local Elysiums in search of powerful and educated patrons. What the Daughters *do* with those patrons is a mystery best left to the darkest recesses of the imagination — at least if you believe the rumors.

SAMEDI

The Samedi of the Camarilla are a curious lot. Solitary by nature, they are seldom offered the option of being gregarious in any case; no one wants to get too close to them. Highly transient, Samedi bounce from city to city and Elysium to Elysium, following the scent of contract work for high-ranking Camarilla officials. Sufficiently distanced observers look on this migratory existence as a survival tactic — stay too long in one place and the locals eventually stop being afraid of you. Familiarity breeds contempt, and for the Samedi, contempt can be fatal.

Camarilla Samedi aren't after acceptance in any case. Rather, they're with the organization for a variety of reasons: dislike of Sabbat tactics, a desire for the protection the Camarilla aegis offers, and sometimes just better pay on the Camarilla side of the fence. Pretty much all of the Camarilla Stiffs, however, share an unrelenting hatred of the Giovanni, and use what influence they have to encourage the Camarilla

to move against the Necromancers. The degree of influence individual Samedi can wield (there is no "organization" of Samedi worthy of the name) is impressive, as many are close to vampires of considerable power.

• Dealings With Others

The average Samedi's appearance is so repulsive — and the wry humor with which the Stiffs invariably present themselves so contrary to expectations — that other vampires can't deal with them without some sort of frame of reference. A Samedi who's in town specifically to serve as a bodyguard for an archon or a prince can be accepted, on a certain level. He's here to do a job, after all, and even the most prejudicial Toreador has to admit that the unique talents of the Samedi let them do certain jobs very well. But to admit a Samedi into normal discourse and society, well, that goes beyond the pale. Nosferatu are ugly, but Samedi are corpselike, revealing a bit too much about the true nature of vampirism for other Kindred to be comfortable around them.

For their own part, the Samedi enjoy keeping everyone else off-balance, as it makes their usual job of bodyguard that much easier. And, as no one can actually afford to offend the Samedi for fear of retribution, the Stiffs push that advantage for all it's worth. Samedi aren't actually contemptuous of their fellows in the Camarilla, just amused by them. Even the monsters find some things a little too monstrous, it seems.

• Roleplaying

Despite their monstrous appearance, Samedi are, in their own way, urbane and civilized — they don't shamble, ooze or moan, and most can hold up their end of a conversation with the best of them. A great many Samedi worked as coroners, morticians and the like, and as such have a long-standing acquaintance with death and other uncomfortable topics. In addition, there's a streak of semi-sadistic humor endemic to the bloodline, and many Samedi simply can't resist subtly playing up their deformity while being as polite as possible, just to watch the Toreador and Ventrue squirm.

When it comes time for business, however, Samedi are more than happy to get their hands dirty. Members of the bloodline have a very low bullshit tolerance; when you look like the stuff at the bottom of the pile in the dumpster, you can't afford to judge anything other than results. While Samedi do show a small preference for spending time in the presence of Nosferatu (whom they generally won't take as targets on assassination contracts) as opposed to any other vampires, they still prefer professional contacts to social ones. It's easier for all concerned that way.

MINOR INCURSIONS

The following clans have few, if any, members who have pledged their allegiance to the Camarilla. Most have professional dealings with the sect, and their presence here is more a matter of completeness than anything else. It is rare, if not impossible, for a member of the Tzimisce, Assamite or Ravnos

clans to proclaim himself a member of the Camarilla. Other allegiances come first.

Some bloodlines, such as the Kiasyd, have absolutely no Camarilla involvement, and as such are not mentioned here.

Assamite

Hassan's childer see the Camarilla as a source of work, nothing more. An Assamite's loyalty is to the clan, first and foremost; the Camarilla offers nothing other than targets or employers to an Assassin. With the Camarilla's strictures against diablerie firmly in place, Assamite existence and the Traditions of the Camarilla would seem to offer little grounds for compromise. Assamites are more than happy to work for Camarilla vampires, but solely as independent contractors. Any childe of Hassan who claims loyalty to the sect is either deranged or running a very weak bluff.

Ravnos

There are a very few Ravnos who proport themselves to be members of the Camarilla and actually mean it. Ravnos of the Camarilla are, to a man, no longer welcome among their clanmates, and take succor where they can. For some, putting up with the humorless elders of the Camarilla is preferable to a quick death, and so they attempt to rein in their socially unacceptable tendencies enough to avoid being staked out by their new playmates as well.

A handful of princes have Ravnos "Fagins" working for them to steal items of power and information from their enemies; a little diablerie in the cause of the prince's work gets ignored or even smiled upon, so long as it's someone from the other side who's getting the bite put on them.

To say that sectarian Ravnos are distrusted by their Camarilla brethren is a vast understatement. Thankfully, there are so few Ravnos in the Camarilla that most vampires never have their prejudices tested in the field. As for those who do mouth off or otherwise make their displeasure known, they often find themselves short a valuable item — such as a piece of jewelry, a document or a favorite ghoul's liver — for their trouble. Just because a Ravnos joins the Camarilla doesn't mean that he's either well-behaved or nice.

Tzimisce

If there are a half-dozen Tzimisce in the Camarilla, it would be a major surprise. The vast majority of the clan belongs to the Sabbat; the rest are apolitical in the extreme. The very presence of the Tremere in the sect guarantees that the Tzimisce have no interest in signing on. Those very, very few Tzimisce who have deigned to join forces with the Camarilla have done so for intensely personal reasons (say, to avenge a mortal insult or to use the Camarilla to dispose of a rival in the Sabbat). However, even under these dire circumstances the Camarilla's few Tzimisce do *not* advertise their presence, do *not* take leadership roles in the sect and do *not* tend to stick around once their personal objectives are accomplished.

Caitiff

Seduced and abandoned by their sires, the Caitiff are everywhere on the fringes of Camarilla society. Clanless and unwanted, the Caitiff are the results of one-night stands, infatuations, frenzied Embraces and outright mistakes. Most have hazy recollections, at best, of sire and Embrace; some have none whatsoever. Stumbling along in the haze of a new existence, each eventually discovered the keys to survival — usually in the form of other Caitiff looking out for the newcomer — or died trying.

A Caitiff's only identifying mark is a lack of identifying marks. Some Kindred theorists posit that some sort of "imprinting" between sire and childe takes place over time, allowing the younger vampire to acquire the physical characteristics of her sire as mandated by the blood. Caitiff, however, have no such distinguishing marks — Caitiff descended from Nosferatu, for example, may be ugly, but rarely do they show the full-blown monstrosity of their vampiric ancestors. Thus it goes for other Caitiff; ones Embraced by Malkavians may be a little quirky but not necessarily prey to full-blown derangements, ones Embraced by Ventrue may have feeding preferences but not full-blown prey exclusions, and so on. An informed observer can generally guess with reasonable accuracy what a Caitiff's lineage might be, but in the end, it's rarely worth even the attempt to do so.

Caitiff fill in the positions in Camarilla society that no one else really wants. While the Camarilla may take the clanless in on occasion out of a vague sense of paternalism, the clans take care of their own first and leave the scraps for the Caitiff. Some Caitiff scorn active participation in city politics as second-class citizens, while others gladly seize any opportunity as a toehold in the establishment. In the meantime, the majority of clanless skirt involvement out of self-preservation, preferring to have the putative benefits of membership in the Camarilla without being drawn into its politics.

Nickname: Trash

Appearance: Caitiff often appear as more poorly dressed versions of their accepted cousins, aping Toreador or Brujah style on a rather limited budget. Few display truly outstanding physical characteristics marking them as descended from one clan or another — disdainful Ventrue have referred to Caitiff as "generic" in appearance, and the Caitiff have seized upon the slight as an ironic badge of honor. A close look at any gang of mortal vampire-wannabes often reveals one or two Caitiff, dressed in their imitative best and enjoying the hell out of the whole scene.

Quote: *I didn't ask to have this done to me. I didn't ask to be a vampire. But since one of you high-and-mighty SOBs did it to me, and I'm one of you now, I'll be damned if I'm gonna be a peon for the rest of eternity.*

Havens: Caitiff make havens wherever and whenever they can. Basement apartments and abandoned tenements are particular favorites, as no one else wants these places and the Caitiff aren't likely to be booted out of them after having set up shop.

Background: Caitiff are primarily a development of the last century, especially the years since World War II. Alarmist Kindred point to the explosion in the numbers of the clanless as a harbinger of Gehenna, but more level-headed vampires see the problem as symptomatic of a breakdown in the traditional social orders.

Caitiff often flock together, forming coteries out of desperation and for defense. Groups of the clanless tend to have short life expectancies; they shatter, fragment and reform on a regular basis. Caitiff come from all walks of life. Most receive the Embrace as an accident of fate, rather than by design, and as such that means that there's no such thing as a "typical" candidate for Caitiffhood. All that the Caitiff share is a knack for having been in the wrong place at the wrong time.

Character Creation: Caitiff have to survive on the streets with little or no help, and a few debilitating conditions that most neonates are in no shape to deal with on their own. While Caitiff are spread across the spectrum of mental, social and physical capabilities, those who survive longest often have Mental or Physical as their Primary. Streetwise, Subterfuge and Survival are common Abilities among Caitiff, but a Caitiff's experience and education can run the gamut.

Disciplines: Any (Default to Fortitude, Potence and Presence)

Weaknesses: Caitiff can purchase any Discipline at character creation, but thereafter have to pay six times current rating for any and all powers purchased with experience points.

On a more basic level, Caitiff suffer a social stigma from not being part of an accepted clan. As a result, more established Kindred feel free to snub or denigrate Caitiff freely. Until a Caitiff establishes herself in a city or social circle, she's at +2 difficulty on all Social rolls with all non-Caitiff vampires.

Organization: Every so often, someone attempts to organize the Caitiff into a clanlike structure. The attempt inevitably fails, in part because of the innate fractiousness of Caitiff society and in part because the established clans have a vested interest in keeping the Caitiff disorganized. On a night-to-night basis, Caitiff organization works, at best, on a local level, and most often not at all.

Stereotypes

Camarilla: *Well, the Sabbat wants us dead, so I can deal with the crap from the Cammies for a while instead. I'd rather get sneered at than shot at, you know? But things are changing. It doesn't matter if they want to keep the power away from us. These days, there are enough of us to take it.*

Sabbat: *Oh, sure, they offer you the world — then they haul off and hit you on the back of the head with a shovel and bury your ass. And that's if they actually bother to stop and talk instead of just trying to kack you right off the bat. I don't like them, don't trust them and would just as shoot them as see them.*

The View from Without
The Camarilla

Well, better that they serve as our buffer and first line of defense than they cross over and join the Sabbat. By allowing the clanless to join us, we protect the Masquerade, defend ourselves and keep the streets quiet. Those benefits are worth the price of occasionally seeing a Caitiff putting in an appearance at Elysium.

— Danielle Foster, Brujah primogen, St. Louis

The Sabbat

Hey, man, the Sabbat is great. You don't have to take any of the crap you get in the Camarilla — over here we're organized. They call us Panders, not Caitiff, and we got a voice! It's so much better than putting up with Toreador attitude and waiting for their table scraps. Just come to one meeting, man — I swear, if you don't like it, you can walk away with no harm done.

— Kai Simmons, recent Sabbat initiate

The Independents

The clanless are a distraction. The trick is to make certain that they distract our opponents, rather than us. A justicar who's busy hunting down a particularly obnoxious gang of Caitiff isn't busy poking into our concerns. It's that simple.

— Rafael Giovanni

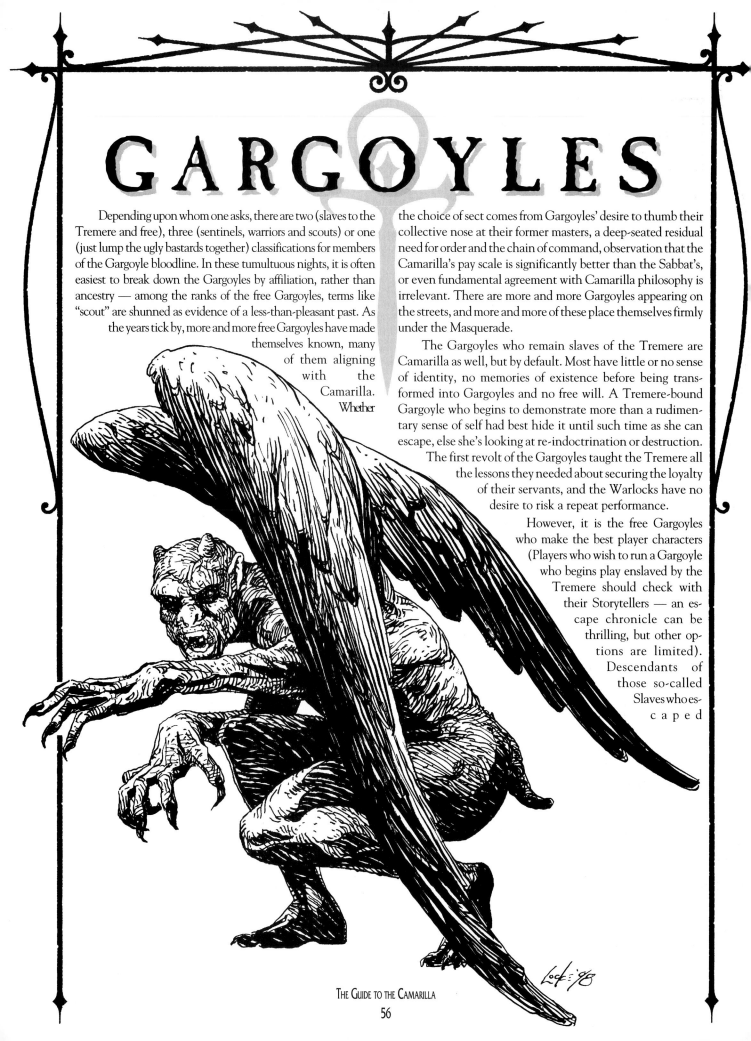

GARGOYLES

Depending upon whom one asks, there are two (slaves to the Tremere and free), three (sentinels, warriors and scouts) or one (just lump the ugly bastards together) classifications for members of the Gargoyle bloodline. In these tumultuous nights, it is often easiest to break down the Gargoyles by affiliation, rather than ancestry — among the ranks of the free Gargoyles, terms like "scout" are shunned as evidence of a less-than-pleasant past. As the years tick by, more and more free Gargoyles have made themselves known, many of them aligning with the Camarilla. Whether the choice of sect comes from Gargoyles' desire to thumb their collective nose at their former masters, a deep-seated residual need for order and the chain of command, observation that the Camarilla's pay scale is significantly better than the Sabbat's, or even fundamental agreement with Camarilla philosophy is irrelevant. There are more and more Gargoyles appearing on the streets, and more and more of these place themselves firmly under the Masquerade.

The Gargoyles who remain slaves of the Tremere are Camarilla as well, but by default. Most have little or no sense of identity, no memories of existence before being transformed into Gargoyles and no free will. A Tremere-bound Gargoyle who begins to demonstrate more than a rudimentary sense of self had best hide it until such time as she can escape, else she's looking at re-indoctrination or destruction. The first revolt of the Gargoyles taught the Tremere all the lessons they needed about securing the loyalty of their servants, and the Warlocks have no desire to risk a repeat performance.

However, it is the free Gargoyles who make the best player characters (Players who wish to run a Gargoyle who begins play enslaved by the Tremere should check with their Storytellers — an escape chronicle can be thrilling, but other options are limited). Descendants of those so-called Slaves who escaped from Tremere domination in centuries past and more recent escapees, the free Gargoyles cluster in isolated communities either in mountain retreats or industrial cities that offer nothing to the Tremere. More adventurous souls flock to Camarilla cities to offer themselves as bodyguards, muscle and other sorts of labor for hire. It is a show of prestige for a prince to have Gargoyle bodyguards at her Elysium, and a show of strength to be able to afford Gargoyle assassins to deal with enemies.

Nickname: Formerly Slaves, now a hodge-podge including Freemen, Runaways and Rockheads, depending on who's using the nickname. Calling a free Gargoyle a Slave is a wonderful way to have a large, stone-encrusted fist punched through your abdomen repeatedly.

Appearance: Like the Nosferatu (with whom they share an Appearance score of 0), Gargoyles are hideously ugly. While the exact features of that ugliness are dependent on the original combination of blood (Nosferatu-Tzimisce, Nosferatu-Gangrel or Gangrel-Tzimisce) that created the Gargoyle's ultimate ancestor, there are certain traits all members of the bloodline share. Warts and other protrusions, batlike wings (that grow as the Gargoyle's mastery of the Visceratika Discipline grows) and a stony countenance are all endemic to Gargoyles, as is a generally "demonic" appearance. Gargoyles move slowly and deliberately except in crisis situations, but there is no truth to the rumor that they leave small piles of dust behind them when they walk.

Haven: Gargoyles employed by the Tremere sleep in closets, basements or wherever else their masters deign to let them rest. Free Gargoyles often request lodging as part of a contract, meaning that the end results can be somewhat haphazard. Those Gargoyles who find their own resting places usually end up in deserted warehouses or factories — the taller the better — or in subterranean cave or sewer systems hewn from solid rock. Bell towers used to be favorites, but the stereotypical nature of the abode made Gargoyles nesting there easy pickings for Tremere ghouls.

Background: The process of creation is particularly intense for Gargoyles, especially for those taken directly by the Tremere. The surge of competing strains of vitae, combined with the magical energy inherent to the transformation even after all of these centuries, serves to wipe away the pre-existing memories and loyalties of a new Gargoyle, leaving a *tabula rasa* on which the Tremere can work. The process is a trifle gentler for Gargoyles Embraced by other Gargoyles, who sometimes retain at least vague senses of their former lives, but even so most of the past just dissolves under the occult onslaught. (**Note**: Free Gargoyles actually Embrace

mortals; the Tremere prefer to take Kindred of the three "root" clans and transform them into Gargoyles.) As for what drives a Gargoyle to Embrace a mortal, most times it's a case of simple obsession. There's neither reason nor rhyme to the matter, and even the most eloquent members of the bloodline shrug and put it down to "gut feeling."

Character Creation: Physical Attributes and Talents should be primary when one is creating a Gargoyle character; the Tremere did not design the bloodline for philosophizing or intrigue. All Gargoyle characters start with at least one dot in the unique Discipline Flight (In essence, this gives the Gargoyles four Clan Disciplines, but there are sufficient disadvantages to level the playing field). No Gargoyle can take the Mentor Background, or have an Appearance greater than 0. Furthermore, no Gargoyle can have a character history that predates 1167, as that was when the Tremere actually created the bloodline.

Weaknesses: As noted earlier, Gargoyles have a slight problem with Appearance. In addition, the nature of the bloodline's origin manifests itself in the fact that Gargoyles are considered to be down two Willpower points when resisting all Dominate or other mind-controlling effects.

Disciplines: Fortitude, Potence, Visceratika, Flight (see page **115**).

LASOMBRA

ANTITRIBU

There are no Lasombra *antitribu*, at least, not according to the Lasombra themselves. The Sabbat Lasombra deny that "traitors" exist, while the so-called *antitribu* see themselves as Lasombra — nothing more, nothing less. Not all Lasombra who disagree with the clan's stance within the Sabbat join the Camarilla — a significant percentage of this relatively small number simply go independent and absent themselves from vampiric politics entirely. The remainder, however, seize for themselves positions of respect and authority — if not prominence — in the Camarilla.

Philosophically, Camarilla Lasombra differ little from their Sabbat compatriots on a basic level. The *antitribu* still fully expect to win the Jyhad; they just see the Camarilla as a more efficient and effective tool for doing so than the Sabbat is. Distaste for the rabble the Sabbat is encased in shows clearly in Camarilla Lasombra's attitudes, as they regard the Sabbat tactic of mass Embraces as wasteful and insulting. Indeed, even the supporters of *antitribu* inclusion in the Camarilla see these vampires as haughty, arrogant and impatient. Few suffer fools or incompetent underlings to live, and the penalty for failing an assignment set by a Lasombra *antitribu* is often death.

The position occupied by these few self-exiled Kindred is an ambiguous one. On one hand, these vampires are Lasombra, the core of the dreaded Sabbat, and no Camarilla vampire is ever completely certain than the defection is a real one. On the other hand, essentially all Lasombra *antitribu* are creatures of undeniable power and presence, and are devoted to the destruction of the Sabbat in a way that few other Kindred are. The Camarilla cannot afford to waste these Cainites' talents, powers and knowledge of the enemy — but cannot afford to trust them entirely, either.

Nickname: None. The Lasombra *antitribu* don't go for that sort of thing. It's not dignified.

Appearance: Lasombra *antitribu* always find a way to look formal, regardless of circumstances. Most are of Iberian or Moorish descent, though a handful of the very newest Embracees are of mixed heritage. The elder Lasombra *antitribu* choose, whenever possible, to wear clothing suitable to the days of their youth; in many cases that means anything from half-armor to the robes of one of the poet-kings of the Andalusian *taifas*. Young Lasombra *antitribu* go more for sharp suits with a hint of Latin style, understated jewelry and sleek black cars that hint at their owners' affluence and power. While all Lasombra *antitribu* understand viscerally the need to keep a low profile (those who don't end up as ashes), they still insist on taking on the world according to their terms. Giving up so small a piece of identity as preferred modes of dress is, in some sense, to *submit* to another's will — and these Kindred would rather die than submit.

Haven: The majority of Lasombra *antitribu* are constantly on the move, the better to avoid being pinned down by their erstwhile brethren in the Sabbat. Many have an apartment or two, preferably in ritzy downtown tower complexes that come complete with extensive security systems and off-street, secure parking garages. Older *antitribu* prefer to dwell outside the cities on large estates, willing to risk the potential depredations of Lupines in exchange for privacy and some separation from nightly struggle.

Background: The Lasombra *antitribu* have existed as long as the Sabbat has, which is to say that more than one clan member agreed with Montano's choice to turn his back on his clanmates. The Sabbat Lasombra have always done their best to deny even the existence of any *antitribu*; such vampires by their very existence give the lie to claims about Sabbat and Lasombra hegemony. As a result, Lasombra *antitribu* are the first target of any Sabbat packs in a given city. The mere rumor of an *antitribu's* presence is enough to whip the local Sabbat Lasombra into a homicidal frenzy.

There are two distinct types of Lasombra *antitribu*. The majority (though still small in number) are older than the Camarilla itself; they are the Lasombra who joined with Montano in turning their backs on the nascent Sabbat. Some of them are still bitter about Lasombra's death; others simply disliked Gratiano and his choice of allies. In either case, these aged defectors are powerful, dignified and in most cases bitter. They have little use for the younger generations of vampires, and less for the Sabbat. Given a chance and a receptive audience, a Lasombra *antitribu* will talk endlessly about the old days, giving his listener a fascinating portrait of times, kings and customs now long gone — but precious little about the Lasombra himself. (**Note**: Almost all Lasombra of this vintage are male; the custom of Embracing women didn't catch on among the Lasombra *antitribu* until quite recently)

The other sort of Lasombra *antitribu* are young, angry and of remarkably low generation for Cainites so new to the Blood. The newer Lasombra *antitribu* are the childer of the aged and vengeful ones, plucked from mortality in accordance with the ancient customs of Lasombra himself. Most often, these mortals are in line to be snatched up by the local Sabbat — particularly Sabbat Lasombra — or remind the elder Lasombra irresistibly of someone from centuries past.

Character Creation: Lasombra *antitribu* tend to prefer exceptional specimens for the Embrace, but regard a quick wit and self-possession as the essential elements of a Lasombra. With that in mind, Social and Mental Attributes come first and second for many Lasombra *antitribu*, and Talents are more important than Skills and Knowledges. Generation is perhaps the most important Background for a Lasombra *antitribu*; they are either old, or the childer of ancient vampires.

Disciplines: Dominate, Obtenebration, Potence

Weaknesses: Like their cousins in the Sabbat, Lasombra *antitribu* have a slight problem with mirrors and other reflective surfaces. Lasombra *antitribu* do not have reflections in the normal sense; they don't show up in mirrors, windowpanes, pools of water or black-and-white photographs. Such a handicap makes Lasombra *antitribu* easy to identify for those who are looking for such, but the wise vampire has long since learned to avoid situations wherein he'd be compromised thus. In addition, since Lasombra are so heavily attuned to shadow, they take an extra level of damage from exposure to sunlight.

The final handicap facing Lasombra *antitribu* (beside the vestigial distrust of the rest of the Camarilla) is the intense hatred that Sabbat Lasombra bear for their straying brethren. A Lasombra *antitribu* is always the first target of a Sabbat pack, and supposedly entire Camarilla cities have been besieged just to get a particularly durable straggler.

Organization: Lasombra antitribu have created for themselves a miniature version of *Les Amies Noir*, the so-called Friends of the Dark. The *antitribu* are so rare, however, and their meetings are so infrequent that most of these vampires fall back on a simple sire-childe relationship. Nine times out of 10, there are no other *antitribu* around.

STEREOTYPES

Camarilla: *Make no mistake, we do not find the Camarilla that much more palatable than the Sabbat — but ours is an existence of inches and degrees. If the Camarilla serves our purposes even infinitesimally better, it has our support.*

Sabbat: *Everything that is corrupt and degraded about Gratiano and his sycophants manifests itself in the Sabbat. Everything that would have made Lasombra himself ill with disgust is there, in plain view. It is time to wipe the slate clean and start over.*

THE VIEW FROM WITHOUT

The Camarilla

Do we dare turn them away? No, for without us they will inevitably be destroyed, and by their mere existence they are a dagger at the Sabbat's throat. Do we dare trust them? How can we?

— Phillippe de Greffuhle, Sheriff of Lyon

The Sabbat

If any of these pathetic fossils still exist — and I doubt that they do — then they are merely marking time waiting for death. Should I learn of any in my domains, I will be certain to make sure they don't have to wait long.

— Francisco Domingo de Polonia

The Independents

Are they curiosities, freaks of unnature? Or is there something more to this most persistent of resistances? By all rights, the *antitribu* should have been wiped out centuries ago. What — or who — has allowed them to survive?

— Leah, Monitor of Sheffield

From the Beginning: Character Creation

That is why we dread children, even if we love them.
They show us the state of our decay.
— Brian Aldiss

Even the mightiest and most populous sect is composed, in the end, of individual Kindred. Each of those Kindred has hopes, dreams, fears and hidden horrors. Each of those Kindred is unique, a single thread in a long and bloody tapestry. But these individuals don't spring fully formed into existence. They must be created.

That's where this chapter comes in. It's a guide to creating characters who are by, for or of the Camarilla. The assumption is made, wrongly, that characters simply default to Camarilla allegiance. This is not true. If a vampire is going to be part of the Camarilla, he's part of it for a *reason*. That reason may be as simple as sheer inertia, but it's there nonetheless. So when you create a Camarilla character, you have to think about why exactly he belongs to the sect.

What you'll find in here is a step-by-step guide to creating a Camarilla vampire (not just a vampire), plus new Traits, Archetypes and other methods of making him a unique individual. Nothing in here is mandatory — you can get along just fine with the character creation chapter in **Vampire: The Masquerade** — but to create a vampire who has a deeper connection to the sect, look here.

Step One: Character Concept

The concept is the wellspring from which the whole of the character arises. Without a good idea as to who and what your character is, all the rest — dots and Disciplines ran-

domly strewn on the page — don't hang together. And if the character doesn't hang together, then stories built around that character won't hang together, and the whole thing comes crashing down.

A character concept doesn't need to be incredibly detailed — if you have your vampire's existence from birth to the present down cold and regimented into five minute intervals, something's wrong — but it should be a basic, strong idea that gets you excited about *being* this person for a while.

It goes without saying that your character concept should be intrinsically tied to the Camarilla somehow. The relationship doesn't have to be lovey-dovey — "anarch trying to take down the prince" is a perfectly valid concept — but it does need to connect *somehow*.

Clan

Your choice of clan is one of the most important decisions you make in creating a character. Your vampire's clan dictates her Disciplines, weaknesses and, to a large portion, the way other characters look at her. With that in mind, the choice of clan should never be made lightly. You can't swap clans the way you can swap jobs, after all. If you don't like being a Brujah, it's not like you can start stockpiling experience to learn how to be a Gangrel.

Your basic choices for clan are the six or seven clans (depending on how one classifies the Gangrel) affiliated with the Camarilla. Brujah, Gangrel, Malkavian, Nosferatu, Toreador, Tremere and Ventrue are the basic options, and

While the six (or seven) core clans make up most of the Camarilla, there are a few other possibilities (as detailed in the clans chapter) available for play. Before a Storyteller allows a player to pick up a Gargoyle, a Camarilla Ravnos or one of the other, even less common bloodlines, she should sit down with the player requesting the unusual character type and make sure that there is a solid story reason for including such an offbeat Kindred in the story. There might be plenty of perfectly valid reasons for having a single Lasombra *antitribu* in a city, but having too many unusual character types in one place at one time stretches credibility. The integrity of the story has to come first.

among them they offer a wide range of character possibilities. As well over 95 percent of the vampires in the Camarilla come from these clans, you should look to them first to see if any of them allow you to express your character concept fully.

In addition to the basic clans, Caitiff characters are also an option. If you're unsure about the concept you have, or aren't quite sold on any of the particular clans, a Caitiff makes perfect sense. Such characters allow for more improvisation of both Disciplines and character concepts — the journey of self-discovery is a lot more literal for Caitiff than for vampires inducted into a solid clan framework — and also provide a roleplaying challenge, as there isn't a stereotypical Caitiff image available to work from. Playing a Caitiff does have certain social consequences in-game, but for an introductory a character, or for a character whose concept isn't quite clear, a Caitiff can be an excellent choice.

NATURE AND DEMEANOR (ARCHETYPES)

A character's Nature and Demeanor are the basic personality types that define her. Nature is the character's true self, the basis for all the details of her personality. Her Demeanor is the face that she shows to the world, the mask she puts on for night-to-night encounters. A character's Nature and Demeanor can be the same, but often a vampire's Demeanor disguises, ever so subtly, what her true Nature is.

Certain Archetype choices are, unsurprisingly, more suitable for Camarilla characters than others. The rules of Camarilla society, need to maintain the Masquerade and other constrictions of Kindred existence make a Monster Demeanor less likely than a Conformist one. A Camarilla vampire can still easily have a Monster Nature, but odds are that he hides his true self well, the better to avoid suspicion. You should think about how well your character's Nature and Demeanor allow her to work within both her coterie and the Camarilla as a whole; acting according to your Nature is all very well and good, but if doing so gets your character killed in the first five minutes of gameplay, that Nature doesn't serve the purpose of helping to create a solid character. After all, you're investing time and

energy in creating your Kindred; building in something that will get her wiped out immediately and waste that investment simply doesn't make sense.

A full list of Archetypes can be found on page 104 of **Vampire: The Masquerade**. Additional ones can be found on pp. 66 of this book.

STEP TWO: SELECT ATTRIBUTES

Attributes define your character's basic capabilities. Divided into Physical, Social and Mental categories, they serve to define your vampire's baseline. All Camarilla vampires start with one dot in each of their Attributes (except Nosferatu and Camarilla-affiliated Samedi, who automatically have a zero rating in Appearance).

When you hand out your vampire's Attributes, the first thing to do is to prioritize the three categories they come in. You then get seven dots to put in your primary Attribute group, five for the secondary, and three for the tertiary in addition to the dots already present. The Camarilla encompasses a wide variety of "types," from Brujah bruisers to Malkavians Embraced as children, so there's no "right" or "Camarilla" way to set up your character's Attributes. Simply try to keep your final arrangement in line with your original concept, and remember that you can come back later and adjust things with freebie points.

STEP THREE: SELECT ABILITIES

The next step in the character creation involves assigning your character's Ability Traits. Abilities range from the basic — like Drive and Brawl — to the more esoteric, which are discussed on page **67**. The way in which you distribute the points for your character's Traits determines what she can or can't do very well, and helps to realize the concept you came up with in Step One. That means that the way you allocate your character's points should line up with the way you envision your character — fragile *artiste* Toreador probably

shouldn't wind up with a rating of Brawl 5, while you might not be able to justify Harley-riding Gangrel anarchs with four dots each in Etiquette and Occult.

Ideally, you should think about who your character is first, then allocate dots to help construct her to match that concept. Filling in the circles on the character sheet, and then scrambling to find a way to make the resultant connect-the-dots puzzle make sense for the character can lead to all sorts of problems.

No vampire can have more than three dots in any given Ability to start with (though this can be adjusted later with freebie points), and the base rating for all Abilities is zero. The Talents, Skills and Knowledges that make up Abilities are learned and studied, not innate; if you don't have one, you don't have it.

SECONDARY ABILITIES

Included in this book (and its counterpart, the **Guide to the Sabbat**) are what are known as Secondary Abilities. While the Skills, Talents and Knowledges in **Vampire: The Masquerade** are the essential ones for gameplay, there are a multitude of other Abilities, from archery to zymurgy, out there that will inevitably be vital to someone's character history and concept. Some of them are refinements of other, broader Abilities (Sense Deception's function is included in Empathy, for example; the former is simply a refinement). Others are narrow enough specialties that they're not likely to be universal in application. Either way, these Secondary Abilities are less pertinent than the basic Abilities in the main rulebook; that's why they're called "Secondary."

Storytellers have three options when it comes to Secondary Abilities. One, they can simply ban them from the game. Doing so restricts character flexibility, but does simplify things.

The second possibility is to reduce the difficulty on all Secondary Ability rolls. A character who's good with Sense Deception should have a better chance to sniff out bullshit than one who's merely a generally empathic guy, after all. In such instances, the difficulty of all rolls based off Secondary Abilities should be a -2 difficulty as compared to what the roll would have been using a Basic Ability.

The final option is to make Secondary Abilities available at a lower cost than normal Abilities. Every point spent on a Secondary Ability during the third step of character creation nets two dots instead of just one. Secondary Abilities bought with freebie points cost only one point per dot, and raising a Secondary Ability with experience costs only the Trait's current rating.

Storytellers should feel free to use any and all, or none, of these approaches. It's your game, after all.

A list of Secondary Abilities available to Camarilla vampires appears in the **Vampire Companion** on page 15. Additional Secondary Abilities can be found in this book, starting on page 67.

Abilities, like Attributes, are broken down into three categories (the aforementioned Talents, Skills and Knowledges), and like Attributes, these are prioritized. Primary Abilities get 13 dots, Secondary get 9 and Tertiary get 5. You cannot take dots from one category and pour them into another, even if you only see three dots' worth of Knowledges that you want your character to have.

Camarilla vampires do have easier access to some Abilities than do Sabbat vampires, but in return some Sabbat-specific Abilities are off limits to Camarilla vampires who don't have a very good reason to have them.

Step Four: Select Advantages

Advantages are what, as much as clan, define a vampire as being such. The term "Advantages" covers Disciplines, Backgrounds and Virtues, and by defining these you finish establishing your character's basics. Advantages are not broken down into categories to be prioritized. You simply get a certain number of dots for each type of Advantage, to spend as you will.

Out-of-Clan Disciplines

There is a temptation, once one reaches the freebie points stage in character creation, to mortgage the figurative farm in order to purchase as many out-of-clan Disciplines as possible. Storytellers should be very careful in allowing characters to purchase out-of-clan Disciplines, though, as a preponderance of Disciplines bundled up in one character can unbalance a coterie very quickly. A chronicle wherein one character starts with six dots in six different Disciplines and another only has three can get lopsided very quickly.

If a player wants to give his character additional Disciplines, he should be prepared to answer a few questions, like:

• Are they really necessary to his character concept, and why does he want them? ("So I can kill more stuff" is the sort of answer that should give most Storytellers pause.)

• Who taught the character? Out-of-clan Disciplines are not instinctive. The character would have had to pick them up somewhere and from someone; such outré powers do need a solid justification in the character's backstory.

Furthermore, there are certain Disciplines (Chimerstry, Melpominee, Mytherceria, Necromancy, Obeah, Obtenebration, Quietus, Serpentis, Thanatopsis, Visceratika, Vicissitude) that should not be available to Camarilla vampires unless their clan origin specifically mandates such. The independent and Sabbat bloodlines are very jealous of their secrets, and aren't about to share them with Camarilla upstarts.

Disciplines

A Camarilla vampire receives three dots' worth of Disciplines initially, though this, too, can be modified with freebie points. Each clan has so-called "clan" Disciplines, vampiric powers that are innate to the bloodline and which can be learned instinctively by even the newest to the Blood. Other Disciplines, those not reflexive to a given clan, can be picked up later in the character creation process (see below), but at this point, the character is restricted to the powers directly linked to her clan. Each clan has three Disciplines in which it specializes, which provide a broad range of supernatural abilities in the physical, mental and social arenas.

Backgrounds

Backgrounds are character history manifested in Trait form. Each character gets five dots' worth of Backgrounds, which can be used in any combination you desire. You can stack up all five dots in one Background, or get one level each of five distinct ones. Your Storyteller can, as always, disallow certain Backgrounds, or keep characters below a pre-set ceiling.

Camarilla vampires generally have a deep and broad investment in their Backgrounds, often using freebie points to add to their ratings. Because of the forced socialization the sect mandates, it's entirely sensible for a Kindred to have Contacts and Allies. The sect's interaction makes a perfectly reasonable justification for Herd, Fame, Resources and Influence, not to mention Retainers. A Mentor also makes for a useful Storyteller character, while Status can be given or taken away by the harpies in the space of a heartbeat.

Virtues

While Camarilla vampires aren't "good guys" in the classic sense of the term, they do cling to a moral center as represented by their three Virtues. Conscience is the character's sense of right and wrong. Self-Control is the measure of how tightly the character controls her Beast and governs her own actions. Courage is self-explanatory, a rating of how well the character controls her fear and stands up to threats — anything from fire to Lupines to a hunter with a stake. These virtues are constants for all Camarilla vampires; even refugees from the Sabbat acquire these Traits.

All vampires begin with one free dot in each Virtue, then seven more to distribute among the three. Virtues are very important to Camarilla vampires. A vampire with a low Self-Control rating is liable to lose control frequently, frenzy and threaten the Masquerade. If he does it too often, he'll be put down. A vampire with a low Conscience rating is liable to indulge in acts that may well encourage other Kindred to avoid her company, leaving her all alone when the hunters come calling. And a Kindred with a low Courage rating isn't going to be much use in a life-or-death situation — which the Kindred face every night.

GENERATION

It can be tempting to put all of your Background points into Generation. That way you get a bigger blood pool and can spend more blood per round, with no drawbacks, right?

That's not necessarily the case. A vampire with all its Backgrounds in Generation has no money, no one to turn to in a crisis, no protector, no feeding reserves and often not much else. That's what having no Allies, no Contacts, no Resources, no Mentor, no Herd and no other Backgrounds means. Players should not automatically assume that they default to comfortable status; without spending the points for a Background, they don't have what the Background mandates.

STEP FIVE: LAST TOUCHES

At this point, you're almost finished with the basics of character creation. All that remains is some bookkeeping and the distribution of freebie points. Remember, though, that finishing with the dots doesn't mean that you've finished creating a character. It just means that you've finished with a character sheet.

HUMANITY

Humanity is the rating of how close a Kindred is to his human side — and how far he is from his Beast. A vampire with a low Humanity rating is too close to his animalistic side for comfort, and is that much nearer to sliding into the abyss permanently. A vampire's Humanity score is the sum of his Conscience + Self-Control ratings, and it can go as high as 10. Humanity is vitally important to Camarilla vampires, especially younger ones. It is through maintaining touch with one's Humanity that one keeps the Beast at bay, and making oneself presentable in polite company.

At its most basic level, Humanity is what separates the Camarilla from the Sabbat. Characters with low Humanity scores are liable to be suspect in Camarilla circles. After all, the drive to keep in touch with one's Humanity is one of the core philosophical stances of the Camarilla, and those who deviate from it or ignore that quest are, in essence, disregarding what the entire sect is about.

WILLPOWER

Your character's Willpower score is equal to her Courage rating. As Willpower has a multitude of uses, from resisting Mental Disciplines to granting automatic successes on rolls, it is recommended that you devote freebie points to increasing your character's Willpower.

BLOOD POOL

Roll a 10-sided die. The result is your character's starting blood pool. It is assumed that any blood in your character's system at the beginning of gameplay is human, unless you and your Storyteller make arrangements otherwise.

FREEBIE POINTS

Freebie points are the 15 additional points you can spend on whatever Traits you like. In addition, you can also buy Merits and Flaws (see page 295 of **Vampire: The Masquerade**, and page 72 of this book for more information on Merits and Flaws) to tweak your character to get it in line with your original conception.

SPARK OF LIFE

At this point, you should have a fully filled-out character sheet — not a fully fleshed-out character. You now need to think about your character's story — who she is, where she came from, why she was made into a vampire and what she's doing with her unlife — before you're ready to play. You need to think about who she knows. If she has Allies, who are they? Other vampires who like her style or her aims? Mortals whom she's kept up an acquaintance with? As for her Abilities, you need to think about why she has that particular skill set. What incident in her past caused her to pick up three dots in Firearms? Why is she good with Dodge, but not particularly skilled at Brawl? Unless you have a reason for handing out each and every dot on the character sheet, those dots remain simply circles. By building a backstory that explains why your character has the Abilities, Backgrounds and whatnot that she does, you make her a real, viable character. If you don't, you just have a collection of dots.

THE PRELUDE

Vampires are made, not born. Each and every Kindred was the result of some other vampire's conscious decision to Embrace a mortal and bring her into the unliving fold. There's a story behind each Embrace, a story called a prelude.

Technically speaking, the prelude is the sequence of events leading up to a character's Embrace. It is recommended that, under normal circumstances, you roleplay out your character's prelude, if for no other reason than to grant some perspective on who she is and where she came from. Roleplaying out the prelude also allows you to establish the relationship between your character and her sire, to firm up the details of her Embrace (was it violent? expected? accidental?) and to define her entry into the world of the Kindred. All of these are pivotal matters for a young vampire. By going through your character's prelude, you work out all of these important details, which gives both you and your Storyteller a better grasp of your character. You'll be able to portray her more realistically, and your Storyteller has more facts on which to hang plot hooks derived from her Embrace.

The circumstances of a Camarilla vampire's Embrace are slightly different from those of other Kindred. Remember, each Camarilla vampire is the result (in theory, at least), of someone's being granted permission to Embrace. That means that there's a vampiric backstory to each character, as well as the mortal's own history. Either you or your Storyteller, depending on circumstance, should know how exactly your character's sire got permission to create her. The Camarilla politics leading to the Embrace can make for fascinating stories, particularly if someone wasn't thrilled with the way the boon of creation was handled. By the same token, the question of why exactly the character was selected for the Embrace needs to be faced. What drew her sire to her? Was she Embraced to fill a particular need in the city's hierarchy, or to spite another Camarilla vampire? Perhaps the Embrace was an accident, or a hasty decision — what will the consequences be for both neonate and sire? The Embrace is a complicated matter for both sire and childe when Camarilla politics get involved, and those politics always do manage to get involved somehow.

COTERIE

Odds are that your character is not going to be working alone. Instead, he'll most likely be part of a coterie, a circle of vampires bound by common interest, common enemies or just plain circumstance. It makes sense before you start play, however, to think about how your coterie fits together and how it fits into the local Camarilla.

Establishing common ground for your coterie is essential. If there's no good reason for your gang to stick together, it won't. That means fragmented storylines, stress for the Storyteller and lots of time spent sitting around as individual plotlines are run. It makes sense, then, to lay the groundwork for a coterie that works together, at least initially. Some good methods of keeping a group of young vampires together include princely fiat, a shared sire, a common enemy (either within or outside the Camarilla) or a mutual interest like music, the arts or travel. The form the coterie takes can be derived from the group's common bond. Vampires who share an interest in music, for example, might form a band, while a princely command to clean up the city might turn the coterie into a *posse comitatus*, complete with a shared look and standardized equipment.

It's also worth figuring out where exactly the coterie fits into the local Camarilla scene. Was the coterie's formation sanctioned by the prince, or the characters' sires? If not, what form will the disapproval of these older Kindred take? Any group of Kindred is a potential power base, and any coterie will have all sorts of other vampires looking at it as a result. With the others see the group as a threat, and if so, what measures will they take? Is there an elder (or two) who wants to use the coterie for his own ends, and what will he do to ensure their cooperation? What is the coterie's ultimate ambition, and does anyone know about it? If the group intends to become the primogen council eventually, the present holders of that office might decide to nip the threat in the bud. By establishing where your coterie belongs in the local Camarilla — if it belongs at all — you set the stage for the types of story to follow.

ARCHETYPES

Archetypes are basic personality types, frameworks on which to hang the details of a character. While a great many Archetypes are listed in **Vampire: The Masquerade** (p. 112), there are some personality types that are endemic to the

FASTER, NEONATE! KILL! KILL!

Occasionally there are coterie combinations that just don't work. Often such oil-and-water arrangements are the product of two characters in particular who simply don't belong together, with neither character's player willing to surrender his creation for the good of the group. Such conflicts can tear a group apart, and wreck a chronicle in the process.

Most situations of this type can be prevented with a little common sense. A good Storyteller keeps an eye on the sorts of characters his players are creating, and if he sees a potential incompatibility brewing, he should step in. Ideally, any players involved in creating a potential problem will be amenable to tweaking their character concepts before investing too much time or energy. Storytellers should take care to avoid the appearance of favoritism when suggesting changes in character concepts, otherwise they run the risk of having resentful players.

If the problem develops after gameplay starts, the best solution is to retire both of the problematic characters and have the players create new Kindred under Storyteller supervision.

Camarilla. A few of those are listed below, for use during the "Nature and Demeanor" section of character creation.

IDEALIST

The Idealist believes — truly, madly, deeply — in some higher goal or morality. The object of his idealism may be something as pragmatic as the Camarilla's eventual triumph or as amorphous as the ultimate good, but the belief is there. Idealists are frequently either very new to the Blood or very old, and many seek after Golconda as the final expression of their idealism. In the meantime, an Idealist tries to reconcile his beliefs with the demands of vampiric existence, often acting contrary to self-interest to do so.

— Regain a point of Willpower any time an action in pursuit of your ideals furthers your goals and brings your ideal closer to fruition.

SOLDIER

The Soldier is not a blindly loyal follower. While she exists for orders, she does not adhere to them unquestioningly. More independent than a Conformist but too tied into the idea of command to be a Loner, the Soldier applies her own techniques to others' goals. While she may seek command herself someday, her ambitions lie within the established hierarchy and structure. The Soldier has no compunctions about using whatever means necessary to do what needs to be done, so long as the orders to do so came from the right place.

— Regain a point of Willpower when you achieve your orders' objectives. The more difficult the orders are to fulfill, the better it feels to accomplish them. At Storyteller discre-

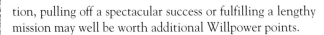

tion, pulling off a spectacular success or fulfilling a lengthy mission may well be worth additional Willpower points.

DABBLER

The Dabbler is interested in everything but focuses on nothing. He flits from idea to idea, passion to passion and project to project without actually finishing anything. Others may get swept up in the Dabbler's enthusiasm, and be left high and dry as a result when he moves on to something else without warning. Most Dabblers have high Intelligence, Charisma and Manipulation ratings, but not much in the way of Wits or Stamina. Toreador are often Dabblers, particularly those afflicted with the derisive sobriquet "Poseurs."

— Regain Willpower whenever you find a new enthusiasm and drop your old one completely.

SCIENTIST

To a Scientist, existence is a puzzle which she can help to reassemble. A Scientist logically and methodically examines her every situation and maneuver, looking for logical outcomes and patterns. This is not to say that the Scientist is always looking for a scientific or rational explanation, but rather, that she examines her surroundings rigorously and with a critical eye. The system a Scientist attempts to impose on the world may be completely ludicrous, but it is a system, and she sticks by it. Scientists have high Mental Attributes, and often hold low-ranking positions in Camarilla city governments.

— Regain Willpower any time a logical, systematic approach to a problem helps you solve it, or information gathered logically is of use in another, similar situation.

SECONDARY ABILITIES

TALENTS

DIPLOMACY

"I'm not sure he's worth it." Adele's face contracted into a sour mask as she pondered the brooding young man at the end of the bar. *"I mean, he's certainly pretty enough, but I'm not seeing anything else here worth preserving. Certainly not his mind."*

Elieser looked up mournfully from the one-way glass window through which he and Adele were peering. "You just don't know him. He's actually quite witty, and rather talented in several fields — his poetry's quite good — and, well, Prince Alexander said I had the right, and I'm choosing him!" The younger vampire's face set in a pout, and his fingers twitched with frustration.

Mentally, Adele sighed. She'd been through this before with Elieser — and Elieser's sire before him. "Now let's not be hasty, Eli. You're right, I don't know him. Perhaps if you brought him into the family, one step at a time? That way I could learn what you see in him." And you'll have time to get bored with him before I get saddled with another mistake, she added silently. Elieser nodded slowly, and Adele permitted herself a small smile.

Diplomacy is the art of handling difficult situations with tact and skill. It is also the ability to negotiate positions, rather than specifics — the latter is the purview of Haggling. You can negotiate policy and treaties, and extricate yourself from unpleasant situations with words, rather than force or use of Disciplines.

- • Novice: You can state your position without driving anyone away from the negotiating table.
- •• Practiced: You clan trusts you to represent it on some issues.
- ••• Competent: Your agenda usually carries the day.
- •••• Expert: You can handle labor strife and cutting deals with the Lupines with equal ease.
- ••••• Master: You can convince nations to alter their policies — and like it.

Possessed By: Diplomats, Seneschals, Politicians, Ambitious Ventrue

Specialties: Settlements, Cease-Fires, Alliance Building, Graceful Exits, Spin Doctoring

HAGGLING

"Absolutely not." Selene Arneault, prince of Boulder, waved agitatedly at her petitioner. "You expect me simply to hand over the entire campus to you and yours in exchange for some rumors about a Nosferatu city? Precisely when did you go insane, and how did I fail to notice it?"

"Your Majesty." Regent Sean Reynolds was, as always, unctuously polite. "I'm not asking for the entire campus — merely that you open up access to the rare documents library and some of the feeding rights to my new childe. In exchange, I offer concrete evidence of something untoward happening in your domain. I have maps, satellite photos, seismic records, eyewitness accounts and—," he paused for effect, "a prisoner."

Arneault sat bolt upright. "Fascinating…. Perhaps your childe wouldn't object to an observer when he visited the documents room?"

"She, Your Majesty. And I'm sure she wouldn't."

You can trade favors, and negotiate costs and other specifics so that transactions come out in your favor. You can judge relative value of goods and services quickly and easily, and know when someone's attempting to rip you off.

- • Novice: You can knock a few bucks off the price of something at a flea market or garage sale.
- •• Practiced: You get used cars for what they're worth, not what they're marked.
- ••• Competent: You can play the game of prestation better than any of your peers.
- •••• Expert: Princes ask you if they're getting a good deal.
- ••••• Master: You can get what you want, when you want it for the price you are willing to pay — always.

Possessed By: Police Negotiators, Anarchs, Purchasing Agents, Household Ghouls, Importers, Nosferatu

Specialties: Swaps, Selling Information, Fine Print, Contracts, Prestation

INTRIGUE

Simon Crabtree had been an angry young man three decades ago; now he was neither a man nor young, but he was still angry. "It's all here, Karp. All of it. She mentions sabotaging my reading, though she barely has room to do so in between these repulsively saccharine endearments she scribbled. This whole goddamned thing is a love note to ruining my career!"

Elias Karp stood impassively, watched his acquaintance impassively and occasionally nodded as Crabtree ranted. It occurred to Karp, as Crabtree tossed off a particularly impressive rhetorical flourish, that perhaps he'd done too good a job in forging that letter. It certainly had been effective in riling Crabtree to the point of homicidal mania (which Crabtree was sure to act on ineffectively, thus getting himself disposed of one way or another). It would surely cause all sorts of trouble for Crabtree's "beloved," whose affairs were bound to come under scrutiny after her beau's mania manifested. It might even win Karp some very hard-to-come-by approval from some very important Kindred who knew what he had done. But was any of that worth listening to Crabtree's interminable rant? The sacrifices one was forced to make....

You can plot and plan effectively. You understand how to manipulate others through trickery and artifice, and you are expert at exposing a target's vulnerabilities. Note that Intrigue is not Subterfuge; the latter involves fieldwork and actual sabotage, while Intrigue operates more on a theoretical and consequential level. Subterfuge is the art of planting a forged letter; Intrigue is the art of knowing whose handwriting to forge for maximum effect.

- • Novice: You maneuver well against a single adversary.
- •• Practiced: You can figure out how to subvert an organized enemy.
- ••• Competent: You can handle multiple plots simultaneously.
- •••• Expert: You've woven a web of double- and triple-crosses, all to your benefit.
- ••••• Master: The rest of the Kindred are just so many puppets, dancing on your strings.

Possessed By: Spymasters, Harpies, Setite Recruiters, Secure Princes

Specialties: Subversion, Isolating Opponents, Corporate Sabotage, Mounting Coups

SCROUNGING

"So what the hell are we looking for, anyway?" The voice came from halfway beneath a pile of wires, vacuum tubes and other, less identifiable components of long-dead machines.

"I have no idea, but I'll know when I find— aha!" Jonah extracted himself from the ruins of what looked to be a fusebox, a handful of wires dangling from his hand. "Bingo."

"Bingo? Looks like crap to me." Katherine burrowed her way out of the mound of junk she'd been excavating. "What exactly are you going to do with those?"

Jonah grinned like a bastard. "Fix a record player."

"A what?"

"A record player. My sire's been bitching for 30 years that his gramophone doesn't work anymore, and he's thrown fatal tantrums any time someone tries to bring him something new. But with these, I can fix his antique and make him very, very happy." He gave a bark of laughter. "And if he's happy with me, odds are I'm going to be happy, too. Worth investing a couple of hours in a junkyard, isn't it?"

With expertise in Scrounging, you can find unusual, outdated or otherwise hard-to-find items. Those items can range from the part needed to repair a Model T Ford to someone skilled at bibliomancy to a rare CD of which only 500 copies were pressed. Scrounging also implies a knowledge of sources for oddball items, and a reasonable ability at turning junk into useful material.

- • Novice: Occasionally you can pluck something off the scrap heap.
- •• Practiced: You know where to look for hard-to-find items — and that includes some hard-to-find sources.
- ••• Competent: You know if something can be found in under 24 hours.
- •••• Expert: You have a network of potential sources for anything and everything you might need on short notice
- ••••• Master: You can find anything, at any time, assuming it still exists.

Possessed By: Researchers, Fixers, Acquisitions Agents, Collectors, Hiring Factors

Specialties: Manuscripts, Electronics and Parts, Talented Individuals, Illegal Items, Occult Items, Improvisational Fixes

SEARCH

The apartment was, to put it politely, a disaster. Everything breakable had been broken, including a couple of the plumbing fixtures. Blood was everywhere, from the linoleum floor of the kitchen to the warped wood of the windowsill. Overhead, a light fixture dangled crazily from a half-snapped chain; only two of the bulbs were working, as the rest had been smashed.

Glass crunched underfoot as Anabelle sniffed the air and frowned. Behind her, her childe snorted in disapproval at the scene. "Looks like the Sabbat got to him first. Nothing here for us." His tone clearly indicated that he was bored with the whole scene, and wanted simply to chalk the whole thing up as a loss.

"Not quite. Everything we need is still here. If whoever did this — and I'm not so certain it was Sabbat — had found what they were looking for, they wouldn't have needed to wreck everything quite so thoroughly. I'll bet you a year off your apprenticeship that what we're looking for is still here."

Devin laughed. "A year? You're on." He crossed his arms and looked smug, right until the time his sire picked up a photograph under a cracked pane. The picture showed a pair of beautiful women in 1890s-style dress; one bore a striking resemblance to Annabelle herself. She neatly popped the remainder of the glass out, then removed the picture. Behind it on the matting was a folded piece of paper, yellowed with age. Anabelle held it up with a grin as her childe sputtered.

"Understanding sentiment was the key to understanding my dear, late friend. Now, Devin, about that extra year...."

You have the ability to examine a person or scene and find what you need. Locating hidden compartments, uncovering wall safes and doping out smuggling techniques are all within your area of expertise. Search also covers both frisking techniques and more generalized searches, such as trying to uncover buried caches or bodies.

- • Novice: You can spot a bulge under a jacket and be reasonably sure what it is.
- •• Practiced: False bottoms and secret pockets can't hide from you.
- ••• Competent: You can find any concealed weapon in a matter of seconds.
- •••• Expert: The proverbial needle in the haystack is no challenge for you.
- ••••• Master: Nothing short of the supernatural can be hidden from you.

Possessed By: Border Guards, Cops, DEA Agents, Sheriffs, Bodyguards

Specialties: Body Searches, Search and Seizure, Vehicle Searches, Uncovering Evidence

Other Possibilities: Artistic Expression, Carousing, Public Speaking, Poetic Expression, Scan, Seduction, Sense Deception and Swimming

Skills

Acrobatics

A lone clothesline was the only connection between the two tenements. Down in the alley below, someone big was moving around, knocking over trash cans and kicking in windows. Who exactly was down there, Shelby had no desire to find out, but odds were that it was one of the sheriff's bruisers.

She knelt down and pulled the clothesline taut. It was 3/4" twine, hardly her favorite to work with, but with the sheriff's men doing a room-to-room search in the building behind her, she didn't have a lot of options. With a quick prayer Shelby took out her knife and slammed it into the roof, then looped the rope around it in order to take up the slack. Then, fingers crossed, she kicked off her shoes and stepped onto the rope. One step at a time, she told herself One step at a time.

You can use your body to perform feats of flexibility that are beyond most individuals' capabilities. You can tumble, swing, flip, balance and otherwise use your body to your best advantage. You may not be the most flexible Kindred in the world, but you use your body's capabilities to their utmost.

- • Novice: You can do a somersault without hurting yourself or others.
- •• Practiced: Flips, rolls and other basic maneuvers are within your range.

- **•••** Competent: You are good enough to amaze crowds or confound foes with your antics.
- **••••** Expert: You are capable of performing gymnastic maneuvers on any surface with whatever equipment is at hand.
- **•••••** Master: You are an Olympic-caliber gymnast.

Possessed By: Trapeze Artists, Contortionists, Athletes, Spies

Specialties: Circus Maneuvers, Contortions, Ducking and Covering, Combat Acrobatics, Tightrope Walking

CAMOUFLAGE

"Sonofabitch said the whole damn caravan pulled over here for the day, but we've got nothing. Nothing." The annoyance in de la Vega's voice was palpable. "That's the last time I trust that lying little turd of a Nosferatu." He turned and kicked a rock. It skittered off into the underbrush at the side of the road with a barely audible clank.

The sheriff of Chattanooga didn't hear, though, being too thoroughly preoccupied with his grumbling. He climbed back into his car, started the engine and roared off into the deepening gloom. The sound of his curses lingered in the air for a moment behind him, along with the scent of his car's exhaust. Then there was nothing but silence.

Deeper within the underbrush, the interior of a well-concealed van exploded with muffled laughter.

You can hide anything through proper application of this skill. You are an expert at disguising things through available (in other words, non-supernatural) means so that they are undetectable by normal methods. Whatever materials are at hand can be put to use hiding whatever you wish to conceal. Camouflage can be used in any locale; the effectiveness of the skill depends on what you wish to hide and what you have to work with.

- **•** Novice: You can hide candy well enough to smuggle it out of convenience stores.
- **••** Practiced: You can use camouflage netting and other tools of the trade.
- **•••** Competent: You can hide a vehicle quickly and well with whatever's at hand.
- **••••** Expert: You can conceal anything from microfiche to military equipment.
- **•••••** Master: With a little preparation and the proper tools, you could hide the Great Wall.

Possessed By: Smugglers, Nosferatu, Fences, Army Rangers, Freedom Fighters, Terrorists

Specialties: Military Hardware, Vehicles, Hiding in Plain Sight, Urban Camouflage

HUNTING

"Look, this place really is too noisy for us to talk. You want to go someplace and get a cup of coffee? My treat." Zander smiled his second-most winning smile, the one that said, "Trust me, I'm harmless."

His prey, a young woman in a black dress that she frankly didn't carry off very well, looked back nervously at her friends. They seemed split on the idea; half gave encouraging smiles while the rest looked worried. Her gaze flicked back and forth from her friends to Zander nervously. She leaned forward and said, as best as she could over the thumping music, "I'm not sure. I mean, would it be OK if my friends came along? Sheila drove, after all, and I'm not real good with directions."

"Of course. They can meet us out front," Zander lied. Mentally, he gritted his teeth. Tonight's hunt was going to take a little longer than he thought.

Hunting is the ability to find and bring down a target of any sort, on any terrain, for any purpose. With a proper application of Hunting, you can do anything from running down deer in the wild to picking a mortal out of the herd for purposes of feeding. This skill also includes manhunting, and can apply to the search for other Kindred

- **•** Novice: You don't need to club your prey over the head first.
- **••** Practiced: You can find dinner with reasonable ease.
- **•••** Competent: Humans are easy to isolate and feed on.
- **••••** Expert: Once you decide on a target, it's only a matter of time.
- **•••••** Master: Human, animal or Kindred — none can escape you.

Possessed By: Alastors, Hunters, Gangrel, Federal Agents, Survivalists, Scourges

Specialties: Animals, Human Prey, The Chase, Manhunting, Cat and Mouse

Other Possibilities: Animal Training, Artillery, Blacksmith, Blind Fighting, Boat Handling, Brewing/Distilling, Bribery, Carpentry, Climbing, Cooking, Dancing, Debate, Escapology, Falconry, Fast-Draw, Fast-Talk, First Aid, Fishing, Forgery, Gambling, Game Playing, Gunsmithing, Heavy Weapons, Hypnotism, Jeweler, Journalism, Leatherworking, Lockpicking, Mechanical Repair, Parachuting, Photography, Pickpocket, Police Procedure, Pottery, Psychoanalysis, Scuba, Singing, Skiing, Speed Reading, and Tracking

KNOWLEDGES

CLAN KNOWLEDGE

"What the bloody hell were they doing out there?" The Regent strode back and forth in a fury, gesticulating wildly with his silver-headed cane and nearly knocking any number of objets d'art off his mantelpiece in the process.

"Making fun of us, obviously." His second in command, a quiet woman dressed severely in a business suit, folded her hands primly in her lap and seemed oblivious to the very real threat of being accidentally whacked with the cane. "I'm told they do that from time to time. Next week, presumably, it will be the Ventrue's turn."

"I don't care what they're doing, Richards!" the Regent roared. "I want to know how the hell they learned so much about us! Everything we do was on display out there!"

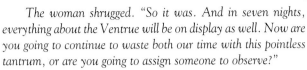

The woman shrugged. "So it was. And in seven nights, everything about the Ventrue will be on display as well. Now are you going to continue to waste both our time with this pointless tantrum, or are you going to assign someone to observe?"

You have knowledge about a particular clan of vampires that no outsider should possess. You are aware of the clan's practices, rituals and secrets, and can put that knowledge to good use. However, members of the clan in question may not like the fact that an outsider has a handle on proprietary information, and may act to plug any such security leaks.

Note: This knowledge only grants information about one particular clan. Clan Knowledge must be purchased separately for each clan of expertise.

- • Novice: You can spot a member of the clan with reasonably accuracy.
- •• Practiced: You know how the clan is set up, and can separate myth from fact.
- ••• Competent: Most of the clan's basic layout and procedure is known to you.
- •••• Expert: You know the clan's secrets as well as anyone.
- ••••• Master: You know more about the clan than most of its members do.

Possessed By: Kindred, Hunters, Ambitious Ghouls, Arcanum Scholars

Specialties: Power Structure, Chain of Command, Secrets, Movers and Shakers

COMPUTER HACKING

Bobby leaned back in his chair, hands clasped behind his head, and grinned the grin of the righteous geek. "Ladies and gentlemen, may I present to you everything you ever wanted to know about where Horatio's banks have been putting our money. I figure we've got about five minutes before the system security boots us out on our collective ass, but in the meantime I've taken the liberty of doing screen shots of everything here. You'll be able to print those out and look at them at your leisure."

Various Kindred crowded around Bobby, trying to get a look at his 21" monitor and jabbering among themselves. Several offered him congratulations; he just looked bashful.

Truth be told, this was his fifth time into Ballard's banks, and at this point Bobby was reasonably certain he could turn them upside down and shake every last penny out of them, if he so desired. But he'd keep that little tidbit to himself. Once you started doing miracles, people expected you to be able to perform them on command, and he'd rather not deal with the pressure.

You can use your computer to insert your virtual presence into systems where you don't belong. With this knowledge, you can crack computer security and some forms of encryption and otherwise perform feats of data piracy and sabotage that would win the approbation of other hackers as well as an arrest warrant from the FBI. Best of all, you can do this while covering your tracks.

- • Novice: You can guess others' passwords.
- •• Practiced: You know all of the basic back doors to popular operating systems.
- ••• Competent: You know how to get yourself root access on a fair number of systems.
- •••• Expert: You can find security loopholes and exploit them within days of a software package's release.
- ••••• Master: You can cut through military security or tap into Wall Street.

Possessed By: Hackers, NSA Agents, Phone Phreaks, Security Specialists

Specialties: Phone Phreaking, Military Security, Financials, Viruses, Encryption, Password Theft, Back Doors

ECONOMICS

"What are you doing?" Bailey gazed uncomprehendingly at the numbers flashing by on his childe's screen. They seemed to be moving at a rapid pace, while she thrummed her fingers on the desk and made "harrumphing" noises.

"Running a simulation."

"Thank you," he said icily. "That answer was technically correct and told me absolutely nothing. Now suppose for a moment you show your sire a little respect, look away from that infernal machine of yours and tell me what exactly you are running a simulation of."

Nicole swiveled her chair to face her sire. (She did not, however, stop drumming her fingers on the desk, a fact which he made a mental note of.) "I'm doing projections as to the effects of bank collapses on certain nations that have been borrowing liberally. Specifically, I'm working out exactly how many financial institutions we're going to have to kick over in order to eviscerate what's left of the East Asian economy."

Bailey raised an eyebrow. "Is that all?"

The younger vampire shrugged. "More or less. It's a project I've been working on for a while. Everyone needs a hobby."

Economics is the study of how money moves and its effects. You can predict, with reasonable accuracy, financial trends and patterns, and you have a leg up on others in matters of investment. You are well-aware of the effects of the Kindred on world markets, and can estimate what sort of effects vampiric dabblings can have on whole industries or nations.

- • Novice: You have a notion of what a capitalist economy is.
- •• Practiced: You know that "the invisible hand" isn't part of an Obfuscated Nosferatu.
- ••• Competent: The Financial News Network makes sense to you.
- •••• Expert: You can spot trends and accurately predict recessions with ease.
- ••••• Master: You know how the world economy works — all of it.

Possessed By: Economists, Brokers, Financial Advisors, Ventrue, Corporate Raiders

Specialties: Macroeconomics, Microeconomics, Game Theory, High Finance, Investment

History

"Aha, here's something good." McLoughlin motioned Dierdre over to his desk. "Read this and tell me what you think."

Dierdre took the photocopy from McLoughlin's hands and read, "'And after the burning the hill was cursed. Nothing would grow there, and sheep that wandered onto it soon took sick and died.' Interesting. Where'd you dig it up?"

McLoughlin took the paper back. "Irish National Folklore Archives. They've spent a fortune recording oral history and folklore. You only get a few stories like this, though, widely scattered over the island. Thoughts?"

His partner frowned. "Well, if I didn't know better I'd say we were dealing with some Tremere problem or other, but as is, I'll have to go with an unpleasant elder taking a dirt nap."

"Right in one." McLoughlin grinned. "Want to go do some field research? Bring the mason jars."

You are familiar with the record of events, mortal and immortal. You can place events in historical context, and even detect Kindred influence on the stream of mortal history. Your expertise may well allow you to uncover evidence of vampiric activity, ranging from resting places of elders to evidence of specific individuals' involvement in affairs.

- • Novice: You know the basics of history without knowing many of the specifics.
- •• Practiced: You can pick out historical errors on television programs and in movies.
- ••• Competent: You have a solid grasp on the field, and have specialized in a particular area.
- •••• Expert: You are a recognized expert in the field; grad students footnote your works.
- ••••• Master: All of the past is an open book to you.

Possessed By: Historians, Elders, Documentary Filmmakers, Academics, Recreationists

Specialties: Military History, Social History, National or Ethnic Histories, Kindred History

Psychology

"So tell me," Helton managed in between gales of laughter, "about your sire." Around him, the rest of the coterie collapsed in helpless hilarity. Jonesie seemed unimpressed by the display. He glanced from vampire to vampire, dismissing each in turn.

"Well," he said, "my sire had a pathological fear of sunlight, to the point of needing to look out the window every half-hour to make sure the Earth hadn't somehow mysteriously speeded up in its rotation and brought morning on early. He also recognized that he had a problem, and dutifully sought help for it — with my encouragement, of course."

The others more or less subsided into snickering. Helton looked up at Jonesie with a smirk. "So what happened to him?"

Jonesie shrugged. "Well, with my help he was finally able to beat his little problem and stop worrying about dawn. In fact, he succeeded so well that he decided to take a little stroll one morning — also with my encouragement — without checking the time before he left. Pity

that the door to the haven got locked behind him, don't you think?"

And suddenly, Jonesie was the only one laughing.

You have a knowledge of psychology in both theory and practice. You are familiar with psychological approaches, counseling techniques and so on. You are also conversant with the pathology of the mind, and can make a diagnosis of a subject's dysfunction given sufficient time to observe him.

- • Novice: You've read the classics of the field.
- •• Practiced: You can separate what Freud actually said from what people think Freud said.
- ••• Competent: You could set up a practice and do reasonably well with it.
- •••• Expert: You are an expert on psychological theory — and know when and how to apply it.
- ••••• Master: You can understand others' thought patterns, motivations and Psychological Flaws from just a few short conversations.

Possessed By: Psychiatrists, Psychologists, Counselors, Social Workers, Marketing Executives, Empowerment Gurus

Specialties: Freudian, Jungian, Lacanian, Pop Psychology, Neuropsychology, Psychopathology, Mob Psychology

Other Possibilities: Accounting, Alchemy, Anthropology, Archaeology, Architecture, Art History, Astrology, Astronomy, Biology, Chemistry, Criminology, Electronics, Engineering, Faerie Lore, Forensics, Geology, Heraldry, Kindred Lore, Literature, Lupine Lore, Mage Lore, Metallurgy, Meteorology, Military Science, Naturalist, Physics, Sprit Lore, Theology, Toxicology and Wyrm Lore

MUNCHKINS AND MINMAX

Sad to say, Merits and Flaws are one of the favorite tools of players more interested racking up kills than in roleplaying. Such players often load up on Flaws they never have any intention of roleplaying, then use the freebies garnered thus to load up on killer Merits, additional Disciplines, and Backgrounds like Generation. Such abuses of the system can lead to severely unbalanced coteries, not to mention lopsided and unenjoyable games.

Storytellers have every right to disallow particular Merits and Flaws, or any combinations thereof. Merits and Flaws are optional, not mandatory, and no character has a God-given right to a *Dark Fate* that he'll whine endlessly about accepting. It is also incumbent on the Storyteller to make certain that his troupe plays out their characters' Flaws. After a few warnings, it is not beyond the bounds of acceptable behavior (or good Storytelling) to strip an unrepentant player's character of points gained through a Flaw the character is ignoring. The system of Merits and Flaws is all about balance; if a player attempts to upset that balance, it is up to the Storyteller to enforce it for the good of the game.

Merits and Flaws

The basic character creation process for **Vampire: The Masquerade** allows you to draw the broad strokes of your character — clan, generation, Attributes and so on. Merits and Flaws, however, allow you to sketch in finer details of your character's capabilities and history within the bounds of the Storyteller system's rules. With Merits and Flaws, you can give a character abilities — or weaknesses — not otherwise covered.

Merits are, unsurprisingly, bonus abilities, knacks, talents, contacts and other pluses that a character might have. Flaws are the exact opposite — weaknesses and liabilities, whether they be psychological, physical, social or even magical. A Merit can cost between one and seven freebie points at the end of character creation, while a Flaw can grant additional freebies in the same range. Characters should never have more than seven points in either Merits or Flaws, and all proposed Traits taken in this fashion are subject to Storyteller approval.

Specifics

There are some Merits and Flaws that are unique to Camarilla vampires. These Traits are mainly social ones, pertaining to personal status and history within the sect, but there are some physical, magical and psychological manifestations that only (or mainly) appear in the Camarilla as well. The Merits and Flaws listed below are intended for Camarilla (or in limited cases, ex-Camarilla vampires) alone; Merits like *Primogen Friendship* (p. 76) generally don't make much sense for Sabbat or independent vampires. By the same token, a Flaw relating to a weakness for the Viniculum generally doesn't make sense for a law-abiding Ventrue neonate. There are always exceptions (say, a Camarilla vampire who's attempting to go undercover with the local Sabbat pack), but common sense should be the ultimate guideline.

Choosing Wisely

Merits and Flaws are part of the last step of the character creation process, the spending of "freebie points." They should be taken as a sort of icing on the cake, rather than as the main thrust of the character's persona. When you select Merits and Flaws (if you do indeed select them), try to keep your character's history and sense of self in mind. If a character's backstory includes the facts that he had a horrifying Embrace and was mistreated by his sire, the Flaw *Nightmares* makes sense; if he was a ghoul trained for decades to take his place in the Camarilla, the Flaw loses its justification. Similarly, if you're going to run a rabble-rousing Brujah, picking the Merit *Sheriff's Friend* makes no sense.

Merits and Flaws are, in the end, optional. There's no shame or weakness in creating a character who has none, nor is a character without Merits or extra freebies from Flaws necessarily at a disadvantage.

With that in mind, below are listed Merits and Flaws that are appropriate for Camarilla characters. Storytellers should feel free to disallow, modify or ignore any of these as their games demand.

Physical

Traits that are designated Physical Merits and Flaws relate to a character's strength, speed, toughness and form.

Bruiser (1pt. Merit)

Your appearance is sufficiently thuglike to inspire fear or at least disquiet in those who see you. While you're not necessarily ugly *per se*, you do radiate a sort of quiet menace, to the point where people cross the street to avoid passing near you. You are at -1 difficulty on all Intimidation rolls against those who have not demonstrated their physical superiority to you.

Friendly Face (1pt. Merit)

You have a face that reminds everyone of someone, to the point where strangers are inclined to be well-inclined toward you because of it. The effect doesn't fade if you explain the "mistake," leaving you at -1 difficulty on all appropriate Social-based rolls (yes for Seduction, no for Intimidation, for example) when a stranger is involved. This Merit only functions on a first meeting.

Twitch (1pt. Flaw)

You have some sort of repetitive motion that you make in times of stress, and it's a dead giveaway as to your identity. Examples include a nervous cough, constantly wringing your hands, cracking your knuckles and so on. It costs one Willpower to refrain from engaging in your twitch.

Dulled Bite (2pt. Flaw)

For some reason your fangs never developed fully — they may not have manifested at all. When feeding, you need to find some other method of making the blood flow. Failing that, you must achieve double the normal number of successes in order to make your bite penetrate properly. A number of Caitiff and high-generation vampires often manifest this Flaw.

Open Wound (2-4pt. Flaw)

You have one or more wounds that refuse to heal, and which constantly drip blood. This slow leakage costs you an extra blood point per evening (marked off just before dawn), in addition to drawing attention to you. If the wound is visible, you are at +1 difficulty for all Social-based rolls. For two points, the Flaw is simply unsightly and has the basic effect mentioned above; for four points the seeping wound is serious or disfiguring and includes the effects of the Flaw *Permanent Wound* (**Vampire**, page 297).

Permanent Fangs (3pt. Flaw)

Your fangs do not retract, making it impossible for you to hide your true nature. While some mortals may think you've had your teeth filed or are wearing prosthetics, sooner or later you're going to run into someone who knows what you truly are. You are a constant threat to the Masquerade, and other

Kindred may take steps to prevent a breach from ever occurring. You are also limited to an Appearance rating of 3 at most.

Glowing Eyes (3 pt. Flaw)

You have the stereotypical glowing eyes of vampire legend, which gives you a -1 difficulty on Intimidation rolls when you're dealing with mortals. However, the tradeoffs are many; you are a walking tear in the Masquerade and must constantly disguise your condition (no, contacts don't cut it); the glow impairs your vision and puts you at +1 difficulty on all sight-based rolls (including the use of ranged weapons); and the radiance emanating from your eye sockets makes it difficult to hide (+2 difficulty to Stealth rolls) in the dark.

Mental

Mental Merits and Flaws help define a character's mental capabilities, strength of mind, native wit and intelligence. Mental Merits and Flaws have nothing to do with a character's state of mind. Rather, they detail what a character can do with her mind instead.

Coldly Logical (1 pt. Merit)

While some might refer to you as a "cold fish," you have a knack for separating factual reporting from emotional or hysterical coloration. You may or may not be emotional yourself, but you can see clearly when others are clouding the facts with their feelings (-1 difficulty on all Sense Deception and related rolls).

Useful Knowledge (1 pt. Merit)

You have expertise in a specific field that makes your conversation intriguing to an older Kindred. So long as your knowledge holds the other vampire's attention, he has a vested interest in keeping you around. Then again, once he's pumped you for every iota of information you possess, that patronage may suddenly vanish. (**Note:** This Merit should be played like a 1-dot Mentor with a specific interest. However, unlike a Mentor, *Useful Knowledge* does not imply a permanent relationship.)

Computer Aptitude (2 pt. Merit)

You are familiar with and talented in the uses of computer equipment. Other Kindred may not understand computers, but to you they are intuitive. All rolls involving computers are at -2 difficulty for you.

Precocious (3 pt. Merit)

You learn quickly. The time for you to pick up a particular Ability (or Abilities, at Storyteller discretion) is cut in half, as is the experience cost.

Impatient (1 pt. Flaw)

You have no patience for standing around and waiting. You want to do things *now*, and the Devil take the hindmost. Every time you are forced to wait around instead of acting, a Self-Control roll is required to see if you go haring off on your own instead.

Unconvinced (1 pt. Flaw)

You fail to see the need for the Masquerade, and have gone on record as saying so. Taking your stand has made you suspect in the eyes of your elders, and may have attracted the Sabbat's attention as well.

Stereotype (2 pt. Flaw)

You buy heavily into all of the vampire legendry you've read and heard. You wear a cape, speak with an accent and otherwise act in a cartoonish fashion. Such behavior is embarrassing in the extreme to other Kindred, who are likely to ostracize or mock you (+2 difficulty to Social rolls with other vampires who don't share your habits). Also, you stand out to hunters, and run the risk of violating the Masquerade every time you take to the streets.

Thirst for Innocence (2 pt. Flaw)

The sight of innocence — of any sort — arouses in you a terrible bloodlust. Roll Self-Control, or else frenzy and attack the source of your hunger.

Victim of the Masquerade (2 pt. Flaw)

The Camarilla's propaganda machine did too good a job on you. Even after your Embrace you refused to believe you were a vampire. You remain convinced that there is some logical explanation for your condition, and spend as much time as you can searching for it. You also have problems feeding, and may insist on trying to eat regular food. None of these habits makes you particularly pleasant company for other Kindred. This Flaw must be roleplayed at all times.

Guilt-Wracked (4 pt. Flaw)

You simply cannot come to grips with the fact that you must drink blood to survive. You suffer horrible guilt over each time you feed (roll Conscience, difficulty 7, or else frenzy every time you feed) and try to avoid doing so as much as possible. This means that you rarely have much blood in your system, leaving you vulnerable to both attacks and hunger-based frenzies.

Social

Merits and Flaws under this heading relate to a vampire's social dealings. Relations within the sect and with the Kindred at large are covered by this category. Note that there are more Social Merits and Flaws listed here than there are of any other category; the intrinsically social nature of the Camarilla mandates such.

Elysium Regular (1 pt. Merit)

You spend an unusual amount of time at the various Elysiums in your city. You see and are seen to such an extent that all of the movers and shakers of Elysium at least know who you are. Extended time spent in Elysium also gives you extended opportunities to interact with the harpies and other Kindred of that stature — and they'll know your name when you approach them.

Former Ghoul (1 pt. Merit)

You were introduced to the Blood long before you were made Kindred. Your long experience as a ghoul gives you insight into and comfort with vampiric society. You are at -1 difficulty on all Social rolls when in the presence of other neonates (particularly those who haven't been educated by their sires), and have a standing -1 difficulty on rolls relating to knowledge of the Kindred.

HARMLESS (1 pt. MERIT)

Everyone in the city knows you, and knows that you're no threat to their plans. While that sort of estimation may seem insulting, it's also what's kept you from being killed. No one considers you worth their time to deal with, and that low opinion keeps you safe. If you start acting in a way that demonstrates that you are no longer harmless, others' reactions to you will likely change as a result.

PROTÉGÉ (1 pt. MERIT)

Your sire watched you for some time before Embracing you, and spoke glowingly of you to acquaintances. These vampires may be inclined to look favorably on you by dint of your sire's recommendation; you are at -1 difficulty on Social rolls with all those who've heard good things about you.

REP (1 pt. MERIT)

Your fame has exceeded the bounds of your sect. Everyone knows who you are, what you've done and what you're supposed to have done (which might not be the same thing). The publicity can be good or bad; what matters is that everybody knows your name. Whether individuals outside of your immediate social circle know enough to match your face to your name is a different matter.

SABBAT SURVIVOR (1 pt. MERIT)

You've lived through at least one Sabbat attack and/or attempted recruitment. Your experience helps you anticipate situations where you might potentially be endangered by the Sabbat once again. You are at -1 difficulty on all Perception rolls when it comes to Sabbat-based matters. This Merit comes into play most frequently as a means of avoiding ambushes and the like.

BOON (1-6 pt. MERIT)

Someone owes you a favor. The vampire in your debt might be the lowliest neonate in the city or might be the prince herself; it all depends on how many points the Merit costs. You only have that single favor owed you (unless you take the Merit multiple times), so using it properly is of paramount importance. Depending on status and other factors, the vampire who owes you a favor may well resent his debt, and might go out of his way to "settle" it early — even going so far as to create situations from which he must "rescue" you and thus clear the slate.

BULLYBOY (2 pt. MERIT)

You're part of the brute squad the local sheriff calls on when he needs some muscle. As a result, you get in on action that others miss entirely, score points with those in power, and occasionally get a chance to act outside of the law. How far outside the law the sheriff is willing to let you go depends on circumstance and how much the sheriff likes you.

OLD PAL (2 pt. MERIT)

An acquaintance from your breathing days was Embraced at the same time you were. Fortunately, your friendship has endured even death and unlife, and you find a constant source of support and aid in your old friend. She expects the same of you, which isn't always convenient, but at least you each have someone to hang onto who remembers the good old nights — and days.

Storyteller Note: An Old Pal should be played as a very loyal Ally.

OPEN ROAD (2 PT. MERIT)

Unlike many Kindred, you like to travel. You have a solid knowledge of safe travel routes and methodologies, not to mention haven space available in any number of destinations. Unless someone out there knows your exact route and is specifically looking for you, you can move between cities unimpeded by random encounters with Lupines, overzealous state troopers and the like.

SCHOLAR OF ENEMIES (2 PT. MERIT)

You have taken the time to learn about and specialize in one particular enemy of the Camarilla. You are aware of at least some of the group's customs, strategies, abilities and long-term goals, and can put that knowledge to good use. This Merit is worth a -2 difficulty for all rolls pertaining specifically to the subject of your specialization. On the other hand, you are at a +1 difficulty when it comes to dealing with other enemies, simply because you're so thoroughly focused on your field.

SCHOLAR OF OTHERS (2 PT. MERIT)

This Merit functions identically to *Scholar of Enemies*, except that it applies to a group that is not necessarily inimical to the Camarilla.

SHERIFF'S FRIEND (2 PT. MERIT)

For whatever reason (maybe your winning smile or perhaps just your superb grovelling technique), the local head lawman likes you. He's inclined to overlook your minor trespasses and let you in on things you're not supposed to know about. He even gives you warnings about occasional crackdowns and times when the prince isn't feeling generous. Of course, abusing this connection might well turn a friendly sheriff into an enemy — and the change might not be apparent until it's too late.

DOMAIN (2-4 PT. MERIT)

The prince has given you exclusive rights to a piece of territory. The size and importance of that territory are in direct proportion to the cost of the Merit. A few blocks' worth of rowhouses might be worth two points, while four square blocks in the city's financial district could be worth four.

While the rights to this territory are yours, there are responsibilities that come along with it. If those responsibilities are not met, the prince may well strip you of your holding.

ALTERNATE IDENTITY (3 PT. MERIT)

In addition to your normal identity, you've taken up an alternate role that allows you to run with another group or sect of vampires. This other self has a believable history and backstory that can stand up to at least cursory checks, and he is accepted at face value (more or less) by his associates. However, your sire, Allies, Contacts, etc. don't know that you maintain this second identity, and treat this "stranger" accordingly.

FRIEND OF THE UNDERGROUND (3 PT. MERIT)

While you're not a Nosferatu, you know your way around the sewers, tunnels, ducts, subway tubes and other subterranean passages of your home town. The local Nosferatu (and any other creatures dwelling down in the muck) may not actually like you, but they're not inclined to kill you on sight when they see you in their territory. You are at -1 difficulty on all Sewer Lore rolls, and any rolls involving the subterranean world (sneaking from place to place underground, finding routes into sub-basements and so on). Nosferatu cannot purchase this Merit.

MOLE (3 PT. MERIT)

You have an informer buried in the Sabbat (or, less likely, one of the independent clans or the Anarch Free States) who funnels you all sorts of information as to what her peers are up to. What you do with the information is up to you, but abusing the knowledge might be a good way to get your informer killed. The other side has spies too, you know….

RISING STAR (3-PT. MERIT)

You're one of the up and comers in your city, a rising star in the Camarilla's firmament. Everyone wants to know you and be your friend, even as those in power groom you for positions of higher responsibility. You are at -1 difficulty on all Social rolls against any Camarilla vampires who aren't actively opposing your ascent.

HOLDER OF OFFICE (3-5 PT. MERIT)

You currently hold one of the official Camarilla positions in your city. The degree of power you possess depends on the cost of the Merit.

CLAN FRIENDSHIP (4 PT. MERIT)

One particular clan (not your own) has a special liking for you. You might have done the clan as a whole a favor at some point, or perhaps you're just a loud voice in support of their aims. Whatever the case, you're at -2 difficulty on all Social rolls involving members of the clan in question. Of course, the reaction your cozy relationship with another clan is likely to draw from your own clan leaders is an entirely different can of worms.

BROKEN BOND (4 PT. MERIT)

You were once blood bound but have have secretly slipped the leash, and you are free to act as you will once more. Your regnant has no idea that you are not in fact bound, and continues to treat you as if you were. At Storyteller discretion, the experience of having been bound once may render you immune to ever being enthralled again.

PRIMOGEN FRIENDSHIP (4 PT. MERIT)

The ruling council of the city values you and your opinions. You are called in to consult on decisions, and your recommendations carry great weight. Your position may not be an official one, but it's powerful nonetheless.

HARPY (5 PT. MERIT)

You count yourself among the harpies, the vampires who rule the roost in Elysium. Yours is one of the voices that mock, exalt, praise or humble the Kindred of the city. Your opinion is very influential, which means that you're going to face all sorts of attempts — from bribes to threats — to change it. You are at -1 difficulty on all Social rolls when acting in your official capacity.

PRIMOGEN (7 PT. MERIT)

You are part of the ruling coterie of vampires in the city in which you reside. Your voice is one of the few to which the prince must listen, and you have tremendous influence in your clan. On the other hand, there are always others plotting to take your place, making your position a precarious one.

BOTCHED PRESENTATION (1 PT. FLAW)

When your sire presented you to the prince of the city, you flubbed it. Now you're convinced His Majesty hates you (whether he does or not). You need to succeed on a Willpower roll (difficulty 7) just to stand in front of the prince or one of his duly authorized representatives without running, blubbering or otherwise making a fool of yourself.

EXPENDABLE (1 PT. FLAW)

Someone in power doesn't want you around. Maybe she wants territory you possess, or is jealous of the attention you're getting from a prize mortal retainer — the details are irrelevant. What does matter is that she has the power to maneuver you into dangerous situations "for the good of the Camarilla," and has no compunctions about doing so.

INCOMPLETE UNDERSTANDING (1 PT. FLAW)

The whole matter has been explained to you, but you're still not quite sure how this whole Camarilla/Masquerade thing works. Your imperfect understanding of the rules and regulations of your new existence means that sooner or later, you're going to make a mistake. It's only a matter of time....

NEW ARRIVAL (1 PT. FLAW)

You've just arrived in your new city of residence, and have done so without knowing anyone in the place. Existing factions may try to recruit or eliminate you, while the harpies size you up and take your measure. Meanwhile, your ignorance of the city's current events, history and politics (not to mention the personality quirks of the vampires already in place) may cause you to make a serious blunder.

NEW KID (1 PT. FLAW)

You're the latest Embracee in the city, and everyone knows it. That automatically puts you at the bottom of the social totem pole. Other neonates take every opportunity to demonstrate your inferiority to you, proving that the dynamics of the schoolyard are alive and well in the Camarilla. Even if someone else is added to the ranks of the unliving, you're still regarded as something as a bit of a geek by your peers — a distinction that can have dangerous consequences if bullets start flying. All Social-related rolls are at +1 difficulty when you are dealing with other neonates.

RECRUITMENT TARGET (1 PT. FLAW)

The Sabbat wants you, and they want you bad. Every effort is being made to recruit you, willing or no, and the press gangs usually show up at the worst possible time.

SYMPATHIZER (1 PT. FLAW)

You have publicly expressed sympathy for some of the Sabbat's goals and policies. Your outspoken views on the subject have made you suspect in the eyes of the city's hierarchy, and you may be suspected of (or arrested for) treason.

BOUND (2 PT. FLAW)

You are blood bound to another vampire. Your regnant may not necessarily treat you badly, but the fact remains that your will is not entirely your own. The knowledge gnaws at you, even as you find yourself lost in devotion to your vampiric master.

CATSPAW (2 PT. FLAW)

You've done dirty work for someone high up in the city's hierarchy in the past — the sheriff, the primogen or even the prince. However, instead of granting you favor, your deeds have made you an embarrassment or a liability. For the moment, your former employer's concern is to keep you quiet. In the long term, it's to get rid of you.

ESCAPED TARGET (2 PT. FLAW)

The flip side of *Rival Sires*, *Escaped Target* means that you had targeted a mortal for the Embrace, but someone else got there first. You cannot stand the humiliation of being cheated of your prize, and fly into a rage (+2 difficulty to avoid frenzy) whenever you see the one who got away. This hatred may lead you into other irrational behaviors, like Embracing enemies of the neonate, creating unauthorized childer or even trying to kill your rival. Furthermore, your petty and irrational behavior is well-known and quite noticeable, and as a result you are at +1 difficulty on all Charisma rolls until the situation is resolved.

FAILURE (2 PT. FLAW)

You once held a title in the city, but failed catastrophically in your duties. Now you are branded incompetent, excluded from circles of power and responsibility and generally ostracized by those on their way up. Your exclusion may make you a target for recruitment by the Sabbat (or so the whispers run, making you even more distrusted). Conversely, the consequences of your error — a breach of the Masquerade, an unauthorized Embrace, a lawbreaker allowed to escape — might come back to haunt you.

MASQUERADE BREAKER (2 PT. FLAW)

In your first nights as a member of the Kindred, you accidentally broke the Masquerade — and were spotted doing so. Someone else covered for your mistake, but holds the favor over you. Now you exist in fear that your error will be revealed. In the meantime, your "savior" takes pitiless advantage of you.

OLD FLAME (2 PT. FLAW)

Someone you once cared deeply for is now with the enemy. He still attempts to play on your sympathies "for old times' sake" while working against you. Unless you succeed on a contested Manipulation + Expression roll against your former friend, you do not act against him unless the situation becomes life-threatening.

Rival Sires (2 pt. Flaw)

Not one, but two vampires wanted to gift you with the Embrace. One succeeded, one failed — and she's not happy about that failure. Either you, your actual sire or both of you have become the target of the failed suitor's ire. Regardless, your persecutor is at +2 difficulty to refrain from frenzy in your presence. In addition, she may well be working actively to discredit or destroy you.

Uppity (2 pt. Flaw)

You are proud of your new status and clan — so proud that you've shot your mouth off to other Kindred and made some enemies. Wiser vampires laugh at you and chalk your rudeness up to youth, but others regard you as arrogant and insulting. These enemies will take action to embarrass or harm you. Furthermore, you are at +2 difficulty on all Social rolls against any vampires you have alienated through your yammering — and you may not know who they are.

At Storyteller discretion, you may also be required to make a Willpower roll (difficulty 6) to keep your mouth shut any time the opportunity presents itself for you to brag about your lineage, your clan or your status.

Disgrace to the Blood (3 pt. Flaw)

Your sire regards the fact that he Embraced you to be a titanic mistake, and has let everyone know it. You are mocked in Elysium, taunted by your peers and actively despised by the one who should be giving you guidance. Any request or petition you make is likely to be looked down upon by friends of your sire, and your achievements are likely to be discounted.

Former Prince (3 pt. Flaw)

Once, you held near-absolute power in a city, but those nights are gone now. Perhaps you stepped down, perhaps you were deposed, or perhaps your city fell to the Sabbat; it matters little in your reduced state. What does matter is that the prince in the city where you now dwell is aware of your prior employment, and has concerns that you might be trying to make a comeback. The machinery of the Camarilla in the city where you now make your home is subtly stacked against you, and if the prince sees an opportunity to get rid of you he just might take it.

Hunted Like a Dog (3 pt. Flaw)

Another sect or group of vampires — be it an independent clan or the Sabbat as a whole — has decided that you're a target for extermination, and pursues you relentlessly. On the bright side, the enemies of your enemy may well wish to help you out, potentially garnering you allies in this one instance.

Narc (3 pt. Flaw)

You are known to be a snitch, an informer firmly planted in the sheriff's pocket. Those on whom you might yet inform loathe you as a result, feeding you misinformation when they can in an attempt to discredit you. Given the opportunity, they might do you mischief. Regardless, your reputation as a full-fledged weasel precedes you, putting you at +1 difficulty on all Social rolls against those who don't agree with your politics.

Sleeping With the Enemy (3 pt. Flaw)

You have some sort of intimate connection with a member of an opposing sect or inimical clan. You may have a lover, a childe, a friend or a contact working the other side of the fence, but regardless of politics you retain a friendly (or more than friendly) relationship with your putative foe. Your close ties to someone on the other side would be regarded as treason by your superiors within the Camarilla, and if you are discovered the penalty will surely be death.

Clan Enmity (4 pt. Flaw)

One clan in particular wants you dead. You have offended the entire clan, from elders to neonates, and as a result every member of that bloodline wants your head on a plate. The effects of the Flaw may manifest as anything from very public snubs and insults to actual attempts on your existence. You are also at +2 difficulty on all Social rolls relating to members of the clan in question.

Loathsome Regnant (4 pt. Flaw)

Not only are you blood bound, but you are also in thrall to a vampire who mistreats you hideously. Perhaps you are publicly abused or humiliated; perhaps your master forces you to commit unspeakable acts for him. In any case, existence under the bond is a never-ending nightmare, with your regnant serving to conduct the symphony of malice.

Overextended (4 pt. Flaw)

You've got your fingers in too many pies, and people are starting to notice. You have too many ghouls, too many retainers and too many influences, which means that a lot of people have a vested interest in trimming back your operations. These enemies take every opportunity to reduce your power and influence, and if that means lying, cheating or killing, so be it. Furthermore, your enemies block every attempt you make to move into new areas of control. You're boxed in, and the box is getting smaller.

Blood Hunted (4-6 pt. Flaw)

You have been made the target of a blood hunt, and for you to return to your home city is death. For four points, this Flaw means that only your home city is off-limits to you. For six, it means that the entire Camarilla is howling for your vitae.

Laughingstock (5 pt. Flaw)

Somehow you've drawn the scorn of the local harpies, who make you their favorite and reflexive target. You are at a +2 difficulty on all Social rolls in Elysium and a +1 anywhere else in the city. In addition, you are at +2 difficulty to use Intimidation or any Dominate powers on anyone who has heard the stories mocking you.

Red List (7 pt. Flaw)

You are either being considered for or are already on the dreaded Red List, the registry of those vampires the Camarilla most wants extinguished. Any Camarilla vampire will either attack you on sight or, more likely, call in for a great deal of help.

SUPERNATURAL

Supernatural Merits and Flaws relate to the unseen world that swirls around mortal existence in the World of Darkness. These Traits tie vampires to the other monsters that stalk the night, as well as granting magical powers — or weaknesses — to Kindred thus afflicted.

DECEPTIVE AURA (1 PT. MERIT)

Your aura is unnaturally bright and colorful for a vampire. You register as a mortal on all attempts to read your aura.

HEALING TOUCH (1 PT. MERIT)

Normally vampires can only seal the wounds they inflict by licking them. With but a touch, you can achieve the same effect.

INOFFENSIVE TO ANIMALS (1 PT. MERIT)

With rare exceptions, animals usually despise the Kindred. Some flee, others attack, but all dislike being in the presence of a vampire. You have no such problem. Animals may not enjoy being in your company, but they don't actively flee from you.

HIDDEN DIABLERIE (3 PT. MERIT)

The tell-tale black streaks of diablerie do not manifest in your aura.

ADDITIONAL DISCIPLINE (5 PT. MERIT)

You can take one additional Discipline (Storyteller discretion) as if it were a clan Discipline. All costs to learn that Discipline are paid out as if it were native to your clan. A character can not take this merit more than once.

COLD BREEZE (1 PT. FLAW)

A chill wind follows you everywhere you go. While it may make for dramatic entrances, this effect also discomfits mortals (+1 difficulty on all appropriate Social rolls) and also endangers the Masquerade. Cold winds sweeping through executive offices or crowded nightclubs can raise all sorts of questions.

BEACON OF THE UNHOLY (2 PT. FLAW)

You radiate palpable evil. Clergy and devout mortals know instinctively that there is something horribly wrong with you, and react accordingly. Churches and other places of worship are barred to you as well.

DEATHSIGHT (2 PT. FLAW)

Everything appears rotted and decayed to you. The world appears to you as a corpse; mortals look diseased or skeletal, buildings seem decrepit, and your fellow Kindred seem to be walking, moldering cadavers. You are at -2 difficulty to resist all rolls based on Appearance, but by the same token you are at +2 difficulty on all Perception-based rolls. In addition, you find social interaction difficult and are at +1 difficulty on all Social-based rolls.

LORD OF THE FLIES (2 PT. FLAW)

Buzzing harbingers of decay swirl around you everywhere. Their constant presence makes it difficult for you to interact socially (+1 difficulty when appropriate) and nearly impossible to sneak up on someone or hide effectively. The buzzing of the flies inevitably gives you away — all Stealth rolls are at +2 difficulty.

POWERS BEYOND UNDERSTANDING: ADVANCED DISCIPLINES

See, I have given you wings on which to hover uplifted high
above the earth entire and the great waste of the sea without strain.
-Theógnis of Mégara, Richard Lattimore, trans.

Most of the outrageous and terrifying vampire myths in the World of Darkness can be traced to uses of the vampiric powers known as Disciplines. Seemingly magical in their manifestation, Disciplines are a means by which vampires can manipulate vitae and the world around them to produce spectacular and often terrifying effects beyond the capabilities of mere mortals.

However, even among the unliving there is a hierarchy of power. Age and strength of blood limit most vampires to the first five levels of the Disciplines (and lineage makes some of those relatively weak abilities harder to learn than others). It is only with power and, more importantly, with proximity to Caine's generation, that the secrets of the higher level Disciplines (levels 6 through 9) are unlocked.

Below are the higher level Discipline powers for the powers normally associated with the Kindred of the Camarilla. Some Disciplines feature multiple powers at various levels; in such cases a vampire with enough experience to learn one of the choices simply picks one. If the character later decides she wants to pick up the other option as well, she can go back and spend the experience to do so.

It should be noted that the powers listed below could easily be abused and used to stomp a chronicle into a bloody pulp. These powers are, for lack of a better word, *powerful*, and should be used with discretion and caution. It should take a great deal of hard work and effort (and by "a great deal," we mean the in-play equivalent of decades or centuries) to master these hideously

potent tricks; Level Five Discipline powers wreak quite enough havoc already. Storytellers should think long and hard about allowing high-level Disciplines into their games (even if the characters are of an appropriate generation to learn them) before giving the go-ahead, and they should always remember that use of powers like Species Speech mark the wielder as being ancient, powerful — and possibly worth diablerizing.

ROLL YOUR OWN

The powers presented below are the most common high-level variations of the vampiric Disciplines, but are by no means the only ones. Once a vampire has sufficient skill and power to learn powers of Level Six and above, she also gains a sufficient understanding of her Discipline's essential nature to allow her to create her own powers. That does not mean that a seventh-generation vampire can suddenly start spewing forth random manifestations of Obfuscate, but rather that she has the ability to craft a new Level Six power and purchase it with experience instead of one of the more common options.

Any new power that a character creates should be cleared with the Storyteller before it ever sees the light of play. Power level, game balance and appropriateness within the bounds of the campaign should be the criteria by which the proposed power should be judged. A Storyteller should feel free to veto a proposed power at any time in the best interests of the game. Just because a character has the potential to create a new power doesn't mean that she can actually do it.

Note: Some Disciplines have more options listed below than others. The disparity does not mean that some are more versatile than others. Rather, it means that there are more commonly known applications of certain Disciplines than there are of others.

ANIMALISM

●●●●●● ANIMAL SUCCULENCE

Most vampires find the blood of animals flat, tasteless and lacking in nutritional value. Some Gangrel and Nosferatu, however, have refined their understanding of the spirits of such "lesser prey" to the point that they are able to draw much more sustenance from beasts than normal Kindred can. This power does not allow an elder to subsist solely on the blood of animals, but it does allow him to go for extended periods of time without taking vitae from humans or other Kindred.

System: No roll is needed; once learned, this power is always in effect. Animal Succulence allows a character to count each blood point drawn from an animal as two in her blood pool. This does not increase the size of the vampire's blood pool, just the nutritional value of animal blood.

Animal Succulence does not allow a character to completely ignore his craving for the blood of "higher" prey; in fact, it heightens his desire for "real food." Every three times (rounded down) the character drinks from an animal, a cumulative +1 difficulty is applied to the next Self-Control roll the player makes when the character is confronted with the possibility of dining on human or Kindred blood.

Animal Succulence does not increase the blood point value of other supernatural creatures (Gangrel, mages, pookas, werecreatures) who have taken animal forms.

●●●●●● SHARED SOUL

This power allows a character to probe the mind of any one animal within reach. Shared Soul can be very disconcerting to both parties involved, as each participant is completely immersed in the thoughts and emotions of the other. With enough effort or time, each participant can gain a complete understand-

HIGH LEVEL DISCIPLINES		
Discipline Level	Cost (Clan Discipline)	Cost (Non-Clan Discipline)
6	30	42
7	35	49
8	40	56
9	45	63

Level 10 Disciplines are only available to vampires of the Third Generation, an exalted state which players' characters are unlikely ever to attain.

Malenkov the Gangrel has fed happily from the herd of deer that forages around his haven 10 times. Venturing into the city for an appointment in Elysium, he comes across the scene of a gun battle and spots a puddle of spilled human blood on the ground. Malenkov's Self-Control roll to keep from diving in and gorging on the blood is made at +3 difficulty. His player rolls well, and Malenkov is sufficiently self-possessed to move on, but next time he might not be so lucky.

ing of the other's mind. Shared Soul is most often used to extract an animal's memories of a specific event, but some Gangrel use this power as a tool in the search for enlightenment, feeling they come to a better understanding of their own Beasts through rapport with true beasts. Too close of a bond, however, can leave the two souls entangled after the sharing ends, causing the vampire to adopt mannerisms, behavior patterns or even ethics (or lack thereof) similar to those of the animal.

System: The character touches the intended subject creature, and the player rolls Perception + Animal Ken (difficulty 6). The player spends a Willpower point for every turn past the first that contact is maintained. Locating a specific memory takes six turns, minus one turn for every success on the roll. A complete bond takes 10 turns, minus one turn for every success on the roll. A botch on this roll may, at the Storyteller's discretion, send the vampire into a frenzy or give the character a derangement related to the behavior patterns of the animal (extreme cowardice if the vampire contacted the soul of a mouse, bloodlust if the subject was a rabid dog, and so forth).

●●●●●● SPECIES SPEECH

The basic power Sweet Whispers (Animalism 1) allows a character to communicate with only one animal at a time. With Species Speech, a character can enter into psychic communion with all creatures of a certain species that are present. Species Speech is most often used after an application of The Beckoning (Animalism 2), which draws a crowd of likely subjects.

System: The player rolls Manipulation + Animal Ken (difficulty 7) to establish contact with the targeted group of animals. Once the character establishes contact, the player makes a second roll to issue commands. There is no practical upper limit on the number of animals that can be commanded with this power, although all of the intended subjects must be in the vampire's immediate vicinity. Only one species of animal can be commanded at a time; thus, if a character is standing in the middle of the reptile house at the zoo, she could command all of the Komodo dragons, all of the boa constrictors or all of the skinks, but she could not simultaneously give orders to every reptile or snake present. Species Speech functions much like Sweet Whispers in all other respects.

(**Note**: Players who get too wrapped up in the species difference between northern diamondback rattlesnakes and south-

eastern diamondback rattlesnakes need to relax and let the point go. At Storyteller discretion, the expenditure of a additional Willpower point allows the character's commands to extend to members of a similar species to the one initially commanded.)

●●●●●●● Conquer the Beast

Masters of Animalism have a much greater understanding of both beasts in general and the Beast in particular. Those who have developed this power can master their own Beasts to a degree impossible for lesser Kindred to attain. Conquer the Beast allows the vampire both to control her frenzies and also to enter them at will. Some elders say that the development of this power is one of the first steps on the road to Golconda.

System: The character can enter frenzy at will. The player rolls Willpower (difficulty 7). Success sends the character into a controlled frenzy. He can choose his targets at will, but gains limited Dominate and wound penalty resistance and Rötschreck immunity as per the normal frenzy rules. A botch on the roll sends the vampire into an uncontrolled frenzy which Conquer the Beast may not be used to end.

The player may also roll Willpower (difficulty 9) to enable the character to control an involuntary frenzy. In this case, a Willpower point must be spent for every turn that the vampire remains in frenzy. The player may make Self-Control rolls as normal to end a frenzy, but if the vampire runs out of Willpower points before the frenzy ends, he drops into an uncontrolled frenzy again. A botch on the Willpower roll raises the difficulty of the vampire's Self-Control rolls by two and renders Conquer the Beast unusable for the remainder of the night.

●●●●●●●● Taunt the Caged Beast

Some Kindred are so attuned to the Beast that they can unleash it in another individual at will. Vampires who have developed this power are able to send adversaries into frenzy with a finger's touch and the resultant, momentary contact with the victim's Beast. The physical contact allows the vampire's own Beast to reach out and awaken that of the victim, enraging it by threatening its spiritual territory.

System: The character touches the target. The player spends a Willpower point and rolls Manipulation + Empathy (difficulty 7). The victim makes a Self-Control roll (difficulty 5 + the number of successes); failure results in an immediate frenzy, with standard rules applying. A botch causes the character to unleash his own Beast and frenzy instead. This power may be used on those individuals who are normally incapable of frenzy, sending ordinary humans into murderous rages worthy of the bloodthirstiest Brujah berserker.

●●●●●●●●● Unchain the Beast

The self-destructive nature of Cainites can be turned against them by an elder who possesses this formidable power. With a glance, the vampire can awaken the Beasts of her enemies, causing physical injury and excruciating agony as the victim's own violent impulses manifest in physical form to tear him apart from within. A target of this power erupts into a fountain of blood and gore as claw and bite wounds from an invisible source spontaneously tear his flesh asunder.

System: The character makes eye contact with the intended victim. The player spends three blood points and rolls Manipulation + Intimidation (difficulty of the victim's Self-Control + 4). Each success inflicts one health level of lethal damage, which can be soaked normally. A botch inflicts one health level of lethal damage on the character for each "1" rolled. This damage can also be soaked normally.

Auspex

●●●●●● Clairvoyance

By using Clairvoyance, a vampire can perceive distant events without using Psychic Projection. By concentrating on a familiar person, place or object, a character can observe the subject's immediate vicinity while staying aware of her own surroundings.

System: The player rolls Perception + Empathy (difficulty 6) and describes the target she's trying to look in on. If the roll is successful, the character can then perceive the events and environment surrounding the desired target for one turn per success. Other Auspex powers may be used on the scene being viewed; these are rolled normally. Clairvoyance does split the vampire's perceptions between what she is viewing at a distance and what is taking place around her. As a result, while using this power, a character is at +3 difficulty on all rolls relating to actions that affect her physical surroundings.

●●●●●● Prediction

Some people are capable of finishing their friends' sentences. Elder vampires with Prediction sometimes *begin* their friends' sentences. Prediction is a constant low-level telepathic scan of the minds of everyone the character is in proximity to. While this power does not give the vampire the details of his neighbors' conscious thoughts, it does provide a wealth of cues as to the subjects' moods, suppressed reflexes and attitudes toward the topic of conversation.

System: Whenever the character is in conversation and either participant in the discussion makes a Social roll, the player may pre-empt the roll to spend a blood point and make a Perception + Empathy roll (difficulty of the target's Manipulation + Subterfuge). Each success is an additional die that can be applied to the player's Social roll or subtracted from the dice pool of the Social roll being made against the character.

●●●●●● Telepathic Communication

Telepathy (Auspex 4) allows a character to pick up only the surface thoughts of other individuals, and to speak to one at a time. With Telepathic Communication, a character can form a link between his mind and that of other subjects, allowing them to converse in words, concepts and sensory images at the speed of thought. Vampires with this level of Auspex can act as "switchboard operators," creating a telepathic web that allows all participants to share thoughts with some or all other members of the network as they choose.

System: The player rolls Charisma + Empathy (difficulty of the target's current Willpower) to establish contact, although a willing subject may allow the vampire access and

thus obviate the need for a roll. The maximum range at which a subject may be contacted and the maximum number of individuals who may be linked simultaneously with this power depends on the Auspex rating of the vampire who initiates contact.

Auspex Rating	No. of Targets	Range
Auspex 6	3 subjects	500 miles
Auspex 7	Perception rating	1000 miles
Auspex 8	Perception + Empathy combined	500 miles for every point of Intelligence
Auspex 9	2x Perception + Empathy combined	1000 miles for every point of Intelligence

•••••• KARMIC SIGHT

The power of Aura Perception (Auspex 2) allows a vampire to take a brief glimpse at the soul of a subject. This power takes Aura Perception several steps forward, allowing a vampire who has mastered Auspex 2 to probe the inner workings of a subject's mind and soul. Knowledge acquired in this fashion can be used in many ways, and a vampire who has developed this power is undoubtedly familiar with all of them.

System: The player rolls Perception + Empathy (difficulty of the subject's permanent Willpower). The degree of success determines the information gained.

No. Of Successes	Effect
Botch	The character gains a Derangement or Psychological/Mental/Supernatural Flaw of the target's for one night, at Storyteller discretion.
1 success	As per five successes on an Aura Perception roll.
2 successes	Subject's Nature, Demeanor and Humanity/Path can be determined.
3 successes	Any outside influences on the subject's mind or soul, such as Dominate or a demonic pact, can be detected.
4 successes	Subject's Willpower, Humanity/Path and Virtue scores can be determined.
5 successes	The state of the subject's karma may be determined. This is a highly abstract piece of information best left to Storyteller discretion, but should reveal the general balance between "good" and "bad" actions the subject has performed, both recently and over the course of his existence. If the plot merits it, the character may receive visions of one or more incidents in the subject's past that radically altered his destiny. With this degree of success, some fate-related Merits and Flaws (e.g. *Destiny* or *Dark Fate*) can be identified as well.

●●●●●● Mirror Reflex

This power was developed by a Toreador elder who made a fearsome reputation through her fencing prowess, acting as a hired champion in dozens of Ventrue duels. Mirror Reflex is similar to Prediction in that it is in essence a low-level telepathic scan of an opponent, but this power taps into physical (rather than social) reflexes, allowing the character to anticipate an enemy's moves in personal combat.

System: The player spends a blood point and rolls Perception + the combat skill the opponent is using (difficulty of the subject's Manipulation + combat skill in use). Each success is an additional die that can be applied to the character's dice pools during the next turn of combat for any actions taken against the scanned opponent. The use of Mirror Reflex does take one combat action, and the power has a maximum range in yards equal to the character's Willpower rating.

●●●●●●● Psychic Assault

Psychic Assault is nothing less than a direct mind-to-mind attack which uses the sheer force of an elder's will to overpower his target. Victims of Psychic Assault show little outward sign of the attack, save for nosebleeds and expressions of intense agony; all injuries by means of this psychic pressure inflicted are internal. A medical examination of a mortal victim of a Psychic Assault invariably shows the cause of death to be a heart attack or aneurysm, while vampires killed with this power decay to dust instantly, regardless of age.

System: The character must touch or make eye contact with his target. The player spends three blood points (and a Willpower point, if assaulting a vampire or other supernatural being) and rolls Manipulation + Intimidation in an contested roll against the victim's permanent Willpower. The result depends on the number of net successes the attacker rolls.

No. of Successes	Effect
Botch	The target becomes immune to the attacker's Psychic Assault for one night per "1" rolled.
Failure	The target is unharmed and may determine that a psychic assault is taking place by succeeding on a Perception + Occult roll (difficulty 6).
1 success	The target is shaken but unharmed. He loses a temporary Willpower point.
2 successes	The target is badly frightened. He loses three temporary Willpower points and, if a vampire, must roll Courage (difficulty of the attacker's Auspex score) to avoid Rötschreck.
3 successes	The target loses six temporary Willpower points and, if a vampire, must roll Courage as above. If this causes him to lose his last temporary Willpower point, he loses a permanent Willpower point and receives

three health levels of bashing damage (soaked normally).

| 4 successes | The target loses all temporary Willpower points and half of his permanent Will power points (round down) and receives three health levels of lethal damage (soaked normally). |
| 5 successes | The target must roll Willpower (difficulty 7). If he succeeds, apply the effect of four successes. If he fails, the Psychic Assault kills him instantly. |

Any result that causes the victim to lose his last temporary Willpower point also renders him unconscious for the rest of the night.

●●●●●●●●● False Slumber

Possibly the source of many Malkavians' conviction that their sire is alive and well on the astral plane, this power allows a Methuselah's spirit to leave his body while in torpor. While seemingly asleep, the vampire is able to project astrally, think and perceive events normally.

System: No roll is needed. This power is considered to be active whenever the vampire's body is in torpor, and astral travels are handled as per the rules for Psychic Projection (Auspex 5). The vampire may not be able to awaken physically at will, however — waking from torpor is handled per the normal rules for such an action (see p. 216, **Vampire: The Masquerade**).

A vampire with this power whose silver cord is severed in astral combat loses all Willpower points, as per the rules for astral combat under Psychic Projection (**Vampire: The Masquerade**, pp. 152), but is not killed. Instead, he loses the use of this Auspex power and half of his permanent Willpower points. Both the Auspex 9 power and the Willpower must be bought back with experience points. The vampire's soul slowly returns to his body over the course of a year and a day, during which time he may not be awakened from torpor by any means.

Celerity

Few Kindred can even conceive of any use for Celerity other than that of speeding up one's actions so that one might pop off a few more TEC-9 rounds in combat. While that approach is all well and good, there are other potential applications of the power available to ancient, learned or clever vampires.

Under normal circumstances, advanced mastery of Celerity means that the normal progression of powers predominates. Unless the character makes a special effort to learn an alternate power or to create one, each additional level of the power from 6 to 9 means that once the Discipline is activated, the vampire simply receives *another* additional action per turn.

If, however, the vampire chooses to take an alternate power, she forfeits that normal progression (which can later be made up through experience) and takes the new manifestation of Celerity instead. She does not gain the extra action in addition to the special power; it's an either/or situation.

Note: Yes, there are fewer alternate Celerity powers listed than there are for any other Discipline (save Potence and Fortitude). No, this is not an oversight — there has been less impetus for practitioners of these three Disciplines to develop variations than there has been on masters of, say, Auspex.

●●●●●● Projectile

Despite the fact that a vampire with Celerity moves at incredible speeds, by some quirk of metaphysics any bullets he fires or knives he throws while in this state don't move any faster than they normally would. Scientifically minded Kindred have been baffled by the phenomenon for centuries, but more pragmatic ones have found a way to work around it. Projectile enables a vampire to take his preternatural speed and transfer it into something he has thrown, fired or launched.

System: Projectile requires the expenditure of a blood point. In addition, the player must decide how many levels of his character's Celerity he is putting into the speed of the launched object. Thus, a character with Celerity 6 in addition to Projectile could decide to put three dots' worth of speed into a knife he is throwing, and use the other three dots as extra actions as per normal. Each dot of Celerity infused into a thrown object becomes an automatic success on the attack's damage roll, assuming the knife/hatchet/spear/bullet actually hits.

●●●●●● Flower of Death

In combat, as in all things, speed kills. A proper application of Celerity in combat can turn even the meekest Cainite into a walking abattoir. How much more deadly, then, is a vampire with the ability to utilize his preternatural speed to the utmost in combat? The answer to that question is "Rather a lot." Flower of Death allows a vampire to take his Celerity and apply it in full to each hand-to-hand or melee attack he makes.

System: Flower of Death costs four blood points, but the spectacular effect is well worth it. Once the power is in effect, a number of dice equal to the vampire's normal Celerity rating gets added to every dice pool for attack the character makes until the end of the scene. The effect is limited to hand-to-hand or melee weapon attacks — firearms, bows and whatnot are excluded — and does not grant the attacker additional dice for damage rolls.

Flower of Death is not cumulative — it is impossible to "layer" uses of the power over one another to create astronomical dice pools.

For Example

Dominic Atter, a seventh-generation Toreador with a taste for trouble, scrapes together enough experience to increase his Celerity expertise to Level Six. However, he decides he wants the alternate Level Six power, Projectile, instead. After spending the experience to pick up Projectile, Dominic is now in a position (once he activates his Celerity) to take five extra actions per turn, *or* to use his preternatural speed to hurl knives, shurikens or whatever else comes to hand with deadly velocity.

●●●●●● ZEPHYR

Zephyr produces an effect vaguely similar to one of the legendary comic book-style uses of enhanced speed, allowing its practitioner to run so fast he can run across water (he's moving so fast he doesn't have time to sink). Particularly successful applications of Zephyr allow a vampire to go so far as to run up walls and, in at least one recorded instance, across a ceiling, though the latter is more of a parlor trick than anything else.

System: Zephyr requires the expenditure of a point each of blood and Willpower. Unfortunately, Zephyr requires such extremes of concentration that it cannot be combined with any form of attack, or indeed, with most any sort of action at all. If a character using Zephyr feels the need to do something else while moving at such tremendous speeds, a Willpower roll (difficulty 8) is required. Needless to say, botches at Zephyr speed can be spectacular in all the wrong ways.

Most times, a vampire moving at such a rate of speed is barely visible, appearing more as a vampire-shaped blur than anything else. Observers must succeed on a Perception + Alertness roll (difficulty 7) to get even a decent look at a Kindred zooming past in this fashion.

DOMINATE

Any vampire with Dominate 6 or higher may employ Dominate upon a character with the Merit *Iron Will*, "burning through" the defender's barriers. An Iron Willed character may spend a Willpower point to raise the difficulty of a Dominate attempt by +2 if the attacker has Dominate ●●●●●●, or by +1 if he has ●●●●●●●. Iron Will provides no benefit whatsoever against the commands of a character with Dominate ●●●●●●●● or higher.

●●●●●● CHAIN THE PSYCHE

Not content with merely commanding their subjects, some elders apply this power to ensure obedience from recalcitrant victims. Chain the Psyche is a Dominate technique that inflicts incapacitating pain on a target who attempts to break the vampire's commands.

System: The player spends a blood point when her character applies Dominate to a subject. Any attempt that the subject makes to go against the vampire's implanted commands or to recover stolen memories causes intense pain. When such an attempt is made, the Storyteller rolls the character's Manipulation + Intimidation (difficulty of the subject's Stamina + Empathy). Each success equals one turn that the victim is unable to act, as she is wracked with agony. Each application of Chain the Psyche crushes a number of resistance attempts equal to the character's Manipulation rating, after which the effect fades.

●●●●●● LOYALTY

With this power in effect, the elder's Dominate is so strong that other vampires find it almost impossible to break with their own commands. Despite the name, Loyalty instills no special feelings in the victim — the vampire's commands are simply implanted far more deeply than normal.

System: Any other vampire attempting to employ Dominate on a subject who has been Dominated by a vampire with Loyalty must spend an additional Willpower point and make all rolls to do so at +3 difficulty.

•••••• OBEDIENCE

While most Kindred must employ Dominate through eye contact, some powerful elders may command loyalty with the lightest brush of a hand.

System: The character can employ all Dominate powers through touch instead of eye contact (although eye contact still works). Skin contact is necessary — simply touching the target's clothing or something she is holding will not suffice. The touch does not have to be maintained for the full time it takes to issue a Dominate command, though repeated attempts to Dominate a single target require the character to touch the subject again.

••••••• MASS MANIPULATION

A truly skilled elder may command small crowds through the use of this power. By manipulating the strongest minds within a given group, a gathering may be directed to the vampire's will.

System: The player declares that he is using this power before rolling for the use of another Dominate power. The difficulty of the roll is that which would be required to Dominate the most resistant member of the target group — if he cannot be Dominated, no one in his immediate vicinity can. For every success past that needed to inflict the desired

FOR EXAMPLE

Domingo is of the Fourth Generation. He wants to command his immediate progeny and their childer to protect the city under which he will soon enter torpor. Domingo's player rolls for the use of this power against a difficulty of 6 (4 + the two generations to whom the command goes out). He succeeds, and members of his brood begins manipulating mortal affairs to ensure the prosperity of Domingo's new home. Several of them take up the reins of power, becoming princes of nearby cities, and all believe that they are acting independently — whimsy or fate made them choose to settle where they did.

Several centuries later, Domingo awakens (in a much larger city, by this point). He soon learns that a close friend of his was destroyed by the Tremere while he slumbered. Overcome with rage, he orders every descendant of his to make the destruction of Clan Tremere an immediate priority, down to those neonates of the 14th Generation. This command spans 10 generations, fifth down to 14th, and thus the difficulty is 14 (4 + 10 generations), or difficulty 10 with five successes. Amazingly, the player rolls five 10s, and hundreds of vampires across the globe slowly begin harboring grudges against the Tremere. Maybe this explains why no one likes the Warlocks….

Note: The above is an example for demonstration purposes only. It is *not* a mandate to create fourth-generation characters.

result on the first target, the player may choose one additional target to receive the same effect *in its entirety*. The vampire needs to make eye contact only with the initial target.

••••••• STILL THE MORTAL FLESH

Despite its name, this power may be employed on vampires as well as mortals, and it has left more than one unfortunate victim writhing in agony — or unable to do even that. A vampire who has developed this power is able to override her victim's body as easily as his mind in order to cut off his senses or even stop his heart. It is rumored that this power once came more easily to the Kindred, but modern medicine has made the bodies and spirits of mortals more resistant to such manipulations.

System: The player rolls Manipulation + Medicine (difficulty of the target's Willpower + 2; a difficulty over 10 means that this power cannot affect the target at all). The effect lasts for one turn per success. The player must choose what function of the target's body is being cut off before rolling. She may affect any of the body's involuntary functions; breathing, circulation, perspiration, sight and hearing are all viable targets. While Still the Mortal Flesh is in effect, a vampire can either stop any one of those functions entirely or cause them to fluctuate erratically.

The exact effects of any given bodily function being shut off are left to the Storyteller. Most mortals panic if suddenly struck blind, but only the shutdown of the heart will kill a target instantly. Vampires are unaffected by loss of heartbeat or breathing, but may be rendered deaf and blind as easily as mortals.

•••••••• FAR MASTERY

This refinement of Obedience (though the character need not have learned Obedience first) allows the use of Dominate on any subject that the vampire is familiar with, at any time, over any distance. If the elder knows where his target is, he may issue commands as if he were standing face-to-face with his intended victim.

System: The player spends a Willpower point and rolls Perception + Empathy (difficulty equal to the subject's Wits + Stealth) to establish contact. If this roll succeeds, Dominate may be used as if the character had established eye contact with the target. A second Willpower point must be spent in order for a vampire to use this power on another vampire or other supernatural being.

••••••••• SPEAK THROUGH THE BLOOD

The power structures of Methuselahs extend across continents and centuries. This power is a powerful tool by which such ancients wield control over their descendants, even far outside their geographic spheres of influence. Speak Through the Blood allows an elder to issue commands to every vampire whose lineage returns to her — even if the two have never met. Thus, entire broods act to further the goals of sleeping ancients whose existences they are completely unaware of. The vampires affected by this power rarely act directly to pursue the command they were given, but over 10 or so years, their priorities slowly shift until the fulfillment of the Methuselah's command is among their long-term goals. Speak Through the Blood, be-

cause it takes effect so slowly, is rarely recognized as an outside influence, and its victims rationalize their behavior as "growing and changing," or something to that effect.

System: The player spends a permanent Willpower point and rolls Manipulation + Leadership. The difficulty of this roll is equal to four plus the number of generations to which the command is to be passed. Unless the character is aware of the location and present agenda of every descendant of his — a highly unlikely event — he may only issue general commands, such as "work for the greater glory of Clan Malkavian" or "destroy all those who seek to extinguish the light of knowledge." Speak Through the Blood can be used by a vampire in torpor. Commands issued through this power last for one decade per success on the roll. Difficulties over 10 require one additional success for each point past 10, making it that much more difficult to issue long-lasting commands stretching down to the ends of one's lineage.

A vampire who has reached Golconda is not affected by this power, and is completely unaware that it has been used. Her childer, however, are affected normally unless they are also enlightened. Ghouls of the victims of this power are also affected, but to a lesser extent than vampires.

FORTITUDE

Vampires have inhuman stamina by mortal standards, capable as they are of withstanding being repeatedly shot, stabbed, crushed, staked and otherwise brutalized without showing much wear. Then there are those Kindred whose powers of endurance cause even other vampires to marvel — or fear. A vampire with sufficient mastery of Fortitude is nigh-indestructible, able to withstand sunlight, flame and other perils that would quickly reduce a mere neonate to ash.

Kindred advance in Fortitude the same way they advance in Celerity, having the option to increase their basic mastery of the Discipline or to take an alternate power such as one of those detailed below.

•••••• PERSONAL ARMOR

Nobody likes to get hit (or shot, or stabbed for that matter), not even Cainites. The easiest way to ensure that one is not hit (or shot, or stabbed) repeatedly is to take the weapon with which one is assaulted away from one's attacker and break it. That's where Personal Armor comes in. This application of Fortitude, derived from one popular in the 12th century, causes anything that strikes a Kindred who employs Personal Armor to shatter on impact.

System: With the expenditure of two blood points, a vampire can add preternatural hardness to his flesh. Every time an attack is made on the Kindred using Personal Armor (one which he does not dodge), his player rolls Fortitude (difficulty 8). If the roll grants more successes than the attacker rolled, then the weapon used to make the attack shatters against the vampire's flesh. (Fetishes, klaives, "magical" swords and so on may be resistant to this effect, at

Storyteller discretion.) The vampire still takes normal damage if the attack is successful, even if the weapon shatters in the process; this damage may still be soaked. If the attack roll botches, any normal weapon automatically shatters.

A hand-to-hand attack causes the attacker equal damage to that suffered by the defender when Personal Armor comes into play. On a miss, the attacker takes one level of bashing damage.

The effects of this power last for the duration of the scene.

••••••• Shared Strength

It's one thing to laugh off bullets, rather another to watch the ricochets mow down everyone around you. Many Kindred have wished, at one time or another, that they could lend their monstrous vitality to those around them. Those few vampires who have mastered Shared Strength can — if only for a little while.

System: Shared Strength transfers a portion of a vampire's Fortitude (one dot for every point of blood the vampire spends) to another being. Activating the power requires a Stamina + Survival roll (difficulty 8, increased to 9 if the target is not a normal mortal), and the expenditure of a point of Willpower. Furthermore, the vampire must mark his target by pressing a drop of his blood onto the target's forehead. This stain remains visible as long as the power is in effect, which is in turn determined by the initial roll.

No. of Successes	Duration
1	One turn
2	One scene
3	One hour
4	One night
5	One week
6	One month
7	One year

The target of this power need not be willing to accept the benefit to receive it. Particularly sadistic Kindred have come up with any number of ways in which a target's "devil's mark" and supernatural endurance can be used to land him in a great deal of trouble.

A vampire can never bestow more levels of Fortitude than he himself possesses on another.

•••••••• Adamantine

Adamantine functions as a more potent version of Personal Armor.

System: This power mimics the effects of Personal Armor, save that the vampire who uses it takes no damage from attacks that shatter on her skin.

Obfuscate

•••••• Conceal

The vampire may mask an inanimate object up to the size of a house (Obfuscate cannot be used to disguise inanimate

For Example

Amelia has earned enough experience points to purchase Obfuscate 6, and chooses Soul Mask as her new power. As the character has no Auspex, she has never seen an actual aura and thus cannot duplicate one. As a result, her use of Soul Mask displays no aura at all. After some time, however, Amelia learns the second level of Auspex from a seemingly friendly Malkavian, and the player also socks away enough experience to purchase a second Level Six Obfuscate power. Now aware of how useful a misleading aura can be, she picks Soul Mask again, this time choosing to display the pure white aura of an innocent mortal child. Amelia can now choose to display her true aura, her "innocent" aura or no aura at all.

objects without the use of this power). If the object is hidden, so are all of its contents. While Conceal is in effect, passersby walk around the concealed object as if it were still visible, but refuse to acknowledge that they are making any kind of detour.

System: In order to activate this power, a character must be within 30 feet of the object to be concealed and the item must hold some personal significance. The Conceal power functions as Unseen Presence (Obfuscate 2) for purposes of detection, as well as the duration and durability of the disguise.

Conceal can be used on a vehicle in which the character is traveling. In this instance, traffic patterns seem to flow around the vehicle, and accidents are actually *less* likely as other drivers subconsciously maneuver away from the concealed auto. A police radar gun still registers a speeding car masked in this fashion, but the officer behind the gun is disinclined to make a traffic stop of the phantom blip. Using Conceal on aircraft is problematic, as the power's range generally doesn't extend far enough to cover air traffic controllers and the like.

•••••• Mind Blank

A vampire with this power is able to shrug off telepathic contact, easily withstanding invasive probes of her mind.

System: Any attempt to read or probe the character's mind first requires a successful Perception + Empathy roll (difficulty of the character's Wits + Stealth). Even if a potential intruder does succeed, his dice pool for the attempt itself is then limited to the number of successes he scored on the initial roll.

•••••• Soul Mask

In addition to concealing her form, a vampire who has developed Soul Mask is able to conceal her aura. She may display whatever combination of colors and shades she wishes, or may appear to have no aura whatsoever. This power is of particular use to those of elder generation who have reached such heights of power through diablerie.

System: The use of this power allows the projection of only one aura (or lack thereof) — the vampire chooses the precise colors to be displayed when she first develops Soul Mask. If the character has no experience with the use of Aura

Perception (Auspex 2), she may not choose an alternate aura, as she has no idea what one would look like, though she can still choose to display no aura whatsoever. Soul Mask can be bought multiple times, if desired, in order to give a vampire multiple alternate auras from which to choose.

Unless the player states otherwise, Soul Mask is always in effect. If the character has bought Soul Mask two or more times, her "default" aura displayed is the first one she learned.

●●●●●●● CACHE

Most Obfuscate powers require the individual using them to be within a short distance of the subjects of the concealment. Cache extends this range considerably, allowing an elder with this power to leave people or objects safely hidden while he goes about his business elsewhere.

System: A character must be within the normal required distance to initiate an Obfuscate power. Once this is done, the player spends a Willpower point, which activates Cache on top of the already functioning use of the Discipline. The concealment will now remain in effect as long as the vampire is within a distance equal to his Wits + Stealth in miles from the object or person he wishes to conceal. The enhanced concealment fades at the next sunrise, or breaks, as always, if the Obfuscate subject reveals himself.

●●●●●●● VEIL OF BLISSFUL IGNORANCE

This power's development is attributed to the Malkavians, but many Nosferatu have also found it to be highly useful. The Veil of Blissful Ignorance allows a vampire to Obfuscate an unwilling victim, removing him from the notice of others. Some Nosferatu use this power to teach a humbling lesson to individuals who take the presence and aid of others for granted, while others utilize it to remove an essential member of a group in the midst of a crisis.

System: The character must touch the victim to activate this power. The player spends a blood point and rolls Wits + Stealth (difficulty of the victim's Appearance + 3). If the roll is a success, the victim is subject to the effects of Vanish From the Mind's Eye for a length of time determined by the number of successes the player rolls.

No. of Successes	Duration
1 success	Three turns
2 successes	One minute (20 turns)
3 successes	15 minutes
4 successes	One hour
5 successes	One night

The victim of Veil of Blissful Ignorance does not necessarily know that he is under the effect of this power. He is only aware that everyone around him has suddenly begun acting as if he were not there. The victim cannot break this effect, even with violence; if he attacks someone, the target ascribes the act to the *visible* individual nearest to him. More than one fatal brawl has been incited by this side-effect. The Veil persists even if the vampire who activated it leaves the area.

Curiously enough, Veil of Blissful Ignorance can never be used on anyone who is ready and willing to accept its effects.

●●●●●●● OLD FRIEND

Many elder Nosferatu have made reputations for omniscience with the secrets they learn through creative uses of this power. A variation of Mask of a Thousand Faces, Old Friend allows a vampire to probe a subject's subconscious and take the semblance of the individual whom that victim trusts over anyone else. Someone using this power does not appear as someone who the victim is frightened of or awed by, but rather someone to whom the victim feels comfortable revealing intimate secrets. Old Friend doesn't necessarily make its user appear as someone who is still among the living; a long-dead friend or relative is just as likely to be the assigned visage, and in such cases the subject remembers the encounter as a dream or a ghostly visitation.

System: The player rolls Manipulation + Acting (difficulty equal to the victim's Perception + Alertness, maximum 10). The more successes, the more convincing the impersonation. Each success also adds one die to all rolls involving the use of the Secondary Talent: Interrogation against the victim. This power only affects one victim at a time; other observers see the vampire as she truly is, unless she also establishes a Mask of a Thousand Faces in addition to using Old Friend.

●●●●●●●● CREATE NAME

Some Toreador call this power the ultimate development of method acting. Create Name allows a character to create a completely new identity; face, speech pattern, aura, even thought processes are constructed according to the vampire's desired identity. The power can be used to impersonate an existing individual, or it can project the semblance of a completely fictional identity with perfect accuracy.

System: A vampire working with Create Name must spend three hours a night in relatively uninterrupted quiet to establish a new personality by means of this power. The player

FOR EXAMPLE

Damon the Malkavian decides that he wants to play doctor, and creates for himself the identity of Dr. Fein, the noted cardiologist. When discussing matters medical with a gang of Brujah who don't know a coronary thrombosis from a cheeseburger, Damon's act is flawless. However, when a Tremere vivisectionist sidles up to the doctor for a little shop talk, with each sentence of technobabble that pours from Damon's mouth it becomes that much more likely that the Tremere is going to figure out something's up. The Storyteller decides to roll Perception + Alertness on behalf of the Tremere once for every three minutes of conversation, and on the third try, the Warlock's suspicions crystallize. Suddenly, the discussion has the potential to get ugly very quickly.

makes an extended roll of Intelligence + Acting (difficulty 8), one roll per night. A total of 20 successes are necessary to construct a new identity, while a botch removes five successes from the vampire's total. Once a new identity has been successfully created, however, the character can step into it at any time without any sort of roll. Any outside observer without Auspex 9 or the equivalent sees the artificial identity. The character's face, aura, Nature, Demeanor, even thoughts and Psychological Merits and Flaws all appear to be those selected and crafted by the character.

The only way to pierce this disguise, other than Auspex 9, is to notice any discrepancies between the assumed identity and the Abilities it by all rights ought to possess. A character with no dots in Medicine should have a hard time pulling off a created identity as a neurosurgeon, for example. The Storyteller should make a secret roll of Perception + Alertness (difficulty 9) for each character who *should* catch a slip made by the impostor.

POTENCE

While flesh and blood have their limits, undead sinews and vitae have a bit more latitude when it comes to feats of strength. Vampires who are close to Caine in descent are sometimes capable of strength-based maneuvers that awe even other vampires. A product of blood and will as much as of muscle and bone, mastery of Potence gives a vampire the ability to do far more than just lift progressively heavier objects — if the vampire himself is willing to learn an alternate way.

Advanced Potence powers can be purchased in the same fashion as advanced Celerity or Fortitude powers. A character can choose to learn an alternate power instead of advancing along the Discipline's normal progression, and can later go back and re-purchase what he's missed.

•••••• IMPRINT

A vampire with extensive knowledge of Potence can squeeze very, very hard. As a matter of fact, she can squeeze (or press, or push) so hard that she can leave an imprint of her fingers or hand in any hard surface up to and including solid steel. A use of Imprint can simply serve as a threat, or it can be used, for example, to dig handholds into sheer surfaces for purposes of climbing.

System: Imprint requires a point of blood to activate. The power remains active for the duration of a scene. The depth of the imprint the vampire creates with Imprint is up to the Storyteller — decisions should take into account how much force the vampire can bring to bear, the toughness of the material and its thickness. If the object the vampire grasps is thin enough, at Storyteller option the vampire might simply be able to push through it (in the case of a wall) or tear it off (in the case of a spear or pipe).

•••••• EARTHSHOCK

According to some pundits, Potence is merely the art of hitting something very, *very* hard. But what do you do when your target is too far away to hit directly? The answer is, if you're

sufficiently talented with the Discipline, to employ Earthshock. On its simplest level, Earthshock is the ability to hit the ground at point A, and subsequently have the force of the blow emerge from the ground at point B, some distance away.

System: The use of Earthshock requires the expenditure of two blood points, as well as a normal Dexterity + Brawl roll. The vampire punches (or stamps on, depending on personal style) the ground, and, if the attack is a success, the force of the blow emerges from the ground as a geyser of rock, stone and whatnot directly underneath the target. The attack can be dodged at a +2 difficulty, as it's a great deal more difficult to time a move away from an underground pulse than it is to duck a punch.

The range on Earthshock is 10 feet for every level of Potence the vampire has, up to the limits of visibility. A failure on the attack roll means that the strike goes errant and is liable to explode anywhere within range; a botch means that the vampire pulverizes the ground beneath him and may well dig himself into a hole in the process.

•••••••• Flick

It is a truism that "the great ones always make it look easy." In the case of Flick, that saying stops being a truism and becomes literal truth. With this power, a master of Potence can make the slightest gesture — a wave, a snap of the fingers, the toss of a ball — and have it unleash the full, devastating impact of a dead-on strike. The attack can come without warning, limiting the target's ability to dodge or anticipate, and thus making Flick one of the most feared applications of Potence known.

System: Flick costs a point of blood, and mandates a Dexterity + Brawl roll (difficulty 6). It also requires that the vampire make some sort of gesture directing the blow. What the gesture is remains up to the player — anything from a snap of the fingers to a blown kiss has worked in the past.

Flick's range is equal to the limit of the Kindred's perception, and the blow struck does damage equal to a normal punch (including all bonuses).

Presence

•••••• Love

The blood bond is one of the most powerful tools in an elder's inventory. However, more and more childer are aware of how to avoid being bound, so alternatives are needed. The Presence power called Love is one such alternative, as it simulates the effects of the bond without any of the messy side effects. While neither as sure a method of control as a true blood bond, nor as long-lasting, Love is still an extremely potent means of command.

System: The player rolls Charisma + Acting (difficulty equal to the target's Willpower). Success on the roll indicates that the victim feels as attached to the character as if he were blood bound to her. Each success also reduces the victim's dice pool by one die for any Social rolls to be made against the character. A botch makes the target immune to all of the character's Presence powers for the rest of the night. This power lasts for one scene and can be applied to the same victim over multiple scenes in the same night.

•••••• PARALYZING GLANCE

Some elders have honed their mastery of Dread Gaze (Presence 2) to such a degree that they are said to be able to slay with but a look. Paralyzing Glance is not quite as effective as all that, but its impact isn't anything to sneeze at, either. The power's name is something of a misnomer, as victims of this power are not precisely paralyzed in a physical sense, but rather frozen with sheer terror.

System: The character must make eye contact with her intended victim. The player then rolls Manipulation + Intimidation (difficulty equal to the target's Willpower). Success renders the victim so terrified that he falls into a whimpering catatonic state, unable to take any actions except curling into a fetal position and gibbering incoherently. The condition lasts for a

length of time determined by the number of successes rolled. If the victim's life is directly threatened (by assault, impending sunrise, etc.), the poor wretch may attempt to break out of his paralysis with a Courage roll (difficulty of the character's Intimidation + 3). One success ends the paralysis. A botch sends the victim into a continuous state of Rötschreck for the rest of the night.

No. of Successes	Duration
1 success	Three turns
2 successes	Five minutes
3 successes	Remainder of the scene
4 successes	One hour
5 successes	Rest of the night
6+ successes	A week (or more, at Story-teller discretion)

•••••• SPARK OF RAGE

A vampire possessing this power can shorten tempers and bring old grudges and irritations to the boiling point with a minimum of effort. Spark of Rage causes disagreements and fights, and can even send other vampires into frenzy.

System: The player rolls Manipulation + Subterfuge (difficulty 8). The number of individuals affected is determined by how many successes are rolled. If this power is used in a crowd, those affected are the people in closest proximity to the character. A vampire affected by this power must spend a Willpower point or roll Self-Control (difficulty equal to the character's

Manipulation + Subterfuge); failure sends the target into a frenzy. A botch sends the character into immediate frenzy.

No. of Successes	No. of Targets Affected
1 success	Two people
2 successes	Four people
3 successes	Eight people
4 successes	20 people
5 successes	Everyone in the character's immediate vicinity

•••••• Cooperation

Any elder knows that Kindred are the most difficult beings in existence to force to work together. Peaceful coexistence is not a common tenet of vampiric society. With that in mind, this power can be used to nudge those affected by it into a fragile spirit of camaraderie. Some cynical (or realistic) Ventrue claim that their clan's mastery of this Presence effect is the sole reason that anything is ever accomplished in Camarilla conclaves. Ventrue who voice this opinion *too* loudly also tend to have numerous chances to test just how effective Cooperation is.

System: To invoke Cooperation, the player rolls Charisma + Leadership (difficulty 8). The number of individuals affected is determined by how many successes the player rolls. Cooperation lasts for the remainder of the scene in which it is invoked, though particularly strong users of Presence may create longer-lasting feelings of non-aggression (at Storyteller discretion) by spending Willpower. While this power is in affect, all those under its influence are more favorably disposed toward one another and are more willing to extend trust or make cooperative plans.

For the most part, players should simply roleplay Cooperation's effects, but there are some concrete ramifications to the power's use. Self-Control difficulties to resist frenzy in response to insults from within the target group are decreased by three. The game effects of appropriate Intolerance Flaws are removed, and Hatred Flaws are treated as if they were Intolerances.

No. of Successes	No. of Targets Affected
1 success	Two people
2 successes	Four people
3 successes	Eight people
4 successes	20 people
5 successes	Everyone in the character's immediate vicinity

••••••• Ironclad Command

Any individual can normally resist the powers of Presence for a brief time through an effort of will. Some elder Toreador and Ventrue have developed such force of personality that their powers of Presence cannot be resisted without truly heroic efforts.

System: This power is always in effect once it has been learned. A mortal may not spend Willpower to resist the character's Presence (For purposes of this power, the definition of "mortal" does not include supernaturally active humans such as ghouls, hedge magicians or those who possess True Faith). A

supernatural being must roll Willpower (difficulty of the character's Willpower + 2; difficulties over 10 mean that the roll cannot even be attempted) the first time he attempts to spend a Willpower point to overcome the character's Presence. He may then spend a maximum number of Willpower points for the rest of the scene equal to the number of successes he rolled. A botch doubles the character's Presence dice pools against the hapless victim for the remainder of the night.

•••••••• Pulse of the City

A Methuselah who has developed her Presence to this terrifying degree can control the emotional climate of the entire region around her, up to the size of a large city. This power is always in effect on a low level, attuning those who dwell in the area to the Methuselah's mood, but it can also be used to project a specific emotion into the minds of every being in the area. Pulse of the City affects residents much more strongly than tourists, and also has a significant impact on those individuals who might be elsewhere at the time but who still have strong ties to the affected city.

System: The player spends a Willpower point and rolls Charisma + Area Knowledge (difficulty 10, and the Area Knowledge used must apply to the city or region in which the power is being used). The number of successes indicates how long mortal residents are affected by the particular emotion that the character broadcasts; visitors with no ties to the area and supernatural beings are affected for a duration one success step lower. The character can choose to terminate this effect at any time before it expires.

No. of Successes	Duration
1 success	One minute
2 successes	10 minutes
3 successes	One hour
4 successes	One day
5 successes	One week

Pulse of the City can be used by a character in torpor.

Protean

••••• Earth Control

An Earth Melded character with this power is no longer confined to the resting place she selected the night before. She can pass through the ground as if it were water, "swimming" through the earth itself. Some elders use this as a means of unobstructed and unobtrusive travel, while others find it a highly effective means of maneuvering in combat.

System: This power is in effect whenever a character is Earth Melded, with no additional roll or expenditure necessary. While in the ground, a vampire can propel herself at half of her normal walking speed. She cannot see, but gains a supernatural awareness of her underground surroundings out to a range of 50 yards. Water, rock, tree roots and cement all effectively block her progress; she can only move through earth and substances of similar consistency, such as sand or fine gravel. If two or more vampires attempt to interact underground, only direct physical contact is possible. All damage dice pools in this case are halved, and dodge and parry attempts are at -2 difficulty. If an underground chase takes place, it is resolved with an extended contested Strength + Athletics roll (see p. 194 of **Vampire: The Masquerade**).

•••••• FLESH OF MARBLE

Tales have long spoken of the combat prowess of Gangrel elders and of their inhuman resilience. Poorly informed individuals believe the stories of swords shattering and bullets flattening against immortal skin to be exaggerated reports of the effects of Fortitude. Those with more reliable information know that such tales result from encounters with Gangrel who have developed Flesh of Marble. The skin of an elder with Flesh of Marble becomes in essence a sort of flexible stone, although it appears no different than normal skin and muscle. Indeed, flesh transformed thus even feels normal to a casual touch.

System: The player spends three blood points to activate Flesh of Marble, which goes into effect instantly. The effects of the power then last for the remainder of the scene. While the power is functioning, the damage dice pools of all physical attacks made against the character are halved (round down). That includes assaults made with fists, claws, swords, firearms and explosions, but not fire, sunlight or magic (unless the magical effect in question is a direct physical attack, such as a rock hurled by means of Movement of the Mind). Additionally, while this power is in effect, a character can attempt to parry melee attacks with his bare hands as if he were holding some form of weapon.

••••••• RESTORE THE MORTAL VISAGE

The Gangrel are of two opinions regarding this power. Those who are politically active, or who associate extensively with mortals, view it as both necessary and acceptable. Those Kindred who embrace their more feral sides, however, see it as a disgusting defiance of the very nature of vampirism. The schism comes because the power allows the elder who possesses it to temporarily return his appearance to what it was before the Embrace, removing the bestial features he has accumulated over the centuries. Restore the Mortal Visage has only been displayed by Gangrel; several Nosferatu elders have attempted to develop it, and it is whispered that they met spontaneous, grotesque Final Deaths when they attempted to take their mortal forms.

System: The player spends three blood points and a Willpower point and rolls Willpower (difficulty 8). Success restores the character's appearance to what it was just before he was first Embraced, erasing all animalistic features gained from frenzies. The power also affects the character's Social Attributes, returning them to their original values (assuming those were higher than the character's current ratings). A botched Willpower roll earns the character another animal feature. Restore the Mortal Visage lasts for the remainder of the scene once activated.

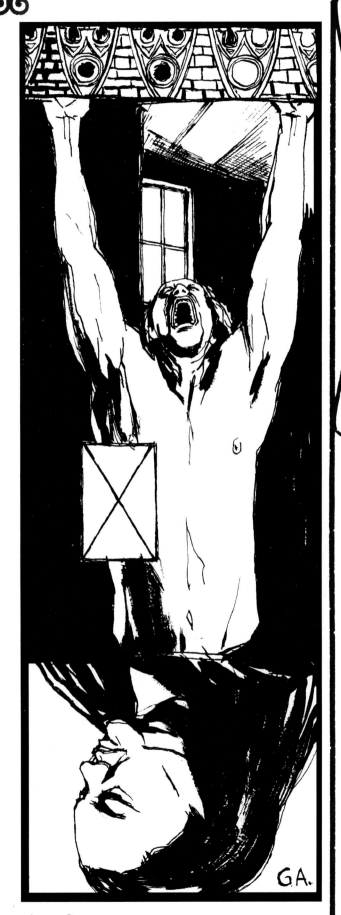

•••••• SHAPE OF THE BEAST'S WRATH

Users of this power are often mistaken for Tzimisce employing the Vicissitude power Horrid Form. The base effect is similar, although no Gangrel who possesses this power takes such a suggestion lightly. A vampire employing this power shifts into a huge, monstrous form, gaining half her height again and tripling her weight. Her overall shape flows into an unholy amalgamation of her own form and that of the animal she feels the closest kinship to (wolves, rats and great cats are the most common manifestations, though ravens, serpents, bats and stranger beasts have been reported). The vampire's new shape does bear some vague resemblance to the war-forms of the werecreatures, but the difference quickly becomes apparent.

System: The player spends three blood points, the expenditure of which triggers the change. The character's transformation takes three turns (the player may spend additional blood points to reduce this time at a cost of one point per turn of reduction). Once transformed, the character remains in this form until sunrise or until she shifts back voluntarily.

The precise Traits of this form are determined when the character first learns this power, as is the animal whose appearance the character takes on. The vampire's new form adds a total of seven dots added to the character's Physical Attributes. At least one dot must go into each Physical Attribute, meaning that no more than five can go into any one (so a character could have +5 Strength, +1 Dexterity, and +1 Stamina, but not +2 Strength and +5 Dexterity). These bonuses are always the same once they are selected; a different allocation requires that the character buy this power a second time and thus purchase another alternate form. Additionally, the character inflicts Strength + two dice of aggravated damage with both bite and claw attacks when in monstrous form. She also gains an extra Hurt health level, and doubles her normal running speed. Finally, the character's perceptions are also heightened. She is assumed to have both the Auspex power Heightened Senses and the Protean power Eyes of the Beast after transformation, with all of the benefits and drawbacks of each.

This form does carry two drawbacks. The first is a lack of communication ability. The character's Social Attributes all drop to 1, or to 0 if they already were 1 (except when making Intimidation rolls) when the transformation occurs. The second problem that a character in this form encounters is the suddenly heightened power of her Beast. All difficulties of rolls to resist frenzy are increased by two for the duration of the power's effect, and the player may not spend Willpower points on such rolls.

•••••• SPECTRAL BODY

This powerful variation on Mist Form (Protean 5) allows a Gangrel to take a shape with most of the advantages of the lesser power but fewer of the disadvantages. A vampire who assumes Spectral Form retains his normal appearance, but becomes completely insubstantial. He walks through walls and bullets with equal ease, and can pass through the floor on which he stands if he chooses to. Although his lungs are no longer solid, the vampire can

still speak, a fact in which some elders of the Daughters of Cacophony bloodline have expressed great interest.

System: The player spends three blood points. The transformation takes one turn to complete, and lasts for the rest of the night unless the character decides to reverse it. When the power takes hold, the character becomes completely insubstantial, but remains fully visible. Henceforth, he is unaffected by any physical attacks, and he doubles his dice pool to soak damage from fire and sunlight. The vampire may even ignore gravity if he chooses to do so, rising and sinking through solid objects if he does not wish to stand on them (although he may move no faster than his normal walking speed while "flying" in this manner). While in this form, the character may also use any Disciplines that do not require physical contact or a physical body. On the down side, while in Spectral Form a vampire can physically manipulate his environment only through the use of Movement of the Mind.

••••••• PURIFY THE IMPALED BREAST

Camarilla records indicate that a disproportionately small number of Gangrel elders were killed by mortals and anarchs during the Inquisition and the Anarch Revolt. This power is one of the primary reasons for the survival of these Kindred. Until recently, the clan practiced a less powerful version of Purify the Impaled Breast, one which only allowed very limited movement. In recent nights, knowledge of a long-lost, stronger version of the power has been disseminated through the clan. An elder Gangrel with this Protean power can expel foreign objects from her body with great force, even excising stakes that transfix her heart.

System: The player spends three blood points and rolls Willpower (difficulty 6, or 8 if the vampire is paralyzed by an object impaling her heart). One success is sufficient to remove all foreign objects and substances from the character's body. Dirt, bullets, even stakes through the heart are instantly and violently removed. The larger the object, the farther away it is hurled by this power. Objects expelled thus are considered to have an attack dice pool of three for any bystanders, and to have a dice pool of one to four (depending on size) for damage.

If the character wishes to leave an object in his body (such as a prosthetic limb) or partially in (expelling a stake from his heart but leaving it sticking out of his breastbone as a ruse), the player must spend a Willpower point when this power is activated.

••••••• INWARD FOCUS

This power has no outwardly visible effects whatsoever. Indeed, its very existence is unknown outside those dozen or so Gangrel Methuselahs who have developed it. The internal effects of this razor-sharp honing of Protean, however, are in some ways more dramatic than any external manifestation. A vampire with this power can heighten the efficiency of his undead body's internal workings to levels undreamed of by lesser Kindred, withstanding inconceivable amounts of injury and moving with blinding speed and shattering strength.

System: The player spends four blood points to activate this power and an additional two blood points for every turn past the first that Inward Focus is maintained. There are three effects of this power. First, the character gains a number of extra actions during each turn equal to his unmodified (by alternate forms or blood point expenditure) Dexterity score. Second, the damage of his physical attacks is increased by three dice per dice pool. Finally, all damage inflicted on the character is halved and rounded down after the soak roll is made (so an attack that inflicts five health levels after soak is reduced to two health levels).

This power may be used in conjunction with other Protean powers that modify the character's combat abilities, such as Shape of the Beast's Wrath (above). It may also be used in conjunction with Celerity, Fortitude and Potence, turning a Gangrel who has mastered this power into a truly terrifying opponent.

THAUMATURGY

The following thaumaturgical paths are practiced primarily by Camarilla Tremere thaumaturges. They may be available to other thaumaturgical practitioners, such as Tremere *antitribu* or Assamites, at the Storyteller's discretion, but are highly uncommon and may be imperfectly taught (+1 difficulty to all uses of the path). All of the following paths use the basic system described in **Vampire: The Masquerade**: the player spends a blood point and rolls Willpower (difficulty of the power's level + 3). A failure indicates that the blood magic does not work. A botch indicates that the character loses a permanent Willpower point.

ELEMENTAL MASTERY

This path allows a thaumaturge limited control over and communion with inanimate objects. Mistakenly believed by many to be related to the four basic elements (earth, air, fire and water), this path is actually closer to an amalgamation of Spirit Thaumaturgy and the Path of Conjuring. Elemental Mastery can only be used to affect the unliving — a vampire could not cause a tree to walk by using Animate the Unmoving, for instance. Thaumaturges who seek mastery over living things generally study Biothaumaturgical Experimentation (see **Dirty Secrets of the Black Hand**) or the Green Path (below).

• ELEMENTAL STRENGTH

The vampire can draw upon the strength and resilience of the earth, or of the objects around him, to increase his physical prowess without the need for large amounts of blood.

System: The player allocates a total of three temporary bonus dots between the character's Strength and Stamina. The number of successes on the roll to activate the power are the number of turns these dots remain. The player may spend a Willpower point to increase this duration by one turn. This power cannot be "stacked" — one application must expire before the next can be made.

•• WOODEN TONGUES

A vampire may speak, albeit in limited fashion, with the spirit of any inanimate object. The conversation may not be incredibly interesting, as most rocks and chairs have limited concern for what occurs around them, but the vampire can get at least a general impression of what the subject has "experienced." Note that events which are significant to a vampire may not be the same events that interest a lawn jockey.

System: The number of successes dictates the amount and relevance of the information that the character receives. One success may yield a boulder's memory of a forest fire, while three may indicate that it remembers a shadowy figure running past, and five will cause the rock to relate a precise description of a local Gangrel.

••• ANIMATE THE UNMOVING

Objects affected by this power move as the vampire using it dictates. An object cannot take an action that would be completely inconceivable for something with its form — for instance, a door could not leap from its hinges and carry someone across a street. However, seemingly solid objects can become flexible within reason: Barstools can run with their legs, guns can twist out of their owners' hands or fire while holstered, and statues can move like normal humans.

System: This power requires the expenditure of a Willpower point with less than four successes on the roll. Each use of this power animates one object; the thaumaturge may simultaneously control a number of animate objects equal to his Intelligence rating. Objects animated by this power stay animated as long as they are within the caster's line of sight or up to an hour.

•••• ELEMENTAL FORM

The vampire can take the shape of any inanimate object of a mass roughly equal to her own. A desk, a statue or a bicycle would be feasible, but a house or a pen would be beyond this power's capacity.

System: The number of successes determines how completely the character takes the shape she wishes to counterfeit. At least three successes are required for the character to use her senses or Disciplines while in her altered form. This power lasts for the remainder of the night, although the character may return to her normal form at will.

••••• SUMMON ELEMENTAL

A vampire may summon one of the traditional spirits of the elements: a salamander (fire), a sylph (air), a gnome (earth) or an undine (water). Some Tremere claim to have contacted elemental spirits of glass, electricity, blood and even atomic energy, but such reports remain unconfirmed (even as their authors are summoned to Vienna for questioning). The thaumaturge may choose what type of elemental he wishes to summon and command.

System: The character must be near some quantity of the classical element corresponding to the spirit he wishes to invoke. The spirit invoked may or may not actually follow the caster's instructions once summoned, but generally will at least pay rough attention to what it's being told to do. The number of successes gained determines the power level of the elemental.

The elemental has three dots in all Physical and Mental Attributes. One dot may be added to one of the elemental's Physical Attributes for each success gained by the caster on the initial roll. The Storyteller should determine the elemental's Abilities, attacks and damage, and any special powers it has related to its element.

Once the elemental has been summoned, the thaumaturge must exert control over it. The more powerful the elemental, the more difficult a task this is. The player rolls Manipulation + Occult (difficulty of the number of successes scored on the casting roll + 4, and the player may substitute Spirit Lore for Occult if he so desires).

No. of Successes	Result
Botch	The elemental immediately attacks the thaumaturge.
Failure	The elemental goes free and may attack anyone or leave the scene at the Storyteller's discretion.
1 success	The elemental probably does not attack its summoner.
2 successes	The elemental behaves favorably toward the summoner and may perform a service in exchange for payment (determined by the Storyteller).
3 successes	The elemental performs one service, within reason.
4 successes	The elemental performs any one task for the caster that does not jeopardize its own existence.
5 successes	The elemental performs any task that the caster sets for it, even one that may take several nights to complete or that places its existence at risk.

THE GREEN PATH

The Green Path deals with the manipulation of plant matter of all sorts. Anything more complex than an algae bloom can theoretically be controlled through the appropriate application of this path. Ferns, roses, dandelions and even ancient redwoods are all equally valid targets for this path's powers, and living and dead plant matter are equally affected. While not as immediately impressive as some other more widely practiced paths, the Green Path (sometimes disparagingly referred to as "Botanical Mastery") is as subtle and powerful as the natural world which it affects.

The origins of the Green Path are thought to lie with the Order of the Naturists (see **Clanbook: Tremere**), a druidic sect within Clan Tremere. Most practitioners of the path are members of the order, and those who are not were more than likely mentored by one. According to those who are familiar with Tremere history, the Green Path is a blood magic-based derivation of some magickal workings formerly practiced by

House Diedne, an order of mortal mages destroyed by the Tremere during the Dark Ages.

• HERBAL WISDOM

With but a touch, a vampire can commune with the spirit of a plant. Conversations held in this manner are often cryptic but rewarding — the wisdom and experience of the spirits of some trees surpasses that of the oracles of legend. Crabgrass, on the other hand, rarely has much insight to offer, but might reveal the face of the last person who trod upon it.

System: The number of successes rolled determines the amount of information that can be gained from the contact. Depending on the precise information that the vampire seeks, the Storyteller might require the player to roll Intelligence + Occult or Intelligence + Intuition in order to interpret the results of the communication.

No. of Successes	Result
1 success	Fleeting cryptic impressions
2 successes	One or two clear images
3 successes	A concise answer to a simple query
4 successes	A detailed response to one or more complex questions
5 successes	The sum total of the plant-spirit's knowledge on a given subject

•• SPEED THE SEASON'S PASSING

This power allows a thaumaturge to accelerate a plant's growth, causing roses to bloom in a matter of minutes or trees to shoot up from saplings overnight. Alternately, she can speed a plant's death and decay, withering grass and crumbling wooden stakes with but a touch.

System: The character touches the target plant. The player rolls normally, and the number of successes determines the amount of growth or decay. One success gives the plant a brief growth spurt or simulates the effects of harsh weather, while three noticeably enlarge or wither it. With five successes, a full-grown plant springs from a seed or crumbles to dust in a few minutes, and a tree sprouts fruit or begins decaying almost instantaneously. If this power is used in combat, three successes are needed to render a wooden weapon completely useless. Two successes suffice to weaken it, while five cause it to disintegrate in the wielder's hand.

••• DANCE OF VINES

The thaumaturge can animate a mass of vegetation up to his own size, using it for utilitarian or combat purposes with equal ease. Leaves can walk along a desktop, ivy can act as a scribe, and jungle creepers can strangle opponents. Intruders should beware of Tremere workshops that harbor potted rowan saplings.

System: Any total amount of vegetation with a mass less than or equal to the character's own may be animated through this power. The plants stay active for one turn per success scored on the roll, and are under the complete control of the character. If used for combat purposes, the plants have Strength and Dexterity ratings equal to half the character's current Willpower (rounded down) and Brawl ratings one lower than that of the character.

Dance of Vines cannot make plants uproot themselves and go stomping about. Even the most energetic vegetation is incapable of pulling out of the soil and walking under the effect of this power. However, 150 pounds of kudzu can cover a considerable area all by itself….

•••• Verdant Haven

This power weaves a temporary shelter out of a sufficient amount of plant matter. In addition to providing physical protection from the elements (and even sunlight), the Verdant Haven also establishes a mystical barrier which is nigh-impassable to anyone the caster wishes to exclude. A Verdant Haven appears as a six-foot-tall hemisphere of interlocked branches, leaves and vines with no discernible opening, and even to the casual observer it appears to be an unnatural construction. Verdant Havens are rumored to have supernatural healing properties, but no Kindred have reported experiencing such benefits from a stay in one.

System: A character must be standing in a heavily vegetated area to use this power. The Verdant Haven springs up around the character over the course of three turns. Once the haven is established, anyone wishing to enter the haven without the caster's permission must achieve more than the caster's original number of successes on a single roll of Wits + Survival (difficulty equal to the caster's Willpower). The haven lasts until the next sunset, or until the caster dispels or leaves it. If the caster scored four or more successes, the haven is impenetrable to sunlight unless physically breached.

••••• Awaken the Forest Giants

Entire trees can be animated by a master of the Green Path. Ancient oaks can be temporarily given the gift of movement, pulling their roots from the soil and shaking the ground with their steps. While not as versatile as elementals or other summoned spirits, trees brought to ponderous life via this power display awesome strength and resilience.

System: The character touches the tree to be animated. The player spends a blood point and rolls normally. If the roll succeeds, the player must spend a blood point for every success. The tree stays animated for one turn per success rolled; once this time expires, the tree puts its roots down wherever it stands and cannot be animated again until the next night. While animated, the tree follows the character's verbal commands to the best of its ability. An animated tree has Strength and Stamina equal to the caster's Thaumaturgy rating, Dexterity 2 and a Brawl rating equal to the caster's own. It is immune to bashing damage, and all non-aggravated lethal damage dice pools are halved due to its size.

Once the animating energy leaves a tree, it puts down roots immediately, regardless of what it is currently standing on. A tree re-establishing itself in the soil can punch through concrete and asphalt to find nourishing dirt and water underneath, meaning that it is entirely possible for a particularly sluggish sycamore to set up shop in the middle of a road without any

warning. Abuses or misuses of this power can very easily lead to breaches of the Masquerade, and the thaumaturge who leaves a row of maples across a major traffic artery is unlikely to have the opportunity to make the same mistake twice.

Neptune's Might

Vampires are rarely associated with the ocean in most mythologies, and most Kindred have nothing to do with water in large quantities simply because they have no reason to do so. Nevertheless, Neptune's Might has enjoyed a small, but devoted, following for centuries among Camarilla thaumaturges. This path is based primarily around the manipulation of standing water, although some of its more disturbing effects depart from this principle.

Once a character reaches the third level of Neptune's Might, the player may choose to specialize in either fresh water or salt water. Such specialization lowers all Neptune's Might difficulties by one when dealing with the chosen medium but raises them by one when dealing with the opposite. Blood is considered neither fresh nor salty for this purpose, and difficulties in manipulating it are unaffected.

• Eyes of the Sea

The thaumaturge may peer into a body of water and view events that have transpired on, in or around it from the water's perspective. Some older practitioners of this art claim that the vampire communes with the spirits of the waters when using this power; younger Kindred scoff at such claims.

System: The number of successes rolled determines how far into the past the character can look.

No. of Successes	Range of Effect
1 success	One day
2 successes	One week
3 successes	One month
4 successes	One year
5 successes	10 years

The Storyteller may require a Perception + Occult roll for the character to discern very small details in the transmitted images. This power can only be used on standing water; lakes and puddles qualify, but oceans, rivers, sewers and wineglasses do not.

•• Prison of Water

The thaumaturge can command a sufficiently large quantity of water to animate itself and imprison a subject. This power requires a significant amount of fluid to be fully effective, although even a few gallons can be used to shape chains of animated water. Mortals subjected to this power's effects can drown if the thaumaturge is not careful (or if she so desires it), and even vampires can be crushed by extreme pressure thus brought to bear.

System: The number of successes scored on the roll is the number of successes the victim must score on a Strength roll (difficulty 8; Potence adds to successes) to break free. A subject may be held in only one prison at a time, although the thaumaturge is free to invoke multiple uses of this power upon separate victims and may dissolve her own prisons at will.

If a sufficient quantity of water (at least a bathtub's worth) is not present, the difficulty of the Willpower roll to activate this power is raised by one.

••• BLOOD TO WATER

The thaumaturge has now attained enough power over water that she can transmute other liquids to this basic element. The most commonly seen use of this power is as an assault; with but a touch, the victim's blood transforms to water, weakening vampires and killing mortals in moments.

System: The character must touch her intended victim. The player rolls normally. Each success converts one of the victim's blood points to water. One success kills a mortal within minutes. Vampires who lose blood points to this power also suffer dice pool penalties as if they had received an equivalent number of health levels of injury. The water left in the target's system by this attack evaporates out at a rate of one blood point's worth per hour, but the lost blood does not return.

At the Storyteller's discretion, other liquids may be turned to water with this power (the difficulty for such an action is reduced by one unless the substance is particularly dangerous or magical in nature). The character must still touch the substance or its container to use this power.

•••• FLOWING WALL

Tales of vampires' inability to cross running water may have derived from garbled accounts of this power in action. The thaumaturge can animate water to an even greater degree than is possible with the use of Prison of Water, commanding it to rise up to form a barrier impassable to almost any being.

System: The character touches the surface of a standing body of water; the player spends three Willpower points and the normal required blood point and rolls normally. Successes are applied to both width and height of the wall; each success "buys" 10 feet in one dimension. The wall may be placed anywhere within the character's line of sight, and must be formed in a straight line. The wall lasts until the next sunrise. It cannot be climbed, though it can be flown over. To pass through the barrier, any supernatural being (including beings trying to pass the wall on other levels of existence) must score at least three successes on a single Willpower roll (difficulty 9).

••••• DEHYDRATE

At this level of mastery, the thaumaturge can directly attack living and unliving targets by removing the water from their bodies. Victims killed by this power leave behind hideous mummified corpses. This power can also be used for less aggressive purposes, such as drying out wet clothes—or evaporating puddles to keep other practitioners of this path from using them.

System: This power can be used on any target in the character's line of sight. The player rolls normally; the victim resists with a roll of Stamina + Fortitude (difficulty 9). Each success gained by the thaumaturge translates into one health level of lethal damage inflicted on the victim. This injury cannot be soaked (the resistance roll replaces soak for this attack) but can be healed normally. Vampires lose blood points instead of health levels, though if a vampire has no blood points this attack inflicts health level loss as it would against a mortal. The victim of this attack must also roll Courage (difficulty of the number of successes scored by the thaumaturge + 3) to be able to act on the turn following the attack; failure means he is overcome with agony and can do nothing.

THE PATH OF CORRUPTION

The origins of this path are hotly debated among those who are familiar with its intricacies. One theory holds that its secrets were taught to the Tremere by demons and that use of it brings the practitioner dangerously close to the infernal powers. A second opinion has been advanced that the Path of Corruption is a holdover from the days when Clan Tremere was still mortal. The third primary theory, and the most disturbing to the Tremere, is that the path originated with the Followers of Set, and that knowledge of its workings was sold to the Tremere for an unspecified price. This last rumor is, of course, vehemently denied by the Tremere, which automatically makes it the favorite topic of discussion when the matter comes up.

The Path of Corruption is primarily a mentally and spiritually oriented path centered on influencing the psyches of other individuals. It can be used neither to issue commands like Dominate nor to change emotions of the moment like Presence. Rather, it produces a gradual and subtle twisting of the subject's actions, morals and thought processes. This path deals intimately with deception and dark desires, and those who work through it must understand the hidden places of the heart. Accordingly, no character may have a higher rating in the Path of Corruption than he has in Subterfuge.

• CONTRADICT

The thaumaturge can interrupt a subject's thought processes, forcing the victim to reverse his current course of action. An archon may be caused to execute a prisoner she was about to exonerate and release; a mortal lover might switch from gentle and caring to sadistic and demanding in the middle of an encounter. The results of Contradict are never precisely known to the thaumaturge in advance, but they always take the form of a more negative action than the subject had originally intended to perform.

System: This power may be used on any subject within the character's line of sight. The player rolls as per normal. The target rolls Perception + Subterfuge (difficulty of the number of successes scored by the thaumaturge + 2). Two successes allow the subject to realize that she is being influenced by some outside source. Three successes let her pinpoint the source of the effect. Four successes give her a moment of hesitation, neither performing her original action nor its inverse, while five allow her to carry through with the original action.

The Storyteller dictates what the subject's precise reaction to this power is. Contradict cannot be used in combat or to affect other actions (Storyteller's discretion) that are mainly physical and reflexive.

•• SUBVERT

This power follows the same principle as does Contradict, the release of a subject's dark, self-destructive side. However, Subvert's effects are longer-lasting than the momentary flare of Contradiction. Under the influence of this power, victims act on their own suppressed temptations, pursuing agendas that their morals or self-control would forbid them to follow under normal circumstances.

System: This power requires the character to make eye contact with the intended victim. The player rolls normally. The target resists with a roll of Perception + Subterfuge (difficulty of the target's Manipulation + Subterfuge). If the thaumaturge scores more successes, the victim becomes inclined to follow a repressed, shameful desire for the length of time described below.

No. of Successes	Duration of Effect
1 success	Five minutes
2 successes	One hour
3 successes	One night
4 successes	Three nights
5 successes	One week

The Storyteller determines the precise desire or agenda that the victim follows. It should be in keeping with the Psychological Flaws that she possesses or with the negative aspects of her Nature (for example, a Loner desiring isolation to such an extent that she becomes violent if forced to attend a social function). The subject should not become fixated on following this new agenda at all times, but should occasionally be forced to spend a Willpower point if the opportunity to succumb arises and she wishes to resist the impulse.

••• DISSOCIATE

"Divide and conquer" is a maxim that is well-understood by the Tremere, and Dissociate is a powerful tool with which to divide the clan's enemies. This power is used to break the social ties of interpersonal relationships. Even the most passionate affair or the oldest friendship can be cooled through use of Dissociate, and weaker personal ties can be destroyed altogether.

System: The character must touch the target. The player rolls normally. The target resists with a Willpower roll (difficulty of the thaumaturge's Manipulation + Empathy). The victim loses three dice from all Social rolls for a period of time determined by the number of successes gained by the thaumaturge.

No. of Successes	Duration of Effect
1 success	Five minutes
2 successes	One hour
3 successes	One night
4 successes	Three nights
5 successes	One week

This penalty applies to *all* rolls that rely on Social Attributes, even those required for the use of Disciplines. If this power is used on a character who has participated in the Sabbat Vaulderie or a similar ritual, that character's Vinculum ratings are reduced by three for the duration of Dissociate's effect.

Dissociate's primary effect falls under roleplaying rather than game mechanics. Victims of this power should be played as withdrawn, suspicious and emotionally distant. The Storyteller should feel free to require a Willpower point expenditure for a player who does not follow these guidelines.

•••• Addiction

This power is a much stronger and more potentially damaging form of Subvert. Addiction creates just that in the victim. By simply exposing the target to a particular sensation, substance or action, the thaumaturge creates a powerful psychological dependence. Many Tremere ensure that their victims become addicted to substances or thrills that only the Warlocks can provide, thus creating both a source of income and potential blackmail material.

System: The subject must encounter or be exposed to the sensation, substance or action to which the character wants to addict him. The thaumaturge then touches his target. The player rolls normally; the victim resists with a Self-Control roll (difficulty equal to the number of successes scored by the thaumaturge + 3). Failure gives the subject an instant addiction to the object desired by the character.

An addicted character must get his fix at least once a night. Every night that he goes without satisfying his desire imposes a cumulative penalty of one die on all of his dice pools (reduced to a minimum of one die). The victim must roll Self-Control (difficulty 8) every time he is confronted with the object of his addiction and wishes to keep from indulging. Addiction lasts for a number of weeks equal to the thaumaturge's Manipulation score.

An individual may try to break the effects of Addiction. This requires an extended Self-Control roll (difficulty of the thaumaturge's Manipulation + Subterfuge), with one roll made per night. The addict must accumulate a number of successes equal to three times the number of successes scored by the thaumaturge. The victim may not indulge in his addiction over the time needed to accumulate these successes. If he does so, all accumulated successes are lost and he must begin anew on the next night. Note that the Self-Control dice pool is reduced every night that the victim goes without feeding his addiction.

••••• Dependence

Many former pawns of Clan Tremere claim to have felt a strange sensation similar to depression when not in the presence of their masters. This is usually attributed to the blood bond, but is often the result of the thaumaturge's mastery of Dependence. The final power of the Path of Corruption enables the vampire to tie her victim's soul to her own, engendering feelings of lethargy and helplessness when the victim is not in her presence or acting to further her desires.

System: The character engages the target in conversation. The player rolls normally. The victim rolls Self-Control (difficulty of the number of successes scored by the thaumaturge + 3). Failure means that the victim's psyche has been subtly bonded to that of the thaumaturge for one night per success rolled by the thaumaturge.

A bonded victim is no less likely to attack his controller, and feels no particular positive emotions toward her. However, he is psychologically addicted to her presence, and suffers a one-die penalty to all rolls when he is not around her or performing tasks for her. Additionally, he is much less resistant to her commands, and his dice pools are halved when he attempts to resist her Dominate, Presence or Social rolls. Finally, he is unable to regain Willpower when he is not in the thaumaturge's presence.

The Path of Technomancy

The newest path to be accepted by the Tremere hierarchy as part of the clan's official body of knowledge, the Path of Technomancy is a relatively recent innovation. It was developed in the latter half of the 20th century, and has not yet spread far beyond the North American Pontifices. The path focuses on the control of electronic devices, from wristwatches to computers, and its proponents maintain that it is a prime example of the versatility of Thaumaturgy with regards to a changing world. More conservative Tremere, however, state that mixing Tremere magic with mortal science borders on treason or even blasphemy, and some European Regents have gone so far as to declare knowledge of Technomancy grounds for expulsion from their chantries. The Inner Council did approve the introduction of the path into the clan's grimoires, but has yet to voice any opinion on the conservative opposition to Technomancy.

• Analyze

Mortals are constantly developing new innovations, and any vampire who would work Technomancy must be able to understand that upon which he practices his magic. The most basic power of this path allows the Tremere to project his perceptions into a device, granting him a temporary understanding of its purpose, the principles of its functioning and its means of operation. This does not grant permanent knowledge, only a momentary flash of insight which fades within minutes.

System: A character must touch the device in order to apply this power. The number of successes rolled determines how well the character understands this particular piece of equipment. One success allows a basic knowledge (on/off and simple functions), while three successes grant competence in operating the device, and five successes show the character the full range of the device's potential. The knowledge lasts for a number of minutes equal to the character's Intelligence.

This power can also be used to understand a non-physical technological innovation — in other words, a new piece of computer software — at +2 difficulty. The character must touch the computer on which the software is installed — simply holding the CD-ROM is not enough.

•• Burnout

It is usually easier to destroy than to create, and sensitive electronics are no exception to this rule. Burnout is used to cause a device's power supply, either internal or external, to surge, damaging or destroying the target. Burnout cannot be used to directly injure another individual, although the sudden destruction of a pacemaker or a car's fuel injection control chip can create a definite health hazard.

System: A character can use this power at a range of up to 10 times her Willpower in yards, although a +1 difficulty is applied if she is not touching the target item. The number of successes determines the extent of the damage.

No. of Successes	Result
1 success	Momentary interruption of operation (one turn), but no permanent damage.
2 successes	Significant loss of function; +1 difficulty to use using the device for the rest of the scene.
3 successes	The device breaks and is inoperable until repaired.
4 successes	Even after repairs, the device's capabilities are diminished (permanent +1 difficulty to use).
5 successes	The equipment is a total write-off; completely unsalvageable.

Large enough systems, such as mainframe computers or passenger aircraft, impose a +2 to +4 difficulty (at Storyteller discretion) to affect with this power. Additionally, some systems, such as military and banking computers, may be hardened against power surges and spikes, and thus possess one to five dice (Storyteller discretion again) to roll to resist this power. Each success on this roll (difficulty 6) takes away one success from the Thaumaturgy roll.

Burnout may be used to destroy electronic data storage, in which case three successes destroy all information on the target item and five erase it beyond any hope of non-magical recovery.

••• Encrypt/Decrypt

Electronic security is a paramount concern of governments and corporations alike. Those Tremere who are techno-savvy enough to understand the issues at stake have become quite enamored of this power, which allows the thaumaturge to scramble a device's controls mystically, making it inaccessible to anyone but him. Encrypt/Decrypt also works on electronic media; a videotape under the influence of this power displays just snow and static if played back without the owner's approval.

System: The character touches the device or data container which he wishes to encrypt. The player rolls normally. The number of successes scored is applied as a difficulty modifier for anyone who attempts to use the protected equipment or access the scrambled information without the assistance of the character. The thaumaturge can dispel the effect at any time by touching the target item; this countermanding costs a point of Willpower.

This power may also be used to counter another thaumaturge's use of Encrypt/Decrypt. The player rolls at +1 difficulty; each success negates one of the "owner's."

The effects of Encrypt/Decrypt last for a number of weeks equal to the character's permanent Willpower rating.

•••• Remote Access

With this power, a skilled thaumaturge can bypass the need for physical contact to operate a device. This is not a form of telekinesis; the vampire does not manipulate the item's controls, but rather touches it directly with the power of his mind.

System: This power may be used on any electronic device within the character's line of sight. The number of successes rolled are the maximum number of dice from any relevant Ability that the character may use while remotely controlling the device. For instance, if Fritz has Computer 5 and scores three successes when using Remote Access on an automated teller machine, he can only apply three dots of his Computer rating to any rolls that he makes through any use the power. Remote Access lasts for a number of turns equal to the number of successes rolled, and can only be used on one item at a time.

If an item is destroyed while under the effects of Remote Access, the character takes five dice of bashing damage due to the shock of having his perceptions rudely shunted back into his own body.

••••• Telecommute

A progressive derivation of Remote Access, Telecommute allows a thaumaturge to project her consciousness into the global telecommunication network, sending her mind through satellite uplinks and ISDN lines and fiber-optic phone cables at the speed of light. While immersed in the network, she can use any other Technomancy power on the devices with which she makes contact.

System: The character touches any form of communications device: a cellular telephone, network card-equipped computer, fax machine or anything else that is connected directly or indirectly to the global network. The player rolls normally and spends a Willpower point. Telecommute lasts for five minutes per success rolled, and may be extended by 10 minutes with the expenditure of another Willpower point. The number of successes indicates the maximum range that the character can project her consciousness away from her body.

No. of Successes	Result
1 success	25 miles
2 successes	250 miles
3 successes	1000 miles
4 successes	5000 miles
5 successes	Anywhere in the world, including telecommunication satellites

While in the network, the character can apply any other Path of Technomancy power to any device or data with which she comes in contact. A loss of connection, usually through the shutdown or destruction of a part of the network through which the character's connection runs, hurls her consciousness back to her body and inflicts eight dice of bashing damage.

A character traveling through the Net by means of this power can use her Path of Technomancy powers at normal difficulty. Using any other abilities or powers while engaged thus is done at a +2 difficulty. Furthermore, there are other denizens of the Net who may not take kindly to Tremere

intrusion, and who may well take steps to remove the riffraff from their electronic doorsteps.

SPIRIT MANIPULATION

Not to be confused with, or perhaps derived from the ancient Path of Spirit Thaumaturgy (see **Dark Ages Companion**, p. 107), Spirit Manipulation is a relatively recent innovation of the Tremere. Created to replace the rituals practiced by the clan in the days when it was a band of mortal wizards, Spirit Manipulation is the art of forcing spirits into actions and situations that would normally be anathema to them. Spirit Manipulation simulates many effects that can be created by Lupine and shamanic mages, but does so by forcing the spirits involved into a grotesque mockery of their normal behaviors. Any botch with Spirit Manipulation not only inflicts the normal loss of Willpower involved with thaumaturgical mishaps but also turns the full force of the spirit's wrath against the offending vampire.

• HERMETIC SIGHT

The vampire can perceive the spirit world, either by gazing deeply into it or by seeing the presence of nearby spirits as a hazy overlay on the material world. This power does not allow the thaumaturge to see into the realms of the dead or into the realms of the fae.

System: One success on the roll is needed for the thaumaturge to perceive spirits, while two allow him to view the spirit realm. With less than four successes, the thaumaturge is at +2 difficulty to all actions performed while using this power due to the distraction of divided perceptions. Hermetic Sight lasts for the duration of the scene or until the thaumaturge deactivates it.

•• ASTRAL CANT

The languages of the spirit world are infinitely varied and mainly incomprehensible to mortal (or immortal) minds. Astral Cant does not teach the thaumaturge the tongues of the spirits, but it does allow him to understand them as they speak to him and to reply in their own languages — in effect, a universal translator for the spirit world. Imprecise use of this power can be disastrous, particularly when a thaumaturge is bargaining with a powerful spirit. The use of this power is not always necessary; many spirits speak human tongues but choose to feign ignorance when dealing with vampires.

System: The number of successes determines the accuracy of the translation.

No. of Successes	Effect
1 success	Pidgin spirit language; very simple words and phrases can be comprehended.
2 successes	Simple sentences are possible; "trade language."
3 successes	Fluent conversation; sufficient for most conversations.
4 successes	Complex issues such as metaphysics can be discussed.

5 successes | Even the most obscure idiomatic expressions and forms of humor come through.

••• Voice of Command

This is perhaps the most dangerous power in the Spirit Manipulation arsenal, for the consequences if a thaumaturge fails can be most unpleasant. Voice of Command allows a vampire to issue orders to a spirit, compelling it to heed her bidding whether or not it desires to do so.

System: The player makes the normal Willpower roll; the target spirit resists with Willpower (difficulty of the thaumaturge's Manipulation + Occult or Manipulation + Lore: Spirits). The degree of success the thaumaturge attains determines the complexity and severity of the command that she can issue.

No. of Successes	Effect
Botch	The spirit is immune to the character's commands for the rest of the night. It reacts however the Storyteller deems appropriate.
Failure	The spirit is unaffected, and further attempts to command it are made at +1 difficulty (cumulative). It may ignore, taunt or even attack the character at the Storyteller's discretion.
1 success	The spirit obeys a very simple command that is no great inconvenience to it.
2 successes	The spirit heeds a relatively straightforward command that it is not innately opposed to performing.
3 successes	The spirit agrees to perform a moderately complex task that does not violate its ethics.
4 successes	The spirit consents to an extended or intricate task that does not place it in immediate danger.
5 successes	The spirit accepts a lengthy or nigh-impossible task, or one that may mean its destruction.

Crafty Storytellers should note that spirits compelled by this power are fully aware that they are being forced into these actions, and may well seek revenge on their erstwhile masters at a later time.

Thaumaturges who issue commands above and beyond what their spirit servants are compelled to perform may find themselves ignored or mocked. Even worse, a spirit in such a situation may "agree" to follow orders without following through, leaving the thaumaturge in a situation of potentially fatal embarrassment.

•••• Entrap Ephemera

This power allows a thaumaturge to bind a spirit into a physical object. This can be done to imprison the target, but is more often performed to create a fetish, an artifact that allows a user to channel a portion of the spirit's power through it to affect the physical world. Fetishes created by this power are often recalcitrant and fail at inopportune moments, as the spirits within are most displeased with their situation and will take any opportunity to escape or thwart their captors.

System: The number of successes rolled determines the power level of the fetish to be created. A fetish is activated by rolling the user's Willpower (difficulty of the fetish's power level + 3). A botch on this roll destroys the physical component of the fetish and frees the spirit that was trapped within.

For more complete guidelines to fetish powers, refer to pages 273-275 of **Werewolf: The Apocalypse**. The Storyteller is always the final authority in determining the powers and mechanics of a fetish created through use of this power.

••••• Duality

The thaumaturge can now fully interact with the spirit world. While using this power, he exists on both planes of existence at once. He is able to pick up objects in the physical world and place them in the spirit world and *vice versa*. Beings and landscape features in both realms are solid to him, and he can engage in any manner of interaction. He can even use Thaumaturgy and other Disciplines in either world. This is not without its dangers, however: One misstep and the vampire can find himself trapped in the spirit realm with no way to return home. Several incautious thaumaturges have starved into torpor while trapped on the other side of the barrier that separates the physical and spirit realms.

System: The number of successes dictates how long the vampire can interact with the spirit world.

No. of successes	Duration
1 success	One turn
2 successes	Three turns
3 successes	10 turns
4 successes	10 minutes
5 successes	The remainder of the scene

Duality can only be used while the character is in the physical world. Note that while Duality is in effect the character is also susceptible to attacks from both realms. Additionally, the player must roll Perception + Occult (difficulty 8) when this power is activated; a roll with less than three successes indicates that all rolls made while this power is active are at +2 difficulty due to the distraction of the character's dual perceptions. The character is still considered to be in the physical world for purposes of basic physics and common sense — for instance, his feet rest on the ground in the physical world, not the ground in the spirit world, and he could thus walk across a spiritual chasm if a physical parking lot overlaid the same space.

A botch on the roll to activate this power tears the vampire out of the physical world and traps him in the spirit realm. The way back the physical realm, if there is one, is left to the Storyteller's discretion, and may constitute an entire adventure in and of itself.

Thaumaturgical Countermagic

This is less of a path than it is a separate Discipline, as the power to resist Thaumaturgy can be taught independently of Thaumaturgy, even to those Kindred who are incapable of mastering even the simplest ritual. However, the techniques of Thaumaturgical Countermagic are not officially taught outside Clan Tremere, for obvious reasons. Any non-Tremere who displays the ability to resist Thaumaturgy quickly becomes the subject of potentially fatal scrutiny from the entirety of Clan Tremere.

System: Thaumaturgical Countermagic is treated as a separate Discipline. It cannot be taken as a character's primary path, and a rating in it does not allow the character to perform rituals. The use of Thaumaturgical Countermagic is treated as a free action in combat and does not require a split dice pool. To oppose a Thaumaturgy power or ritual, a character must have a Thaumaturgical Countermagic rating equal to or greater than the rating of that power or ritual (which means that rituals of Level Six or greater cannot *ever* be countered with this power). The player spends a blood point and rolls the number of dice indicated by the character's Thaumaturgical Countermagic rating (difficulty equal to the difficulty of the power in use). Each success cancels one of the opposing thaumaturge's successes.

Thaumaturgical Countermagic can only be used against Tremere Thaumaturgy at full effectiveness. It works with halved dice pools against non-Tremere blood magic and mortal "hedge wizardry," and is completely ineffective against non-vampiric magics and powers.

Thaumaturgical Countermagic can be learned by characters who are unable to learn Thaumaturgy (e.g. those with the Merit *Magic Resistance*). Any non-Tremere character with a rating in this power automatically gains the Flaw *Clan Enmity (Tremere)*, receiving no freebie points for it. This power cannot be taken during character creation and cannot be spontaneously developed. It costs the same as any other non-clan Discipline to learn.

- • Two dice of countermagic. The character can attempt to cancel only those powers and rituals that directly affect him and his garments.
- •• Four dice of countermagic.
- ••• Six dice of countermagic. The character can attempt to cancel a Thaumaturgy power that affects anyone or anything in physical contact with him.
- •••• Eight dice of countermagic.
- ••••• Ten dice of countermagic. The character can now attempt to cancel a power or ritual that targets anything within a radius equal to his Willpower in yards, or one that is being used or performed within that same radius.

Weather Control

Command over the weather has long been a staple power of wizards both mortal and immortal, and this path is said by many to predate the Tremere by millennia. The proliferation of usage of this path outside the clan tends to confirm this theory; Weather Control is quite common outside the Tremere, and even outside the Camarilla. Lower levels of this path allow subtle manipulations, while higher stages of mastery allow a vampire to call up raging storms. The area affected by this power is usually rather small, no more than three or four miles in diameter, and the changes the power wreaks are not always immediate.

System: The number of successes rolled indicates how long it takes the weather magic to take effect. One success indicates an entire day may pass before the weather changes to the thaumaturge's liking, while a roll with five successes brings an almost instant effect.

The difficulty of the Willpower roll necessary to invoke this power may change depending on the current local weather conditions and the weather the character is attempting to create. The Storyteller should impose a bonus (-1 or -2 difficulty) for relatively minor shifts, such as clearing away a light drizzle or calling lightning when a severe thunderstorm is already raging. Conversely, a penalty (+1 or +2 difficulty) should be applied when the desired change is at odds with the current conditions, such as summoning the same light drizzle in the middle of the Sahara Desert or calling down lightning from a cloudless sky.

For Example

Jaeger is a Tremere archon with Thaumaturgical Countermagic 5. He is facing Nadine, an infernalist with Lure of Flames 5. Nadine attempts to use her Lure of Flames to hurl a fireball at Jaeger and rolls two successes against a difficulty of 8. Jaeger rolls 10 dice of countermagic against a difficulty of 8, the same difficulty against which Nadine rolled, and scores three successes, completely neutralizing the attack.

Jaeger's partner Nathaniel has Thaumaturgical Countermagic 4. If Nadine had attacked Nathaniel, he would have been completely unable to counter the fireball, as his Thaumaturgical Countermagic rating is lower than that of the power being used against him. Likewise, if Nadine used her Movement of the Mind 4 to hurl a stake at Nathaniel, he would have been unable to oppose it because he cannot yet counter spells that target things that he is not touching.

Playing Indoors

Weather Control is not the sort of power that lends itself well to indoor application. While certain of the path's uses (changes of temperature, high winds and possibly even fog) do make a certain amount of sense in interior settings, others (precipitation of any sort, lightning) don't. The difficulty for all rolls to use Weather Control indoors is at +2, and the Storyteller should free to disallow any proposed uses that don't make sense.

If the character tries to strike a specific target with lightning, the player must roll Perception + Occult (difficulty 6 if the target is standing in open terrain, 8 if he is under shelter, or 10 if he is inside but near a window) in addition to the base roll to use Thaumaturgy. Otherwise the bolt goes astray, with the relative degree of failure of the roll determining where exactly the lightning strikes.

Effects of the power default to the maximum area available unless the thaumaturge states that he's attempting to affect a smaller area. At Storyteller discretion, an additional Willpower roll (difficulty 6) may be required to keep the change in the weather under control.

Individual power descriptions are not provided for this path, as the general principle is fairly consistent. Instead, the strongest weather phenomenon possible at each level is listed.

- • **Fog:** Vision is slightly impaired and sounds are muffled; a +1 difficulty is imposed on all Perception rolls that involve sight and hearing, and the effective ranges of all ranged attacks are halved.

Light breeze: A +1 difficulty is imposed on all Perception rolls that involve smell.

Minor temperature change: It is possible to raise or lower the local temperature by up to 10 degrees Fahrenheit.

- •• **Rain or snow:** Precipitation has the same effect as Fog, but Perception rolls are impaired to a much greater extent; the difficulty modifier for all such rolls rises to +2. In addition, the difficulty on all Drive rolls increases by two.

- ••• **High Winds:** The wind speed rises to around 30 miles per hour, with gusts of up to twice that. Ranged attacks are much more difficult: +1 to firearm attacks, +2 to thrown weapons and archery. In addition, during fierce gusts, Dexterity rolls (difficulty 6) may be required to keep characters from being knocked over by the winds. Needless to say, when gale-force winds are in effect, papers go flying, objects get picked up by the winds and hurled with abandon, and other suitably cinematic effects are likely.

Moderate temperature change: The local temperature can be raised or lowered by up to 20 degrees Fahrenheit.

- •••• **Storm:** This has the effects of both Rain and High Winds.

- ••••• **Lightning Strike:** This attack inflicts 10 dice of lethal damage. Body armor does not add to the target's dice pool to soak this attack.

THAUMATURGY RITUALS

LEVEL ONE RITUALS

BIND THE ACCUSING TONGUE

This ancient ritual is said to have been one of the first developed by the Tremere and a primary reason for the lack of cohesive opposition to their expansion. Bind the Accusing Tongue lays a compulsion upon the subject that prevents him from speaking ill of the caster, allowing the

thaumaturge to commit literally unspeakable acts without fear of reprisal.

System: The caster must have a picture or other image or effigy of the ritual's target, a lock of the target's hair and a black silken cord. The caster winds the cord around the hair and image while intoning the ritual's vocal component. Once the ritual is complete, the target must score more successes on a Willpower roll (difficulty of the caster's Thaumaturgy rating + 3) than the caster scored in order to say anything negative about the thaumaturge. The ritual lasts until the target succeeds at this roll or the silk cord is unwound, at which point the image and the lock of hair crumble to dust.

Engaging the Vessel of Transference

This ritual enchants a container to fill itself with blood from any living or unliving being who holds it, replacing the volume of blood taken with an equal amount previously held inside the container. When the ritual is enacted, the vessel (which must be between the size of a small cup and a gallon jug) is sealed full of the caster's blood and inscribed with the Hermetic sigil which empowers the ritual. Whenever an individual touches the container with his bare skin, he feels a slight chill against his flesh but no further discomfort. The container continues to exchange the blood it contains until it is opened. The two most common uses of this ritual are to covertly create a blood bond and to obtain a sample of a subject's blood for ritual or experimental purposes.

System: This ritual takes three hours to enact (reduced by 15 minutes for each success on the casting roll) and requires one blood point (although not necessarily the caster's blood), which is sealed inside the container. The ritual only switches blood between itself and a subject if it is touched bare-handed — even thin cotton gloves keep it from activating.

Individuals with at least four dots in Occult or three in Expert Knowledge: Mage Lore recognize the Hermetic sigil with two successes on an Intelligence + the appropriate Knowledge roll (difficulty 8).

Incantation of the Shepherd

This ritual enables the thaumaturge to mystically locate all members of his herd. While intoning the ritual's vocal component, he spins in a slow circle with a glass object of some sort held to each of his eyes. At the end of the ritual, he has a subliminal sense of the direction and distance to each of his regular vessels.

System: This ritual gives the character the location relative to him of every member of his herd. If he does not have the Herd Background, Incantation of the Shepherd locates the closest three mortals from whom the thaumaturge has fed at least three times each. This ritual has a maximum range of 10 miles times the character's Herd Background, or five miles if he has no points in that Background.

Purity of Flesh

The caster cleanses her body of all foreign material with this ritual. To perform it, she meditates on bare earth or stone while surrounded by a circle of 13 sharp stones. Over the course of the ritual, the caster is slowly purged of all physical impurities: dirt, alcohol, drugs, poison, bullets lodged in the flesh and tattoo ink are all equally affected, slowly rising to the surface of the caster's skin and flaking away as a gritty gray film that settles within the circle. Any jewelry, makeup or clothes that the caster is wearing are also dissolved.

System: The player spends one blood point before rolling. Purity of Flesh removes all physical items from the caster's body, but does not remove enchantments, mind control or diseases of the blood.

Level Two Rituals

Blood Walk

A thaumaturge casts this ritual on a blood sample from another vampire. Blood Walk is used to trace the subject's Kindred lineage and the blood bonds in which the subject is involved.

System: This ritual requires three hours to cast, reduced by 15 minutes for each success on the roll. It requires one blood point from the subject. Each success allows the caster to "see back" one generation, giving the caster both the True Name of the ancestor and an image of his face. The caster also learns the generation and clan or bloodline from which the subject is descended. With three successes, the caster also learns the identities of all parties with whom the subject shares a blood bond, either as regnant or thrall.

Burning Blade

Developed during Clan Tremere's troubled inception, Burning Blade allows a thaumaturge to temporarily enchant a melee weapon to inflict unhealable wounds on supernatural creatures. While this ritual is in effect, the weapon flickers with an unholy greenish flame.

System: This ritual can only be cast on melee weapons. The caster must cut the palm of her weapon hand during the ritual — with the weapon if it is edged, otherwise with a sharp stone. This inflicts a single health level of lethal damage which cannot be soaked but may be healed normally. The player spends three blood points which are absorbed by the weapon. Once the ritual is cast, the weapon inflicts aggravated damage on all supernatural creatures for the next few successful attacks, one per success rolled. Multiple castings of Burning Blade cannot be "stacked" for longer durations. Furthermore, the wielder of the weapon cannot choose to do normal damage and "save up" aggravated strikes — each successful attack uses one aggravated strike until there are none left, at which point the weapon reverts to inflicting normal damage.

Donning the Mask of Shadows

This ritual renders its subject translucent, her form appearing dark and smoky and the sounds of her footsteps muffled. While it does not create true invisibility, the Mask of Shadows makes the subject much less likely to be detected by sight or hearing.

System: This ritual may be simultaneously cast on a number of subjects equal to the thaumaturge's Occult rating; each individual past the first adds five minutes to the base casting time. Individuals under the Mask of Shadows can only be detected if the observer succeeds in a Perception + Awareness roll (difficulty of the caster's Wits + Occult) or if the observer possesses a power (such as Auspex) sufficient to penetrate Level Three Obfuscate. The Mask of Shadows lasts a number of hours equal to the number of successes rolled when it is cast or until the caster voluntarily lowers it.

WARDING CIRCLE VERSUS GHOULS

This ritual is enacted in a manner similar to that of Ward versus Ghouls (see **Vampire: The Masquerade**, p. 184), but creates a circle centered on the caster into which a ghoul cannot pass without being burned. The circle can be made as large and as permanent as the caster desires, as long as she is willing to pay the necessary price. Many Tremere chantries and havens are protected by this and other Warding Circle rituals.

System: The ritual requires three blood points of mortal blood. The caster determines the size of the warding circle when it is cast; the default radius is 10 feet, and every 10-foot increase raises the difficulty by one, to a maximum of 9 (one additional success is required for every 10-foot increase past the number necessary to raise the difficulty to 9). The player spends one blood point for every 10 feet of radius and rolls. The ritual takes the normal casting time if it is to be temporary (lasting for the rest of the night) or one night if it is to be permanent (lasting a year and a day).

Once the warding circle is established, any ghoul who attempts to cross its boundary feels a tingle on his skin and a slight breeze on his face — a successful Intelligence + Occult roll (difficulty 8) identifies this as a warding circle. If the ghoul attempts to press on, he must roll more successes on a Willpower roll (difficulty of the caster's Thaumaturgy rating + 3) than the caster rolled when establishing the ward. Failure indicates that the ward blocks his passage and inflicts three dice of bashing damage on him, and his next roll to attempt to enter the circle is at +1 difficulty. If the ghoul leaves the circle and attempts to enter it again, he must repeat the roll. Attempts to leave the circle are not blocked.

The Tremere have access to several other Warding Circle rituals: Warding Circle versus Lupines (Level Three), Warding Circle versus Kindred (Level Four), and Warding Circles versus Spirits, Ghosts, and Demons (Level Five). Each Warding Circle ritual must be learned separately. The material components required for each warding circle are the same as those needed for the corresponding ward, but in larger amounts. The effects against the targeted beings are the same as for Warding Circle versus Ghouls.

LEVEL THREE RITUALS

FLESH OF FIERY TOUCH

This defensive ritual inflicts painful burns on anyone who deliberately touches the subject's skin. It requires the subject to swallow a small glowing ember, which does put off some thaumaturges with low pain thresholds. Some vain Tremere use this ritual purely for its subsidiary effect of darkening the subject's skin to a healthy sun-bronzed hue.

System: Flesh of Fiery Touch takes two hours to cast (reduced by 10 minutes per success). It requires a small piece of wood, coal or other common fuel source, which ignites and is swallowed at the end of the ritual. The subject who swallows the red-hot ember receives a single aggravated health level of damage (difficulty 6 to soak with Fortitude). Until the next sunset, anyone who touches the subject's flesh receives a burn that inflicts a single aggravated health level of damage (again, difficulty 6 to soak with Fortitude). The victim must voluntarily touch the subject; this damage is not inflicted if the victim is touched or accidentally comes in contact with the subject.

This ritual darkens the subject's skin to that which would be obtained by long-term exposure to the sun in a mortal. The tone is slightly unnatural and metallic, and is evidently artificial to any observer who succeeds in a Perception + Medicine roll (difficulty 8).

SANGUINE ASSISTANT

Tremere often need laboratory assistants whom they can trust implicitly. As Tremere often trust no one whom they know and no one whom they do not, this ritual allows the intrepid thaumaturge to conjure a temporary servant. To cast the ritual, the vampire slices open his arm and bleeds into a specially prepared earthen bowl. The ritual sucks in and animates whatever random unimportant items the wizard happens to have lying around his workshop — glass beakers, dissection tools, pencils, crumpled papers, semiprecious stones — and binds the materials together into a small humanoid form animated by the power of the ritual and the blood. Oddly enough, this ritual almost never takes in any tool that the thaumaturge finds himself needing during the assistant's lifespan, nor does it take the physical components of any other ritual nor any living thing. The servant has no personality to speak of at first, but gradually adopts the mannerisms and thought processes that the thaumaturge desires in an ideal servant. Sanguine Assistants are temporary creations, but some Tremere become fond of their tiny accomplices and create the same one whenever the need arises.

System: The player spends five blood points and rolls. The servant created by the ritual stands a foot high and appears as a roughly humanoid shape composed of whatever the ritual sucked in for its own use. It lasts for one night per success rolled. At the end of the last night, the assistant crawls into the bowl used for its creation and falls apart. The assistant can be re-animated through another application of this ritual; if the thaumaturge so desires, it re-forms from the same materials with the same memories and personality.

A Sanguine Assistant has Strength and Stamina of 1 and Dexterity and Mental Attributes equal to those of the caster. It begins with no Social Attributes to speak of, but gains one dot per night in Charisma and Manipulation until its ratings are equal to those of the caster. It has all of the caster's Abilities at

one dot lower than his own. A Sanguine Assistant is a naturally timid creature and flees if attacked, having only four health levels, though it will try to defend its master's life at the cost of its own. It has no Disciplines of its own, but has a full understanding of all of its master's Thaumaturgical knowledge and can instruct others if so commanded. A Sanguine Assistant is impervious to any mind-controlling Disciplines or magic, so completely is it bound to its creator's will.

SHAFT OF BELATED QUIESCENCE

This ritual turns an ordinary stake of rowan wood into a particularly vicious weapon. When the stake penetrates a vampire's body, the tip breaks off and begins working its way through the victim's flesh to his heart. The trip may take several minutes or several nights, depending on where the stake struck. The stake eludes attempts to dig it out, burrowing farther into the victim's body to escape surgery. The only Kindred who are immune to this internal attack are those who have had their hearts removed by Setites.

System: The ritual takes five hours to enact, minus 30 minutes per success. The stake must be carved of rowan wood, coated with three blood points of the caster's blood, and blackened in an oak-wood fire. When the ritual is complete, the stake is enchanted to act as described above.

An attack with a Shaft of Belated Quiescence is performed as with a normal stake: a Dexterity + Melee roll (difficulty 6, modified as per the normal combat rules, as the attack does not need to specifically target the heart — the stake takes care of that) with a lethal damage rating of Strength + 1. If at least one health level of damage is inflicted after the target rolls to soak, the tip of the stake breaks off and begins burrowing. If not, the stake may be used to make subsequent attacks until it strikes deep enough to activate.

Once the tip of the stake is in the victim's body, the Storyteller begins an extended roll of the caster's Thaumaturgy rating (difficulty 9), rolling once per hour of game time. Successes on this roll are added to the successes scored in the initial attack. This represents the tip's progress toward the victim's heart. A botch indicates that the tip has struck a bone and all accumulated successes are lost (including those from the initial attack roll). When the shaft accumulates a total of 15 successes, it reaches the victim's heart. This paralyzes Kindred and is instantly fatal to mortals and ghouls.

Attempts to surgically remove the tip of the shaft can be made with an extended Dexterity + Medicine roll (difficulty 7), rolled once per hour. The surgeon must accumulate a number of successes equal to those currently held by the shaft in order to remove the tip. Once surgery begins, however, the shaft begins actively evading the surgeon's probes, and its rolls are made once every 30 minutes for the duration of the surgery attempt. Each individual surgery roll that scores less than three successes inflicts an additional unsoakable level of lethal damage on the patient.

Shaft of Belated Quiescence may be performed on other wooden impaling weapons, such as spears, arrows, practice swords and pool cues, provided that they are made of rowan wood. It may not, however, create a Bullet of Belated Quiescence — wooden bullets are not large enough to absorb the full amount of blood required for the ritual.

WARD VERSUS LUPINES

This wards an object in a manner identical to that of the Level Two ritual Ward Versus Ghouls (see **Vampire: The Masquerade**), except that it affects werewolves. Other versions of this ritual are rumored to have been created to affect different species of werecreatures.

System: Ward versus Lupines behaves exactly as does Ward versus Ghouls, but it affects werewolves rather than ghouls. It does not affect Nuwisha, Bastet or any Changing Breed other than Garou. The ritual requires a handful of silver dust rather than a blood point.

LEVEL FOUR RITUALS

HEART OF STONE

A vampire under the effect of this ritual experiences the transformation suggested by the ritual's name: his heart is completely transmuted to solid rock, rendering him virtually impervious to staking. The subsidiary effects of the transformation, however, seem to follow the Hermetic laws of sympathetic magic: the vampire's emotional capacity becomes almost nonexistent, and his ability to relate to others suffers as well.

System: This ritual requires nine hours (reduced by one hour for every success). It can only be cast on oneself. The caster lies naked on a flat stone surface and places a bare candle over his heart. The candle burns down to nothing over the course of the ritual, causing one aggravated health level of damage (difficulty 5 to soak with Fortitude). At the end of the ritual, the caster's heart hardens to stone. The benefits of this are that the caster gains a number of additional dice equal to twice his Thaumaturgy rating to soak any attack that aims for his heart and is completely impervious to the effects of a Shaft of Belated Quiescence (see above), and the difficulty to use all Presence powers on him is increased by three due to his emotional isolation. The drawbacks are as follows: the caster's Conscience and Empathy scores drop to 1 (or to 0 if they already were at 1) and all dice pools for Social rolls except those involving Intimidation are halved (including those required to use Disciplines). All Merits that the character has pertaining to positive social interaction (e.g. *Animal Magnetism* or *Sanctity*) are neutralized. Heart of Stone lasts as long as the caster wishes it to.

SPLINTER SERVANT

Another ritual designed to enchant a stake, Splinter Servant is a progressive development of Shaft of Belated Quiescence. The two rituals are mutually exclusive, which is fortunate for many, because a Splinter Servant of Belated Quiescence would be a truly terrifying weapon. A Splinter Servant consists of a stake carved from a tree which has nourished itself on the dead, bound in waxsealed nightshade twine. When the binding is torn off, the Splinter Servant leaps to life, animating itself and attacking whomever the wielder commands — or the wielder, if she is too

slow in assigning a target. The servant splits itself into a roughly humanoid form and begins single-mindedly trying to impale the target's heart. Its exertions tear it apart within a few minutes, but if it pierces its victim's heart before it destroys itself, it is remarkably difficult to remove, as pieces tend to remain behind if the main portion is indelicately yanked out.

System: The ritual requires 12 hours to cast, minus one per success, and the servant must be created as described above. When the binding is torn off, the character who holds it must point the servant at its target and verbally command it to attack during the same turn. If this command is not given, the servant attacks the closest living or unliving being, usually the unfortunate individual who currently carries it.

A Splinter Servant always aims for the heart. It has an attack dice pool of the caster's Wits + Occult, a damage dice pool of the caster's Thaumaturgy rating, and a maximum movement rate of 30 yards per turn. Note that these values are those of the thaumaturge who created the servant, not the individual who activates it. A servant cannot fly, but can leap its full movement rating every turn. Every action it takes is to attack or move toward its target; it cannot dodge or split its dice pool to perform multiple attacks. The servant makes normal stake attacks that aim for the heart (difficulty 9), and its success is judged as per the rules for a normal staking (see **Vampire: The Masquerade**, page 214). A Splinter Servant has three health levels, and attacks directed against it are made at +3 difficulty due to its small size and spastic movement patterns.

A Splinter Servant has an effective life of five combat turns per success rolled in its creation. If it has not impaled its victim by the last round of its life, the servant collapses into a pile of ordinary, inanimate splinters. Three successes on a Dexterity roll (difficulty 8) are required to remove a Splinter Servant from a victim's heart without leaving behind shards of the stake.

WARD VERSUS KINDRED

This warding ritual functions exactly as do Ward versus Ghouls and Ward versus Lupines, but it inflicts injury upon Cainites. It does not harm *kuei-jin* (see **Kindred of the East**), although Tremere researchers are promising their elders a Ward versus Cathayans ritual "any night now."

System: Ward versus Kindred behaves exactly as does Ward versus Ghouls, but it affects vampires rather than ghouls. The ritual requires a blood point of the caster's own blood and does not affect the caster. As noted above, this ward does not harm *kuei-jin*, and there is currently no "Ward versus Cathayans" in existence.

LEVEL FIVE RITUALS

ENCHANT TALISMAN

This ritual is the first taught to most Tremere once they have attained mastery of their first path. Create Talisman allows the thaumaturge to enchant a personal magical item (the fabled wizard's staff) to act as an amplifier for her will and thaumaturgical might. A Tremere's talisman is a great source of personal pride, and any insult directed against a talisman is an insult at the thaumaturge herself. Many talismans are laden with additional rituals (such as every ward known to the thaumaturge). The physical appearance of a talisman varies, but it must be a rigid object close to a yard long. Swords and walking sticks are the most common talismans, but some innovative or eccentric Tremere have enchanted violins, shotguns, pool cues and classroom pointers.

System: This ritual requires six hours per night for one complete cycle of the moon, beginning and ending on the new moon. Over this time, the thaumaturge carefully prepares her talisman, carving it with Hermetic runes that signify her True Name and the sum total of her thaumaturgical knowledge. The player spends one blood point per night and makes an extended roll of Intelligence + Occult (difficulty 8), one roll per week. If a night's work is missed or if the four rolls do not accumulate at least 20 net successes, the talisman is ruined and the process must be begun again.

A completed talisman gives the thaumaturge several advantages. When the character is holding the talisman, the difficulty of all magic or magick that targets her is increased by one. The player receives two extra dice when rolling for uses of the character's primary path and one extra die when rolling for the character's ritual castings. If the talisman is used as a weapon, it gives the player an additional die to roll to hit. If the thaumaturge is separated from her talisman, a successful Perception + Occult roll (difficulty 7) gives her its location.

If a talisman is in the possession of another individual, it gives that individual three additional dice to roll when using any form of magic or magick against the talisman's owner. At the Storyteller's discretion, rituals that target the thaumaturge and use her talisman as a physical component may have greatly increased effects.

A thaumaturge may only have one talisman at a time. Ownership of a talisman may not be transferred — each individual must create her own.

Escape to a True Friend

One of the few rituals available to the Tremere that allows a form of teleportation, Escape to a True Friend allows the caster to travel to the person whose friendship and trust she most values. The ritual has a physical component of a yard-wide circle charred into the bare ground or floor. The caster may step into the circle at any time and speak the True Name of her friend. She is instantly transported to that individual, wherever he may be at the moment. She does not appear directly in front of him, but materializes in a location within a few minutes' walk that is out of sight of any observer. The circle may be reused indefinitely, as long as it is unmarred.

System: This ritual takes six hours a night for six nights to cast, reduced by one night for every two successes. Each night requires the sacrifice of three of the caster's own blood points, which are poured into the circle. Once the circle is complete, the transport may be attempted at any time. The caster may take one other individual with her when she travels, or a maximum amount of "cargo" equal to her own weight.

Some Tremere have servants or allies whom they wish to make exempt from the damage and subsequent avoidance compulsion inflicted by the various "Ward versus" and "Warding Circle versus" rituals (Ward versus Ghouls, Lupines, Kindred, Spirits, Ghosts, and Demons). This technique is taught to all Tremere who are taught any of these rituals. It requires either the presence of each individual who is to be exempt from the ward or a point of their blood when the ward is cast. The difficulty of the roll to cast the ward is raised by one (to a maximum of 9). The thaumaturge may exempt a maximum number of individuals equal to his Thaumaturgy rating from each ward he casts.

The caster of a warding circle can also temporarily enchant a specific being to pass through a warding circle cast by that thaumaturge. This requires five minutes, one point of the subject's blood and an Intelligence + Occult roll (difficulty 8). If this succeeds, the subject is exempt from the warding circle for one night per success.

Ward versus Spirits

This warding ritual functions exactly as do Ward versus Ghouls, Ward versus Lupines and Ward versus Kindred, but it inflicts injury upon spirits. Several other versions of this ward exist, each geared toward a particular type of non-physical being.

System: Ward versus Spirits behaves exactly as does Ward versus Ghouls, but it affects spirits (including those summoned or given physical form by Thaumaturgy Paths such as Elemental Mastery). The material component for Ward versus Spirits is a handful of pure sea salt.

The other versions of this ward, also Level Five rituals, are Ward versus Ghosts and Ward versus Demons. Each of these three Level Five wards affects its respective target on both the physical and spiritual planes. Ward versus Ghosts requires a handful of powdered marble from a tombstone, while Ward versus Demons requires a vial of holy water.

VISCERATIKA

The exclusive possession of the Gargoyle bloodline, Visceratika is an extension of the Gargoyles' natural affinity for stone, earth and things made thereof. Certain Visceratika powers also closely resemble some aspects of Protean and, to a lesser extent, Vicissitude. Tremere in a position to know insist that this is pure coincidence, but the few among the Gargoyles who retain scholarly aspirations maintain that the Gangrel and Tzimisce blood used to create the bloodline still maintains a certain hold over its members.

Clan Tremere recently released a report stating that, contrary to popular belief, the appearance and wings of the Gargoyles are results of the Gargoyle Embrace or creation process, not side effects of Visceratika as was previously believed. The implication is that other Kindred can learn

Visceratika and retain human appearance. The Gargoyles, however, are understandably unwilling to share one of their primary survival tools, and few other Kindred are willing to risk it in any case.

• SKIN OF THE CHAMELEON

This basic power has saved countless Gargoyles from committing breaches of the Masquerade — and has allowed just as many to ambush unsuspecting intruders. When Skin of the Chameleon is in effect, the Gargoyle's skin takes on the color and texture of the surrounding environment. This coloration changes reflexively as long as the Gargoyle maintains a walking pace or slower speed. More rapid movement causes the Gargoyle's appearance to blur, negating the camouflaging effect. If this power is used while the Gargoyle is in flight, his skin becomes a reasonable facsimile of the night sky (though it will not shift to mimic nearby skyscrapers or star patterns, and a black silhouette against a brightly lit skyline is likely to be noticed).

System: The player spends one blood point. For the rest of the scene, the Gargoyle's Stealth dice pool is increased by five dice. This power is subject to the limitations described above; any ground movement faster than a walk negates this power's effect, as does flight (at the Storyteller's discretion).

•• SCRY THE HEARTHSTONE

The backbone of the Gargoyles' strength as guardians of havens and chantries, this power allows the user to maintain vigilance over part or all of an enclosed structure. The Gargoyle gains an innate sense of where all beings are located within the structure, even those who are hidden by Obfuscate or other supernatural concealment.

GARGOYLE FLIGHT

The Gargoyles' ability to fly is one of their more noticeable traits. Although Gargoyles do gain enormous strength via Potence, and they do sprout wings as a result of being Embraced or converted, their enhanced body density (some Gargoyles have been recorded as weighing over 800 pounds) makes natural flight an impossible proposition — they don't have enough thrust-to-weight ratio to do more than glide like a brick with a couple of sheet-metal wings taped on. The more biology-minded among the Kindred have been wondering about this for some time.

The truth of the matter is that Gargoyles *shouldn't* be able to fly. Their ability to perform aerial maneuvers is unnatural (even for the Kindred) and is a direct result of Tremere experimentation. The initial thaumaturgical process that created the Gargoyles incorporated a highly refined variant of Movement of the Mind as a fundamental component of the subjects' magical makeup, making one application of this one thaumaturgical path second nature to them. This instinctive magical ability has been passed along through their blood for centuries. The Tremere scholar who gave the Gargoyles their flight capability in this manner was destroyed in the Gargoyle Revolt, and it's unknown whether anyone else knew what he did. Thus, the secret of Gargoyle flight is most likely lost forever.

For characters with more natural airborne forms, such as Gangrel in bat-form, Flight is a specialty of the Athletics Talent, or at Storyteller discretion can be listed as a Secondary Ability instead. Gargoyles, however, use a unique Discipline called Flight that is only available to them. All Gargoyles start with one dot in Flight in addition to their initial three Discipline dots; further levels of Flight must be bought like any other clan Discipline. As the character's Flight rating increases, so does her maximum speed.

• The character cannot fly *per se*, but can soar like a vulture or a hang-glider — as long as he's not trying to carry anything. Maximum speed equals the prevailing winds, or 15 miles per hour in calm air.

•• The character can make running takeoffs and can carry a maximum payload of 20 pounds. Maximum speed equals 30 miles per hour.

••• The character can perform a straight vertical ascent if unencumbered, or can make longer takeoff runs carrying up to 50 pounds. Maximum speed equals 45 miles per hour.

•••• The character can carry up to 100 pounds aloft, though vertical takeoff is impossible with more than 50 pounds of baggage. Maximum speed equals 60 miles per hour.

••••• The character can lift up to 200 pounds, which should be sufficient for most player characters — or prey. Maximum speed of 75 miles per hour.

Every dot in Flight past the fifth adds an additional 100 pounds and 20 miles per hour to the Gargoyle's maximums. Celerity cannot be used to enhance flight speed. Although Flight did originate as a modification of Movement of the Mind, it is *not* considered Thaumaturgy; Gargoyles with high Flight ratings may have slightly effervescent auras, but they certainly can't perform rituals using Flight. Remember — *only* Gargoyles can learn this Discipline, and they're not aware that it's a Discipline at all. To the character, her wings and her ability to fly are just part and parcel of her existence as a Gargoyle.

Players who want to know what their characters are capable of doing to devastate opponents from the skies are directed to page 82 of the **Book of Storyteller Secrets** for **Vampire: The Dark Ages**.

System: The player spends a Willpower point to activate this power, which remains in effect as long as the Gargoyle is within or in contact with the target structure, or until the next sunset. Scry the Hearthstone may be used on anything up to the size of a large castle, including a cave complex, a theatre, a parking garage or a mansion. The character gains an innate sense of the location and approximate size and physical condition of all living (or unliving) beings within the structure. To pinpoint a specific individual's location with this power, the player must succeed in a Perception + Alertness roll (difficulty 6). If the subject is attempting to hide, he may oppose this roll with a roll of Wits + Stealth (difficulty 6).

Scry the Hearthstone may be used to detect the presence of characters who are under the concealment of Obfuscate or similar powers. In this case, the Gargoyle only knows that there is someone present — she cannot actually see the individual in question. To determine the Gargoyle's ability to detect Obfuscated characters, compare the relative levels of the Gargoyle's Visceratika minus one and the intruder's Obfuscate as per the rules for Auspex in **Vampire: The Masquerade**.

••• Bond with the Mountain

Similar to the Protean power of Earth Meld, Bond with the Mountain allows a Gargoyle to seek shelter within stone (or building materials that are stonelike, such as cement). The merge produced by this power is not as complete as that made by Earth Meld, however. A faint outline of the Gargoyle's shape can be seen by the sharp-eyed observer.

System: The player spends two blood points, and the merge, which may only be performed upon bare rock or a similar substance, takes four turns to complete. This power functions in a fashion similar to the Protean 3 power of Earth Meld. However, the Gargoyle does not sink fully into the substance with which he merges, and his outline can be detected within the stone with a successful Perception + Alertness (difficulty 9) roll. A Gargoyle attacked while Bonded with the Mountain has triple his normal soak dice pool against all forms of attack. However, if he sustains three lethal health levels of damage from a single attack, he is forced out of his bond and suffers disorientation similar to that experienced by an Earth Melded character whose slumber is interrupted.

•••• Armor of Terra

This power, combined with the unnatural resilience granted by Fortitude, is the source of the Gargoyles' ability to withstand assaults that would tear lesser Kindred to shreds. An individual who has reached this level of Visceratika finds her skin to have become immeasurably tougher than it once was, and gains a higher pain threshold. She also acquires a limited amount of immunity to fire (though she is no less terrified of it).

System: This power is automatic and requires no roll; it is always in effect. A vampire with Armor of Terra has one extra soak die for all aggravated and lethal attacks and two for all bashing attacks, reduces all wound penalties by one, and halves the damage dice pool of any fire-based source of injury. However, the difficulty of all touch-based Perception rolls is increased by two due to the desensitization of the character's skin.

••••• Flow Within the Mountain

A Gargoyle who has attained this level of Visceratika is no longer confined to the location in which he Bonded with the Mountain (above). He may now travel through stone and concrete as if they were no denser than a thick liquid. Gargoyle guardians use this power to devastating effect when intercepting intruders, while more subtle individuals find it to be a highly effective method of gaining access to "secure" areas. This power is of more limited use in this age of girder construction than it was when buildings were made of solid stone, but it still sees nightly use.

System: Once the character has used Bond with the Mountain, the player spends two more blood points to activate Flow Within the Mountain for the duration of the scene. The Gargoyle can move within stone and cement under the same rules used for a character under the effect of the Protean 6 power of Earth Control, with the exception of the medium through which the character can "swim."

The character can also use this power to walk through a stone wall and emerge on the other side without first using Bond with the Mountain. In this case, the player spends one blood point and rolls Strength (difficulty 8, Potence adds successes normally). The Gargoyle may flow through a maximum thickness in feet equal to the number of successes rolled. If the wall or barrier is thicker than this, the character is trapped within it until he is chiseled out or uses Flow Within the Mountain to escape.

Creating Combination Disciplines

Just as characters should be able to work up their own high-level Discipline powers, there are cases where it *may* be appropriate for them to create their own high-level combination Discipline powers. Moments like this are best treated like moments when a player asks to create his own Discipline powers, but with even more caution. Combination powers are very potent, and an incorrectly designed one can unbalance a game immediately. It is suggested that if a player wants to come up with his own combination power, that power should never involve more than two Disciplines. Furthermore, the player should have to spend extensive time roleplaying his research or being tutored in this new art by a Storyteller character who happens to possess the knowledge the character wants — new ground is being broken here, and that should never be easy. Finally, the experience spent for the new power should be removed immediately, not at the end of the training/research period. In any event, the Storyteller should feel free to reject any proposed combination Discipline powers for any reason whatsoever.

Combination Disciplines

Some elder Kindred have advanced their mastery of the basic physical Disciplines — Celerity, Fortitude and Potence — to such a degree that they have developed powers inconceivable to vampires of lesser ability and strength of blood. The following powers are available to those characters who have developed the listed Disciplines to the required degree. These powers cannot be developed spontaneously — they must be taught.

Elemental Stoicism

Although no vampire can resist the sun's light indefinitely, those elders who have mastered the powers of Fortitude to this advanced degree can stave off death for a few crucial moments. Elemental Stoicism also offers some degree of protection against fire.

Required: Fortitude 8, Obfuscate 4

Cost: 40 experience points, once the prerequisite levels of Fortitude and Obfuscate have been reached.

System: This power is involuntary and cannot be turned off. Every hour that the character is exposed to fire or sunlight, the player *must* spend one blood point. All damage inflicted on the vampire by fire or sunlight during that hour is changed from aggravated to nonaggravated lethal damage and may be soaked as such. This blood point use does not count against the character's maximum expenditure per turn. A character whose blood pool is emptied by this power falls into torpor immediately and begins taking damage normally if she is still in contact with the damage source. This power does not protect the vampire's clothing or belongings against such damage — she may be able to walk through a burning building, but she'll most likely walk out of it wearing nothing but ashes.

Martyr's Resilience

Reputedly pioneered by the Salubri bloodline, this power has been demonstrated by members of several other clans as well. Martyr's Resilience allows the vampire to choose to absorb injuries inflicted upon anyone whose blood he has tasted. This power is not necessarily used for selfless means — several Ventrue in London command small criminal armies of ghouls who seem to possess a disturbing degree of immunity to bullets.

Required: Auspex 4, Fortitude 7

Cost: 35 experience points, once the prerequisite levels of Fortitude and Auspex have been reached.

System: The vampire must have ingested at least one blood point of the subject's blood within the past year to employ this power, and must be within eyesight of the subject when the injury is inflicted. The player spends a blood point to activate this power, and the action must be declared before the initial victim rolls to soak the damage. As a result, a number of health levels of damage equal to the character's Stamina are transferred from the initial target of the attack to the character. This damage is considered to have been inflicted directly on the character and is soaked nor-

Martyr's Resilience: An Example

Randall, a Gangrel elder (Stamina 8), and Christopher, Randall's newly Embraced childe, are accosted by a group of woefully unprepared Inquisitors. One of the vampire-hunters shoots Christopher in the face with a shotgun, inflicting a total of 14 health levels of lethal damage. As Randall does not want to lose the companionship of Christopher, Randall's player spends a blood point and transfers eight health levels of lethal damage from Christopher to Randall. Christopher is left with six health levels of lethal damage to soak, which is still painful but considerably more manageable. Both players make their respective characters' soak rolls, pantomime spitting out some teeth, and prepare to teach the Inquisitors a lesson in dealing with elders.

mally. Any damage in excess of the character's Stamina is inflicted on the initial recipient of the damage, who soaks it normally as well.

The use of this power is completely voluntary — a character cannot be forced to use it, even through Dominate or other powers of that sort.

Unassailable Parry

According to the Sabbat, one of the primary advantages that younger Kindred have in battling their elders is modern technology — firearms, to be precise. Many overconfident elders have fallen to packs of diablerists with automatic weapons. Some few ancients, however, have honed their reflexes and hand-eye coordination to an edge fine enough to stop a bullet, or at least to deflect one.

Required: Auspex 3, Celerity 7

Cost: 42 experience points, once the prerequisite levels of Auspex and Celerity have been reached.

System: This power allows a character to parry projectiles. The player spends one blood point and rolls Dexterity + Athletics (difficulty and number of successes required are shown below) to parry or catch a thrown weapon, arrow or bullet. Only solid physical projectiles may be deflected in this manner — Unassailable Parry has no effect on a stream of liquid from a fire hose, for instance.

Missile	To parry	To catch
Rock or grenade	4	5
Knife or shuriken	6	7
Spear	5	5
Hatchet	7	7
Arrow	7	8
Crossbow bolt	8	9
Bullet	9	9 (two successes)

If the player scores less than three successes on any roll to parry or catch a bullet, the character still takes the gun's base damage. Any missile hurled with Projectile is considered a bullet for the purposes of deflecting or catching it with Unassailable Parry.

The Rhythm of Immortality: Tactics and Systems

Death is no threat of people who are not afraid to die: But even if these offenders feared death all day, Who should be rash enough to act as executioner?

-Lao Tzu, *The Way of Life*, Witter Bynner, trans.

There are many observances and customs that are indigenous to the Camarilla, most of which are shrouded in tradition and antiquity. However, the exact procedurals of these customs has gotten a bit foggy at times. Everyone knows that the Embrace is a big deal, but not everyone is as sure as to how one might go about it. There are certainly penalties attached to breaking the Traditions, but how those penalties are enforced or what they might be has been something of a mystery. Below, then, is a discussion of some of the most important traditions and customs of the Camarilla, with attention paid to their details and niceties.

A Note

This is not a traditional systems chapter, in the sense of "If you want to do this, spend X points and make Y roll at Z difficulty" for every action imaginable under the moon. Rather, this chapter details the way things are done by the Camarilla, with an emphasis on roleplaying rather than dice rolling. The niceties and procedures of the blood hunt and prestation demand attention if they're to be fully fleshed out parts of a chronicle. Hence, the following discussion.

The Embrace

The Embrace is the process of creating new vampires from mortals. It works only on human beings or (exceedingly rarely) creatures so close to human as to pass for them. The right to Embrace new vampires is jealously guarded by the elders of the Camarilla, who fear both overcrowding and the prospect of a sea of hungry neonates seeking elder vitae. Even the details of how the process is accomplished are sometimes hidden from the thin-blooded youth of the Camarilla, creating an ignorance which prevents some accidents but produces gruesome mistakes in other cases.

Obtaining Permission

The Camarilla operates under the Masquerade, a concerted effort to hide the existence of vampires from the mortal world. A logical derivation of that statement is the fact that the more vampires there are, the harder it is to hide them — so it's best for the Masquerade to keep the numbers low. But vampires will be vampires, and one of the basic drives the Kindred have is to Embrace others. As a result, the Camarilla has come up with an ornate procedural for obtaining permission to Embrace. Were those guidelines not followed, the vampiric population would increase exponentially, shattering the Masquerade in the process. While no one actually likes the way the process is currently arranged (the most common gripe being that the Ventrue and Toreador seem to be favored), agreement is more or less universal that it beats the alternative.

A vampire who wants to create progeny needs to go directly to the top, namely, the prince. The prince holds the right of creation and destruction in his city, meaning that he alone has the actual right to create childer. It is within his power, however, to bestow that right temporarily on one of his subjects. This is often done as a reward for exceptional service, such as fending off a Sabbat attack, uncovering an infiltrator or preventing a particularly dangerous breach of the Masquerade. At other times the right of creation is held out as a bribe to potential allies, or a way of juggling the power of the primogen. If the Brujah elder, who sits in opposition to the prince, has a few too many childer, it may behoove His Majesty to grant the right of creation to the as-yet unaligned Nosferatu primogen. Doing so bolsters the Nosferatu's forces and renders him indebted to the prince; all in all, an entirely satisfactory result.

On rare occasions, Kindred trade prestation debts for the right of creation. The right to create a new vampire is never given away cheaply. The vampire petitioning for such a boon must bring a great deal to the table, either incurring tremendous debt to the prince or offering to release the prince from immense obligations he has incurred.

Once the right of creation has been granted (often in a public ceremony at Elysium; more infrequently in private if a prince is quietly supporting an ally or increasing his own brood), it cannot be rescinded. The Kindred who receives this boon has as long as she wishes to exercise it, though most vampires already have someone in mind for the Embrace when they go seeking the boon. Sometimes there is an observation period mandated by the prince, during which approval can be given or denied for a particular candidate for the Embrace. More often than not, however, the vampire with the mandate to create is on her own as regards her choice.

Why Create Childer?

While mortals are driven by biology to perpetuate the species, vampires don't have any such excuse. On a basic

Unlife During Wartime

In wartime situation, the restrictions on creation are often relaxed. With the Sabbat pounding on the door and casualties constantly mounting, the need for reinforcements sometimes overrides the demands of protocol.

CARE AND FEEDING

The Traditions state that a sire is responsible for his childer until he turns them loose as responsible "adults." Bringing up neonates can be a weighty task, especially for a vampire embroiled in simmering intrigues. Most sires teach the basics of vampiric existence — the clans, the Traditions, the Masquerade and the things that can or cannot kill a vampire — and then hopes that the neonate picks things up on her own. The Tremere and Nosferatu are notable exceptions, as their clan support structures mandate an intensive education of all new members for the good of all. Ventrue often plug their neonates into their roles, teaching them just enough to get along so they don't get any ideas about advancement.

A vampire who doesn't teach his childe properly runs a tremendous risk. All of the childe's actions while he is still "in training" are laid at the sire's doorstep; ignorance of the law is no excuse. Furthermore, even once a neonate is let go, if he demonstrates a profound ignorance of custom or habit, it reflects poorly on his sire. A loss of status is certain; if the neonate's ignorance becomes dangerous, more stringent penalties may apply.

level, it doesn't make sense to Embrace mortals. A new vampire is more competition for food, a hindrance during his education and, eventually, a potential rival. Furthermore, within the guidelines for creation established by the Camarilla, Embracing a mortal is expensive. The cost of the right of creation is a valuable boon or the forgiveness of a massive prestation debt; the permission to add to Caine's childer does not come cheap.

With all of these drawbacks, then, why do the vampires of the Camarilla continue to add to their ranks? There are several answers which combine to provide some justification for the act, but none is entirely satisfactory on its own.

First and foremost, the act of creating progeny gives a vampire an automatic ally (should he choose to impose the blood bond). Even in cases where the bond is not employed, odds are that the neonate will walk a long way with his sire before choosing his own path, giving the elder vampire support and someone to watch his back in the murderous intrigues of the Camarilla. Many childer do eventually grow to rival their sires, but that is a process of decades or centuries, and in the meanwhile the benefits of a reasonably loyal ally are incalculable. Some Kindred go so far as to create large broods of childer, bonding them and their childer in turn, but this practice is frowned upon by the rest of the sect; no one wants to see any one vampire build up too much of a personal power base, after all.

Second, creating a childe may be a matter of logistics. Kindred who have had their claws in a particular mortal industry for a hundred years may find that the business has expanded beyond their ability to manipulate effectively. In such cases, an assistant and protégé is required, and there are times when a ghoul just won't do (for example, if the vampire's control of that business is being actively challenged, or if the

business has opened a new division involving technology beyond the Kindred's comprehension). In similar fashion, older vampires sometimes realize that they're behind the times on matters like telecommunications, computers and so on, and Embrace mortals knowledgeable with such subjects to serve as tutors or subordinates. The problem with this practice is that such tech-specific Embracees tend to have a limited shelf life; within a few years of the Embrace their knowledge often becomes outdated, and they, in turn, become expendable.

There are even Embraces out of spite, or to deny an enemy a promising childe. Often one vampire will Embrace another Kindred's favorite mortal, wreaking havoc on long-laid plans and rendering the neonate useless to his former patron. While such maneuvers don't amount to that much in the Jyhad, they still provide pleasant moments of spite for the new sire; what worse punishment is there for an enemy than to see his prized pupil and would-be childe blood bound to someone else? Such Embraces do have their business side, though — by their very nature they disrupt other vampires' best-laid plans nicely.

Some vampires do Embrace mortals for less pragmatic reasons. Toreador in particular have a habit of trying to immortalize mortal beauty through vampirism, though other vampires grumble that they wish the Toreador paid more attention to their childer's personalities and less to their looks. On rare occasions, love does blossom between living and unliving souls; one possible outcome of this sort of romance is for the mortal partner to be Embraced. Such romances usually end unhappily, but that doesn't keep optimists from trying. Occasionally, outstanding mortals (again, the Toreador have made a particular hobby of this) are "rewarded" for their accomplishments with eternal life. Composers, scientists, artists, writers and others of this ilk are thus brought into the fold, willing or no.

And sometimes, just sometimes, a vampire succumbs to the overwhelming loneliness of her condition and Embraces a mortal whom she think might be sympathetic company through the centuries. Such moments of creation are usually poohpoohed or explained as something else by the embarrassed sire, but they happen more frequently than one might think.

WHAT GOES WRONG

The basics of the Embrace are simple. The would-be sire drains his potential childe of mortal blood, then allows some of his own to pass her lips. If all goes well, the victim soon awakens, ravenously hungry for blood. She has become one of the Kindred.

In real life (or the World of Darkness), though, nothing's that simple. There are complications and mistakes, errors and tragedies that make the process of turning a mortal into a vampire painfully complicated. Some of those problems can be planned for, some can't, and all make the creation of a childe an adventure.

The first, and most obvious complication comes when a mortal, for whatever reason, refuses the Embrace. While not common, this problem does occur, and it leaves the frustrated sire with any number of problems. The local prince may rule that the very attempt is enough to cancel the vampire's right to creation; the vampire is left with nothing to show for having expended his boon. More immediately, there's the question of a drained corpse with vampiric blood in its lips to deal with; police forensic procedure is certainly good enough to draw all sorts of interesting conclusions from that body of evidence. Finally, there's the question of the effect the frustrated Embrace has on the sire denied his progeny. Frenzy is always a possibility, and under the circumstances of a failed Embrace that loss of control might be disastrous for the Masquerade.

On a similar note, there is a small but significant percentage of neonates who suffer permanent psychological damage from the Embrace. The experience of dying and then being reborn through the blood is not a pleasant one, and any number of new vampires have been twisted by it. The observed effects vary, ranging from mild phobias to full-blown dementia. Oddly enough, Malkavian neonates seem largely immune to the mind-warping aspects of the Embrace itself; it is the members of the other clans that need to watch their childer's transitions carefully.

Less pressing, but with longer-term consequences, is the peril of doing too much damage to a potential childe before the Embrace. In theory, the new vampire's sire drains his blood through a single bite. In reality, things can get messy. If the victim resists, or the vampire gets particularly energetic in his feeding, permanent damage can be done to the neonate's cadaver before the Embrace. Unfortunately, this injury can become permanent and be carried across into unlife, resulting in a vampire who is eternally crippled and awakens every night with his wounds freshly reopened. Such an unlucky vampire is unlikely to be well-disposed toward his sire.

Once the new vampire awakens, there is the question of food. New Kindred are inevitably ravenous. This is understandable, as the only blood they have in their systems is that donated by their sires, who are usually loath to give up too much. As such, a neonate surges into her new existence in the midst of a hunger-driven frenzy, and will attack whatever source of blood is handy. A wise sire keeps something (or someone) handy for just such an occasion, but as always there are complications. When an Embrace is a spur-of-the-moment decision, there usually isn't a convenient food supply around, and that means the neonate is frenzying on the streets. On the other hand, particularly malevolent sires may indeed take care with the food they stockpile for their childer — friends, lovers and family members offered up for slaughter make an excellent means for alienating the new vampire from his former existence.

Battlefield Promotions

A significant percentage of off-the-cuff Embraces occur in the midst of firefights and other hazardous scenes. A favorite ghoul or human is mortally wounded in the fray, and the vampire has the choice of letting him die or Embracing him. Such Embraces are seen as more forgivable than the usual ruck and run of impromptu creations, and in such instances the sire often gets off with a relatively light (as compared to, say, being staked out for the sun) punishment.

Accidents

It would seem nearly impossible to Embrace someone by accident. After all, the process is a lengthy and involved one; few Kindred are so clumsy as to cut themselves accidentally and then somehow manage to spill that vitae in just the right place. Still, Caitiff come from somewhere, and there are more and more every night.

Most "accidental" Embraces are the products of pity or remorse. The scenario is a common one: Vampire feeds (often while in frenzy), kills his vessel, and, stricken by guilt or sorrow, attempts to make amends by bestowing immortality on his victim. Of course, the sire in these cases usually comes to his senses just as his childe is shuddering her way back to consciousness, and more often than not abandons his charge before she can fully awaken. The error is thus compounded; a ravenous neonate, unaware of the Masquerade, now wanders the streets while her sire cannot educate or protect her. To do so is to admit his violation of the Traditions, which brings with it the risk of destruction. The very laws of the Camarilla prevent it from protecting its wayward children, ironically placing the Masquerade at risk as well.

The vast majority of accidental Embraces are created by young vampires — 12th- or 13th-generation Kindred — or more powerful vampires who have only been under the Blood for a short while. Such inexperienced Kindred are rarely educated properly in the ways of creating progeny, and few take the threatened penalties seriously. As a result, they have an unfortunate habit of screwing up, then abandoning their mistakes to the streets. Such "mistakes" usually find a way to remove themselves from the vampiric community (through the offices of the scourge, if nothing else), but woe betide the sire of the Caitiff whose lineage gets traced. The punishments for unauthorized creation are real and do get levied with stern regularity.

Older and more powerful vampires occasionally create childer by accident as well. Unfair though it may be, such Kindred usually have enough favors tucked away, or are valuable enough allies for a prince to have that they can usually work some sort of deal to avoid the ultimate penalty.

Presentation

One of the most important customs of the modern Camarilla is that of presentation. When a vampire enters a city, she is obligated to present herself to the local prince and request his permission to reside in his domain, even temporarily. While the "permission" is almost always a formality (refusal on the part of a prince is a major event, and can even bring an archon calling to investigate the disruption of usual routine), the procedure itself is one of the backbones of the sect.

The primary purpose that presentation serves is that it allows a prince to see just who is in his city. Information has power, and this way the prince at least has the knowledge of who all of his subjects putatively are. Furthermore, the formal presentation, with its request for permission to remain, clearly reinforces the power dynamic between prince and subject; the process is designed to reinforce the prince's stature.

Conversely, a vampire who refuses to present himself to the prince sets himself up for the attentions of the scourge or sheriff as an interloper. Kindred who avoid the ritual greeting clearly don't want to be identified as being in the city (or are just too damn lazy to present themselves), and as such, probably deserve a visit from the city's law enforcement in any case to keep them in line.

PROCEDURALS

There is every chance that a vampire who is new to a city doesn't know who the prince is or where Elysium might be. (The fact that this ignorance might be remedied by a little research on the part of the character — it's always wise to check out the lay of the land before you travel — isn't worth worrying about.) Vampires who do know where to go and what to do before arriving in a new city generally take care of their obligations right away, presenting themselves to the local prince and, if they're wise, to the elders of their clans as well.

Those vampires who don't know where to go, however, have a slightly trickier process. They must hunt down other Kindred in the city and get the information on where to go and what to do — and do so before the local sheriff zeroes in on them. If the law finds an unpresented vampire, even one who's making a serious effort to learn where Elysium might be, then it can become open season on strangers. The sheriff might take pity on the newcomer and take him to the prince himself, or he might just take the opportunity to beat the hell out of the "criminal" instead.

If the newcomer is lucky and good, she finds out where she needs to go and lays low until the prince's next court at Elysium. At such a time, she makes a beeline for the court, in hopes of getting there without incident or interference from other Kindred (who may be waiting en route, looking for their last chance to pick off "fair game"). Should things go well, she is presented, granted permission to stay in the city, and leaves the prince's presence a resident of that locale. If it goes poorly, she may not get an audience or might be refused permission to stay. In that case, the vampire had best duck for cover or get out of town immediately. She can try again at the next Elysium, but surviving until then may be difficult.

REFUSING PERMISSION

While it's not common for a prince to refuse a new vampire the right to stay in a city, it is permissible. Some reasons for refusal include:

• Overcrowding;

• The postulant has a bad reputation elsewhere;

• A favor to another prince or elder, who wants the newcomer kept on the run;

• Evidence that the new Kindred supports one of the prince's rivals.

The actual process of presentation is short. The postulant gives her name to the seneschal, who announces her to the prince when the latter's agenda permits. The newcomer is then ushered into the prince's presence and formally presents herself, stating her name and clan and requesting permission to stay (or just visit) in the city. Often the prince asks about her business and lineage, with her answers assiduously taken down by the seneschal for later referencing. After that, if all goes according to plan, the prince recognizes the suitor and turns her loose on his city. From that point on, it's up to the individual vampire to make her way.

DESTRUCTION

Deep down, on some atavistic and predatory level, every vampire secretly wants to be the only one in existence. However, acting on this nagging little impulse tends to cause all sorts of problems with the Camarilla social order. As a result, the destruction of other vampires (at least those belonging to the sect) is strictly forbidden, save in the most exceptional and unusual of circumstances.

WITHIN THE SECT

Murder of other Camarilla vampires is one of the most severe crimes one of the Kindred can perform. A murderer of fellow vampires can expect to face Final Death in an extraordinarily painful manner if she is caught, both to punish her and to warn others against repeating her mistake. The stated reason for such draconian penalties is that killing a sectmate weakens the Camarilla's defenses against its enemies, which makes perfect sense. Kill a Camarilla vampire and you save the Sabbat the trouble of doing the same. Then again, there are other, unspoken reasons for the prohibition, most of which stem from the elders' fear of being overwhelmed by a tide of younger Kindred. By legislating so heavily against murder and by inculcating a loathing of the act in their childer, the elders work to keep themselves from becoming targets.

Kindred who murder other Camarilla vampires can expect little help from anyone besides their closest friends and allies. Enemies of the victim may offer some token assistance or protection, but most will be content to reap the benefits of the murder while allowing the actual murderer to take the fall. In the meantime, the prince and all his officers swoop down on the offender like avenging angels, making

GREASING THE SKIDS

Kindred who have supporters, sires or allies in a city find the process of presentation to be an easy one. Such vampires are escorted by their sires or patrons, and are usually recognized immediately. By doing so, the prince avoids angering the postulant's supporters. At the same time, the presence of said supporters indicates that the newcomer has a place waiting for him in the city. The latter is important, as it assures the prince that he's getting a reasonably responsible new subject, as opposed to an anarch or rabble-rouser who might well prove a threat.

punishment swift, deadly and public. Doing so is a necessity, otherwise the supporters of the victim may decide to take matters into their own hands and trigger a bloodbath. Such a feud can tear a city apart in a matter of nights, making the metropolis easy prey for the Camarilla's enemies.

OUTSIDE THE SECT

The rules about murder change when the putative victim isn't a member of the Camarilla. Sabbat vampires are fair game almost all of the time; the more dead Sabbat there are, the happier the Camarilla authorities are likely to be. Dealing with the independent clans is a bit trickier. While the Camarilla doesn't necessarily like the Setites, Ravnos, *et alia*, it does need to avoid alienating them to the extent that they become die-hard enemies. That means treading carefully around the independents, especially as regarding touchy subjects like murder and the like. A Camarilla vampire who decides to rid himself of a pesky Giovanni permanently had best be sure to hide all of the evidence — including the ghost of the deceased — or risk being turned over to those he has wronged as punishment should he be caught. On the other hand, if he's not caught, those in the know about his deed may well offer subtle congratulations, and even raise their estimation of the successful assassin.

WALKING THE BEAT

There are those Kindred whose titles put them in positions where they may well have to kill, and kill repeatedly. Scourges and sheriffs in particular face this situation. Scourges are often licensed to kill (as it were), armed with a mandate to remove a city's surplus population. Abuse of that privilege ("That was your childe, Your Majesty? I'll be hanged if he didn't look just like a Caitiff to me.") can get the scourge on the hit list himself, but most scourges are at least careful about when they overstep their bounds.

Sheriffs face a slightly different problem, as they're more likely to be confronted with kill-or-be-killed situations when observing breaches of the Masquerade or apprehending criminals. In those cases, if the sheriff can at least offer a solid explanation for why he felt it was necessary to bring the hammer down, he usually gets off scot-free. Many princes see paying attention to neonate claims of brutality by a sheriff as giving the rabble too much credence, and are more inclined to trust their appointees than they are to listen to the vampiric masses. So long as a sheriff (or scourge) picks his targets well and doesn't destroy someone with a powerful patron or protector, the odds are that he won't even be interfered with. A wise prince has someone watching both his scourge and his sheriff to keep an eye out for abuses, but both positions come with wide latitude when it comes to eliminating other Kindred.

BLOOD AND DIABLERIE

The main reason that most vampires get the urge to murder others is blood. Kindred vitae is more potent than that of mortals; it tastes better, is more satisfying and under certain circumstances can temporarily increase the powers of the vampire who drinks it. That's why the practice of murdering for

BLOODBATHS

Every so often, the pressure in a Camarilla city builds up to the point where the only possible escape valve is an explosion of violence. The combination of restrictive princes, powerful elders and excessive numbers of childer seems to be the perfect recipe for this sort of outbreak, which consumes both mortal and vampiric society in chaos and flame. Chicago in particular has been prone to these spasms of bloodshed, during which vampires make open war on the streets and the casualty lists run long. Usually the violence lasts for a week or so, during which time the prince and sheriff are too busy trying to clamp down on the city as a whole to prosecute individual murders. That doesn't mean that any acts committed during the rioting won't be prosecuted later, but in an odd way these outbreaks have a Mardi Gras-style feel of permissibility to them. A killing done among the frenzy of a Kindred-style riot is somehow more likely to be excused or let off lightly by a prince than a single premeditated act of homicide that disrupts a careful peace.

blood is even more severely frowned upon than the practice of murder itself; Kindred who get a taste for the hard stuff run the risk of becoming addicts and turning into serial cannibals.

Worst of all is the practice of diablerie. A diablerist (instantly identifiable by the black threads in his aura) can expect nothing less than Final Death if caught. A policy of benign neglect sometimes applies to the notion of diablerie on outsiders (if nothing else, it's tremendous motivation to get the youngsters hunting Sabbat vampires), but diablerie within the sect is forbidden. That doesn't mean that some Kindred don't try the act or even succeed at it, but they brand themselves with the evidence of the crime and run the risk of prosecution thereafter. A prince who catches a diablerist often makes a tremendous spectacle of the offender's death, which again serves as an object lesson for other Kindred who might have been getting ideas about supplementing their diets.

NIGHT COURT

The laws at the heart of Camarilla society are the Traditions. Everything else is variation or elaboration. However, some 4000 years of history and tradition carry their own weight, and when order is called in the courts of the Camarilla, 40 centuries are looking down on the sect's adherents.

Princes are traditionally charged with keeping the law in their cities, and until well into the Renaissance, many princes and warlords did just that. Absolute in their authority, the princes of the Kindred dispensed justice and punishment like King Solomon, or more often Hammurabi and Draco. Over the years, as cities grew larger and princes found themselves with more responsibilities, many princes farmed out some of the tasks of law enforcement to other officers, most often the sheriffs and keepers of Elysium. In these modern nights, sheriffs, keepers and some primogen

It Gets Worse

Implicit in punishment from one's sire is what some neonates call "Wait 'till your father gets home!" meaning, "Take your medicine from your sire and smile, because if he hands your ass to the prince, you'll really get it." Those caught by an officer of the city and handed over to the prince go right to "father," and it's all downhill from there. In such cases, the sire is also hauled up on the carpet at this time, and punished right alongside his errant fledgling. Needless to say, a sire punished thus is not going to be well-disposed toward his childe afterward.

(usually Ventrue) carry the burden of enforcing the laws that the prince decrees. In the higher echelons, the justicars are responsible for enforcing the laws of the Camarilla over the entire sect, assisted by any archons they choose.

Most Kindred laws specific to a particular city deal with circumstances and situations specific to that city. Such modifications to the Camarilla's basic legal code are meant primarily to keep the Masquerade and the peace (although sometimes there's very little difference between the two). Such laws are usually just variations on the Traditions, as they relate to conditions unique to the city. For example, the First Tradition is considered essentially inviolate, but a prince may further rule on contact between mortals and vampires, such as decreeing that a Kindred may walk among mortals so long as she does nothing that would mark her as unnatural, or that even casual contact between mortals and Kindred (beyond feeding) is out of bounds. In a sprawling city like Houston, the Second Tradition may be interpreted with regard to one's haven and the haven's environs to a one-block radius, while in crowded San Francisco, only the haven applies. In truth, princes have nearly *carte blanche* when it comes to creating legislation. Most justicars are unlikely to make an issue of examining the minutiae of every city's laws, so long as the Masquerade is enforced and things are otherwise running smoothly. Sheriffs and keepers are expected to be aware of changes in the local legal code and to pick them up without a change or disruption. Primogen are told to inform their clans regarding each law as it is made, and sires are expected to teach their childer.

If the Inner Circle decides to rule on a Tradition's interpretation, it expects that the decree will be obeyed, and it does not need to send around the justicars to make certain. In truth, most princes are too busy running their cities to worry about following the newest proclamation to the letter. Princes commonly do their best to implement the new rulings, but in these days, it's not uncommon to find a city that has chosen to ignore the proclamation due to extenuating circumstances.

Busted!

How exactly does a Kindred get caught *in flagrante?* Patrolling the streets is not included in a sheriff's job description, and even with a cadre of deputies, there's no way he and his posse can be everywhere. Law enforcement, therefore,

It Gets Worse

Implicit in punishment from one's sire is what some neonates call "Wait 'till your father gets home!" meaning, "Take your medicine from your sire and smile, because if he hands your ass to the prince, you'll really get it." Those caught by an officer of the city and handed over to the prince go right to "father," and it's all downhill from there. In such cases, the sire is also hauled up on the carpet at this time, and punished right alongside his errant fledgling. Needless to say, a sire punished thus is not going to be well-disposed toward his childe afterward.

often runs largely on tips from other Kindred in various stations. A keeper of Elysium may watch for violations of Elysium or the Masquerade in her purview, while the scourge tracks those violating Tradition and city law in the barrens, and the sheriff's deputies are informed to watch around them at all times. A few times, mortal television cameras or observant ghouls reading the newspaper have caught wind of Kindred law-breakers. A neonate who happens to look up at the right moment and see the crime may go to his primogen or elder with the information (which often results in the elder's taking credit for the tip-off.) The majority of arrests and seizures are based on tips to the sheriff or prince, often complete with set-ups to ensure the proper authorities catch the offender red-handed. When the Kindred in question is considered to be "troublesome" by the prince for whatever reason, the authorities can be inclined to utilize normally untrustworthy sources or even entrapment — anything to get the offender. There is no *habeas corpus* among the Kindred; the prince's law is absolute and how he chooses to enforce it is his business.

This is not to say that Kindred don't get away with crime — they often do. Those who do know exactly where the prince's purview stops, where they are likely to be unobserved, and what can be done under cover of shadows. They also often know what the sheriff's price is, or failing that, his weaknesses.

What happens to a Kindred caught breaking the law? That can vary greatly according to both the circumstances of the crime and when the errant one gets before the bench.

If the delinquent is lucky, his elder or sire catches him first and deals with him. Publicly, the sire does as much as possible to sweep the incident under the rug or at least soften the blow. A slap on the wrist and the proper hang-dog attitude can go a long way in Elysium. As the sire can be held responsible for his childe's actions, the less people are thinking about a wayward childe's actions, the less people are likely to turn on the sire. The prince will want to make certain that no breach of the Masquerade has been incurred, but is unlikely to make too great an issue of it. Behind closed doors, however, is a completely different scenario. The sire makes *very* certain that the childe understands what he did wrong, how much the sire did to clean up the mess, and how much the childe will have to do to repair the damage. A plethora of apologies and some groveling contrition is only the first step in the offender's rehabilitation. The sire may also demand that the childe perform certain acts of retribution or "ground" her, allowing her out only to hunt and then only if she is in the sire's company. More severe discipline, often involving physical punishments (such as breaking every bone in the offender's hand every night for a week) or private humiliation, is also common, particularly if the sire in question is well-distanced from his fading Humanity. If the childe treats the matter like a lark and shows no contrition (indeed, if she acts like her only mistake was to be caught), the sire is perfectly within his rights to punish her even more severely.

Trials depend entirely on the whim of the prince and precedent; there is nothing in the Traditions or laws that gives an

Shysters

Shakespeare might have advocated killing all the lawyers, but a lot of the most infamous shysters end up in the Camarilla's considerable system. Public defenders are often selected as potential childer by Brujah, entertainment and copyright lawyers find their ways into the Toreador, and corporate lawyers and district attorneys are chosen by Ventrue. Once inside, these advocates often pick up right where they left off, learning as much as they can about the Camarilla's laws, the ins and outs of a given city's body of law, and every imaginable loophole in the Traditions. Often, those who are very serious about further study learn with the law-givers of old, from Greek solons to Enlightened thinkers and even a select few "modern" lawmen (rumored to include such luminaries as Daniel Webster and William Jennings Bryan). Some who have taken study at the Academie in Lichtenstein recall nights spent honing debating skills under the watchful eyes of former Roman consuls and Sanhedrin members. Graduates of the Virginian reminisce about the time that Clarence Darrow, fresh from the Scopes trial, was brought in for a guest lecture (whereupon his mind was wiped of the encounter by the school's president).

Those legal eagles who served as defenders in life often continue their crusades during their unlives as well, offering their services to those Kindred who have no recourse or at the behest of the Kindred's clan. As in life, those who work as solicitors can command exorbitant fees for their help, and a clan can be faced with the choice of acquiring a lawyer for their clanmate and thereby practically selling themselves into slavery, or hoping the clanmate can help herself. Self-proclaimed "public defenders" are rare, but finding one is the greatest good luck a desperate Kindred might have. Many times, the defenders are known only through word of mouth and the occasional tattered business card that has been carefully passed from hand to hand. Chances are that these advocates work the courts for the rush of victory rather than money. One Toreador lawyer described closing-statement oration to be an art form no less beautiful or awe-inspiring than painting a portrait, while a Brujah attorney claimed the thrill of victory to be better than any vitae he'd ever drunk. While these advocates rarely request money — most of their clients are indigent with equally indigent clanmates — a wise Kindred finds some way to express her "gratitude." Commensurate boons (major or life), loans of Influences, assistance, information, heirlooms, blood dolls, the teaching of new Disciplines or Abilities, even service — all have been offered as payment at one time or another.

accused any sort of rights. A prince may decide to let the accused languish in an oubliette, and none could gainsay his choice. Traditionally, the prince, with the primogen counseling, acts as judge. The clan of the accused may levy for an elder outside the city or even an archon to preside, if the clan carries sufficient clout, the crime is sufficiently serious (anything which might end in Final Death as punishment is deemed sufficiently serious), and enough doubt is engendered regarding the prince's capacity for judgment. The last is a tricky gamble; accusations of incompetence can spiral off into completely separate quarrels, while prejudice is very difficult to prove. Some modern Kindred attempt to call in the "pre-trial publicity" gambit, but these are usually laughed out of Elysium. All offenders are deemed guilty until proven innocent, with the burden of proof on the accused. The guilty one is usually expected to defend herself, unless she or someone in her clan can procure a Kindred willing to act as her advocate. If the prince is not sitting the bench, then she and her keeper of Elysium may be acting as prosecution.

When vampires have the ability to mold the minds of others or create illusions of events, digging out the truth can be difficult. A person on the stand or her defender may request that her aura be examined during questioning, or that her memories be searched for evidence of a block or tampering. If it becomes evident that the accused is telling the truth (as she believes it, regardless of whether or not it is actually true), circumstances demand that she be allowed to have the block examined. Unfortunately, the most skilled at such activities tend to be Tremere and Malkavians, and even the threat of death may not be enough to persuade the accused to allow either clan into her thoughts. Those who search the minds of witnesses are ordered to swear that they will not interfere or tamper with anything else, but there have been incidents where other information was extracted during the investigation or the block being examined was merely tamped down even further and more seamlessly.

A prince may attempt to place an offending elder on trial, but many elders sneer at a prince's authority, refusing to appear in court and sending the sheriff back in several boxes for the temerity of such a demand. In such cases, a prince may appeal to a justicar for assistance, whereupon the justicar determines if the charges merit a conclave. If they do, the justicar calls for a small conclave for the purposes of a trial, usually holding it in the city concerned. Such a meeting is not as widely announced and advertised as a regular conclave, being reserved specifically for trial purposes and not intended for any other business. The elder may choose to have an assistant help her with defense; otherwise, she's on her own. When a prince breaks the law, the matter is considered one for the conclave, no questions asked. Princes are expected to be the bulwarks of the Camarilla in the cities, and one who shows disregard for the law needs to be made a very public example. Those who have broken the Traditions in some widespread, spectacular fashion that affects a region or nation are also placed on trial at conclave. Trials meant for conclaves may be held in reserve to wait for one of the annual ones, or may be called within the city strictly for trial purposes with little other business.

As per the Fourth Tradition, a childe's sire is punished if the childe breaks the law. Most punishments of this sort are usually very public and visible, a firsthand look for the childe at what will happen to her and a visceral reminder of the change in her circumstances. The impetus is on the sire to raise and guide his childe appropriately so this sort of thing doesn't happen. Chances are, if the sire survives his punishment, the childe *will* learn her lesson if she hasn't already. The sheriff and prince usually handle these breaches within the city.

When on trial, an accused can usually expect to sit quietly (sometimes gagged or Dominated into silence), listen to the accusations thrown at her as fact, and then respond to them as best she may. If she has legal assistance, the lawyer may call witnesses or request that her client's memories be examined for tampering. Some primogen have been known to needle at certain issues on their clanmate's behalf, long enough to plant seeds of doubt in the other primogen's (and sometimes the prince's) minds. A prince may, however, by right of her station, deny the offender any chance to speak and pass sentence at once. Those on trial at a conclave are of sufficiently high station to garner themselves some chance to speak, and they do not waste it. A moving oration has been known to save many a prince from a midnight pyre or the next sunrise, although how she will face her city later is another matter.

Trials can be nightmarish affairs on many levels. For the accused, it means enduring slander, the scorn of peers, having one's memories rifled through, and the real threat of Final Death in as painful a method as possible. Is it any wonder, then, that all the stops are pulled out as things grow more desperate? During this time, the Kindred on the stand learns exactly who her worst enemies and greatest friends are. Clanmates and friends may dig themselves into extraordinary debt through bribing and favor-currying with the prince or primogen body to be allowed to speak on the defendant's behalf, while trying to outbid the enemies who wish to ensure that they do not have the chance to do so. The Kindred's primogen may call upon years of prestation debt to ensure a more reasonable outcome of events. Officers who are clanmates or friends are often torn in several different directions, instructed not to "abuse" their authority by the prince, wanting to help a friend in trouble with information granted by their position, and often having their persistence threatened by higher powers. Not a few Kindred can recall crucial pieces of evidence suddenly going missing due to a prestation debt called in or a witness who "took a trip" down into the sewers at the wrong time.

Paying the Price

Punishments in Kindred society are very public, and meant to drive home a message about the wheels of justice and the Camarilla's willingness to use any means to keep order. Most punishments given by princes and archons can be divided into the social, the physical and the creative; what the sires and clan leaders choose to do privately with their offenders is up to them entirely.

Social punishments are the sort most often inflicted on sires whose unreleased childer have offended, and on those whose crimes are not serious enough to warrant physical punishment. Such crimes include a bad judgment call in dealing with a mortal or another Kindred who was likewise in the wrong, or failing to follow proper etiquette in dealings with other Kindred. The criminal can expect to be called on the carpet in Elysium and embarrassed before all and sundry. The harpies usually strip him of part or all of his reputation, and may even go to work spreading word of his foolishness as punishment. Any city positions he held he must relinquish immediately to his second. He can expect to be left off guests lists for a long while and generally ignored and snubbed, all the while being watched like a hawk for his next such slip. Socially oriented clans, such as Toreador and Ventrue, fear such punishments dreadfully.

Physical punishments call to mind the old methods of marking criminals — cutting off hands, branding, scarring, flogging and the like. These tend to be reserved for anarchs (if those offenders aren't killed outright) and clans like the Brujah, although a prince may choose to levy this sort of penalty against any she chooses. To ensure the visibility of the punishment, the offender may not grow back the missing body part for a specified amount of time, or must return every night to have the brand reapplied, or some such. Those who attempt to dodge their punishments or who ignore them are often subject to the blood hunt, as they've proven themselves to be incorrigibly recalcitrant, and thus not worth saving.

The creative punishments are the ones that make any Kindred with half a brain cringe. This could be anything from giving the offender over the clan he wronged (fatal in the case of Brujah and Tremere, terrifying in the case of Malkavians) to sending him on a Diogenes-like quest. Creative punishments can produce some… interesting results. One unruly Brujah, ordered to clean his elder's library and work through a reading list in response to some bad behavior in another's domain, discovered he actually liked reading many of the classics he'd been given, and was last seen attempting to track down Kindred who were mortal contemporaries of Jonathan Swift. Usually, however, "creative punishment" is semantically equivalent to "creative torment;" few princes are as interested in rehabilitation as they are in emphasizing their authority and extracting vengeance.

Those tried at conclave face far more serious punishment in accordance with their crimes. The accused, however, is not without options. She may challenge the ruling by requesting an ordeal, created for her by the justicar. An ordeal may be quite literally any exacting task imagined, mandated with a specific time limit for completion. If the accused does not complete her assigned task to the justicar's satisfaction, she must accept his sentence. Should the crime be considered too heinous to allow the offender an ordeal, she may challenge one of her accusers to ritual combat. Like the ordeals, a trial by combat can include practically any bizarre detail, from blindfolds to forbiddance of weapons or Disciplines. Many times, though, these combats are stacked from the beginning, and the accused sees the option as a way to die on his feet rather than on his knees. (If he gets lucky, he might even get to take out one of the Kindred who screwed him over in the process.)

On the rare occasion that a defendant has bested his accuser, his sentence is usually reduced. The reduction itself is not always great, and most times clemency simply means death instead of exile. Even victory in a trial by combat is not a sure route to escape, however; there are plenty of stories of victorious combatants who were killed anyway because the spectacle of the bloody combat whipped the crowd into frenzy.

THE CONCLAVE

The conclave is the greatest event in vampire politics to which every vampire can be privy. It serves as the highest court of Camarilla Kindred, as the legislative body which chooses the Camarilla's direction and considers the sect's place in both mortal and vampire societies, and as a stage on which to reaffirm the principles of the Camarilla. For the elders, it is a salon without peer, an opportunity to meet others of their station, socialize and deal with them without constant interruptions from the "children." For the ancillae and neonates, it is a social scene to meet clanmates and friends, a place to swap gossip and (if one has the courage) to venture into the world of vampire politics on a grand scale. Conclave is also one of the few perks that continues to keep many young vampires from defecting to the anarchs and Sabbat, or simply abandoning the Camarilla altogether, as it is a time when the young may speak directly to the elders and

have a chance of being heard, as well as being an opportunity to vote on the direction that the Camarilla takes

Normally, only Camarilla Kindred who hear the call to conclave are welcome to attend; however, some friendly independents are welcomed as well, since the conclave's business can relate to the Kindred as a whole. The announcement of an impending conclave is typically made in Elysium, with the news

COMMON ORDEALS

- Withstanding sunlight or flame for a pre-ordained time.
- Feats of strength, such as withstanding a weighted press.
- Going without feeding for a pre-ordained time; if the accused frenzies at any point during the ordeal, he fails.
- Walking a gauntlet of other Kindred who are free to insult or attack the accused. If the accused responds in any way, she fails.
- Finding something (such as a scrap of the *Book of Nod* or a star sapphire) for the justicar within a pre-ordained time limit.
- Sitting in vigil for a day without falling asleep or otherwise breaking concentration.

Ordeals are a serious business, and their creation is not something justicars take lightly. Any Kindred suggesting a frivolous or obviously impossible ordeal may find himself serving as a guinea pig instead.

carried back to absentees via childer and coterie mates. Only a justicar may call for a conclave; with a few notable exceptions (such as the former Gangrel justicar's septennial New Orleans party), they are rare and erratic events. The logistics involved with running one of these gatherings do not make it a thing to be announced on a whim; by the same token, canceling a conclave is only done under the greatest duress. Because so many of the attendees are frequently elders and other potent-blooded luminaries, the location of the gathering is often kept secret for as long as possible, even as the conclave's organizers try to keep in mind the travel times and needs of those who may be coming from a great distance.

Justicars only call conclaves to deal with dire circumstances — individuals or situations that threaten or regard the Camarilla as a whole. The logistics of travel, accommodations and the Masquerade make this a requirement. In addition, a conclave frequently makes rulings regarding the Traditions, taking the opportunity that having such an assembly to discuss issues presents. At the annual conclave of '94, the matter of the Internet was discussed with regard to the Masquerade, along with the Second Tradition as it related to Web sites. A number of elders saw an advantage in including the great many attending neonates and ancillae who were more versed in the technology in the discussion; certain of the younger Ventrue acquired tremendous prestige as a result of their performances.

Some conclaves are called as trials of powerful Kindred, to contain destructive quarrels between elder Kindred or to depose corrupt princes, such as the Minneapolis Conclave of 1887 when the despotic Prince Cyril Ximenes was brought to trial for his unrealistic demands regarding the Masquerade and even more outrageous means of enforcing such.

Not all who attend conclave are strictly regarding business, though — many vampires attend conclave in order to meet others of their clan and sect, both for business and pleasure. The hustle and bustle of a conclave with so many vampires in attendance makes it an ideal place to meet contacts for back-room deals, or for groups of elders to gather for meetings that do not look any more suspicious than their usual social soirees.

For young vampires, the conclave is one of the few benefits that Camarilla membership can offer. The opportunities to socialize and network at a conclave can boggle the mind, and for a number of neonates, this becomes their first look at the much greater world to which they belong. Not a few sires bring their childer here to introduce them to more of the clan, perhaps grandsires and great-grandsires, or to give them a firsthand lesson in the political structure of the Camarilla. Young vampires may speak in assembly and voice their opinions, and a well-spoken neonate with a sharp mind can impress potential mentors while buttressing her own sire's reputation. The young ones may vote, and by this believe that they have some small amount of control over their destiny in a society that limits their benefits according to their vampiric age. Most ancillae and elders agree that by these small things (and they are small indeed by comparison to the larger scope of vampiric society) the young ones are kept a little more content, are made less likely to start another Anarch Revolt, and may be carefully guided into becoming the next generations to carry on tradition (and Tradition).

Making Arrangements

For as quickly as they can be called, conclaves can be logistical nightmares for even the most experienced hosts. Few vampires attending rarely have any idea of the scrambling that went on behind the scenes to reach the point wherein the conclave is actually a working event.

Security

When a justicar calls for conclave, he usually publicly announces the location a month before the event proper. Princes and harpies in cities around the nation often have news of the event before it is officially named, but announcing things before the justicar does so rouses righteous ire, both for the breach in protocol and because of the potential for alerting enemies. This is primarily due to concerns regarding Sabbat and anarch attacks — the less time the enemy has to prepare, the less likely they are to mount anything organized enough to succeed. The news of a conclave is typically given first in Elysium and spread along the lines of gossip (of which there are many in any city). Those who might not attend Elysium can still receive the news from friends, clanmates and childer, and only the most isolated Kindred (or demented Malkavians) are unlikely to hear the call. In years when the Sabbat have been excessively active, double bluffs regarding location are not uncommon, but this can be tricky and dangerous for those attendees who miss the latest news (along with the Sabbat packs) and end up walking into a large-scale trap as a result. One such disaster occurred in 1957 when a conclave was called for Rotterdam, then revealed to be taking place in Brussels a little too late and a little too secretly for a collection of visiting American elders. These unfortunate tourists learned too late that the Sabbat in Europe are just as vicious as their American counterparts, and that they don't take well to being tricked.

Some have debated (under the guise of security concerns) changing tradition so that only those invited may attend conclave. This notion has been vetoed as often as it has come up, primarily because tradition demands that any who hear the call may attend (and changing tradition is considered to be slightly easier than stopping Niagara Falls), and secondly because of the concerns over putting out enough invitations. Someone would be forgotten, insults would be perceived, and things would inevitably and rapidly deteriorate from there. Those who support the younger vampires also fear that the conclaves would lose some of their liveliness without the young ones' debating and partying. If nothing else, the parties and clan meetings assure the elders that the "children" are kept constructively busy.

In the modern nights, security at conclaves has become steadily tighter in every way possible. With the Sabbat's attacks becoming more frenzied, and more outside threats to worry about, the Camarilla is naturally concerned about the potential for catastrophe so inherent in having so many potent-blooded elders sitting in one place. Not a few like-minded Kindred have made jokes about this, ranging from "Ground Zero" to "the meat market" to "accident waiting to happen." Such jokes are not spoken too loudly when a city is in conclave. A sheriff in a city neighboring one hosting conclave heard a group of neonates making similar remarks, and decided to take no chances; the group was staked and put in storage until conclave had passed without incident.

The head of security detail is often hand-picked by the justicar who calls for the conclave. The individual thus chosen may be an archon, an elder or the sheriff of the hosting city. She is responsible for making certain that the wrong people don't get in, that those people who are in don't cause trouble and that everything runs safely and without incident from Sabbat, anarchs, Lupines or anyone else. Running security can be one of the most important tasks of conclave, and the justicar chooses carefully, well-aware that the deaths of dozens of high-ranking elders will look bad on even her record. Those who have served previously as security tell stories that border on grim comedies of errors about trying to contain a threat without breaking the Masquerade or alerting those within as to the bubbling crisis.

A chief of security may choose deputies to assist him, usually selecting to have a broad range of skills at his disposal. Multi-talented individuals are more likely to be picked than "one-hit wonders"; a Brujah who can fight decently and who has a good grasp of Kindred society while being an excellent investigator is considered a much better choice than one whose greatest and only talent is hitting things and making them fall down. A wise chief also chooses from several different clans to avoid too much conflict over "persecution." People are more disposed to obey a request from those like them, and a Malkavian can make a clanmate understand that his ravings are attracting too much attention in a way that a Tremere or Gangrel never could. Security chiefs recruit from both their own towns and across their networks of contacts in various cities, dependent on the circumstances of the conclave. If the conclave is strictly for trial purposes in the city, the chief chooses only locals, but a national or international conclave requires a more diverse palette. Many times, security procures the services of a harpy to assist with certain matters of etiquette to ensure that things go quietly.

Security has considerable clout due to the immense danger that surrounds a conclave. They have the right to detain nearly anyone who is causing a disturbance or who is threatening the proceedings. Many justicars grant security license to use deadly force against any enemies of the conclave, which can include anarchs, Sabbat, Lupines, any other supernatural threats and even overly rambunctious young Camarilla Kindred. Security's powers are occasionally stymied by the elders, but if the chief has a legitimate concern and voices it to the hosting justicar, he can expect that the grievance will be addressed and dealt with. Often, the prince loans security the use of certain of his powers, such as contacts in the police force and city administration, to assist during the conclave.

During these nights, younger vampires have brought security up to date from the days when a couple of burly Brujah with swords stood guard at the door with the Tremere reading auras. Discreetly placed metal detectors, heat sensors, infrared cameras and closed-circuit cameras are stock in trade now for any security director worth his salt. While the elders are disturbed by such technological toys, they find it difficult to argue their effectiveness in keeping out weapons and hunters. Some have grumbled that these devices place the elders at the mercy of their younger counterparts, but a few princes have actually told the more paranoid ones to stay home if they don't like the electronics. Such measures have the harpies scrambling to figure out the new ramifications and matters of etiquette, such as the propriety of asking an elder to submit to a wand search after he's set off one of the threshold detectors or where to place certain cameras.

TRAVEL

Vampires traveling to conclave come by literally every means available to them. Those still able to mingle with mortal society may fly in coach class, take trains, book passage on ocean liners (a frequent means of travel for European

A COMEDY OF ERRORS

One such tale is told by Allen Two-Timer, a Gangrel from Milwaukee, regarding a conclave in that city in 1932. The hotel chosen to host one of the conclave's sessions had also been chosen by a collective of rumrunners to discuss their business and sample a few wares. The barrels of rotgut and an elder's private vintage became confused on the loading docks, and were only discovered after Allen licked some leaking vintage off his hand that turned out to be bathtub gin. Realizing the error, he dispatched two deputies to retrieve the missing vitae while he stalled the session. The deputies, both Brujah, recall going through several different ideas, including disguising themselves as waiters, bum-rushing the door and setting off a fire alarm. Finally, the deputies decided to tip off their police contacts to arrest the rumrunners, and walked themselves into the fray and out with the necessary casks. While the elder was very perturbed about the delay and gave Allen a proper tongue-lashing, none except Allen and the deputies were the wiser about the near-miss to the Masquerade. Furthermore, three of the rumrunners who proved particularly resistant to arrest later ended up working for Allen, and one eventually became his childe.

elders who have never quite adjusted to planes), drive or even hitchhike on occasion. Packs of Brujah and Gangrel arriving on motorcycles can make the highways look like biker conventions, while well-preserved vintage autos and limousines ferry Ventrue and Toreador. Malkavians may carjack their transportation, Dominate unfortunate mortals into hauling them, or simply take Greyhound buses (which offer the added bonus of allowing them to frighten their fellow passengers).

Those with special travel needs (such as largely inhuman Kindred, monstrous Gangrel, some Nosferatu) need to plan a little more thoroughly. Many Gangrel choose to travel in mist or animal form to spare themselves the worry about commingling with mortals. Nosferatu and other Kindred who cannot travel by conventional means arrange to have themselves shipped to their destination and having retainers meet their boxes at the docks to prevent any accidental openings. A keeper of Elysium in a conclave city can find herself signing for a great many large packages during the nights just prior to the first meetings.

Retainers can be invaluable during travel, always a difficult proposition at best and often more so during a conclave. A ghoul can see to securing ground transportation after a flight, or lead her morning-groggy companion out of the sun while ushering her to a limo or taxi. Other ghouls pack their masters into boxes to be shipped and meet them on the loading docks. Competent ghouled limo drivers are worth their weight in gold, while a single mortal or ghouled com-

panion who can take daylight shifts of driving can be invaluable for those who need to use less luxurious means of travel.

Accomodations

The amount of time a city has to prepare for conclave varies according to the kind of event planned. A small conclave called for a trial or regarding a single city is usually announced only a month or so in advance. Since the event is concerned with a smaller audience, it needs less preparation. On the other hand, a regional, national or international conclave that is intended as one of the annual events is usually announced to the public approximately three to four months before the conclave's opening date. A select few in the city, however, have most likely learned the date at least six months before. Some even claim that annual conclave sites are chosen a full three years in advance to allow the prince time to have new hotels built and ensure that there are no conflicting mortal events on the calendar. The hosts of annual conclaves usually inform the prince themselves via formal letter, which requires an equally formal reply. Smaller events receive notice via an archon's visit, which heralds the justicar's arrival. It is an honor for a prince's city to be chosen for conclave, as it reflects the prince's work in keeping the peace and defending against enemies like the Sabbat. Cities under siege or at war are too busy with other concerns to host a conclave, besides being terribly unsafe.

It might seem ideal to host conclave in a city already bustling with other mortal events. After all, the feeding supply is ample, there are enough strangers in town that suspicions cannot be roused by a few more, and another event in an busy town won't attract the attention of hunters or other enemies. However, in a town cramped for living space, such quarters can rapidly become too close. A city's resources become strained to the limit, and the prince of the hosting city is the one who feels the pinch later. Should a mortal visitor or two go missing, the hosting city's tourism and commerce suffers. If one is looking for protective camouflage, a careful balance must be struck between too many mortals and not enough.

A prince who's just been informed that his city is about play host to the world promptly goes into a flurry of activity. Hotels are evaluated for such things as defensibility, staff and room quality with regard to lightproofing (as well as pliability of staff). On occasion, those with influence in the chamber of commerce and tourism industries are requested to have new hotels built. The problem of feeding so many vampires is scrutinized, particularly with consideration of the number of Kindred entering the city and straining resources. Current safety and security are put under the microscope, with troublemakers either put on ice or bribed to stay out of the way. Much in the same way that a city's chamber of commerce puts together a sheet for mortal conventioneers, so does the prince's staff (the keeper of Elysium and sheriff) inform the prince of the city's resources so that he may inform the justicar.

It is rare, but some cities do refuse the honor of hosting conclave. The concern most often cited is sheer numbers. If the city cannot safely support so many visiting vampires' feeding habits without risking the Masquerade, the justicars — who are the bastions of the Traditions — often accept the explanation. Lupine and Sabbat incursions or otherwise compromised security is another troubling matter. If a justicar believes that the prince is refusing on the grounds that there is some potentially dangerous (and illegal) business afoot, however, he may choose to investigate the refusal personally. If the excuses of Lupines and feeding problems show themselves to be without substance, the justicar may then rephrase his request as a command. After all, nothing is out of order for hosting a conclave — why should the prince continue to balk? The prince now has the unpleasant choice of either refusing the command (and thus putting himself and his city hard under suspicion) or allowing the conclave to take place, swallowing whatever happens and finding new living arrangements afterward.

Robert's Rules of Order

Conclave follows a very specific order, based on ancient judicial and monarchical court systems, with Greek democracy, modern developments and vampiric tradition grafted onto the existing frame. The result is a somewhat staid and slow, but effective, administration in action. Those who were members of legislative bodies in life often claim that they feel quite at home in the midst of conclave. As a general rule, vampires are reminded that conclave is to be treated like Elysium, with all the privileges and responsibilities therein.

Seating is traditionally based on age, with the gathered harpies assigned to monitor the proceedings. Clans, especially the Nosferatu and Gangrel, find strength in numbers and arrange themselves as a clan, grabbing a block of seats and filling as members arrive. The youngest vampires are seated in the "cheap seats," which usually have a terrible view of proceedings and make it difficult for the neonates to be seen and heard (which is how many elders claim they like it). Coteries do their best to stay together, but one that has mixed ages may find itself being broken up due to the age-related seating. The only time a younger vampire may be seated with an older one is if she is being escorted by an elder or is herself a particularly noteworthy ancillae, and then she had better be on her best behavior. Neonates and ancillae fill in the "second tier" seating, and a younger vampire is expected to give way to an older one if a seat is in contention. Fighting over a chair is not viewed with humor, and the disagreeing parties are likely to be barred from the session for such bad behavior. Guests — such as ancillae and neonates making presentations — are usually seated near the elders, but not too closely, lest someone take offense. Elders and archons typically sit in front with the best view of the proceedings. The hosting justicar and any others of his standing usually face the assembly, seated and perhaps behind a long table. Ghouls are almost never permitted in during assembly, and never during a trial except for reasons of security or testimony.

For a young vampire, entering conclave session without an experienced guide can be a nerve-wracking experience. Sitting in the section reserved for the elders can be potentially fatal if a touchy elder takes great offense at the mistake, while the harpies

Running Conclaves

Having read about conclaves, you find the idea intriguing. Wouldn't it be neat to introduce your young players to a world far vaster than they realized? And now that you've thought about that, you think about the logistics and shudder. How are you going to Storytell this unwieldy thing? How are you going to keep perhaps 300 or more vampires straight? What if everyone decides to ignore the major event and thinks it's just a party?

First of all — relax! Running a conclave can be a challenge, but it need not be the one that breaks you. The keys to running a successful in-game conclave are organization, opportunity and atmosphere. Grab your notebook or sit down at the computer and start putting thoughts together.

Who's calling this conclave, and more importantly why? The matters at hand will have a considerable impact on the theme and mood of your story. Who's coming to this event? What clans will be represented? Sketch out who your biggest movers and shakers will be from the top down; they won't all be elders and justicars. Will there be a few starry-eyed neonates gawking at all the powerful vampires? Will there be a would-be anarch trying to rally the youth around his banner by pointing out that they're not invited to the councils? Will there be a few ancillae who are quite powerful (such as regents or lieutenants), but who are still treated snippily as "children"? Will there be spies and infiltrators from the independent clans, anarchs and Sabbat? You don't have to detail *everyone*, but at least have some ideas what the characters can expect of those of their clans who attend.

Consider how deeply your players are getting into the scene. Are they planning on sitting in on the sessions? Are they working security detail? Are they simply there for the party? Find out what your players' characters plans are before you go too far into crafting. What sorts of things will they gravitate toward and what will they ignore? It makes little sense to put *all* the best clues and fun things into events and scenes the characters are unlikely to attend. Just because they miss the major event doesn't mean that they won't be in the thick of things, though; the news will find ways to filter into party conversations, security briefings or simply talking with clanmates. Also, don't plan on getting through this in one night, unless the conclave was called for a very specific sitting (such as a single trial). If your players are going in 50 directions, and you're doing this with a single friend or by yourself, you will go batty and end up glossing over too much. Plan out a fairly specific time table (such as three sessions) and when it's over, it's over;

there's enough going on at a major conclave that could easily fuel several months' worth of sessions.

Be assured, you will need to wear a *lot* of hats if you're Storytelling this by your lonesome. There will be vampires trying to talk on the floor, vampires coming through the metal detectors, vampires hosting some killer room parties — plus ghouls, plus Sabbat infiltrators and any other things you feel like throwing in. Here is one time you will probably not want to struggle through this on your own. Draft a Narrator or a couple of outside players to help with roleplaying work. This option leaves you free to run the major points of the story while those characters who chose to do something else have an option besides sitting on their thumbs. You may even want to consider recruiting your players to do double-duty (if someone's character is sitting in session — and temporarily out of play — have him play the rakehell Toreador that another character is encountering at a party). If you're considering having your players do double-duty, take into consideration what information you're giving the secondary characters; if your players can be weasely about where they acquired their information, be careful about which parts are given out. Give your helpers a thorough write-up on their new personas, including goals and motives, and a little time to read it over and ask any quick questions before throwing them into play.

So why go through all this work for a conclave? What's it worth to the players? Quite a lot, if it's presented properly. Chances are very good that your characters have never been out of their city governments or very far afield, and the opportunity to meet others of their clan who are not the same old faces may give them a new perspective on the scope and breadth of vampire society. It's a great place to plant seeds for new stories with new acquaintances and enemies made or old ones renewed. Maybe the characters learn of matters that will soon be arriving in a plot, such as a hunted criminal or the mysterious Eastern vampires. Seeing a Kindred on trial firsthand may bank the fire of a would-be anarch's runaway enthusiasm (which has been disrupting the game) or inflame a staid conservative out of his complacent belief that the people upstairs know what's best for everyone. If you want to get your vampires a little more experienced in the ways of the world, a conclave gives them the opportunity to meet almost *anyone*. A character who has a run-in with a Setite at conclave will remember his kind when they come calling in his city, while another seeking information must learn to play diplomat when she goes to visit an elder who may be able to help — for a price.

watch and make catty comments without offering much help. Most often, a lone vampire who wishes to ensure she makes no howling gaffes watches others seat themselves first and follows their example, taking note of any sidelong looks or facial expressions to gauge her progress. Certainly, any blunders made come back to haunt the young one later in the form of harpy barbs, or perhaps in unwelcome attention from elders in and out of clan.

Mistakes in seating and sundry other etiquette sound like trivial offenses, and not a few ancillae and neonates find the matter utterly ridiculous in relation to the business of conclave itself. Others point out that the conclave and Elysium are events in Kindred society that have true pedigrees, and that these procedures carry the weight of tradition with them. As Elysium has so mutated over the years until it is only somewhat recognizable as a descendant of its original form, there is a sense that at least the conclave must be preserved as closely as possible to its old form. Not a few elders impress on their childer and grandchilder that a conclave is truly like living history. When one considers that a vampire might meet his ancestral line up to the clan's founders, debate in session or clan meetings with brethren Embraced before his mortal great-grandparents were born, or encounter luminaries from history, the notion gains credibility.

The hosting justicar opens proceedings and addresses the assembly, informing them of the business at hand and what must be accomplished at conclave. Any vampires who wish to speak may do so, provided that at least two other members of the assembly support them. This is perhaps the strongest reason for clans and coteries to sit together, as it provides any would-be speaker with supporters at hand; on the other hand, it can easily become a monumental embarrassment if no one chooses to recognize the speaker (and harpies do note those elders and ancillae who have been so snubbed by their peers; neonates so embarrassed are usually let off lightly with just the experience itself as their punishment). That even young vampires may address the conclave (if they have the courage and support to do so) is something that many Camarilla advocates have fought fang and talon to keep; the perks for the young ones are few enough, and those elders who think to take such away from the "children" may risk those children turning their backs on the Camarilla and siding with the anarchs or Sabbat.

Speakers are expected to talk in a reasonable tone and not interrupt one another. An elder may occasionally override a young one, though, and few argue the matter. Arguments may become passionate, but violence is not tolerated. When fisticuffs (or worse) break out, the head of security himself usually arrives to escort the combatants outside or to the brig and waiting stakes. If someone takes passionate offense to a speaker's remarks and the argument is not a productive rebuttal, the two are requested to table any arguments for later or remove themselves from proceedings. Occasionally duels have been fought between Kindred whose disagreements started in conclave session.

Disruptions are not looked on kindly. When the doors to the chambers are closed and business gets underway, the secu-rity chief usually finds a good seat that allows him to monitor the entirety of the proceedings. At the first signs of a scuffle, argument or other potential interruption, the chief immediately inserts himself into the matter to ensure that things are either cooled down without incident or the combatants are shown the way to the door. Hecklers are another matter. A heckler who is annoying everyone in general is bounced without mercy, while a heckler who is playing Devil's Advocate is usually requested (with icy politeness) to make his opinions on the floor. Such people either shut up immediately or accept the challenge and are promptly set up to fall on their faces. Those with merit to their arguments who impress the right people and survive their abrupt call to debate get off lightly for disrupting things and a guarantee that they will be watched in the future by a number of factions; a particularly quick-witted heckler can even gain status through his grandstanding.

Voting on issues is a simple matter — each member of the assembly gets one vote. Voting may be accomplished either by raising one's hand at the right time or marking one's vote on a sheet of paper and placing it in a ballot box. This is another of the perks frequently proffered to the young, one which wise leaders do not try to take away. For all the powerlessness that may plague them otherwise, the youth receive (or believe they receive) some measure of control in shaping their futures, which is one of the surest ways to entice anyone. Most of the elders, however, are well-aware that for every neonate or ancilla who votes as she chooses, there are a dozen who are voting to further an agenda, curry favor or save their skins; in fact, most of the elders present are probably watching certain pawns to ensure they follow previously laid plans and vote as they have been instructed.

A conclave called for purposes of trial or a single matter is usually accomplished relatively swiftly and dispersed without too much fanfare. What the attendees do out of chambers is largely up to their own devices. Those conclaves called as annual events or to discuss multiple matters take time to work through a docket of business, then may open the floor for any matters that Kindred may wish to address. Not a few Kindred take this time to bring up problems in their cities and regions that have stymied them, such as abusive elders, growing interference from Setites or Giovanni, or mortals who are proving too powerful and visible for just one city to deal with. Speaking may then be limited by the hosting justicars based on the matter. A call to force a destructive or powerful prince's abdication may result in a request that those who dwell in the prince's city first discuss the matter in chambers, while a prince who is requesting assistance in dealing with

QUIET, PLEASE

The right to speak is not the right to speak interminably. The host retains the right to inform a long-winded speaker that she must either conclude or be seated. And, with debate time in such short supply (especially during summer conclaves), filibustering is frowned on as a waste of precious minutes.

particularly troublesome enemies may receive a bevy of interested responses from old and young alike.

Conclaves as Trials

A conclave called for the purposes of a trial is focused sharply on the business at hand, and the justicar presiding allows nothing to interrupt that business. Such is far less about granting the accused a speedy trial and more about getting things done and over with, as such trials can gobble up a great deal of a justicar's valuable time. Because of the problems with security and the time involved, a justicar who finds out his time has been wasted by a frivolous charge can be extremely harsh in his dealings with the accusers; most times they are punished severely, occasionally with Final Death if the justicar is angry enough.

There is nothing in the Traditions body of law that grants a Kindred the right to a trial. Likewise, when trials are permitted, there is nothing particularly modern about the forms. The defendant is automatically assumed to be guilty, and the burden of proof rests with her and any legal defense she is permitted. Only after the charges have all been presented may she begin the arduous task of proving her innocence. In truth, many conclave trials end up being show trials for the Camarilla's mighty fist of justice. Those on trial at conclaves are most often abusive, despotic princes and elders, or Camarilla traitors whose guilt has been conclusively proven in the field. A trial where there is actually doubt in the minds of attendees regarding guilt of the accused is a rare and exciting event.

During a trial, any who have something to contribute to the matter at hand, who have support from at least one other person, and who have sufficient courage may speak up either for or against the defendant. Of course, supporting an unpopular defendant is a risky business, and those who do are usually well-aware of the need to seek out other living arrangements in the event that the defendant is found guilty. It has been known to happen that someone with particularly damning evidence in a case may step up to speak, but certain powers-that-be (such as a prince, powerful elders or a concerted clan's efforts) threaten any who would support her. The justicars frown on witness intimidation, and if they believe that a witness is being threatened, they will stand for her support to speak and may even offer her protection. Such protection, however, is usually only good for as long as the justicars and their agents are in a city, and tends to be conveniently forgotten once the justicars have left.

Trials involving ritual combat or ordeals are frequently very ritualistic, very flashy in a somber manner and very much focused on finding a suitable fate for the accused. Those accused who have chosen to challenge a court's ruling are either desperate or too angry to care, and they will drag as much as they can out of the spectacle. Sometimes, the best they can hope for is a spectacular death that leaves many questions in the minds of its viewers.

The Lextalionis

Kindred existence is marked with blood, and so is the punishment for breaking the laws of that existence. Most Kindred scholars can date the Lextalonis to the time of Caine, as it follows the Old Testament precept of "an eye for an eye, a tooth for a tooth." It may well be that this is the only certain pronouncement of Caine's that continues to survive into the modern age without becoming corrupted by time. Among the youth and less tradition-minded of the Kindred, the practice is called the blood hunt.

The Lextalionis is tied directly into the Sixth Tradition, and probably has been since its inception. The Sixth Tradition orders that only the eldest shall call the blood hunt, with "eldest" being taken to refer to the prince. While there may be other elders in the city who might attempt to call a hunt, they have neither the right nor the authority to do so. The calling of the hunt remains a prince's purview, and a prince is perfectly within her rights to punish one who would usurp her Tradition-given right. Any Kindred foolish enough to follow an overly presumptuous elder's call are often subjected to the same punishment they would have inflicted on another, although rare exceptions have been made for neonates and childer who have never been taught otherwise.

The blood hunt may be called for numerous crimes, including:

- Kin-slaying;
- Diablerie;
- Wide-scale breach of the Masquerade or continuous offenses regarding such;
- Invasion of domain that has resulted in kin-slaying or breaches of the Masquerade;
- Any behavior deemed a sufficient threat to the safety of the Masquerade and the Kindred of the city.

The hunt is formally declared in Elysium, with primogen and those present expected to carry news of the declaration back to their clanmates, or at least to pass it along the so-called barking chain. All who hear the call must participate at least nominally in the hunt, even if they find the activity distasteful or wrong. Fortunately for those who might object to a hunt, in these fallen times "participating" can mean simply staying out of the pursuers' way and not interfering with their business. Some Kindred find the hunt exhilarating in the same way as they might once have enjoyed a foxhunt, reveling in the thrill of the chase and bringing the quarry to ground. There are few greater excitements than predators hunting predators, according to these eager hunters, and every city seems to have one or two Kindred who place themselves at the forefront of the hunting pack. Such excessive enthusiasm is looked on with some trepidation by a few elders. After all, over-excitement during the chaos of a blood hunt seems to some to be an open invitation to a figurative tiger pit. You never know who might "accidentally" be killed along with, or instead of, the actual quarry.

Aiding and abetting the quarry of a blood hunt is dangerous, and often a sure means of becoming the next to be hunted. As a result, calling a hunt is an excellent way of separating the quarry from her allies and supporters; they can but watch or risk becoming hunted themselves. This can be a dangerous card for a prince to play, however. Too blatant a use of the hunt as a tool for excising political rivals or isolating dangerous opponents tends to get the local citizenry thinking about replacing the one calling the hunts.

For the most serious of crimes (such as aiding the Sabbat or deliberately and repeatedly violating the Masquerade), the prince has the option of declaring that every Kindred in the city must take active part in the hunt or risk being declared accomplices of the quarry. Particularly paranoid princes make mandatory active participation a condition of all of their hunts, but again, abuse of this perogative is taken as proof of unsatisfactory leadership by many Kindred.

The blood hunt is not called lightly, although the last decade has seen a significant upturn in its use. Any prince calling the hunt does so with full knowledge that the Camarilla may examine her judgment of the situation in conclave. Such a threat has been enough to keep a prince from calling a hunt if her motives are even the slightest bit questionable. If the conclave determines that the prince has called a hunt without cause, she usually suffers a profound loss of status among her peers, and may well be saddled with an archon "observer" to keep her on the straight and narrow. If too many hunts are being called in a city, a justicar may choose to call for a conclave and have the offending prince deposed, assuming the angry residents don't remove her themselves first.

It has happened that new evidence comes to light during the conclave, evidence which clears the hunted one of wrongdoing. Too often, though, the acquittal comes after the fact, and tradition demands that once the hunt has been called, it cannot be stopped. In such circumstances, the prince or conclave may suggest that certain measures be taken in reparation; while no one may make an outright attempt to call the hunt off, the pursuit of the quarry may become rather less vigorous as a result of a conclave's findings. The hunted may also find himself receiving surreptitious aid from clanmates and friends; a guard may "casually" look the other way at just the right moment, or a convenient window may be left serendipitously open to facilitate escape.

On occasion, the blood hunt is used as a means of enforcing exile, of literally hounding someone out of the city. Such an option is extended by some princes who must exile a Kindred in response to an outraged populace or when the accused's crime does not warrant a death penalty but still demands punishment. The hunted may then flee and seek a new haven in another city, but she does so knowing that she may never return home. No matter who rules after this prince, the blood hunt remains in effect until her Final Death. The names of those exiled are often kept by sheriffs and keepers of Elysium, and are marked in the annals of city histories by those who style themselves lore-keepers.

THE MISBEGOTTEN HUNT

It has happened that a prince has called a blood hunt that either outrages the populace so thoroughly that they refuse to attend, regardless of any threat levied, or that the elders unite

against the prince and inform the populace that any who stand with him are the next targets. In either case, the situation means blood in the streets. If the populace as a whole refuses to support the prince on a blood hunt, his reign is ended then and there. Chances are very good that the justicars have had their eyes on him already, and even if he is found not guilty at conclave, the Kindred of the city have already demonstrated they have no respect for him. They will not follow him if he returns; his reign as an effective leader is over. The prince may try to maintain his hold through force, but such efforts are doomed to failure. In such situations it is more than likely that he instead falls prey to a hunt declared by his successor — who may already be styling himself prince.

If the elders alone stand in the way of a hunt, things become considerably more tricky. In the best of all situations, a conclave may be ordered to sort out the chaos, with the hunt on hold until the matter is resolved. However, rarely does common sense thus prevail because rarely is the blood hunt itself the real issue in these instances. Perhaps a particularly powerful elder has chosen to square off with the prince, and she is using the contested blood hunt as a touch-point. Then again, it could be that the primogen council is forcing the populace to stand down in an effort to further their agenda against the prince. Such political machinations muddy the waters of the Camarilla's justice system considerably, and often the actual merits of the case are lost in the confusion. At such times, the accused generally takes advantage of the chaos to absent herself from the city and watch the sorting-out process from a safe distance.

Miscarriages of Justice

The Camarilla's justice is a rough and simple thing, but that doesn't prevent it from being subverted left, right and center. The process of the blood hunt, from inception to execution, provides innumerable opportunities for misconduct, and cunning Kindred have taken advantage of all of them.

The first place things can go wrong, of course, is the actual declaration of the hunt. It is sufficiently easy to frame a vampire for a breach of the Masquerade or some other heinous crime, particularly when powers like Dominate come into play. More than one prince has been tricked into issuing a blood hunt on a perfectly innocent Kindred on the basis of spurious or forged evidence. Real masters of the art of inciting blood hunts can turn a prince's edict on his allies and childer, tricking him into removing his own supporters one by one. A prince tricked repeatedly in this fashion rapidly beomes an ex-prince, or more often, a pile of ashes.

Two can play at that game, however, and for every prince tricked into calling a hunt on an innocent, there's another who set out to call a spurious hunt deliberately. Such hunts are called to eliminate rivals, demonstrate princely power or just exercise a prince's sadistic tendencies. They also tend to keep the population jumpy, for while such behavior tends to destabilize a prince's reign, no one wants to be martyred while waiting for the prince to be deposed.

Dirty Pool

Just as the blood hunt process is sometimes hijacked for unscrupulous means, so too can a conclave's review be subverted. Even if a prince has called blood hunts for perfectly good reasons, persistent complaints to archons from the prince's enemies can lead to a justicar's review. As many justicars operate under the "where there's smoke, there's fire" principle, enough complaints — especially from Kindred of high standing — *will* inevitably lead to some sort of inquiry. Once the review is called, then it becomes open season on the prince, and things get interesting indeed.

On the other hand, no justicar is likely to appreciate being used thus, and attempting to manipulate a justicar into deposing a prince is a very dangerous game.

Both hunters and hunted can take advantage of the hunt in unscrupulous ways as well. One of the hardest parts of any blood hunt is the preservation of the Masquerade during the chase. Quarries, particularly those being hunted for breaches of that Tradition, often rip the Masquerade wide open during their flight. Such behavior distances them from their pursuers, who are mandated (even in the grip of the hunt) to preserve the Masquerade first and foremost. Other targets of a hunt deliberately lead the chase across their enemies' domains, merrily causing their pursuers to trample everything underfoot. Particularly vengeful targets of a blood hunt attempt to turn the tables on the hunters, ambushing and destroying as many pursuers as possible. A vampire who is successful at taking out two or three of those theoretically hunting him can cause an entire hunt to bog down in paranoia and chaos. A hunt that's collectively jumping at shadows isn't likely to provide effective pursuit.

On the other hand, participants in a blood hunt can play dirty pool as well. Accidents happen, and hunts wherein more than just the quarry goes down beneath the hunters' fangs are common. Many of the most eager hunters love to use the hunt as an opportunity to settle scores, take out rivals or even indulge in unauthorized diablerie. The pursuit of a hunted vampire also provides plenty of chances to plant evidence, frame rivals or "accidentally" sneak peeks at rivals' domains under the guise of searching for the guilty party.

Diablerie on the Hunt

On occasions of the blood hunt, diablerization of the quarry is most often treated with a sort of benign neglect. As the target of the hunt is a heinous traitor (else he would not be the subject of a hunt now, would he?), he deserves the utmost penalty, and having one's essence subsumed by one's killer fits that description pretty neatly. On the other hand, if the hunt is really just a disguised exile, diablerizing the quarry can draw down the prince's ire, and it is a given that a prince frustrated in this manner *will* seek to extract revenge.

The tradition of the blood hunt does state that the successful hunter does get to take the blood of the quarry, though nowhere is it stated that diablerie is either mandated or permissible. If the target of the hunt has particularly potent vitae, the prince may declare diablerie off-limits in order to prevent strengthing a hunter unduly; in other cases, the prince may insinuate in the very declaration of the hunt that the quarry may be thus destroyed. Such a declaration is music to the ears of bloodthirsty neonates, who commonly flock to such hunts as a means of advancing in generation and power.

In the end, diablerie on the hunt is handled on a case-by-case basis, with permission often assumed to be implicit in the hunt. In many cases, a prince may fail to block the diablerization of the target, then use evidence of the "offense" as leverage on the successful hunter.

TECHNIQUES

The term "blood hunt" conjures up images of a horde of vampires storming the streets of the city, pitchforks, torches and Uzis in hand as they look for their victim. In truth, the actuality of the event is far from the stereotype. While a great many Kindred may get involved in a single hunt, usually it is only the neonates who flock together, and they do so for protection against the more potent vampires they are hunting. Hunts are more often conducted by individuals and coteries, combing the city for evidence of the target's presence and using ghouls, mortals and even animal servants to flush the prey out into the open.

Once the hunt is declared, there is often a rush for the accused's usual haunts or haven, in hopes of catching him before he hears about (and prepares for) the hunt. If that tactic fails, the wise blood hunter takes the measure of the victim's ghouls, allies and coterie. Often useful leads can be garnered from a successful interrogation of this sort, while a thorough search of the target's haven or havens can also be helpful. Other experienced hunters prefer to head straight for major transit points (highways, train stations, airports) in order to catch the accused on his way out of town. With the advent of the automobile and the helicopter, such tactics are less useful than they used to be, but the number of hunted Kindred who still manage to stumble straight into such traps is astonishing.

ALTERNATE TECHNIQUES

All things being equal, it should be nearly impossible to track down an intelligent, determined vampire who wants to get out of town. There are too many roads to take, too many places to hide and too many ways to avoid detection. Things are rarely equal among the Kindred, however, and there are any number of strategems and powers that can be brought to bear to track down a fugitive.

The most effective tools the Kindred have at their disposal are their Disciplines, of which Auspex and Thaumaturgy are the most effective on the blood hunt. The latter offers the possibility of scrying, at the very least, and assorted rituals designed to bring prey to heel. The former is more useful when one is directly on the trail of the prey. Heightened Senses and Psychometry in particular are useful for keeping the pursuit hot, though Astral Projection can work as well as thaumaturgical scrying.

If the target isn't caught within the first few hours of the hunt, then the chase becomes a giant game of many cats and one mouse. The fact that the mouse in question is as deadly as any of the cats adds a certain spice to the affair, and a vampire on a blood hunt who is disabled or knocked into torpor by his target is apt to lose a great deal of status while he recovers. However, an extended hunt often boils down to the fact that no hunter wants to share the spoils of victory (i.e., the chance to diablerize or otherwise make use of the quarry) with anyone else. Greed tends to keep hunting expeditions small.

THE RED LIST

The Red List has been called, with some accuracy, "The Kindred's Most Wanted." It is the list of the most grievous, powerful and troublesome offenders against the Camarilla and its Traditions, those vampires whom the Camarilla most wants to see reduced to ash and brightening sunsets over half a hemisphere. Vampires on the list, called Anathema, have been formally accused of crimes ranging from traffic with demons to diablerie, breaches of the Masquerade to mass murder. They are, in short, monsters, and the Red List is a method by which these creatures may be brought to heel.

In order to be placed on the Red List, a vampire must commit crimes of a legendary nature. Merely belonging to the Sabbat and leading an attack is nothing; leaving a thousand-mile trail of dismembered ghouls and destroyed vampires is

STORYTELLERS: HUNTING ANATHEMA

A group of neonates going to hunt an Anathema is roughly equivalent to a bunch of kindergarteners toddling off into the woods to hunt a grizzly. If they're very, very lucky, they won't find anything. Otherwise, they may suffer the extreme bad luck to locate exactly what they were looking for. The consequences of such are not pleasant, but they are usually brief.

Anathema make it onto the Red List for a reason. They are powerful, vicious and murderous. The average generation of an Anathema is sixth, and all have mastered a truly awe-inspiring spectrum of Disciplines. Then throw in their homicidal manias, their perversions and their general nastiness, and the full horror of the scenario becomes apparent.

In other words, a bunch of 12th-generation neonates stand a snowball's chance in Hell against one. While it is certainly possible to include younger characters in a "hunting the Anathema" plotline, even to the point of allowing a character to admister the *coup de grace*, be sensible in how you handle things. Players' characters are much more likely to get involved in the events peripheral to the hunt for an Anathema (say, drawing an alastor's suspicion of aiding a Red List vampire) than they are to be part of the hunting expedition itself. In the end, remember: The Anathema are dangerous, to both your characters and your storyline, and should be treated as such.

more on the scale of the villainy required. Membership on the List is not limited to Sabbat vampires, either; infamous Kindred of all clans and sects have made their way onto the charts.

Alastors

If the archons and justicars are the law enforcement agencies of the Camarilla, the alastors are the secret police. Moving unseen and unnoticed through the Camarilla, they serve a variety of purposes at the Inner Circle's command. Mostly, however, the alastors hunt the Anathema relentlessly. While the anonymous existence of the alastors can be a difficult one, it does have its rewards, specifically a more-or-less universal immunity to prosecution from local princes. This immunity is occasionally honored in the breach instead of the observance, and there have been any number of trials of princes who uncovered and executed alastors for crimes committed while on the job. The balance is gradually shifting toward giving these roving investigators more leeway, however, as the importance of tracking down the sect's foes increases in urgency.

Alastors are usually archons of exceptional talent, who are secretly recruited by the Inner Circle for promotion into the secret service. As most archons are blood bound to their justicars, the mechanisms of such elevation would be grounds for all sorts of speculation — if anyone besides the Inner Circle and a few others actually knew the alastors existed.

Even among the elite alastors, there are degrees of eliteness. The best of the best (those who have taken down an Anathema from one of the top five positions on the Red List) are known as the Red Alastors, and they apparently exercise greater authority and powers than their fellows.

The Trophy

Every alastor who destroys an Anathema (and any vampire who nails a member of the Red List gets recruited to be an alastor, willy-nilly) receives the Trophy (sometimes called the Mark of the Beast by the cynical), a tattoo of ink and blood on the right palm. Alastors with the Trophy always wear gloves to hide this fact, as unlike normal tattoos, the Trophy never leaves a vampire's flesh. The mark made by the Trophy is recognizable to high-ranking archons and other sufficiently trained Kindred (even through gloves); apparently this flaw was built into the Trophy so that someone could watch the Camarilla's watchmen. If an alastor is easily identifiable to an archon, an alastor who defects can easily be found and destroyed.

Equal Opportunity

You don't have to be a vampire to get on the Red List, but it helps. On very rare occasions, members of other species have clawed their way onto the list. Ghouls and Lupines are the most common suspects, but over the years a handful of particularly dangerous mortals and other, less common creatures have made appearances. However, it must be noted that the Red List is at its core, by vampires, for vampires and most especially, composed of vampires. Adding too many other boojums is an invitation to chaos for all concerned.

There are benefits to the Trophy, however, not the least of which being the automatic aid it compels from princes and other Kindred in a position to know what the mark means. There are also other rewards, including:

- Immunity to blood hunts
- The severance of any existing blood bonds
- Permission to create progeny
- A Life boon
- Financial or territorial rewards
- Sanctioned diablerie under certain circumstances
- Instruction in Disciplines
- Amnesty for past transgressions
- Sanctioned slaying of enemies within and without the Camarilla (within limits)
- Clan friendship
- Safe passage, hospitality, feeding rights and haven
- Retainers and permission to create ghouls

Not all of these rewards are necessarily given to every alastor, nor are all of the rewards announced. However, receiving the Trophy can be a very lucrative proposition.

Note that the hunting of the Red List is not a duty restricted to the alastors. It is theoretically every Camarilla vampire's duty to hunt these monsters, as they are all considered to be under permanent and universal blood hunt. It is simply that the alastors are provided with the resources and support to make a full-time go of it.

The Kill

A hunter who brings down a member of the Red List gets the Trophy, and is also granted all of her prey's possessions. As the Red List vampires are usually quite old and very powerful, the deceased's effects can turn out to be quite valuable. What a successful hunter is not allowed to do, however, is diablerize the Anathema. The Inner Circle takes great care to spread rumors about taints and diseases in these creatures' blood, warning younger vampires away from drinking or even touching it. (It is even rumored that the bizarre stories about "Souleaters" came out of a misguided attempt of this sort when it looked like a Tzimisce Anathema might be brought to ground.) In truth, the rumors are probably just that, and the Inner Circle is just taking steps to keep potent vitae out of the hands of relative youngsters.

Getting on the List

It's not easy to get on the Red List. There are all sorts of monsters among the Kindred, and to achieve the sort of sick fame that demands the title "Anathema" takes time, effort and a truly warped set of actions. It is only the worst of the worst that make it onto the list, the vampires whose whispered names freeze even elders' blood.

In order to put a name on the List, the justicars of two clans must agree to prosecute this action, one bringing the name of the potential Anathema forward and the other witnessing the fact. The vampire's crimes are then read to the assembled

justicars and other witnesses, and unless anyone can mount a sufficient objection (an unlikely event), the document of Anathema is signed and a new name is added to the list. Once a vampire is put on the Red List, the only way off is death.

THE CAMARILLA AT WAR

According to official Camarilla doctrine, the Sabbat does not exist. After all, the Camarilla claims hegemony over all vampires, including those who don't want any part of the sect. Technically, then, the vampires of the self-proclaimed Sabbat are really just members of the Camarilla in massive denial of their true affiliation.

Needless to say, expounding on this question of logistics while a Sabbat pack is pouring into your haven, guns blazing, is about as effective a defensive tactic as putting a bag over your head and shouting, "Nanny nanny boo boo." Either is a good way to get turned into a small pile of ash posthaste.

Regardless of the technicalities, the Sabbat is out there — as are the Lupines, Cathayans, the Risen Dead and any number of other enemies, all hell-bent on the destruction of the Camarilla. As a result, the Camarilla has been forced to create tactics and strategies for every contingency from a full-scale Sabbat invasion of a city to the extraction of a prisoner already buried up to her eyeballs for Creation Rites. Declared or not, the Camarilla is in

a war — a constant war for its very survival — and if its methods of defending itself aren't up to snuff, then the sect is doomed.

Make no mistake, the Camarilla's approach on the battlefield is effective. The sect has lasted half a millennium, after all, even in the face of constant assaults. The recent reverses the Camarilla has suffered notwithstanding, the sect's generals and tacticians know what they're doing, and are very, very good at what they do.

They have to be. The price of failure is extermination.

STRATEGIES

OFFENSE

On a grand scale, the Camarilla's strategy is much the same as the Roman Empire's was — the idea is to make the world Camarilla, to assimilate rather than conquer. Ergo, the Camarilla doesn't mount offensives, and doesn't seek to take Sabbat cities by storm. That's not the Camarilla way — for one thing, open combat in the streets is akin to taking the Masquerade out back and shooting it. For another, it is a truism that while the average Camarilla vampire is older, stronger and more powerful than the average Sabbat vampire, on any given battlefield there are going to be a lot more Sabbat vampires than there are Camarilla ones. Numbers will tell, and in stand-up fights, too often Camarilla vampires get swamped by the sheer weight of the opposition.

So, instead, on those rare occasions when it's on the offensive, the Camarilla resorts to subtler techniques. Often,

Camarilla offensives work through mortal and ghoul pawns. A favorite tactic is to locate a neighborhood in a Sabbat city that is home to a particularly annoying pack, buy up the real estate and pour money into a high-profile "urban renewal" project there. A few ghouls get tucked into the construction crew to clear out any "obstacles" to the project, and *voila*, the Camarilla takes the pack's haven and stomping grounds out from under them and buries them — along with a member of the pack or three — under tons of nice, shiny new concrete and steel. The idea behind this, and other, similar tactics is to crowd the Sabbat back, neighborhood by neighborhood, taking out handfuls of combat effectives each time. The process is efficient, quiet and deadly, and when done properly serves to eliminate the Sabbat advantage in numbers. By the time the constriction finishes, the Sabbat leadership is boxed in without reinforcements and can be picked off from a position of strength.

In a nutshell, the Camarilla's ultimate offensive strategy is nothing more than a process of slow subsumption, rather than fast assault. Pitched battles tend to make the mortals paranoid (or dead), often spark riots and other catastrophes among the kine that make it difficult to keep a city functioning, and lead to massive conflagrations that can make vampiric existence extremely unpleasant. It's far better from every perspective to strangle the Sabbat out of a city and have a city left behind afterward.

DEFENSE

Unfortunately, there are few occasions these days when the Camarilla can afford to go on the offensive. While Europe's perpetual stalemate plods on toward the millennium, fierce battles are raging in North America, and the Camarilla is losing them. On the East Coast, the Sabbat is taking city after city, going on the offensive after years of tentative aggression. On the West Coast, the so-called Anarch Free States (ultimately friendly to the Camarilla, for all their bluster) are being overrun by Cathayan invaders, and to the south squats the Sabbat stronghold of Mexico City. North lie the endless forests and acres of tundra that the remaining Lupines call home. In North America, the Camarilla is in a box, one that's getting smaller all the time.

With the situation as dire as it is, the Camarilla is determined to hold on to every last inch of ground that it can. The sect's strategy is primarily a defensive one these days, and one that is in some senses hamstrung by the necessity of maintaining the Masquerade and otherwise upholding the Traditions, even in the midst of war. A defense of a city that blows the lid off the vampiric presence is worse than losing the city to the Sabbat; no single city is worth the price of irrevocably breaking the Camarilla's oldest and most sacred Tradition. Such a move would, in the end, cost the Camarilla the city in any case, and the rest of the world not long after.

So the cordon must be drawn and the perimeter established early. If the Sabbat never sets foot in a city, there's no chance that the Masquerade will be broken by those defending the city from the Sabbat. Rather than focusing on driving the Sabbat out of occupied territories, the Camarilla prefers to do its utmost to keep its enemies from infesting any more of its territory. An ounce of prevention is worth several pounds of cure, especially under these circumstances.

Moreover, the Camarilla's strategy is predicated on big pictures, not little ones. Individuals, apart from rare exceptions, are ultimately expendable; cities and real estate are more important. Vampires are, in the end, replaceable. A Camarilla vampire who is captured should not expect rescue; the Camarilla's strategists learned the hard way that it's not worth losing three vampires and a half-dozen highly trained ghouls just to get a single prisoner out. These days the Sabbat doesn't even bother kidnapping Kindred for bait, except when the head of the local Camarilla forces is extremely inexperienced or gullible. The place and the sect are what matter in Camarilla strategies, not the individual. In the end, the Sabbat must be kept out of the cities and the sect must be maintained; all else must in the end be sacrificed to that goal.

CHAIN OF COMMAND

The Camarilla is not now, nor has it ever been, a military organization. There is no standing army of vampires waiting for the call to battle. Vampire generals don't call their soldiers onto some darkling plain, there to stand in military formation until ordered to march forward at their highest rate of Celerity. If nothing else, pitched battles with phalanxes and

BENDING THE RULES

Every good commander needs reinforcements. In the end, numbers do tell. This military truism holds as well for vampires as it does for mortals. Unfortunately, the Traditions forbid the most effective method of creating reinforcements, while the Sabbat is under no such restrictions. That means that every Camarilla field commander goes into the fight knowing she's at a disadvantage — and her enemies know it, too.

That's why, during wartime, the restrictions on the Embrace tend to get loosened just a little bit. Princes have been known to offer limited *carte blanche* to their sheriffs and other key allies to Embrace as many mortals as they need (so long as no one gets greedy) and to worry about the paperwork afterward. More often, the prince takes it on himself to create — and bond — the reinforcements. The Camarilla corridor in New York is a prime example of this tactic in operation; should the Sabbat abandon the city tomorrow, it would be awash in the Ventrue progeny of the prince, all of whom have been Embraced in the last three years as battlefield "promotions."

An additional benefit to this tactic is the fact that odds are, the "reinforcements" created thus have a fairly powerful Kindred of relatively low generation siring them. As a result, even if the fresh meat isn't particularly well-trained in the art of being a vampire, there's still a lot of innate power that the neonate can draw upon in the interests of self-preservation. In a tussle between an eighth-generation Ventrue neonate created by the local prince and a 13th-generation Brujah *antitribu* created as part of a mass Embrace by a street-level pack member, you'd do well to put your money on the Ventrue every time.

whatnot present definite violations of the Masquerade, and as such are worthless to the Camarilla cause. A Ventrue primogen may have *known* Tacitus or Trajan in the flesh, but isn't in a position to use any of their suggestions.

In most cities, military or pseudo-military affairs are left to a city's sheriff and his childer, though as a matter of course the sheriff is granted leave to "deputize" other Kindred to help him in whatever matters are pressing. In reality, situations like that often emulate the recruitment practices of the golden age of the British Imperial Navy, with neonates plucked from the street and pressed into service.

It is only in extraordinary circumstances that the prince himself takes a hand in issuing orders; that's what he has a sheriff for, after all. When the prince himself has to start fighting in the streets, everything's already gone to hell. More commonly, the prince comes up with a general strategic overview of how he wants the city protected, what (and who) he considers most important and what's expendable, and then leaves the tactics to the sheriff.

Things don't always run smoothly in the heat of battle, and complicating factors like lingering conditionings from uses of Dominate and the power of the blood bond can make giving orders an exercise in frustration for even the most exceptional tactician. While defense of the city does take precedence over most personal rivalries, it's not always easy to get the impedimentia of peacetime out of the way so that war can be waged most efficiently.

FRONTS

Camarilla tacticians know that they are beset on all sides. They also know that the Camarilla does not have the resources for a multiple-front war, even if that is the specter currently confronting them. With that in mind, the Camarilla makes a conscious effort to turn its enemies on one another, or at least to keep them off-balance to the point where the attacks come one at a time, rather than all at once.

To that end, the Camarilla's scions make more than occasional deals with the Devil. In a hundred cities, the dance goes on every night. Bargains are struck with incautious Lupines for swatches of territory that house Setite temples or Sabbat advance bases, or with a Sabbat pack far from home to "ally" against a marauding couple of *kuei-jin* (all the while attempting to maneuver the pack to the front lines to take the brunt of the enemy offensive, of course). Such short-term alliances are never carved in stone — treachery and the appearance of new threats means that these alliances are *always* short-term; the old ally is expendable to help deal with the new danger. The idea, in the end, is to preserve the Camarilla. Everything else is secondary — destruction of enemies is a method of safeguarding the Camarilla's security. There are even a fair number of important Camarilla figures (more than one might immediately suspect) who honestly would not care what the Sabbat did *so long as it left the Camarilla alone.* Alas, then, that vampiric population pressure, age-old rivalries and the manipulations of the masters of the Jyhad ensure that such a state can never come to pass.

TACTICS

ON THE ATTACK

It is rare for the Camarilla to go on an all-out offensive, as there just isn't the manpower (or reasonable facsimile thereof) to do it properly. Furthermore, the average Camarilla vampire is firmly attached to her unlife — she's been a vampire long enough to know exactly what she's risking by charging the tenement that the local Sabbat has had time to turn into a deathtrap. On the other hand, the Sabbat troops that invading Cammies are likely to run into are fresh out of the grave and haven't yet had it sink in that they've got all of eternity in front of them; ergo, they're more than willing to mount suicidal defenses. What it boils down to is that Camarilla vampires are naturally cautious, none more so than those who know that they're in enemy territory. Any offensives that these overly cautious vampires launch, then, are likely to be more than overly cautious. No one wants to risk his immortal skin unless it's absolutely unavoidable, and even younger Camarilla vampires aren't overjoyed about being ordered into dangerous spots, unless compelled by supernatural or other means.

As a result, Camarilla offensives are slow ones, marked by long periods of subversion beforehand and spearheaded by mortals and ghouls. If the sect's vampires are lucky, they never have to fire a shot or raise a talon in order to accomplish their aims. When the problem is just a single Sabbat pack, roving the countryside in a souped-up van, there's no need for actual vampires to dirty their hands. A phone call to a ghouled state police supervisor here, a small bribe administered there, and suddenly there are state troopers crawling all over the offending vehicle an hour after sunrise. The matter is taken care of, a little bit more of highway is safe for Camarilla vampires to travel once again, and no one important was threatened — at least to the Camarilla way of thinking.

Even when more direct measures are called for, Camarilla tacticians prefer to go for Sabbat support mechanisms — havens, feeding grounds and the like. Clean up a neighborhood, and all of a sudden a pack's depredations stand out to the city's *gendarmes*. Put up a building on an empty lot, and suddenly the *antitribu* don't have any place for their rites any more. Nudge the local diocese to send a few priests who *really* believe into a Sabbat-infested neighborhood, and there's going to be a True Faith-flavored surprise for any Lasombra who gets too cocky. And while each of these steps may not seem like much, they add up — and with minimal risk to the vampires pulling the strings. The Camarilla has far greater mortal resources than its opponent does, and is not afraid to use them. Better a half-dozen police officers get killed in flushing out a basement haven than a single loyal Kindred.

There are times, however, when vampire-on-vampire conflict is unavoidable. Even in these cases, Camarilla agents try to protect and surround themselves with heavily armed and armored ghouls, blood bound and eminently willing to die to

Attacks on Sabbat positions provide one of the few chances for sanctioned diablerie that a Camarilla vampire is likely ever to see. While there is no official Camarilla policy on the matter, the unofficial rule has always been, "Take care of business first — and don't let us catch you at it."

protect their "patrons." Camarilla strategists do prefer surgical fights as opposed to protracted sieges. They'd rather pick a target, isolate it, then hit it hard with everything they have and overwhelm the opposition through a precise application of force. Ideally, there is only one target to hit at a time, as Camarilla forces can't afford to be stretched too thin or they'll be swamped under the seemingly endless numbers that the Sabbat can bring to bear. So, once a building is targeted, it's taken floor by floor, starting from the ground up, with a ring of support "troops" on surrounding buildings and covering escape routes. Camarilla assaults are thorough, efficient and bloody; the attackers make certain of their kills before moving on to new targets. Once a building is reduced, the strike team moves onto the next one, and then the next — speed is of the essence. The Camarilla cannot win a war of attrition, so its offensives need to be fast and deadly.

Camarilla pushes are also bound by the necessity of keeping up the Masquerade, and armed assaults on Sabbat strongholds are by necessity not terribly subtle. As such, Camarilla attack teams need to have some sort of cover in place, as they can't burn down the building they've just emptied every time. At moments like this, the Camarilla's decided advantage in mortal resources comes into play. A noisy but ineffective shootout between the forces of two Camarilla-controlled drug lords makes for perfect camoflauge for a vampiric operation, as any witnesses are more than likely to see the entire action — humans and vampires both — in terms they understand. Getting construction crews, transit authority workers, gas company employees and other mortals in positions that give them access to lots of yellow tape that reads "Do Not Cross" to cordon off zones of conflict also serves Camarilla purposes — any banging, shouting, shooting or other loud noises can be explained as part of the "problem" necessitating the clearance of the area.

DEFENDING THE CITIES

Defense of Camarilla territory is ruthless. It is the cities, more than any individual vampire, that the Camarilla must defend in order to remain a viable entity. One can always Embrace new Kindred, but there are just so many cities available to be occupied, and not enough places to put new ones. Many younger Camarilla vampires don't understand the sanctity of territory, thinking it's better to retreat to another city and fight another night. The elders, the wise ones who have seen the game played out for a half a millennium, know better. Every city is at once an armory and a source of supplies, not to mention a nigh-limitless source of new recruits. Moreover, vampires are

creatures of place and habit. In addition, Caine's childer, particularly those who have seen a few decades on the other side of the grave, prefer security and comfortable surroundings. To such vampires, the loss of a home is more than just a matter of moving a line on a map a few miles. It is the loss of identity, the violent uprooting of tendrils that have been carefully laid down over decades. For all these reasons, and more, the Camarilla defends its own with the fury of a lioness defending her cubs.

Defensive tactics put into play against the Sabbat are simple: Figure out what and who in a city is expendable. Defend the rest to the Final Death. Use mortal and ghoul forces to keep relentless daytime pressure on Sabbat encampments. Burn down as many buildings as you have to in order to get the invaders, and blame it on an arson wave — have your ghouls smile for the news crews while lighting the flames, if necessary. The area can always be rebuilt later, providing opportunities and rewards for whatever neonates and ancillae distinguish themselves in the city's defense.

Speed of response time is also key to Camarilla defenses. If the Sabbat gains a foothold in a city, then the sect can start mass-creating shock troops within the contested zone. Not only does this produce more opposition at a nigh-exponential rate, but it also threatens the Masquerade. If the Sabbat is allowed to get "energetic" in its recruiting, the defenders' resources need to be split between actual defense of the city and protecting the Camarilla's veil of secrecy. The pressure only increases as time goes by. If the infection is not burned out quickly, it may never be burned out at all.

If truth be told, the Camarilla almost welcomes frontal assaults from the Sabbat. Yes, Kindred may be destroyed, property smashed and resources used up, but in such cases the enemy is visible, recognizable and ultimately driven off. Infiltration by deep-cover Sabbat operatives, on the other hand, is

WAR COTERIES

The war coterie is a relatively recent invention, with the credit (or blame) going at the feet of the late Lodin of Chicago. Essentially sanctioned privateers (or the land-going, bloodsucking equivalent thereof), war coteries are bands of neonates and the occasional ancilla who's feeling constricted in her current position, given *carte blanche* to go out onto the mean streets and wreak havoc upon the sect's enemies. War coteries operate under only the loosest guidelines from the local sheriff or prince, who essentially wind the coteries up, point them at a convenient enemy and let them go. If the coterie manages to do something effective, there's cheering all around and the survivors find themselves rewarded (though potentially targeted to do the same thing all over again the next time there's a need). If the coterie goes down in flames, well, that's one fewer batch of potential troublemakers around, and everyone else in the city gets an object lesson in why haring off after the Sabbat without strict direction is a bad idea.

every prince's nightmare. The slow cancer of subversion rots out many a city that might be strong enough to withstand any frontal assault. As a result, any prince worth her salt is constantly in a state of nigh-certafiable paranoia. Which ancilla is dissatisfied enough to deal with the enemy? What neonates haven't received enough guidance from their sires, and have been seduced by the promises of an infiltrator? What primogen member, believing the Sabbat's hollow promises that the invaders will withdraw "once this current prince is toppled," is planning a coup? It's hard to tell, and oftentimes the paranoia that the threat of an infiltrator engenders does as much for the Sabbat cause as an actual mole would have.

Therefore, most princes have in place elaborate counter-intelligence measures. Options range from bribing anarchs to hang with the Sabbat to bring back information, to kidnapping neonates and ancillae for Dominate-enhanced interrogations (with all memories wiped afterward, of course) to giving sheriffs broad powers of enforcement to deal with suspected traitors. The latter, to no one's surprise, rarely works, but stubborn princes keep on trying it anyway.

Dealing With the Menagerie

The Sabbat isn't the Camarilla's only enemy, just its most prominent and dangerous one. However, conflicts with the independent clans, Lupines and whatnot rarely require all-out war. Instead, brushfire conflicts are the norm. The Camarilla and Lupines, while far from any official accord, both know the rules of the game they play: The cities belong to the vampires, the country to the Garou, and anyone who trespasses is fair game. More geopolitically aware Kindred refer to the arrangement as a "Good Fence," and try not to rock the boat.

Dealing with the independent clans is a bit trickier. While either the Camarilla or the Sabbat could, presumably, crush the independents one at a time, the victor would be weakened and easy prey for the opposite sect as a result. Conversely, the support of one of the independents as an ally is a valuable weight on the scales of conflict, and as such the Camarilla finds itself often wooing the independents to the point of overlooking trespasses that would not be tolerated in, say, a Toreador. Eventually, though, the Setites, Giovanni or what have you cross the line of acceptable behavior and need to be taught a lesson. Often, the fatal debate is over a lucrative Camarilla-run business that an independent is encroaching upon (drugs, porn and numbers are the prime grounds for conflict with the Setites, for example). Less frequently, members of independent clans flout their non-Camarilla status by violating the Traditions, leaving the aggrieved prince of the city no choice but to act — regardless if there's any real evidence or not. In such cases, the general principle behind Camarilla action is to resolve the matter quickly: Send in overwhelming force to deal with the problem vampires, annihilate them, and make apologies and token concessions to appease the offenders' clan leadership. Unlike hostile dealings with the Sabbat, when it comes to the independents the Camarilla does have the advantage of numbers, and it likes to use it.

Open and armed conflict, however, is rare. The local prince is much more likely to impose "feeding sanctions," mount a harassment campaign through mortal catspaws, or even extract concessions from clan leadership to make recompense for the "offenses" of the interlopers. Aggressive warfare on anyone's part, though, is infrquent. It's just too expensive for all concerned.

PRESTATION

While power may be the true currency of the Kindred, boons and favors also enjoy a healthy trade. The process of trading, repaying and incurring favors (called prestation), is the lifeblood of the vampiric economy. A wise vampire grants favors; a foolish one incurs them and becomes beholden to his benefactors. A vampire who requests assistance often enough soon finds his entire existence dictated by the obligations he has incurred; in exchange for whatever tokens of help he requested, he becomes a puppet of his benefactors.

ACCRUING DEBT

The process of racking up a prestation debt is a simple one. Either a vampire asks another of her kind for assistance in a matter, in return for a favor of some sort at a later date, or a vampire renders another assistance in a crisis, with it being understood that the help will be repaid later. Sensible Kindred keep very close tabs on whom they owe favors to, and take great care not to rack up more debts than they can afford to pay back at any given time. Prestation debts can be called in at literally any time, so it pays to make sure that you have the resources to pay, regardless of circumstance. Some Kindred do make a habit of racking up as many debts as possible as a form of protection, operating on the theory that their manifold creditors will want to keep them in one piece in order to collect.

Not all debts are accrued voluntarily, however. Elders are past masters at maneuvering younger Kindred into positions where they have no choice but to ask for help, thus placing themselves in an elder's thrall. For example, a corporation controlled by an elder might purchase the building a promising neonate lives in and immediately start harassing her with maintenance checks, surprise inspections, fumigations and the like. Eventually the neonate has no choice but to seek relief, which leads her to the elder's doorstep. The favor is extended, and the neonate has placed her first foot on the elder's spiderweb.

Expert players at the game of prestation also like placing potential debtors into perilous situations and then rescuing them dramatically, thus placing the "hapless victims" in their debt. A favorite tactic involves letting knowledge of a vampire's haven slip to a hunter, then swooping in as the hunter makes his move. From the rescue it's only a short step to helping the neonate find a new haven ("This one is clearly unsafe,"), and, inch by inch, the victim is thus ensnared.

INTEREST

It is not in a vampire's best interest to cash in the favors she has acquired immediately. After all, a vampire who is known to owe you a favor is likely to come under suspicion if you disappear (see page **149**), with potentially fatal consequences. As a result, any Kindred is as safe as can be expected from any of her debtors.

Surety of safety isn't the only reason to hang onto a favor. As long as one of the Kindred has a debt hanging over him, he must always be aware of the possibility of having his marker called in. He can't act as freely as he might otherwise, for fear of being called on to repay his debt. Holding a debt over a vampire and insinuating that repayment might be due at any moment is a superb method of paralyzing a Kindred, stripping him of his maneuverability and forcing him to reserve some of his resources against the possibility.

Furthermore, a vampire who owes another a debt is perceived as being inferior to the vampire whom she owes. This perception only applies to those who know about a debt — but any Kindred who gets a line on a powerful peer lets the whole world know about it as quickly as possible. As a result, the creditor gains prestige, the debtor loses it. Even better, the longer the debt can be sustained, the more prestige accrues to the creditor. It is in the interest of the vampire holding the favor to hang onto it as long as possible, then, though most creditors take care to avoid yanking their debtors' leashes too hard or too often. Once the debt is discharged, it's socially permissible for an abused debtor to take vengeance on an overly harsh creditor.

PAYING OFF

Few Kindred like the idea of having lingering debts. It's embarrassing socially, painful financially and potentially hazardous. As a result, most vampires attempt to pay off their prestation debts as soon as they can safely do so. As creditors have a vested interest in stringing those debts out, the result can be a game of cat and mouse, with the debtors frantically attempting to do their creditors favors and the creditors dodging anything that might conceivably be construed as a kindness from their debtors.

Debts among the Kindred rarely take specific shape, as it were. It is uncommon for a vampire to request a detailed service. Rather, debts are kept nebulous — "I'll simply ask for your help with something down the road." This ambiguity works both for and against the creditor. The indistinct nature of the debt helps keeps those on the short end of prestation on their toes, as they never know what they might be asked for. On the other hand, since the nature of the debt is fuzzy, it is common for Kindred to perform some sort of favor for their creditors in hopes of canceling the prestation debt. Particularly energetic or devious vampires maneuver their creditors into situations wherein they can appear on the scene and render assistance, thus wiping out the imbalance. Such attempts should be made very carefully, though — if they backfire or are found out, the instigator just sinks deeper into debt and becomes a target of derision as well.

What form payback takes depends on the size and type of debt incurred. It is considered bad form to ask for excessive repayment of minor debts; in such cases, the debtor is usually free to laugh off the request, and the debt itself is canceled, more often than not. On the other hand, no vampire wants to let a debt go frivolously by asking for too little. Doing so is a sure path to being made a target by the harpies, more than canceling any status gain made by acquiring the debt in the first place.

In truth, the actual repayment of the debt is almost incidental to the process of prestation. It is the debt that matters, the artistry of the creation or dispersal of the obligation and the webs of allegiance strung by favors owed. Actually paying off whatever is demanded is somehow anticlimactic in all but the most dire circumstances.

When a debt is finally repaid, however, more often than not it is done so publicly. Sample forms of payments include boons (especially that of creation, if the prince is the debtor), favorite ghouls or mortal pawns, assistance in financial or martial arenas, tutoring in Disciplines or even just the performance of publicly humiliating acts. Often favors involve one Kindred lobbying another on a third vampire's behalf, usually as regards matters of creation or interference in the mortal world. Asking for a service that is overly hazardous, or demanding that one's debtor break the Traditions is forbidden by long custom; if nothing else getting one's debtor killed ensures that you can't use him again. On the other hand, a sufficiently subtle vampire can get around these restrictions, and prestation has been used to eliminate any number of incautious Kindred. The harpies usually end up being the ultimate arbiter of whether the repayment is suitable, though they hold no official capacity in this matter.

SWAPS

As with everything else, the Kindred trade prestation debts like children trade baseball cards. They are constantly swapped, retrieved, dangled and otherwise moved around so that it becomes dizzying to keep track of who owes what to whom. While there is no formal system for trading favors — all such arrangements operate more along the lines of, "Hmm, Desmond owes me some consideration; I'll tell him to talk to you if you let Reese know that I could use his assistance with my little Gangrel problem." — there is one *sine qua non* involved in the process. The vampire whose debt is being traded must be informed as to his new creditor, otherwise he runs the risk of blowing off a perfectly valid request for what he thinks is a perfectly valid reason, and instead causing the whole system to break down.

Besides, letting an inferior know that you didn't even feel his debt was worth hanging on to is a wonderful way of reinforcing his social status beneath you. The transmission of debt is as much a part of the game of prestation as anything else.

FORMALITY

At first glance, it seems that the weight that the Kindred place on incurred favors and the like is completely ludicrous. Don't like owing a Nosferatu a favor? Blow him off! He's only a Nosferatu! He can't do anything if you don't pay up, right?

Wrong.

Defining Boons

Most young Kindred learn the art of prestation (if they're lucky) as the art of giving and granting favors; 20th-century vampires define it as "you scratch my back, I scratch yours." Unfortunately, more often the neonates come to prestation only through being taken advantage of by skilled elders, giving them no chance to learn under more "forgiving" conditions.

Many an inexperienced Kindred (youth and elder alike) has dug themselves into horrendous debt due to their ignorance of the levels of prestation. This is not entirely through their own making; not a few harpies brokering deals have assisted the matter by choosing not to inform a Kindred about his potential mistake or by deliberate misinformation when it suited them (this of course gives them the opportunity to "help" the unfortunate one by leveling another debt to have the first one renegotiated).

The levels defined below are what passes for definition across most of the Camarilla; regions, ages of the Kindred in question, previous working relations and extenuating circumstances (such as war) may all play a part in the negotiations.

- **Minor boon** — This is given in return for some small favor, such as the loan of something and its return, or for political support that did not risk or inconvenience the giver's standing. It is expected that the receiver will return the favor in similar fashion. While minor boons may not sound like much to worry about, a collection of them carefully placed and called in can be the prelude to a devastating gambit. Most vampires of any sect or clan consider the acts of granting and returning minor boons to be common politeness, and a vampire who does not do so is considered to be beyond even the harpies' scorn.

- **Major boon** — A major boon is collected in return for items loaned that did not return or returned damaged (such as ghouls, weapons, artwork), political support that involved considerable risk and/or inconvenience to the giver or his standing, and for physical assistance during an assault that was not life-threatening. Major boons can be quite handy to have in the political arena during conclaves, or during wartime to force the hand of Kindred who have been slow to offer resources or support.

- **Life boon** — A life boon entails the spectacular debts that prestation is famous for. In most cases, the debtor literally owes his continued unlife to the boon-holder, and the boon-holder can demand quite a bit before considering the debt paid — how much is the debtor's life worth to him? The collection of a life boon at a crucial moment can force a debtor to vote against his own dearly held cause or to betray a friend.

The sanctity of the prestation system is very important to the Camarilla, especially to the elders who have spent centuries carefully accruing favors from others. If it suddenly becomes acceptable to welch on one's prestation debt, then suddenly those elders' stockpiles of favors become worthless. Needless to say, the elders in question don't intend to allow that to happen. Those investments in favors are valuable, major resources in the mini-Jyhads the elders play. As such, they have a vested interest in keeping the formality of the prestation system intact.

Any attempt by a Kindred to wriggle out of a prestation debt is met with immediate and overwhelming response. As soon as the harpies hear of the affair, the offender's reputation is effectively trashed. He loses status and finds himself followed by derisive gossip. Alliances, particularly those based on favors given in the past, wither. Enemies spread slander about what *other* agreements the offender is unlikely to honor, paying homage to the time-honored Camarilla tradition of kicking a man when he's down. Other Kindred to whom the vampire owes favors call those favors due, daring him to break his word again and dig himself in even deeper. The offender has a choice of paying back all the favors he owes at once or cementing his reputation as untrustworthy. The former can place the vampire in a dangerous or exposed position, and certainly has the potential to drain his resources to a critical point. The latter offers the chance to make a whole new round of enemies, as Kindred denied their due are rarely forgiving.

Furthermore, the reputation one gets for welching on favors is not easily shaken, and the stench of it will follow the offender for decades. In the meanwhile, he finds obtaining help from anyone to be nigh-impossible, unless he's willing to pay usurious rates for assistance. Vampires are by nature a cautious race, and a Kindred who breaks faith is the sort of risk no Camarilla investor wants to assume.

Dead Files

While the Kindred who attempts to get out of a debt has it bad, the one who kills his creditor to avoid paying gets infinitely worse treatment. As it is the elders who hold most of the debts, they're the most likely targets for assassination if this practice is allowed to flourish. As a result, they come down *hard* on those who kill to escape paying. The best a Kindred who takes this route can expect is a blood hunt; the worst is unspeakable — but rest assured that the stories get around, so as to discourage other would-be killers.

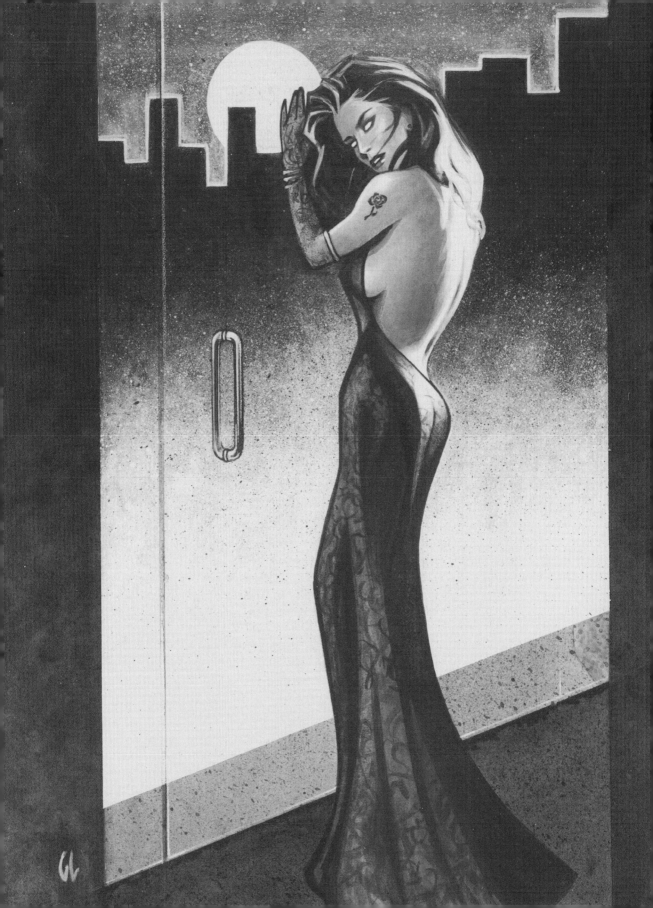

THE CITY BY NIGHT: BUILDING YOUR SETTING

The city of right angles and tough, damaged people.
— Pete Hammill

Vampires are, by definition, urban creatures, and the Camarilla takes this tendency to extremes. Away from the sheltering streets and skyscrapers, the Kindred find themselves out of their element. There are no sewers for the Nosferatu along the interstates, no Elysiums in small towns or highway rest stops. To make matters worse, there are matters of survival to consider — the scarcity of prey and proliferation of Lupines away from the cities offer double incentive for Kindred to keep to their home territory.

As a result, the vast majority of **Vampire** chronicles, especially those involving the Camarilla (the Sabbat pack mentality lends itself to a bit more experimentation outside the city limits), are bounded by the borders of the metropolitan area. With that in mind, it behooves the Storyteller of a Camarilla-based chronicle to have as detailed a city setting as possible, one that allows for a wide variety of stories without descending into caricature or chaos. This chapter is a guide to building a city for a Camarilla chronicle literally from the ground up — or to co-opting one that already exists and bringing it into the World of Darkness.

Note: This chapter is intended for Storyteller use only.

THE BASICS

If you are going to create a city to hold your game, there are a great many questions you're going to have to be prepared to answer about it. Remember, your characters will go places in the city you don't expect them to. They will ask where the dumpsters are and if there are alleys they can duck down, which directions the streets run and how much local phone calls cost. Unfortunately, you can't map out absolutely everything — if you did you'd have precious little time for anything silly like eating or sleeping — but there are steps you can take to prepare for moments when the story wanders into *terra incognita*.

The better and more fully realized your city is, the easier it is for you to extrapolate on the fly the details you haven't mapped out yet. The work and care you put into preparing your setting for play invariably pays off during your chronicle, when knowledge of your creation allows you to let the character wander its streets freely. Nothing wrecks the mood of a chronicle more completely than a Storyteller saying, "You can't go there," as a way of covering up for incomplete preparation. Vampires are lords of the night — the streets are their domain and they can go wherever they wish. The loss of a neighborhood (or even a building) to nothing in particular diminishes both the vampires' unholy swagger and the reality of the chronicle.

To avoid moments like that, you need to know your city. You need to know its mood, its feel, its architecture, its industries and more. It's a lot of work, yes, but the process is a rewarding one.

LAYING THE GROUNDWORK

Before you create the first vampire with whom to populate your metropolis of the night, you need to ponder the most central character in your chronicle: the city herself. Her history, mood, theme and very existence are what make up the bedrock of your chronicle. If you can't answer the following questions, your city isn't ready for your players yet, and any scenario you try to create will eventually collapse under its own weight.

Real or Imagined?

The first decision you have to make is whether or not your city is a real one. There are benefits and drawbacks to either choice. If you decide to set your chronicle in the World of Darkness equivalent of a real world city, a lot of the hard work has already been done for you. The city's geography and the basics of its history are already in place, and all you have to do is apply vampiric shadings. On the other hand, centuries of established history makes for a lot of research and limits your options to an extent; if your players are familiar with local history, they're going to take umbrage at your rewriting it too cavalierly.

On the other hand, building your city literally from the ground up gives you a blank canvas on which to work. History, location, street maps — all of them await your whim. The fictional city is completely your creation, from top to bottom. Unfortunately, that means that you have to create everything in it — and that's a great deal of work. There's more to a city's history than edited highlights and more to a city's map than a few main highways and a financial district. Once you make the commitment to create a city, there's no doing things halfway.

Home or Away?

If you choose to use an existing city as a base, you also need to decide whether to use your home town. While it can be tempting to do so, looking at your neighborhood with rose-colored mirrorshades can limit your options. With roughly 100,000 mortals required to support a single vampire, setting your campaign in a small city — even if you know it intimately — can severely limit your Storyteller character options. If your city can only support three Kindred and you have five players, certain problems of population present themselves. If your home town can support a reasonable game, however, it does give you a tremendous hand with Storytelling.

One of the main advantages of using your home city as the basis for your chronicle is the fact that you have in-depth knowledge of the place. Knowing where the clubs, the burned-out crack houses and the skyscrapers are reflexively allows you to move your chronicle to those places smoothly and rapidly. Being familiar with hangouts, restaurants and local slang lets you drop pertinent and real details into your story, and give it the sort of *verite* that adds to your players' immersion and enjoyment.

If you choose a city that's not your own, it's always a good idea to research it thoroughly first — and to make sure that it will spawn enough story ideas to sustain your chronicle. There's little sense in investing the time to learn a place satisfactorily, only to discover that the city doesn't hold interest for your players.

Travel books make excellent resources for this sort of research, as do the brochures and pamphlets that a city's tourist bureau is more than happy to send out. Many cities also have web sites these days, allowing for instant access to history,

Eminent Domain

So you want to run a chronicle set in your home city, but there's already published material on it. Even worse, the material that's in print doesn't jibe with what you want to do with your home town — how can your characters aspire to the princedom if a book states very clearly that there's an angry sixth-generation Ventrue who's laid claim to the throne and who brooks no dissent?

Fear not — you have plenty of options. You don't have to accept the published continuity if you don't want to — if your St. Louis doesn't jibe with our St. Louis, well, it's your game and you won't hurt our feelings by changing it. Your chronicle is implicitly yours, to do with as you wish, and that's all there is to it.

On the other hand, there's a lot of work that's already been done for you when you decide to run a game in a pre-created setting. If the setting as it stands doesn't work for you, but you don't want to rebuild the city from the ground up, there are compromises that you can make. The easiest is to run through the published setting, see what you like about it, and simply replace the rest. Another is to see where the city is, decide what you want it to be, and have the plot of your game be the progression from actual to ideal. Instead of simply removing a Storyteller character, you can have him assassinated in play and the characters put to the task of investigating. In that fashion, your exercise in world-building becomes the players' plot twist. You get what you want out of your setting while the players get to game without waiting for you to recreate the entire city.

Just don't stress about what you "can" and "can't" do. It's your game and your city. Do with both what you will.

tourist attractions and street maps. Having an idea of the city's high points allows you to concentrate the action in regions you know while buying time for you to do further research.

What Is The Mood?

Above and beyond the propaganda that tourist center brochures proclaim, each city tends to have a mood and a personality. Identifying your city's mood is a key step in identifying what sort of chronicles will run well there. A history of warfare and sprinkling of monuments give a city one flavor; urban renewal with lots of glass, chrome and steel provides another. If you look at your city's downtown region and see looming gothic architecture, narrow streets and weathered gargoyles, the locale probably lends itself better to chronicles of intrigue and conspiracy than it does to random gun battles in the streets.

Why Is It Camarilla?

The easy answer to this question is "Because the book says so," but that doesn't do a lot to help your chronicle along. Instead, you should look at the resources the city has to offer to see reasons the Camarilla wants to maintain control of this place. Perhaps there's a high-tech belt to the west of the city

THE PISSING MATCH

The most common pitfall attached to using your home town as the site of your chronicle is the know-it-all player, who invariably attempts to use his superior knowledge of the setting to derail the story. Getting drawn into arguments as to what exactly the name of the restaurant at 4th and South is, or how long ago a particular club closed, is extremely detrimental to your chronicle. The other players get bored, or worse, get involved in the debate. And if everyone's debating the minor details of city geography, no one's roleplaying.

The best thing to do if stuck with this sort of player is to remind him, gently, that the city in the World of Darkness is not the real city, and that things have changed a little bit. After all, this is your version of your home town, not his, and you have every right to let him know who's in charge.

that the younger Ventrue have decided is the key to their future success, or the city's port is a strategic point for smuggling Kindred in and out of the country. Maybe the city holds fond memories for certain elders, and they're not willing to relinquish the place, or perhaps a slumbering Methuselah has commanded in dreams that this city be maintained for her.

By cataloging what the city holds to keep the Camarilla in place, you're also cataloging what there is of interest to vampires in the city. Knowing what areas of control are possible allows you to start thinking about the Kindred who control them. Knowing what's out there that's attractive lays the groundwork for populating the city, and also thinking about the possible conflicts within the city itself. If a city loses its heavy manufacturing sector, the Brujah who controlled that industry and fed off its successes suddenly finds himself without a power base. At that point, he may seek to take away the domain of another Kindred, or his enemies may seek to annihilate him when he's at his weakest ebb.

QUESTIONS OF GEOGRAPHY

The physical makeup and layout of your city dictates in large part what sort of stories you can run comfortably in your game. If your city has just undergone a major urban renewal, complete with revitalized downtown area and gentrified neighborhoods, it may not necessarily be suitable for a game based around a the struggle to revitalize a declining manufacturing base in the face of Ventrue opposition.

WHAT DOES THE MAP LOOK LIKE?

Before doing anything else, get a map of your city (or create it, if you have to) and look at the town's physical layout. Get familiar with major access routes and important landmarks (airports, city hall, hospitals, police headquarters, etc.), and estimate how long it roughly takes to reach them when one is in a *Rotschreck*-fueled hurry. Note neighborhood and district divisions — being able to tell the run-down parts of town from the trendy shopping districts is important when it comes to placing your fictional landmarks. Finally, think about which

parts of town your players' characters are likely to be comfortable in and which ones will find them out of their element.

WHICH PLACES MATTER?

Not all sites are created equal. This is a truth so obvious it hardly seems worth repeating, but when it comes to mapping out your city it's important to remember that fact. Some chunks of real estate are more desirable to Kindred than others. Some afford financial or temporal power; others offer easy access to feeding or prime candidates for ghouling. Then there are transportation hubs, important parts of the city's physical plant and so on. A Nosferatu who has his talons in the city's water treatment station has a great deal more actual power than a Toreador who owns a dozen trendy clubs; the former can bring the metropolis to its knees, while the latter offers mortals a hip and happening good time.

It is important to figure out which buildings and institutions in the city matter to your vampires, and from there to determine which sites are relevant to which individual Kindred. City hall, police headquarters and the like are obvious places to start, but they're just starting points. If a mortal institution has power or influence, a vampire is going to want to get her hands on it. So establish which places might conceivably afford a vampire an advantage to inhabit or influence, and work from there. Some possible examples:

• **Prisons** — They offer extensive feeding possibilities, assorted underworld connections and potential ghouls with all sorts of useful skills

• **Airports** — Airports offer rapid transportation in and out. They also provide tremendous smuggling opportunities, and can be a great way to bottleneck arriving Kindred. If a city has multiple airports, there may well be a power struggle to control all of the air routes into or out of the city.

• **Train and Bus Stations** — Like airports, only less so. More important for snagging anarchs and refugees.

• **Freight Yards and Working Ports** — Smuggling, organized labor and access to and from a city without the need for a passport.

VISUALIZATION TOOLS

Often it's helpful to imagine the defining anima of a city as an individual. Think about the city's history, industry, population and architecture, and then collate all of that into the image of a single person. Try to avoid stereotypes — not everyone in Minneapolis talks like an extra from *Fargo*, for example. Then again, the defining moments of a city's heritage do need to be addressed. Atlanta may have been burned 13 decades ago, but the matter still subtly informs many residents' attitudes even today.

Once you achieve a working personification of a city's soul, it can get easier to work up other details of the city. It's often a lot simpler to figure out what goes well with a person than with a city as a whole. Remember, what you're going for is generalities and basics. If you try to work in all of the details this early in the process, you'll never finish.

• **Higher Education** — A city's colleges and universities, particularly those with good party scenes, make for excellent feeding opportunities. Outstanding students and graduate students can be targeted for ghouling or even the Embrace, and if the school has any sort of research wing, there's access to grant money and the fruits of that research as well. Then again, a supposed community of scholars might be of interest to Kindred with an interest in Noddist or other lore….

• **Local Branches of Government Departments** — The ability to call in audits, levy fines or shut down plants and businesses cannot be overestimated. Even something seemingly as unrelated to vampires as the EPA can be used to hamstring a business with astonishing speed.

• **Newspapers and Local Television** — These mortal institutions are a must-have for those interested in protecting the Masquerade. The ability to kill or alter stories — or to insert them to serve the Kindred's ends — makes influence in these areas powerful indeed.

• **Hospitals** — For the squeamish, hospitals offer cached blood. For the ghoulish, they offer feeding. For the careless, they offer places to dispose of mistakes.

• **City Hall** — For obvious reasons.

• **Police Stations** — Kindred with influence over the local police can call backup to deal with pesky opponents, or maneuver so that there are certain places that the police just know to leave alone….

• **Parks, Public Areas and Stadiums** — Wide open spaces offer space to host meetings or conclaves, and generally offer plenty of hiding places.

• **Trendy Clubs and Restaurants** — These places to see and be seen offer plenty of business opportunities, feeding for Kindred of discriminatory taste and excellent sources of income. Peripheral businesses (narcotics, fencing, etc.) also often come with the territory.

• **Industrial and Manufacturing Centers** — Manufacturing plants are still the economic backbone of their cities in many cases. They also have connections to organized labor, links to shipping and often ties to financial institutions as well.

• **Stockyards** — If your city has anything of a livestock industry, it has a perfect last-ditch hiding place and all-night cafeteria for losers in local brawls.

• **Homeless Shelters and Relief Agencies** — Shelters offer plenty of victims who won't necessarily be missed. For the less immediately homicidal, surpassingly effective ghouls can be plucked from the residents of such places.

• **Real Estate Companies** — Being able to buy, sell and have listings on havens is an advantage many Kindred would gladly pay for.

• **Fire Departments** — Having the ability to delay the hook and ladder truck's arrival at a rival's burning haven is worth a great deal to some Kindred.

• **Local Charities** — These can be touchstones for many local businesses. Someone with a stranglehold on the local office of a major charity gets to deal with all of the businesses who contribute….

• **Service Industries** — Power meter readers, phone technicians *et alia* get into everyone's home. *Everyone's.* That sort of access is power, and that's before you get into things like tracing or tapping cell phone calls, cutting off service at strategic times and so on.

• **Major Employers** — The notion of the company town is not dead. Even today, some companies employ (directly or indirectly) large segments of a city's population. Microsoft's impact on Seattle and Mercedes-Benz's on Stuttgart makes that sort of thing worth taking advantage of.

• **Financial Centers** — Controlling individual branches of banks is fine for getting petty cash or breaking into safe deposit boxes, but local stock exchanges or corporate headquarters are where the real money is. A little fiddling with the local stock index can do wonders — or horrors — for firms that are thus listed.

• **The Morgue** — A well-trained medical examiner is a vampire's best friend. Even the best-intentioned Kindred makes mistakes sometimes, and inevitably one of those mistakes gets picked up. Having a finger on the man who writes the death certificates can be a valuable asset in preserving the Masquerade.

• **Underworld Businesses** — The local numbers shop. Places that sell guns with the serial numbers filed off. Places to get assault rifles, explosives and illegal narcotics. The Kindred don't worry too much about going to jail, but they do worry about being able to kill, mutilate, drug or explode things on occasion.

…and so on. Note that this isn't be be-all end-all of what sorts of places are of interest to Kindred — there's always a chance that someone will decide to take an interest in the zoo or a local sports team — nor will every one of the places listed above have a vampire squatting malevolently behind it. Instead, just consider which of these and similar places might matter to your Kindred, and pick and choose from there.

When you're handing out places for Kindred to control, it also makes sense to establish which sites and institutions they don't have a handle on. Working out what these places are and why the Kindred don't at least influence them can produce interesting stories later on, when the characters try to establish control of these as-yet virgin territories. In the meantime, knowing why no one seems to have a handle on, say, the utilities (too many rivals maneuvering for it? princely edict? the local Monitor's haven? another supernatural protector?), you can sprinkle hints and ominous rumors into your chronicle.

WHERE DO THE KINDRED GO?

There's a world of difference between places the Camarilla likes to have a pallid finger on and those where individual vampires like to spend their time. Just because a Brujah has consolidated his influence in a city's labor unions doesn't mean that he necessarily enjoys whiling away his evenings at organizational meetings or in factories. There are places where vampires gather and hunt (the so-called "Rack"), and that's ground zero for most vampire-on-vampire interaction in a given city.

Defining your city's Rack takes more than just setting up a hip neo-Goth club and letting things go at that. If your vampires do frequent clubs, what sort of clubs are they, and who owns them? There's a very good chance that the Gangrel aren't going to hang out where the Toreador do, for example. As a result, you'll have to set up more than one club or bar in order to avoid artificially forcing all of your vampires under one roof. Don't take the time to set up a club that's frequented by each clan, though — it's a waste of time and defeats the purpose of having a club as a central meeting/interaction point. If all of the Tremere can go hang out at Club Etrius in one part of the city, they're never going to go anywhere else. And if they don't go anywhere else, you lose a valuable tool for introducing new characters and kicking off plots.

When you establish a club that's a vampiric hangout or hunting ground, make sure to give it something of a unique identity. People attend particular clubs for particular reasons, after all — playlists, DJs, ambiance, decor — and you need to create reasons for vampires (the pickiest of the picky consumers, especially when you figure in Auspex) to attend. Private space, places for unobtrusive feeding, ghoul doormen who let Kindred in automatically, aesthetics that are pleasing to Auspex-enhanced senses and so on are all reasons for Kindred to flock to a particular nightspot. Without amenities like these, vampires will simply move on to another place that caters to their whims.

On the flip side, lay out how the club deals with the Masquerade and breaches thereof. Any place that attracts flocks of Kindred on any given night is a magnet for trouble. Frenzies, fights, accidental killings during feeding and other crises will arise, and they'll all need to be dealt with quickly, quietly and efficiently. If a club gets a reputation as a trouble spot, if patrons disappear or get shot on a regular basis, then the cops are going to move in and the lowly mortals who make up the place's real customer base are going to move on. It's not like the *Kindred* are paying for their drinks, after all. So ponder your mythical club's cleanup, cover-up and defenses. You don't want

CHOPPING UP THE TOWN

It's fine to divvy up sections of your city to Kindred left and right, but restraint is as important as thoroughness in this instance. This is a Camarilla city, after all. The vampires who pull the strings of mortal institutions don't do so directly; they work through mortals to achieve their ends. Furthermore, vampiric control is always subtle and often imperfect; a Ventrue doesn't casually stroll into the local paper's city room and delete files at random. Instead, he calls the editor of the section, who may be a ghoul or may just be a mortal beholden to him, and requests that the offending story be killed. He may offer recompense in the form of additional ad revenue for that section that day, or he may "create" another newsworthy incident to fill the space. The desired effect is achieved without bloody constraint.

So remember that when you hand out sections and institutions, you're handing out influence, not total and direct control. Plan your plots accordingly.

BAD NEIGHBORHOODS

It's easy to dismiss the bad parts of town. It's simple to sketch them simply and use them as convenient feeding grounds, nothing more. But it's not necessarily right to do so.

If you're going to take your story into the less savory parts of town, show respect for your subject matter. Poverty and despair are powerful, dreadful things, and cavalierly using them as justifications for cheap feeds sends the wrong message. If a neighborhood goes to hell, there's a reason — plant closings, neglect or malice from city government, infestation by dealers — and there are real human beings affected by that decline. Even if your Kindred plumb the worst depths of your city, remember to ascribe some basic human dignity.

to be caught unprepared when the local mob of Brujah decides to tear the club's mysterious owner a new one.

While the clubs are the heart of your city's Rack, they're not the entire thing. Is your city's prime hunting ground a club district, or does it tend more toward shopping and restaurants? Outlining the Rack also lays out what sort of prey vampires are likely to find there. A ritzier, shopping-based Rack is likely to have more middle- and upper-class patrons, and these people are more likely to be taken seriously when they talk about being attacked. A club-based Rack, however, has younger and possibly inebriated or otherwise chemically altered patrons, and such mortals don't necessarily carry great credibility. Pick your spots and expand upon them.

Clubs and the Rack aren't the only places that Kindred spend their time. Elysium is also important to establish. For more information on setting up Elysiums in your city, see page XX.

WHERE ARE THE HAVENS?

At this point in the process, you've laid out where the Kindred go to "work" and where they go to eat and play. What's left is where they live. In other words, it's time to figure out whose havens are where.

Many Kindred, particularly experienced, wealthy and paranoid ones, have multiple havens. As a result, trying to pinpoint where each haven of every vampire in your city might be is a fine way to drive yourself mad. Instead, decide where the main havens of a) the important Kindred, and b) the vampires your characters are likely to bump into might be. You might also want to sketch out the details and defenses of havens that your players' coterie are likely to visit or invade. If the plots that you're cooking up make it look likely that the characters are going to have to go beard the Malkavian elder in his den, it only makes sense to know ahead of time what they're going to have to get past in order to get there.

Even if you don't pick street addresses and apartment numbers for the havens you're designing, you should at least know what general neighborhoods they're in, and why they're there. Having a haven next door can do strange things to a community — police patrols might drop as a result, leading to higher crime, or perhaps the Kindred sees fit to ghoul a few of his neighbors as a precaution….

How Do You Get There?

An overlooked aspect of a city's geography involves access. How do mortals get in and out — is there a busy airport (and which airlines use it as a hub)? What about train lines, buses or major highways? If there's only one main road leading into or out of town, a single traffic accident at a strategic time can wreak havoc on Kindred travel plans. A massive snarl an hour before sunrise can trap a vampire far from his haven with nowhere to hide. As an extension of this, it makes sense to take a quick look at the city's traffic maps. Main streets, parkways, traffic bottlenecks and construction projects are all good to know about, particularly if you anticipate high-speed chases in your chronicle.

Just as important is figuring out how vampires get smuggled in and out of the city. Kindred travel arrangements can get peculiar, and more than one vampire has made a fortune by shipping his fellow bloodsuckers like cargo. Ports, air freight terminals, railroad freight yards and the like all deserve attention as potential points of entry for Kindred.

Where Don't They Go?

The flip side of picking out where the Kindred of your city do go is delineating the places where they don't go. That's more difficult than looking at a map, figuring out what the quote-unquote "bad neighborhoods" are, and X-ing them off your game map. What might be a bad neighborhood to you or me isn't so much of a hassle to an unliving killing machine who can shrug off bullets like they're mosquito bites, after all.

Instead, it takes effort to figure out why a particular part of town is inhospitable to Kindred. A tightly knit Catholic neighborhood might have enough ambient True Faith to keep most vampires at bay. Parks or other less heavily developed spaces might have other supernatural inhabitants who aren't vampire-friendly. Or maybe there are just vampiric rivalries — one line of Brujah has its havens firmly settled in the neighborhoods in

The 'Burbs

Your city is not just the city itself. There's the entire metropolitan area to consider. Which neighborhoods do the wealthy suburban squires retreat to at the end of the day, and can the Kindred get there without being ambushed by Lupines along the way? Gated communities can serve as private hunting preserves, or they can be death-traps. It's all a matter of perspective.

Fortunately or unfortunately, the Kindred don't much like the suburbs. There's a little too much open space, there aren't enough places to hide, and the residents still sometimes call the cops when they hear screaming coming from neighbors' houses late at night. An active neighborhood watch association is surprisingly good at picking up breaches in the Masquerade.

A few Kindred do like to have suburban havens, far from the hustle, bustle and armed robbery of the city streets, but they're in a distinct minority. For even the ever-wary Kindred, there's safety in numbers.

the southern part of the city, while their rivals are established to the west, and never the twain shall meet. Take the time to figure out which parts of your city aren't safe for any vampires (and why), which ones aren't safe for your important Storyteller characters and which ones aren't safe for the players' characters.

What Does the Place Look Like?

While not strictly a question of geography, the matter of the physical appearance of your city, right down to its base architectural style, should be addressed at some point. A city's façade affects the mood it establishes — a skyline of mirrored glass and steel creates a different mood than does one of stately turn-of-the-century skyscrapers encrusted with gargoyles, or one marked by medieval or even Roman ruins. A city wherein every building and terrace is marked by beetling, glowering statuary generates an oppressive, paranoiac feel, while the ultra-modern look of glass, chrome and steel makes for a depersonalized, alienated setting. Furthermore, no city's decor is uniform; the breakdowns run neighborhood by neighborhood, with dilapidated row homes cheek-by-jowl with freshly yuppified condos and trendy shops. Figure out which feel you want to emphasize in your game and play that look (and those neighborhoods) up. Remember, this is your city, and you don't have to stick that closely to "reality" in matters like this.

Building style is also a matter that is more important than it seems. Vampires are creatures of the side alley and the boardroom, and you need to figure out the proportions thereof. While it's all well and good for the characters to want to duck down an alley and hide behind a dumpster after killing a Ventrue's prized ghoul, skyscraper districts tend not to have too many alleys. Define what the regular features of your city's landscape are. Are there trees planted in front of every building, or is there trash in the streets? How about alleys — how many, how often, how deep and do they have sewer tunnel access for the Nosferatu? Does the city spring for bright, white street lamps, or are the roads lit in dingy yellow and orange (if they are lit at all)? This sort of thinking extends to the human aspects of the landscape as well. Do the cops walk their beat on foot, or do they stick to cars and in pairs?

Questions of Elysium

Part of what makes a city definitively Camarilla is its Elysiums. These places, cultural centers where violence is forbidden against all, rest at the heart of a city's intellectual unlife. Without knowing a city's Elysiums — where and what and how numerous they are — you can't know a city. Therefore, defining your city's Elysiums is a matter of paramount importance.

Where Is Elysium?

Elysiums are the rocks of a city's foundations, the safe and strong places that remain inviolate even when all around them is chaos. You should put thought and consideration into your selection of Elysiums, because by selecting Elysium so you affect everything that happens *around* Elysium as well. It may seem obvious just to go ahead and pick your city's largest art museum as Elysium and letting it go at that, but the obvious choice isn't always the best one. Choosing multiple, unexpected or just plain strange places to serve as Elysium helps give your city an identity rooted in specifics.

Just the sheer number of places marked Elysium has a profound impact on a city's feel. A city that has but a single museum declared Elysium is a very different place from one with a half-dozen sites — the latter is clearly a more prosperous and peaceful domain, its Kindred have more time for contemplation of the arts, there is more culture fostered in the city by mortal and immortal alike, and multiple Elysiums offers more opportunities for intriguing on safe ground. On the other hand, the city with but a single museum or theater demonstrates that the prince's priorities lie elsewhere, that the city doesn't have the resources to support multiple Elysiums, and that the Kindred of the metropolis have other, more pressing concerns than the cultivation of art.

There are other, more subtle effects on the city to be considered as well. For example, the more locales the prince recognizes as Elysium, the more bases of power the local harpies have. More Elysiums also means fewer prime pieces of downtown to be handed out as prize domains to the local Toreador, not to mention more places lawbreakers can duck into for sanctuary.

By plotting out how many sites in a city are designated Elysium, you can also establish the city's attitude toward culture and keeping up the appearance thereof.

What Is Elysium?

The places chosen for a city's Elysiums say a great deal about both the city and those who dwell there. The effects of labeling a place Elysium are both obvious (here is where the vampires can be found) and subtle (a museum not chosen as Elysium is liable to enter a precipitous decline). Defining the Elysiums of your city, not to mention the effects of your choices, makes a tremendous difference in establishing your setting.

The stereotypical image of Elysium is that of the art museum open after hours, Kindred strolling to and fro while making snide comments and sipping vitae from wine glasses. While that image certainly can hold some truth, you should think about whether it holds enough truth for your game. Is the art museum your Kindred's Elysium of choice? If so, why — tradition, a specific collection of Impressionists or artifacts, fond memories relating to a particular piece ("*I was in Paris when George painted that one. It was the year I finally left my sire's household and I was looking for someone I could sponsor to gain entrance into a certain salon…*") or some reason esoteric beyond human understanding? There's certainly nothing wrong with choosing a city's art museum as your core Elysium. After all, it has a variety of exhibits to please the eye, plenty of space for intriguing with or avoiding others, and a central location — all vital elements to a proper Elysium. However, picking the art museum because you think it's expected, and not for the merits that the particular place holds, shortchanges your story and your city.

So if your central Elysium is to be located elsewhere, what sort of place should you pick? An opera house or academy of music is a superb choice. Most are decorated in a suitably rococo style to appease even the most perfectionistic Toreador; many have sweeping lobbies as well as secluded boxes and numerous back stairwells, all excellent places to conduct vampiric business or to hold court. Furthermore, there's always the prospect of intrigues conducted subtly, through hand gestures, passed notes and urgent whispers while the orchestra plays madly and the opera's action crashes to a climax onstage.

Beyond libraries and music halls, there are other potential choices to consider. Theaters, particularly ones with some sort of history to them, work well. Many cities have central libraries of renown that can also offer the amenities essential to an Elysium, ranging from exhibits to statuary to suitably ornate decoration. Art galleries offer many of the same amenities of museums, but in more intimate surroundings. European cities may have Roman amphitheaters or other landmarks still in functioning condition. Manors and castles turned into museums and left behind by their original residents often fit the bill — particularly if the city's Kindred visited those houses centuries earlier and seek comfortable surroundings.

The trick when selecting a site for a central Elysium is to make sure it offers enough — enough space, enough culture, enough to amuse visitors and enough respect to keep Kindred from ignoring the place's status. Just labeling something "Elysium" is no guarantee that the name will stick — good luck enforcing Elysium status for a comedy club or even for an experimental theater that's a little too experimental for the local harpies' taste.

That being said, you certainly don't have to restrict yourself to just one Elysium. If a city has several sites worthy of the title, or the prince simply wants to show off how cultured and sophisticated he might be, any number of locales can end up as an Elysium. What matters is that you know which Elysium is the main one — the one where the harpies gather and where the prince receives petitioners. You also might want to consider whether the prime Elysium rotates its location, or what is happening at the other sites on the nights when the central Elysium is dull and quiet.

It Can't Rain All the Damn Time

While it may seem very moody and gothic to have your chronicle constantly backlit by jagged forks of lightning, it's not always necessary. If nothing else, the constant rain would flood out the Nosferatu and produce all sorts of interesting rumblings in the city's power structure. Use symbology like lightning to your advantage, which is to say sparingly and only at appropriate moments.

Your city's weather and climate can help your stories along. Unnatural hot streaks can make mortal and immortal alike irritable and prone to violence. Blizzards and cold snaps can seal mortals in their homes, leaving slim pickings for Kindred on the streets. Droughts can lead to fires, and to slow or inadequate responses from city fire departments. Heavy rains and flooding might do unpleasant things to Kindred with subterranean havens. And a city with clear night skies might prove a hazard to stargazing Toreador, who stand, enraptured, staring in awe at the beauty of the heavens.

Finishing Touches

Once you have the where and the what (not to mention the why) of your Elysiums set up, there are a few other questions that need answering.

• **What sort of security is there?** Does the prince rely on the tradition of Elysium to protect the site, or are there armed guards? What about supernatural protections?

• **Who benefits from having this place as Elysium?** Did a vampire suggest this site to His Majesty? If so, what was her reward? What about those museums and theaters snubbed — what's happening to them, and who's suffering as a result?

• **What can you do with this place?** Is the building hosting Elysium big enough for audiences and mass meetings? What sort of space does it offer for plotting? If there are dangers, what are they?

• **What is the local attitude toward Elysium?** Does the prince simply tolerate it as a necessary evil, or does he embrace the notion? What about his subordinates, and what are they willing to do to push their agendas about the place?

Questions Of Historical Import

It is no understatement to say that many Kindred dwell exclusively in the past, to the point where they refuse to acknowledge the very existence of the present. History, then, is of paramount importance to these creatures, and that means that history should matter to your newly hatched city as well. By establishing your city's history — and the role the local Kindred played in creating it — you lay the groundwork for the vampiric rivalries and vendettas of the present. Without knowing where your Kindred have been, you can't get a handle on where they're going.

So What Happened?

The first step in establishing a city's history in the World of Darkness is to learn the city's real history. (Of course, if you're creating a city from whole cloth, it's up to you to make up the mortal history as well.) Once you have that under your belt, you can start looking for highlights, incidents of importance in the city's story that look as if they might have been "adjusted" by outside influences. Riots, battles, mysterious murder sprees and other violent moments are a great place to start, but there are other options as well. What about notable elections, massive donations of land to the city, building projects and the like? Just because the Kindred revel in blood doesn't mean that all their works are immediately soaked in it.

Gaining familiarity with a city's history isn't the same thing as becoming a world-renowned expert on it. Don't feel you have to know everything about a city, from the political affiliation of its 14th mayor to the names of its turn-of-the-century semipro athletic teams, to have a handle on a city's past. Don't worry about not knowing everything. Just make sure you've learned enough that you can ground the current events you're creating in some sort of historical context. If your city has a history of gangland violence, you can take that trend and use it to inform what you're

doing now. Perhaps two of the feuding gangsters were Embraced, and carry on their deadly rivalry from beyond the grave. Or maybe the course of the fighting took out one Kindred's entire ghoul support network, leading to her downfall. Now, decades later, she's looking to extract payback from the vampires who supported the killers. Then again, the entire thing may have been sparked by the maneuvering of some Kindred using mortal pawns to undercut the other, and the conflict is simply awaiting the appropriate time to renew itself. In all three cases, what has been, once given a vampiric twist, now fulfills two functions. It fits nicely into the city's supernatural history, and it sets up future plots that are well-grounded in the "historical" past.

How Much Influence?

The vampiric influence on human history in the World of Darkness has consistently been overstated, both by the vampires themselves and by outside observers (i.e. folks reading and playing the game). History happens, driven by the great mass of humanity. Vampires, with very few exceptions, cannot alter that flow of events; they can merely hope to divert it, to forestall or trigger events or to ride the crest of the wave to a profitable result. There are simply too many humans with too much historical momentum for the Kindred to muck about with things willy-nilly.

That being said, in order to see what role vampires have historically played in your city, you have to figure out how much of that city's history they were behind — and why. It does no good to say that vampires were behind a particularly bloody strike in the 1920s unless you can figure out why — who benefited from the strike and the subsequent brutal strikebreaking? Why would they instigate such events? What did they stand to gain? Vampires, like anyone else, have motivations for doing things. It doesn't matter if those things are as insignificant as choosing a dress or as momentous as instigating an assassination — there has to be a reason for something being done. Ascribing actions to the Kindred without ascribing motives makes those actions nonsensical. Bear in mind that the vampire behind the scenes may not have had good or intelligent reasons for what he did, but as long as there was a reason that made sense to him, the whole sequence of events becomes much more believable.

Behind Closed Doors

You should think beyond the public spaces when creating your Elysium. There's more to a museum than galleries — there are restoration facilities, storage and warehouse spaces, offices and more far from the public eye. Similarly, an academy of music offers rehearsal spaces, costume chambers, dressing rooms, ticket offices and the like. Libraries have document chambers, microfiche storage rooms, preservation facilities, closed stacks, rare book collection rooms and other places that aren't necessarily obvious, but which can provide a wealth of plot hooks. Once you designate a site Elysium, you might as well get as much out of your Elysium as you can. That means using every available inch of the place, and not ignoring any of it.

What Have the Vampires Done?

Though vampires exist at a slower pace than mortals do, they're not always idle or in torpor. Over the centuries or even millennia your city has existed, there has been a shadow history of vampiric doings running parallel to the record of mortal events. Knowing what the human beings were doing for all those years is only half the story; you have to know what the Kindred were doing as well.

Note that your vampiric history should not simply be a matter of "here's when the vampires fought, and here's how they covered it up." Instead, keep track of who arrived when, and where they came from. Establish Embrace dates for your major characters, not to mention the stories behind their Embraces. Which vampires died along the way, how did they die, and what happened as a result? Often it makes sense to establish the vampiric power dynamics of today and then work backward to see how they got that way.

Just remember that your shadow history has to be masked by the real one. A hundred years of vampiric warfare might make for excellent backstory, but if it coincides with a century of peace and prosperity in the real world, the incongruity will strain players' credulity.

Wars

One of the most devastating things that can hit a city is the tide of war. As bloody and brutal as warfare has been in the real world, the influence of supernatural monsters in the World of Darkness might even make it worse. What is certain, however, is that warfare touches the unliving population of a city as well as the living one, and that ignoring the effect of warfare on your city's vampires can be a serious mistake.

Mortal Wars

Most of the cities on the planet have been involved in some sort of warfare, and the effects of that sort of action on the local Kindred population need to be examined carefully. It's a mistake to worry about which vampires were behind which side. Rather, think about how war affected your city directly. Was it burned to the ground, like Dresden or Moscow? If it was, how much of the vampiric population was caught in the firestorm? Did enemy troops occupy it, making it harder for Kindred to feed, or did total chaos reign? How about the reconstruction of

the urban area afterward — which vampires had a hand in rebuilding the city to their liking? Mortal wars provide a storytelling opportunity to change the course of your city's shadow history; take advantage of it if you can.

Immortal Wars

Vampires wage war as well, thought not on the direct scale that mortals do. Even if two of the most powerful vampires in a given city decide to go at it, you're not going to see tens of thousands of Kindred lined up in ranks, waiting for the order to charge. Instead, war between vampires is a more subtle thing, played out by mortal pawns and vampiric catspaws. Gang wars, political upheavals, riots, overthrows of governments and the like all provide excellent cover for deadly struggles between Kindred. The overlaying violence serves to mask the more vicious tactics that each feuding vampire puts into play.

If you decide that two or more Kindred went to war in your city's past, it makes sense to look for upheaval in the mortal world that could have provided camouflage for the deadly struggle. If you can find an instance in which the unruly mortals more or less matched the philosophies of the Kindred you scripted as going at it, so much the better. Otherwise, think about when it makes sense for there to be immortal combat in your setting, and pick a moment in history to fit.

Note: You may want to wait on this particular aspect of building your city until after you've filled in the vampiric population (see below).

What About Tidbits?

While it's not necessary to know absolutely everything about your city's past to run a good chronicle in it, knowing the odd bit of historical trivia can certainly serve its purpose. Putting factoids from 10 or 12 centuries past into the mouths of your older Kindred serves nicely to establish the realism of their age. Having a vampire stroll onto the scene and announce that he's three centuries old stretches credulity — the moment seems staged, and as a result the character doesn't acquire the respect his age should garner him. But having him walk into Elysium, garbed impeccably in the wardrobe of yesteryear and dropping conversational tidbits about the measures he and a friend had helped institute to control the outbreak of yellow fever among the kine back in the 1790s, he acquires a bit more of the aroma of historicity.

In addition, every city's history is full of bits of just plain old-fashioned weirdness — rains of frogs, the odd political suicide or socialite disappearance, rich eccentrics building strange houses and the like — that can fit nicely into a campaign as evidence of vampiric maneuverings gone awry. The rain of frogs can be laid at the feet of an incompetent local Tremere, the disappearances and suicides might be the evidence of anything from abuses of Dominate to cover-ups for Embraces and so on.

Also, remember this: Just because a vampire might have influenced an event doesn't mean that things turned out the way the Kindred wanted. Vampires screw up, too, and sometimes to absolutely spectacular effect.

Nights of Old

While cities in the Western Hemisphere are younger than the Camarilla, much of the rest of the world boasts metropoli that predate the sect by centuries or millennia. For places like Athens, Cairo, Jerusalem and so on, the reasons the city went down the Camarilla path need to be laid out clearly. The vampires who inhabit these places, many of whom predate the sect as well, also need to establish why they chose the Camarilla. If there was a sectarian struggle in your city's past, map it out and decide why things went the way they did.

It might even be worth wondering if someone out there wants a rematch.

Questions of Population

No city is suitable for a vampire game without a population of vampires. As detailed as your history might be, as fascinating as your setting is, without a suitable flock of living dead in place to provide allies, enemies, informants and other bodies for your players to interact with, your city isn't complete. You need to know who lives in your city, who visits it, where the residents are likely to be found and where they stand on a whole host of issues. Otherwise, your detailed cityscape is simply so much gorgeous scenery.

Who Lives There?

The first thing you need to do in creating your city's population is to establish how many vampires the city actually supports. A good rule of thumb is one Kindred per 100,000 mortals, and population statistics are generally pretty easy to find. Note that this number can be adjusted up or down, depending on the feel you want to establish in your setting. If you decide that your city should have a wide-open, sparse feel to it, drop the number of Kindred. On the other hand, if you're going for a feverish, overcrowded ambiance, increase the vampiric population. Just be careful not to increase it *too* much, or else be prepared for an in-play culling.

Once you know how many vampires are in your city, think about the clan breakdown. As your city is Camarilla, the six main clans should easily predominate, with a few straggling Gangrel as well. Minor clans, bloodlines, Sabbat invaders and so on should make up a tiny fraction of the Kindred population.

The Prince and Population

In large part, your city's clan breakdown is determined by what clan the prince is. As the prince alone has the right of unlimited creation, it only makes sense for her to reinforce her position by Embracing enough progeny to protect herself properly. Furthermore, the right of creation makes an excellent favor to bestow on those to whom the prince owes boons; odds are that many Kindred thus gifted are from the prince's clan.

Who Made Who?

After you get a rough breakdown of numbers in place, it's time to think about lineages. This step is more important than one might think. While the Toreador might have five members in your fictional city, how exactly those five are related can make a tremendous difference in the clan's power. A clan comprised of one elder with four progeny certainly presents a different face to the city than does a "family" of five Toreador of successive generation. Mapping out how the vampires of a single clan are related, if indeed they are, also helps you establish the relative power of the various clans.

Note: At this point in the process, you should probably be giving at least preliminary names to your Kindred. This serves as a tremendous aid in keeping the tangled web of vampiric relationships straight.

Sires and Childer

As important as knowing who spawned whom is knowing how the parties relate afterward. Poor sire-childe relations can weaken a clan's hold on a city; strong ones can unify the clan into a nigh-unstoppable force. Also take into consideration blood bonds, voluntary and otherwise, and their effects on childer's affection. (Some of those bonds might be fragile or broken, which is always good to know.) Finally, it's worth thinking about siblings in the blood — multiple childer of the same sire — and any rivalries that might exist there.

The Unwanted

Bear in mind that not every childe is acknowledged. Caitiff aren't part of anyone's equation, but they do need to be taken into account when you're populating your city. How many Caitiff there are, who created them, and how likely it is that the act will be traced back are all questions to ponder. A Caitiff's quest for her parentage can make for an interesting plot thread, especially if the trail leads back to the corridors of Elysium. Remember, the creation of a Caitiff is a violation of the Traditions and is theoretically punishable by death. Building that sort of ticking time bomb into your city's foundations gives you something earthshaking to spring on your players later on.

The Lessers

Vampires aren't the only ones intimately wound in the city's Camarilla web. There are ghouls to consider as well. While a ghoul isn't necessarily as important a part of the city as one of the Kindred (particularly if he's part of a particular vampire's large stable), it make sense to know where the ghoul numbers stack up in your city as well. The more ghouls a clan has, the longer its reach in the daylight hours, the more eyes it has in place in the city and the more soldiers it can call upon in times of crisis.

If there are particularly prominent ghouls (police officers, reporters, politicians, etc.) in your city, it often makes sense to figure out whom they're beholden to. Mapping the web of favors and allegiances down to the mortal — or mostly mortal — level goes a long way toward figuring out who's inclined to help your players' characters and who isn't.

The Disloyal Opposition

After the basic framework of the city's Camarilla population is established, then you can start thinking about who doesn't fit in. That designation includes anarchs, members of the unaffiliated clans like the Giovanni, and Sabbat packs and infiltrators. Needless to say, you don't want to stock up too heavily on any of these, otherwise your Camarilla city abruptly ceases to be Camarilla.

If your city has an anarch population, make a note of how many of the anarchs are homegrown (and who their sires are) and how many are imported rabble-rousers; a blood hunt following an anarch from his home city onto your prince's turf can make for an interesting story. The independents' connections and targets in the city need to be delineated; knowing which Kindred the lone Setite is dealing with and which ones he's got in his pocket is an important difference. As for the Sabbat, knowing where it's holed up, what it's after and whom it's targeted or subverted already sets up Sabbat-related plotlines down the road.

TRANSIENTS

If your game is set in a small city, your players' coterie might well be 50% of the vampiric population. This can make for short-lived chronicles, with the coterie ganging up on the rest of the city's Kindred and taking them out one by one.

A possible solution lies in bringing in transients. Think about which vampires are frequent, infrequent or even vaguely regular visitors. A pack of roving Gangrel, an archon who has a centuries-old romantic entanglement with a member of the primogen council or a rabble-rousing anarch who thinks the city's an easy mark can all beef up your vampiric numbers temporarily without overstuffing the city.

JOB DESCRIPTIONS

Since your city is held by the Camarilla, it should have a prince, sheriff, primogen, harpies and so on. Establishing which clans and which characters fill those roles is imperative. The entire vampiric population of the city takes its cues, positive or negative, from the prince. Start defining the power structure at the top, and the rest flows downhill from there.

WHO'S THE PRINCE?

Before you fill out the rest of the Camarilla hierarchy, you need to define and establish your prince. Who is she? How old is she? What is her clan, and is this her first time holding a city? If not, why did she leave her last post — and who pushed her out of it? If so, how did she climb to power, and who's plotting vengeance as a result?

THE WEIRD ONES

It can be tempting to treat your city like a salad bar, taking one vampire from each clan or bloodline. One of each can't hurt, right?

Wrong. You only have so much space for vampires in this city, and by the time you finish including all of the minor and extremely rare lineages, you won't have room for the Brujah, Ventrue, Toreador and others who should be making up the meat of your story. In addition, one of the defining characteristics of the Gargoyles, Lasombra *antitribu*, etc. is that they are extremely rare. Having one in a city is enough to excite comment and cause speculation; having several in place for anything short of a conclave is beyond the bounds of coincidence.

It's wiser and easier to stick to the basics, seasoning lightly with one or perhaps two of the rarities. Otherwise, you run the risk of having the sideshow become the main event, and having your plot crowded right off the stage.

Answering the above questions gives you a good idea of who the prince is, but what remains to be defined is her relationship with her city. Is she strict in enforcing her laws, and has she added any legislation to the basic Traditions? How harsh is she on lawbreakers, and how likely is she to call a blood hunt? Which clans beside her own does she favor, and which does she frown upon? What are her solutions to the so-called anarch problem? Caitiff? The Sabbat? Lupines? Does she trust her seneschal, the primogen or any of the other officers of the city? Map out the answers to these questions, and you draw yourself a political map of your city.

WHO ARE THE PRIMOGEN COUNCIL?

Few princes have absolute power in the strictest sense of the term. Most rule in conjunction with, if not on the sufferance of, the city's primogen. Theoretically the primogen council is the city's council of elders, a gathering of the oldest and wisest representatives of the clans. To no one's surprise, it rarely works out that way. Politics and jealousy make for compromise candidates, and a strong prince can ramrod his candidates through if there isn't anyone else in the city strong enough to stop him.

Ideally, your primogen should comprise the elders of the various clans. If you want to deviate from this basic setup, think about how and why you want to change things. If your primogen is going to consist of five Brujah and a Malkavian, you need to have a good reason for setting things up that way. Your city has to *function* night to night, after all.

PRIMOGEN AND PRINCE

An important thing to watch is the relationship between your prince and his city's primogen. In some cities, it is the primogen who select the prince; in others matters run precisely opposite. Establish how the balance of power tilts. A city with a primogen council full of yes-vampires who belong to the prince's clan runs a little differently than does one wherein the prince is beholden to his "advisors" for everything he has.

The next order of business is to define how much power the primogen council has, and what it's actually doing as opposed to what it's supposed to be doing. Detailing the primogens' subversions (or lack thereof) matters just as much as detailing what the council is supposed to be doing. More than one prince has been surprised by a revolt fomented by his "advisory" committee.

WHAT ABOUT THE OTHER TITLES?

There are titles beyond prince and primogen in a city. While it's important to know at least theoretically who the seneschal is, etc., the priority lies with establishing those Kindred who are most likely to interact with your player's coterie. In most cases, that means the sheriff, the keeper of Elysium, the harpies and possibly the scourge, assuming your city has one. As the characters are likely going to interact with any and all of these Kindred, those characters need to be drawn up in detail. They're going to

ECONOMY

If you establish your web of character relationships and find that there are two or more that essentially have the same allies, enemies and functions, it's worth your while to combine the two. You only have so many Kindred to play with, and redundancy wastes one of your most valuable resources.

be on stage a great deal in your campaign, which means that they'd better be ready for the spotlight. The politics of these lesser figures don't matter as much as their personalities do. They don't make policy so much as they enforce it, and as a result figuring out who they are and how they're likely to react to the characters is of paramount importance.

THE UNTITLED

The ruck and run of the Kindred population of your city is left without titles, which is as it should be. However, that doesn't mean that those left out in the cold aren't thinking about climbing the ladder of power. You should think about which of your Kindred are actively ambitious (and whose positions they're targeting) and which ones are content where they are. Clan ties may play into this as well; the Tremere elder may frown on a younger clan member's desire to be sheriff, for example, but may encourage his protégé to take the role of scourge.

POLITICS: WHO HATES WHOM?

Once you have a rough idea of who the vampires in your city are, the last step is to figure out how they all fit together. Establishing friendships, alliances, patronages and favors owed primes future plots based on those vampires' interactions.

In a sense, what this part of city creation boils down to is writing the personal histories and ambitions of your horde of characters. The trick is to make sure that if you've got 30 Kindred in your city, you don't have 30 free-floating individuals. Make a goal of having each and every Kindred link to at least three others. If there's a good reason for a character to have only one connection (say, an illegitimate childe whose existence is known only to his sire), that's fine, but a character who only seems to work well with one or two other Kindred doesn't lend himself to enough stories for you to keep him around. Not all of the relationships you establish between characters should be amicable (conflict is every Storyteller's friend), but they should be real, passionate and vital. Vampires are creatures out of time. Their hatreds and rivalries are nurtured over the centuries with each insult and dig, every setback and petty triumph. That intensity of relationship has to come through when you map out how your Kindred feel about one another. Mild dislikes and vague affection have no place in the web of vampiric relationships; such delicate emotions are reserved for mortals.

Some of the questions you'll probably want to answer at this point are:

Who supports the prince? Who doesn't, and who's willing to do anything about it?

Who's been talking to the Sabbat, or other outsiders? Conversely, who's loyal, and to whom?

Who owes other Kindred favors? The pecking order of prestation is important in determining who can lean on whom.

Who loves whom? Love blossoms even among the unliving, but a spurned suitor can take a terrible vengeance.

Whose politics jibe with whose? Who are the anarchs? The traditionalists? The wild cards? Conversely, who's willing to kill to buttress his position?

Who are the diablerists, and who died in that fashion? Is anyone looking for vengeance, or even those tell-tale streaks in the aura?

Who is ambitious, and who's a target for that ambition? What Kindred are seeking to climb in the power structure, and what are they willing to do to get there?

These simple questions, and the questions that their answers raise, should help you establish a solid framework for your city's Camarilla politics.

WHERE DO YOU GO FROM HERE?

By this point, you should know where your city is, what it's like, what it looks like, what's important in it, what happened in there, what *really* happened there, who lives there, what they control, whom they like and dislike and what they're trying to do about it. While creating every detail of a fiction (or even fictionalized) city is the work of many lifetimes, by this point you've done enough to have at least a workable setting for your chronicle. You've done your preparation. Now it's time to use the conflicts you've set up and the history you've established to start telling stories.

TEMPLATES

Below are statistics and very basic writeups for archetypal characters who are likely to be found in a Camarilla city. The statistics, descriptions and other traits are only a starting point, and you should feel free to modify them as you wish when populating your chronicle setting. Bear in mind, however, that so-called "stat creep" is one of the most insidious enemies a chronicle can have, and that the characters presented here are designed with their stats as is for a reason.

CHARTS

A tremendous help in clarifying your vampires' tangled relationships is the so-called coterie chart. First, space out your major characters' names on a sheet of paper. Then draw arrows between those vampires who interact. Finally, write descriptives along those arrows, establishing how each half of the equation feels about the other. You'd be amazed at how easy this sort of quick reference makes things.

Street Caitiff

Background: Seduced and abandoned, a street-level Caitiff is a vampire by default. He's spent his brief time as a vampire ducking from the sheriff, the scourge and anyone else he imagines is after him. Desperate for an ally but afraid to trust anyone, he sleeps where he can, feeds when he can and waits for the inevitable end.

Image: Street chic is the best a Caitiff can hope for — shirts, jeans, jacket and boots scrounged from a thrift store — or worse. A haggard face and haunted eyes are the hallmarks of a lone Caitiff on the streets, and odds are he's got a visible air of nervousness about him.

Roleplaying Hints: Trust no one, and keep an eye on the exits at all times. The whole world is out to get you, and your only hope of survival is to keep running. You desperately want to find someplace to belong, but no one will have you. So instead you run.

Clan: Caitiff
Nature: Rebel
Demeanor: Survivor
Generation: 13th
Physical: Strength 3, Dexterity 3, Stamina 4
Social: Charisma 2, Manipulation 2, Appearance 2
Mental: Perception 3, Intelligence 2, Wits 3
Talents: Alertness 3, Brawl 2, Dodge 2, Intimidation 1, Streetwise 3, Subterfuge 2
Skills: Drive 2, Firearms 2, Melee 1, Security 2, Stealth 3, Survival 2
Knowledges: Academics 1, Computer 2, Law 1, Medicine 1
Disciplines: Fortitude 1, Potence 1, Presence 1
Thaumaturgical Paths: None

Backgrounds: Allies 1, Contacts 5, Resources 1
Virtues: Conscience 3, Self-Control 4, Courage 4
Humanity: 7
Willpower: 7

Angry Anarch

Background: Embraced without warning and thrust into the Camarilla against her will, the anarch bided her time until she could escape. Now she's out on the mean streets looking for revenge and blood, working to gather a gang with whom she can take down her hated sire and all he stands for.

Image: Radiating tough from head to toe, an anarch's every glance is a challenge. She wears whatever looks good and protects her well — biker jackets are a particular favorite, as are motorcycle or combat boots. An anarch always goes armed — a nice shiny pair of .45s, worn visibly, can prevent a lot of arguments.

Roleplaying Hints: Anywhere you go is your property. Defend your turf with everything you've got, and make sure to spit in authority's eye while you do so. You don't have a cause, you've got an agenda, and the difference is important. You won't die for what you believe in; you're more interested in finding a way to survive so you can win.

Clan: Brujah
Nature: Rebel
Demeanor: Bravo
Generation: 13th
Physical: Strength 4, Dexterity 4, Stamina 3
Social: Charisma 3, Manipulation 3, Appearance 2
Mental: Perception 3, Intelligence 2, Wits 3
Talents: Alertness 2, Brawl 3, Dodge 2, Expression 2, Intimidation 3, Streetwise 3, Subterfuge 3

Skills: Animal Ken 1, Drive 3, Firearms 2, Melee 2, Security 2, Stealth 2, Survival 2

Knowledges: Computer 1, Investigation 1, Law 1, Medicine 1, Politics 1

Disciplines: Celerity 2, Potence 2, Presence 1

Thaumaturgical Paths: None

Backgrounds: Allies 2, Contacts 3, Resources 2

Virtues: Conscience 3, Self-Control 3, Courage 4

Humanity: 5

Willpower: 8

NEONATE

Background: Just brought into the world of the Camarilla, the neonate is still working from a jumble of half-truths, myths and misconceptions. He's not quite sure what he's supposed to be doing yet, only that the consequences of failure are terrible indeed. Just beginning to understand his new status, the neonate is taking the first few steps toward coming into his true power.

Image: The neonate dresses much as he did in life; conservative suit, power tie, black shoes and a neat mustache (though he's finally abandoned his glasses). He's just starting to realize that he has other options, and is beginning to experiment — though the stereotypical cape and cravat are miles beyond what he'd conceive of trying.

Roleplaying Hints: Lord it over the humans, but cower before your sire and his peers. You don't know much, but you know your place on the food chain — and it's near the bottom. Search for allies among vampires of your age and generation, but look over your shoulder for your sire's approval all the while. Flinch from garlic, running water, crosses and the rest — but once you

discover that the legends are only stories, you run the risk of getting cocky.

Clan: Ventrue

Nature: Traditionalist

Demeanor: Conformist

Generation: 12th

Physical: Strength 3, Dexterity 2, Stamina 2

Social: Charisma 3, Manipulation 4, Appearance 3

Mental: Perception 2, Intelligence 2, Wits 2

Talents: Alertness 2, Empathy 1, Intimidation 3, Leadership 2, Streetwise 1

Skills: Drive 1, Etiquette 2, Firearms 2

Knowledges: Bureaucracy 2, Computer 2, Finance 3, Investigation 2, Law 2, Politics 3

Disciplines: Fortitude 1, Presence 3

Thaumaturgical Paths:

Backgrounds: Generation 1, Herd 1, Influence 1, Resources 2

Virtues: Conscience 3, Self-Control 3, Courage 4

Willpower: 5

Humanity: 6

Willpower: 7

ANCILLA

Background: Having dwelt behind the Masquerade for a century, the ancilla is comfortable with his existence and his potential. He looks to advance himself within his home city's power structure, struggling to carve out a niche and a domain. Whip, sheriff, even prince — these are the goals to which the ancilla aspires, and he is laying careful plans in order to attain them.

Image: Dressed in the style of decades long gone. the ancilla looks as if he has stepped straight from a Frank Capra film. In appearance he looks to be a sad

little man, with a sad little smile and soft hands that don't look like they've ever seen a day's hard work. Only the ancilla's eyes — cold and hard and predatory — reveal his true nature.

Roleplaying Hints: Agree with those of higher station while exercising your authority over those beneath you. Watch for rising stars to befriend, and be careful to disassociate yourself from those who are out of favor. Keep your eye on your ultimate goal; every move and alliance you make is merely a step on the road to power. In the end, everyone and everything is expendable to your ambition.

Clan: Tremere

Nature: Conniver

Demeanor: Architect

Generation: 10th

Physical: Strength 2, Dexterity 4, Stamina 3

Social: Charisma 2, Manipulation 4, Appearance 2

Mental: Perception 4, Intelligence 3, Wits 4

Talents: Alertness 3, Brawl 2, Empathy 2, Leadership 2, Subterfuge 3

Skills: Drive 1, Etiquette 3, Firearms 2, Stealth 2

Knowledges: Bureaucracy 2, Finance 3, Camarilla Lore 4, Law 2, Politics 3

Disciplines: Auspex 3, Dominate 3, Thaumaturgy 2

Thaumaturgical Paths: Blood 2, Weather Control 1

Backgrounds: Contacts 4, Generation 3, Herd 2, Influence 2, Resources 3, Retainers 3, Camarilla Status 3

Virtues: Conscience 2, Self-Control 5, Courage 3

Humanity: 5

Willpower: 5

HIDDEN SOURCE

Background: The hidden source sees everything that goes on in the city — or at least she talks to people who do. When it's information that's needed, she's the one everyone turns to, or at least everyone who can meet her price. Those whom she trusts know how to get in touch with her; everyone else just has to hope that, if they need her, they're lucky enough to find her.

Image: Average for a Nosferatu, she wears voluminous clothes and a floppy hat to cover up her appearance as much as possible. Marked and stained by the sewers, her garb is practically unidentifiable. A pity the same can't be said for her face — wrinkled and covered with warts, her bald visage is something out of a nightmare. Fortunately, most of the time the Nosferatu wears visages other than her own — Obfuscate has its cosmetic uses as well as its tactical ones.

Roleplaying Hints: Don't come out of the shadows unless you have a deal pending. Trade information for favors or more info, but always keep the balance of trade decidedly

in your favor. Use your appearance as a weapon, to shock and confuse vampires who can't see past a person's looks. Keep a very small soft spot for the underdog — you know what it's like to be hated and kicked down.

Clan: Nosferatu

Nature: Loner

Demeanor: Curmudgeon

Generation: 11th

Physical: Strength 2, Dexterity 4, Stamina 2

Social: Charisma 2, Manipulation 3, Appearance 0

Mental: Perception 4, Intelligence 2, Wits 4

Talents: Acting 3, Alertness 3, Brawl 1, Dodge 2, Empathy 2, Streetwise 1, Subterfuge 1

Skills: Etiquette 2, Firearms 1, Security 1, Stealth 1

Knowledges: Bureaucracy 2, Camarilla Lore 3, Computer 2, Finance 2, Investigation 3, Linguistics 2, Politics 1, Sabbat Lore 2

Disciplines: Fortitude 1, Obfuscate 3, Potence 2

Thaumaturgical Paths: None

Backgrounds: Generation 2, Contacts 3, Influences 1

Virtues: Conscience 3, Self-Control 3, Courage 2

Humanity: 6

Willpower: 5

SCOURGE

Background: His Majesty the prince's choice to rid the streets of annoying anarchs and other rabble, the scourge has the power of life and death over unauthorized Kindred. Always traveling with backup, he has the prince's mandate to enforce at least a few of the Traditions in fatal fashion. Hated and feared by those with something to hide (such as themselves), the scourge is one of the most despised Kindred in the city. It's a good thing for him, then, that he loves his work.

Image: The scourge affects a tougher-than-thou image — dark sunglasses, black hat, leather duster and shotgun — for purposes of intimidating idiot neonates and anarchs. When he goes to work, he dresses less stylishly, but with much more of an eye toward ease of movement. At any given time, the scourge has at least one ghoul or subordinate backing him

up, not to mention a small arsenal secreted somewhere on his person.

Roleplaying Hints: Judge each target and treat him accordingly. Have no compunctions about lying, cheating, stealing or terrorizing to get what you want — and you honestly do enjoy putting those pain-in-the-ass anarchs out of their misery.

Clan: Gangrel
Nature: Director
Demeanor: Bravo
Generation: 10th
Physical: Strength 4, Dexterity 4, Stamina 3
Social: Charisma 2, Manipulation 3, Appearance 1
Mental: Perception 4, Intelligence 3, Wits 3
Talents: Alertness 4, Athletics 3, Brawl 3, Dodge 2, Intimidation 3, Streetwise 2
Skills: Drive 2, Firearms 4, Melee 2, Security 1, Survival 2
Knowledges: Camarilla Lore 3, Investigation 2, Sabbat Lore 3
Disciplines: Animalism 2, Celerity 1, Fortitude 3, Protean 2
Thaumaturgical Paths: None
Backgrounds: Camarilla Status 2, Generation 3

Virtues: Conscience 1, Self-Control 4, Courage 5
Humanity: 5
Willpower: 7

Loyal Ghoul

Background: Service, loyal service, is all that the ghoul knows now. By day he still holds his day job, but the charade of office and bureaucracy wears thinner every day. Night, when it's time to serve the master's wishes with his meager skills — that's when the ghoul feels alive. He'll do anything to make his regnant happy. Anything.

Image: A slightly disheveled businessman, the loyal ghoul is vaguely attractive, in a fleshy, middle-aged sort of way. His suit is a few years out of fashion, his glasses a bit thick and his hairline receding, but he radiates an air of competence. He carries a pistol, which he of course has no idea of how to use.

Roleplaying Hints: You know your chosen field very, very well, and have no trouble slapping down anyone who questions your expertise. Well, anyone except your regnant, the one whose blood is so very, very sweet. For him you'll kill without hesitation, steal without a second thought and lie in a heartbeat. Someday, if you're very, very good, he might make you a vampire as well, but in the meantime you're content to do what you can to make him happy and protect him.

Clan: N/A
Nature: Masochist
Demeanor: Conformer
Generation: N/A
Physical: Strength 2, Dexterity 3, Stamina 1
Social: Charisma 2, Manipulation 4, Appearance 2

Mental: Perception 3, Intelligence 3, Wits 3

Talents: Alertness 2, Intimidation 3, Leadership 3, Subterfuge 1

Skills: Drive 2, Etiquette 3, Security 1

Knowledges: Camarilla Lore 3, Finance 3, Investigation 2, Law 3, Linguistics 2, Politics 3

Disciplines: Auspex 1, Celerity 1

Thaumaturgical Paths: None

Backgrounds: Allies 2, Contacts 3, Influence 1, Resources 2

Virtues: Conscience 3, Self-Control 4, Courage 3

Humanity: 7

Willpower: 5

SHERIFF

Background: Every anarch's nightmare and every primogen's whipping boy, the sheriff is responsible for enforcing the laws of the city. He does this with an iron hand inside a velvet glove that's showing a lot of wear — anarchs and troublemakers understand only one thing these nights, and that's force.

Image: The sheriff is a looming, hulking presence — six-and-a-half feet of muscle and mean. While he can dress up for Elysium or audiences with the prince, the sheriff's scarred and ugly mug is more at home in a Kevlar-and-denim ensemble. A shotgun is his weapon of choice; it's got more stopping power than any mere machine gun, and it's great for Kindred crowd control.

Roleplaying Hints: Play stupid and let the anarchs get overconfident. There's no sense in showing them that you've outsmarted them until it's time for the game to end. Insults roll right off you; you do your job and you do it well, and the whining from those vampiric brats is proof. Uphold the city's law to the letter, and add a few codicils that you think are worthwhile.

Clan: Brujah

Nature: Judge

Demeanor: Monster

Generation: 9th

Physical: Strength 4, Dexterity 3, Stamina 5

Social: Charisma 2, Manipulation 5, Appearance 1

Mental: Perception 4, Intelligence 3, Wits 5

Talents: Alertness 3, Brawl 3, Dodge 2, Intimidation 4, Leadership 3

Skills: Animal Ken 1, Drive 3, Firearms 4, Melee 2, Security 3, Stealth 1, Survival 2

Knowledges: Camarilla Lore 4, Politics 2, Sabbat Lore 3

Disciplines: Auspex 3, Celerity 4, Fortitude 3, Potence 4, Presence 4

Thaumaturgical Paths: None

Backgrounds: Allies 2, Camarilla Status 3, Generation 4, Herd 3, Resources 2

Virtues: Conscience 2, Self-Control 5, Courage 4

Humanity: 6

Willpower: 8

TREMERE INTERROGATOR

Background: The Tremere interrogator serves both her clan and her city, though the former takes precedence at all times. Through a combination of thaumaturgical expertise and a detailed understanding of pain and its applications, she makes sure that those whom fate delivers to her unveil all of their secrets. Not everyone has access to her talents, but those who do find her invaluable.

Image: Thoroughly modern in her appearance, the interrogator prefers severe business suits, and lab coats for when she gets down to work. Her face is all angles and edges, giving her a raptorlike visage. Her fingers, on the other hand, are slender and graceful, and she always wears black leather gloves to protect them.

Roleplaying Hints: You have many interests and talents, but your work supersedes them all. In conversation, you're the one who asks the questions — long-winded stories bore you, and you prefer to get straight to the point. You're hard to like, but easy to work with, at least from the outside. Your patients probably find you less charming.

Clan: Tremere

Nature: Autocrat

Demeanor: Perfectionist

Generation: 11th

Physical: Strength 3, Dexterity 3, Stamina 3

Social: Charisma 4, Manipulation 4, Appearance 2

never, ever let yourself grow predictable. You hold the reputation of everyone in the city in your hands, and you know it.

Mental: Perception 4, Intelligence 3, Wits 3

Talents: Acting 2, Alertness 3, Empathy 3, Intimidation 3, Leadership 2

Skills: Etiquette 2, Firearms 1, Music 1, Repair 1

Knowledges: Bureaucracy 3, Camarilla Lore 4, Computer 2, Finance 2, Investigation 4, Law 3, Politics 3, Sabbat Lore 3

Disciplines: Auspex 3, Dominate 3, Fortitude 2, Presence 2, Thaumaturgy 3

Thaumaturgical Paths: The Lure of Flames 3, Hands of Destruction 2, Blood 1

Backgrounds: Camarilla Status 3, Contacts 4, Generation 2, Herd 2, Influence 1, Resources 2, Retainers 2

Virtues: Conscience 3, Self-Control 5, Courage 3

Humanity: 4

Willpower: 6

HARPY

Background: The harpy is the arbiter of style and status in the city. With a flock of her peers, she peers out from Elysium to bestow good fortune or venomous malice with but a word. Everyone courts her favor — especially those who despise her.

Image: A vision of supernatural and predatory loveliness, the harpy always makes a statement with her appearance. Gowns from centuries past, exquisitely tailored to play up her beauty, are standard apparel for her when she wants to be seen — and she is never seen when she does not want to be.

Roleplaying Hints: No one is your equal. You are judge, jury and social executioner, and anyone who dares contradict or insult you has committed an unpardonable crime. Respond well to flattery — if it's done well — but

Clan: Toreador

Nature: Gallant

Demeanor: Celebrant

Generation: 9th

Physical: Strength 2, Dexterity 3, Stamina 3

Social: Charisma 4, Manipulation 4, Appearance 4

Mental: Perception 3, Intelligence 2, Wits 3

Talents: Acting 3, Alertness 3, Empathy 3, Intimidation 4, Leadership 3, Subterfuge 3

Skills: Etiquette 3, Firearms 1, Music 3

Knowledges: Camarilla Lore 3, Linguistics 3, Occult 2, Politics 3

Disciplines: Auspex 3, Celerity 3, Presence 3

Thaumaturgical Paths: None

Backgrounds: Allies 2, Camarilla Status 3, Contacts 3, Fame 2, Generations 4, Influence 2

Virtues: Conscience 3, Self-Control 5, Courage 4

Humanity: 4

Willpower: 8

KEEPER OF ELYSIUM

Background: The unliving can appreciate grace, beauty and art far better than can the living, who have but a few brief decades to contemplate it. The keeper of Elysium preserves that for the Kindred, enforcing the laws of Elysium and carefully gathering the artifacts of culture and inspiration for the vampires of the city's pleasure.

Image: The keeper of Elysium dresses soberly, but in expensive clothing than can come from any era of human history, depending on her whim. Her demeanor is sober and reserved, but she sees everything that goes on in her domain, and deals harshly with those who would violate Elysium's sanctity.

Roleplaying Hints: Elysium is your garden. Share your treasures with those who show a genuine interest and feed the frauds to the harpies. The peace and tradition of Elysium are paramount to you, and you deal harshly with any violators. You can call on the might of the entire city to do so, and have resorted to that tactic on multiple occasions.

Clan: Toreador
Nature: Celebrant
Demeanor: Pedagogue
Generation: 9th
Physical: Strength 3, Dexterity 3, Stamina 3
Social: Charisma 4, Manipulation 3, Appearance 3
Mental: Perception 4, Intelligence 4, Wits 4
Talents: Alertness 3, Empathy 2
Skills: Etiquette 3, Firearms 1, Melee 1, Music 3, Security 2
Knowledges: Camarilla Lore 2, Computer 1, Finance 3, Law 3, Linguistics 4, Politics 2, Science 1
Disciplines: Auspex 3, Celerity 1, Presence 4
Thaumaturgical Paths: None
Backgrounds: Camarilla Status 1, Generation 4, Herd 1, Influence 2, Resources 3
Virtues: Conscience 5, Self-Control 4, Courage 2
Humanity: 6
Willpower: 5

THE LOYAL OPPOSITION (PRIMOGEN)

Background: It has taken centuries, but the primogen has finally clawed her way to the top of the local branch of her clan. Now she speaks for all the Malkavians in her city, and her word carries a great deal of weight on the primogen council. She doesn't agree with the current prince on, well, on much of anything, but isn't ready to move against him — yet. In the meantime, she moves in council to thwart his aims, never crossing the irrevocable boundary of open rebellion.

Image: The Malkavian primogen dresses as a prim and proper woman of the mid-1800s, modestly garbed and with downcast countenance. She has always appeared this way, so far as anyone in the city remembers. Perhaps she always will.

Roleplaying Hints: You did not achieve your age or position by wandering around in bunny slippers and pajamas. Your madness is a cold and terrifying thing, twining perfectly around your ambition to help you achieve the bloody heights of the primogenship. You are not ready to move openly against the prince, but in the meanwhile you enjoy nothing more than thwarting his will.

Clan: Malkavian
Nature: Fanatic
Demeanor: Penitent
Generation: 8th
Physical: Strength 3, Dexterity 5, Stamina 3
Social: Charisma 3, Manipulation 4, Appearance 4
Mental: Perception 4, Intelligence 4, Wits 4
Talents: Alertness 4, Dodge 3, Empathy 3, Intimidation 3, Leadership 4, Streetwise 2
Skills: Animal Ken 2, Etiquette 4, Firearms 2, Music 3, Stealth 3

Knowledges: Bureaucracy 4, Camarilla Lore 4, Investigation 3, Law 3, Linguistics 1, Medicine 2, Politics 3

Disciplines: Auspex 4, Celerity 3, Dominate 5, Obfuscate 4, Protean 3

Thaumaturgical Paths: None

Backgrounds: Camarilla Status 4, Contacts 5, Herd 3, Generation 5

Virtues: Conscience 4, Self-Control 3, Courage 5

Humanity: 3

Willpower: 8

SENESCHAL

Background: The prince may rule the city, but the seneschal is the one who keeps it running from night to night. He who would see the prince must first convince the seneschal of the urgency of his business; the seneschal is the keeper of the keys to the prince's presence. Publicly subservient but never craven, he controls far more of the city than even his master suspects.

Image: Tall, gray-haired and impeccably groomed, the seneschal is the very picture of gentility. His suit is black and immaculate, his cane silver-handled and his manner precisely polite.

Roleplaying Hints: You know where everyone stands in the city, and where all of the bodies are buried as well. Always be polite, but leave no doubt as to who really runs the city. You have the prince's trust and his permission to use his authority; use both wisely and make sure not to abuse either.

Clan: Ventrue

Nature: Director

Demeanor: Conformist

Generation: 10th

Physical: Strength 3, Dexterity 3, Stamina 3

Social: Charisma 3, Manipulation 5, Appearance 2

Mental: Perception 5, Intelligence 4, Wits 4

Talents: Acting 1, Alertness 4, Brawl 2, Dodge 4, Empathy 3, Intimidation 4, Leadership 4, Subterfuge 4

Skills: Drive 1, Etiquette 4, Firearms 4, Music 2, Security 4, Stealth 4

Knowledges: Bureaucracy 4, Camarilla Lore 4, Finance 4, Investigation 4, Law 4, Linguistics 1, Occult 2, Politics 3, Sabbat Lore 3

Disciplines: Auspex 4, Celerity 4, Dominate 4, Fortitude 3, Obfuscate 2, Presence 4, Protean 3

Thaumaturgical Paths: None

Backgrounds: Allies 3, Camarilla Status 4, Contacts 3, Generation 2, Herd 3, Influence 3, Mentor 4, Resources 3, Retainers 3

Virtues: Conscience 4, Self-Control 5, Courage 4

Humanity: 5

Willpower: 9

PRINCE

Background: The prince has been a part of the city for centuries, even though he has only been prince for a bare handful of decades. He has spent his entire unlife here climbing from the ranks of the swarming neonates, and now he holds the entire city in his grip. Within his domain, his is the power of life and death, of creation and destruction, and he uses that power as he pleases.

Image: The prince cuts a terrifying figure. He prefers hand-tailored suits of the latest fashion, cut to accentuate his looming figure. His hair is cut short in imitation, perhaps, of the style of his living days, and he rarely smiles. His eyes are a steely but deceptively mild blue, and few can meet his gaze for long.

Roleplaying Hints: You are the prince. Your word is law. Brook as little opposition as possible. While the primogen and others must be respected, you make the final decisions and you make them stick. If anyone argues, you have the option of calling the blood hunt — and you never let your enemies forget it.

Clan: Ventrue

Nature: Autocrat

Demeanor: Visionary

Generation: 8th

Physical: Strength 4, Dexterity 4, Stamina 4

Social: Charisma 5, Manipulation 4, Appearance 4

Mental: Perception 5, Intelligence 5, Wits 5

Talents: Alertness 4, Athletics 3, Brawl 3, Dodge 3, Empathy 4, Intimidation 4, Leadership 5, Subterfuge 3

Skills: Drive 1, Etiquette 3, Firearms 2, Melee 3, Stealth 2

Knowledges: Camarilla Lore 4, Finance 3, Law 5, Linguistics 2, Politics 4, Sabbat Lore 3

Disciplines: Auspex 3, Celerity 4, Dominate 5, Fortitude 3, Presence 4, Protean 4

Thaumaturgical Paths: None

Backgrounds: Allies 3, Camarilla Status 5, Contacts 5, Generation 5, Herd 4, Influence 4, Resources 4

Virtues: Conscience 4, Self-Control 5, Courage 5

Humanity: 4

Willpower: 9

ROVING ARCHON

Background: It's been a half-century or more since the roving archon had a home city. Since then, she's been in the employ of a justicar, traveling from city to city to investigate whatever her superior tells her to. Her presence is always accompanied by fear, for an archon is both a power in her own right and a potential harbinger of a justicar's fatal attentions.

Image: Dressed for travel, the archon certainly looks unimpressive. Her sandy-colored hair is cut raggedly short, and her clothing is drab khakis that have seen too many miles. She carries a single gun, loaded with silver bullets, for safety between the cities, but she never uses it on Kindred. After all, she doesn't need to.

Roleplaying Hints: Everyone has something to hide. Your mission is to discover whether what they're hiding actually matters. You have a low bullshit tolerance and a short fuse — you've seen every scam and every ruse before, and they're not going to start working now. If you see a problem, you are more than capable of dealing with it yourself. Call for backup only if things are about to go completely to hell; otherwise you're utterly self-reliant.

Clan: Toreador

Nature: Judge

Demeanor: Martyr

Generation: 9th

Physical: Strength 5, Dexterity 5, Stamina 5

Social: Charisma 3, Manipulation 3, Appearance 2

Mental: Perception 5, Intelligence 4, Wits 4

Talents: Alertness 4, Athletics 4, Brawl 5, Dodge 4, Empathy 2, Intimidation 4, Streetwise 4, Subterfuge 4

Skills: Drive 2, Firearms 4, Melee 2, Repair 3, Security 3, Stealth 4, Survival 3

Knowledges: Camarilla Lore 4, Investigation 5, Law 3, Medicine 3, Politics 3, Sabbat Lore 4

Disciplines: Auspex 3, Celerity 4, Fortitude 3, Obfuscate 3, Presence 3

Thaumaturgical Paths: None

Backgrounds: Camarilla Status 3, Contacts 3, Generation 4, Resources 2

Virtues: Conscience 3, Self-Control 4, Courage 5

Humanity: 5

Willpower: 10

JUSTICAR

Background: Elected by the Camarilla's Inner Council, the justicar has the power to bring even a rogue prince to heel. Invested with the authority to strip a prince of his authority or destroy an entire generation of Kindred, the justicar is the Camarilla's court of last resort. When the justicar arrives in town, it's already too late — all hell has broken loose and it's time for the cleanup to commence.

Image: The justicar is well over six feet tall and carries the weight of centuries with him. He dresses with the times, but is most comfortable in the tunic and palla of his breathing days centuries ago. When in public, however, the justicar dresses for effect, dominating any room he is in with his presence.

Roleplaying Hints: You are all business — the Camarilla's business — and woe betide anyone who tries to stop you. You have no compunctions about using any and all of your powers (legal, supernatural or physical) to do what needs be done. You only deal with problems of an earthshattering nature, so whatever has drawn you to the city is serious indeed.

Clan: Malkavian

Nature: Competitor

Demeanor: Pedagogue

Generation: 6th

Physical: Strength 5, Dexterity 5, Stamina 5

Social: Charisma 6, Manipulation 7, Appearance 3

Mental: Perception 6, Intelligence 4, Wits 6

Talents: Alertness 5, Athletics 4, Brawl 3, Dodge 5, Empathy 2, Intimidation 5, Leadership 3, Subterfuge 2

Skills: Animal Ken 1, Etiquette 4, Firearms 4, Melee 4

Knowledges: Bureaucracy 4, Camarilla Lore 5, Investigation 4, Law 5, Politics 4, Sabbat Lore 4

Disciplines: Auspex 4, Celerity 4, Dominate 5, Fortitude 3, Obfuscate 5, Potence 5, Protean 3

Thaumaturgical Paths: None

Backgrounds: Allies 2, Camarilla Status 4, Contacts 5, Generation 7, Herd 2, Resources 4

Virtues: Conscience 4, Self-Control 4, Courage 4

Humanity: 5

Willpower: 9

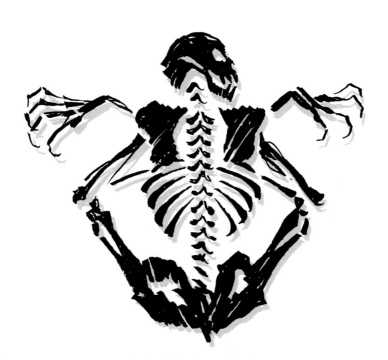

Tales of Imagination and Mystery:
Storytelling

We use ideas merely to justify our evil, and speech merely to conceal our ideas.
— Voltaire, *Dialogue XIV*

There is a natural assumption that a game of **Vampire** is, by default, a Camarilla game. The book is called **Vampire: The Masquerade**, after all, and who else practices the Masquerade but the Camarilla? The connection seems logical enough, but it's still not necessarily correct. There are matters of tone, style, mood, theme and definition that make a chronicle uniquely Camarilla. After all, if the Camarilla were all there was to **Vampire**, we wouldn't have to worry about that pesky Sabbat now, would we?

At the Heart of Things

There are several core elements to Storytelling: mood, theme, plot and conflict. To Storytell a chronicle based around the Camarilla requires integrating those elements with the demands of using a sect that hides behind a Masquerade while pulling the strings of the mortal world. There are things that make the Camarilla unique — the Masquerade, the Traditions, the Inner Circle, the justicars and so on — and all of these can be used to make your chronicle unique as well. The trick is to use those tools that are essentially Camarilla to make your game essentially Camarilla as well.

Captain Vampire to the Rescue!

As has been stated earlier in this book, the vampires of the Camarilla are most emphatically not nice. They have a vested interest in avoiding wholesale slaughter of humans, but that's about it — it's a long way from that position to casting the Kindred as noble, unliving protectors of humanity. Vampires, even those vampires who follow the Path of Humanity, are not superheroes; they don't stalk the night looking for bad guys to beat up and leave them, a pint low, for the local *gendarmes* to find. While individual vampires may work to protect individual humans, the Camarilla as a whole does *not* work to protect humanity as a whole. Altruism is an expensive weakness among the Kindred, and any vampire who puts others' good ahead of his own is exposing himself dangerously to his enemies.

Roleplaying and Rollplaying

There's much more to Storytelling a game of **Vampire** than simply setting up the next turn's worth of bloody combat. While situations wherein characters are forced to use their assorted skills (represented in the game system by rolling dice) do come up, they shouldn't be the whole game. Every time 10-sided plastic polyhedrons hit the table, the illusion of the story is shattered, and you as a Storyteller must reconstruct your players' suspension of disbelief all over again. One of **Vampire's** strengths is its capacity to support chronicles of intrigue and emotion, and Camarilla-based stories lend themselves to that sort of thing especially well. The traditions, customs and built-in conflicts of the Camarilla give you a wide palette of Storytelling tools, and by restricting yourself to using just one, you're shortchanging both your players and yourself.

Furthermore, you should recognize that the most important aspect of Storytelling a Camarilla chronicle is not devotion to the rules and rolls, but rather making your game enjoyable. If the coterie comes up with a brilliant plan to save themselves in the face of overwhelming opposition, but the dice roll falls just short, it might make sense to allow the characters to succeed in any case. If the characters are ambushed and you roll so well that the entire coterie would be dropped without getting off a single shot in response, it might behoove you to fudge the rolls in favor of your players so as to make for a better game. If necessary, you can always work this sort of *deus ex machina* mercy into your plot later — perhaps you can later hint that the ambushing party was under orders not to wipe out the entire coterie, but rather just to put a scare into them — and thus advance your chronicle even further.

Finally, you should think about the very meaning of success and failure in your chronicle. When a player produces a handful of 3s and 4s on a roll with difficulty 6, it's easy to say "OK, you failed. Next!" Instead, try to make those failures mean something. Perhaps the character's shots went wide, shattering windows all along the street and covering the area with broken glass. Maybe the failure was on an attempt to leap from rooftop to rooftop, and by failing the character ended up crashing through the window of a top-floor apartment instead. By ascribing context to failures on rolls of the dice (and successes as well), you make those rolls a part of the story. By leaving them just as failed rolls, you lose an opportunity to draw your players even further into your story.

MOOD

The mood of your game can best be described as the single emotion that best sums up your chronicle. While any chronicle worth its salt has more than one mood to it — hot and heavy combat shouldn't evoke the same emotional response as playing politics in Elysium, after all — each story should have an overarching sense to it. Giving your chronicle an emotional unity helps you be consistent as a Storyteller. If you know the sort of emotion you're trying to invoke, you can direct your plots and play your characters in such a way as to emphasize that feeling. On the other hand, if you go into a chronicle with no clear idea of what the underlying mood should be, there's a good chance that this lack of direction will manifest itself in areas of plot, character motivation and more.

While **Vampire** is a versatile game, the Camarilla by definition lends itself better to certain sorts of moods than others. This is a sect built on tradition and respect, on well-disguised ferocity and obsession and contempt. There is a sense of restraint to the Camarilla (at least in front of others), a willingness to abide (however grudgingly) by the laws laid down theoretically for the protection of all. With the adoption of the Path of Humanity by the sect's vampires, there is a mood of regret or longing — at least among those Kindred young enough to remember what it was to be mortal. And there is bitter hatred for those who would tear down the Masquerade and destroy the sect. All of these senses and feelings should be taken into consideration when you're working up the basic mood of your chronicle.

WHITTLING IT DOWN

While you should consider the entire gamut of moods that the Camarilla can inspire for your game, eventually it's best to select a single one to serve as the core emotion of your chronicle. Often this decision goes hand-in-hand with any decisions you make about your plot. Chronicles with a mood of sadness or longing probably shouldn't be combat-intensive; wistful Kindred moping around firefights have a way of becoming casualties in short order. By the same token, a chronicle centered on hatred might be a bit awkward if the central plot is about a vampire's quest to protect his mortal descendants. It's certainly possible, with some effort, to reconcile those two elements, but you shouldn't make a habit of making more work for yourself than you have to.

The primary criterion in selecting the essential mood of your chronicle is whether or not you can sustain that mood throughout the entire storyline. A mood that works terrifically for single scenes might not be strong enough to sustain the whole chronicle. For example, if vengeance is at the heart of your story, you may find yourself hard-pressed to keep the game going if the characters settle their old scores by the third session of play. While setting up instances centered around other moods is an excellent Storytelling technique — a steady diet of regret or hatred or anything else can get tiresome very quickly — you want to avoid confusing the main flavor of your game with the seasoning.

A few moods that work well for Camarilla-centered games include:

• Fear

The Sabbat is coming. The elders are whittling down the ranks of their childer. The Antediluvians might be waking. The Lupines are growing bolder in their raids on the city. Anarchs are inciting younger Kindred to revolt. Any and all of these worries can and should make for a heady brew of paranoia among your city's Kindred, allowing you to establish a mood of fear that permeates your chronicle.

• Regret

Your players' coterie watches mortal existence recede into the dim and distant past. Parents, friends, lovers and children grow old and die — all without the characters.

Occasionally there is a reminder of humanity, perhaps in the form of a mortal who reminds a character of what he used to be, but that reminiscence just emphasizes the characters' loss once it passes. Chronicles with a mood of regret often center on characters' attempts to hang onto the last shreds of their Humanity, often in the face of the inhuman demands of existence among the Kindred.

• Mystery

The characters have entered an entirely new existence. Everything about their very being is strange to them, let alone the customs and perils of their new world. Playing up the aspect of alienation and confusion that mystery presents can make for extended chronicles of discovery, especially if other Kindred are trying to keep the truth from the coterie.

• Hatred

The entire myth of how the Kindred came to be is rooted in hatred, and the Camarilla does little to disgrace that legacy. Childer hate their sires for plucking them into a state of unlife. Sires hate their ambitious progeny, who look with hungry eyes at their elders. The clans war with each other, when not uniting to confront the hated Sabbat. Just as deadly is the unspoken self-loathing many Kindred feel, driving them to commit acts that risk destruction.

• Ambition

Mortal concerns pale when a human receives the Embrace, but immortal ambitions can make for an acceptable substitute. The desire to rise in generation, in status, in power or in rank can drive a vampire to commit acts both unspeakable and superhuman. A sense of ambition can drive your players' characters to greater and greater heights of achievement — or can lead them to crushing weights of failure.

• Respect

The Camarilla is built on respect for tradition (and Tradition). A chronicle can easily be constructed around neonates' attempts to deal properly with their elders and the strictures of their sect, particularly when defying either might be an easy way to get ahead.

• Loyalty

Loyalty can be a difficult thing to situate at the heart of your chronicle, but when used properly it can drive dynamic storylines. The loyalty of childe to sire, of members of a coterie to one another and to their clans, and the overriding loyalty each vampire should feel to the sect — any and all of these can be called into question or tested at a moment's notice. What happens, for example, when a neonate is offered prime hunting grounds in exchange for setting up a member of his coterie for destruction? The stresses and demands of loyalty — particularly when the blood bond comes into play — make for fertile material for a wide range of chronicles.

THEME

If mood is the central emotion of your chronicle, then the theme is the central idea. Whereas the mood can be

summed up by an emotion, the theme can usually be summed up as an abstract idea — tradition, for example, or antiquity. The events of your plot should support your theme and highlight it, using the mechanisms of the story to get across the central point of your chronicle.

THEME AND THE CAMARILLA

Certain themes lend themselves better to Camarilla chronicles than do others. The very makeup of the sect — older vampires dictating policy to younger ones — fairly screams for themes of rebellion and oppression. The fact of the elders' existence speaks more to themes of age and remembrance; chronicles that contrast the Kindred's past with their present often have such themes. Political games can center on themes of intrigue and betrayal, while horror is another perennial favorite when the characters are up against Kindred more monstrous than they are.

With its heritage of formality and tradition, the sect does offer innumerable tools for reinforcing any theme you choose. The indifference of an elder to a neonate's plot can be used to spur the youngster's incipient revolt, or to demonstrate the elder's age and perspective. The timeless elegance of a meeting at Elysium plays up the sect's tradition to some, while exposing stagnation to others. Use what the Camarilla gives you, and you'll find plenty of material to support your chronicle's themes.

PLOT

The plot of your chronicle is nothing less than the story itself, the sequence of events that propels and supports your chronicle. Without a plot, all you have is a disconnected scattering of events with no coherent framework or direction. With a strong plot, however, you have a skeleton on which to drape the other elements — mood, theme, character development — of your chronicle.

SINGULAR OR PLURAL?

While having only one plot going at a time offers the pleasures of simplicity, you might want to explore the notion of having multiple plots running simultaneously. Bear in mind that in a sect like the Camarilla, wherein open warfare is theoretically prohibited, plotting is the only way to get ahead of one's rivals. You, as Storyteller, should take your characters' plots (as determined by their personalities) and make them your chronicles' plots as well.

Consider this notion: The Kindred aren't going to stand around courteously and wait for one another's schemes to come to fruition before initiating their own, after all. Why shouldn't the Nosferatu primogen be working to undermine a particularly snobbish keeper of Elysium at the same time two Ventrue are struggling over control of a new hi-tech corporate campus and a Malkavian neonate is trying to survive in the face of new legislation that closes down mental institutions, dumping his entire herd onto the street? Bear in mind that just because your characters are plotting doesn't mean that their plots will impact your players' coterie all the time, or even any of the time. After all, if your chronicle travels from boardroom to museum to luxury suite, odds are that the plight of the lone Malkavian won't be a matter of much concern. On the other hand, knowing what that Malkavian is up to and making sure to advance his storyline (to yourself, at least) means that if one of the player's characters takes a bite out of that Lunatic's exclusive property, the machinery to make a story out of the incident is already in place.

Running multiple plots also lets you give players options. If your Elysium plot doesn't appeal to half of your troupe, then perhaps starting a second plotline involving a power struggle on the streets might pique their interest. There's also the appeal of differently paced plots, wherein one plotline only pops up every third session or so, while the vampires' night-to-night activity deals with entirely different matters. For example, the coterie might be caught up in a struggle to influence the city's newly burgeoning Russian community, which requires nightly immersion in that world as well as constant challenges from rivals. At the same time, however, those same vampires might be under observation by a local Tremere elder, who decides to test them every so often in his own inimitable fashion. The two plots co-exist and occasionally interact (when, for example, the Tremere aids and abets the coterie's rivals to see how the group handles adversity), but they appear with different frequencies. One serves as a change of pace for the other, and as a reminder that Kindred existence is much more complicated than just getting from point A to point B.

Remember, the Kindred are creatures of machination. Some have spent decades, if not centuries or millennia developing their schemes, working through others who often don't even know they're part of some elder being's plans. These ancient schemers are your creations within the boundaries of your chronicle; every Kindred's personal agenda should double as a potential plotline for you to use.

BIG PLOT, LITTLE PLOT

The scale of your plot is something to consider carefully. On its basic level, the Camarilla functions city by city. As a result, most plotlines should operate within the boundaries of a single city. Whether those plots are as grandiose as attempts to overthrow princes or visits from angry justicars, or as personal as a single vampire's quest to earn permission to Embrace a terminally ill loved one is a matter of taste, but the city is the unit by which most Camarilla plots are measured.

Whether such plots are "big" or "small" generally depends on how many other Kindred are involved, and thus what the consequences of the plot might be. An attempt by the coterie to overthrow the local prince, for example, is effectively a "big" plot, as the prince has enemies, allies and childer (all of whom have their own agendas to be satisfied) that the storyline must bring into the mix. Such chronicles frequently have large casts of Storyteller characters and complex webs of character interaction, and they can be difficult for inexperienced Storytellers to run well. The bigger the plot (and the more earthshaking its potential consequences), the more complex it is likely to be to run.

On the other hand, "small" plots usually only involve a few individuals, and are much less complicated. They can be roleplaying or combat intensive — a vampire's relationship with his mortal family, or the coterie's struggle to establish itself in a small city with only a few resident Kindred — but they are generally less complex and less demanding than "big" plots. Bear in mind, however, that a small plot doesn't have to stay small together. The mortal who spends too much time checking in on his family might draw the ire of his clan elder, who decides to teach him and his friends a lesson, or the small city the coterie settles could become the target of an archon's fact-finding mission. However, small plots serve as an excellent way to practice for bigger ones, in addition to making for good chronicles by themselves.

Camarilla plots are not limited to the city scale, however. In theory, the sect encompasses every vampire in the world, and its members can reach thousands of years of age. Plots involving the sect as a whole, or the schemes of elders and Antediluvians, certainly qualify as "big" plots. Conclaves, hunts for vampires on the dreaded Red List, bold moves in the Jyhad — all of these work through the institution of the Camarilla on a grand scale. If you're going to create a narrative on this scale (and the framework of the game can certainly support doing so), just be prepared to do the legwork necessary with such an ambitious chronicles. A conclave (see page 130.) is much more than just throwing a few thousand vampires into a single room and letting them go; you have to work out the arrangements, agendas and problems that go with the conclave as well. On the other hand, a plot that uses such grandiose devices can, if done well, inspire awe and some spectacular roleplaying. Just make sure you're up to the challenge before trying it.

Plotting the Camarilla

Using the Camarilla as the starting point for crafting your plot means that certain of your narrative choices are already defined for you. If you're going to run a Camarilla chronicle, there are functions and traditions of the sect — the Masquerade, the Traditions, the city's vampiric hierarchy and so on — that must be taken into account when you're constructing your plot. Rather than being a handicap, these pre-existing constructions can work for you, giving you the building blocks of a solidly constructed narrative.

Plots centered around the sect usually have one of three main foci:

• Defending the Camarilla

The easiest plots to construct, stories that revolve around defending the sect can be out-and-out action fests, with your players' characters going toe-to-toe with the Camarilla's enemies. Such plots can be simple slugfests or cat-and-mouse chases after infiltrators. Either way, though, the plot revolves around the Camarilla being on the defensive.

• Advancing the Camarilla

Stories to advance the Camarilla can involve improving the sect in terms of territory, power or policy. A plot to advance the

Staying At Home

Observant Storytellers will no doubt notice that at the rate experience points get handed out, even the slowest-learning characters acquire ludicrous amounts of power in a few short months. Extrapolating that trend across the thousands of years that elders have existed, one comes up with staggering numbers of dots' worth of powers.

Then one looks at the statistics provided for pre-made characters, and doesn't see quite so many dots as all that. The discrepancy can be troubling.

There is, however, a reason for the differential: Vampires don't spend all their time running around doing things that, in game terms, garner them experience. Scouring the streets fighting the Sabbat, meddling with elders and otherwise exposing one's self to mortal danger is not standard vampiric behavior. With immortality a certainty, what vampire is going to risk his eternal existence any more than necessary? Most Kindred spend the vast majority of their time hiding behind ghouls and mortals, tending to their concerns and plots and resolutely avoiding danger. As a result, they don't rack up knowledge of new skills too quickly.

Player characters, needless to say, are the exception to this trend. They're out in the trenches, doing deeds of daring and otherwise picking up new Abilities and Disciplines. Bear in mind when Storytelling that your players' characters are advancing at a much faster rate than their peers in the city, and don't let them get too far ahead of everyone else too fast.

Camarilla can range from an assault on a Sabbat city to an attempted assassination of a particularly competent Lasombra bishop. There are less obvious ways to center plots on the notion of advancing the Camarilla as well: Struggles to remove incompetent elders or princes, attempts to make sect policy or ways to modernize fossilized practices all fall under this rubric, and all offer interesting challenges for characters.

• Working With the Camarilla

Working with (or within) the sect can cover any number of plot ideas. Attempts by the characters to advance politically, machinations by elders to use or abuse their lessers, situations where the Masquerade must be defended and other such stories all fall into this category. Such plots are marked less by open conflict and more by politicking, intrigue and subtle uses of Disciplines.

Signature Devices

One of the best ways to make your game distinctively Camarilla is to use the traditions and customs of the sect as core elements of your plotting. There's no sense making your game Camarilla if you don't take advantage of some of the story elements that the Camarilla has to offer. Consider the following:

• The Masquerade

In many ways, the decision to create and maintain the Masquerade is the defining feature of the Camarilla. Much of the sect's energy can be tied up in the maintenance of this veil to hide the fact of vampiric existence from the vast seas of humanity. Plots can revolve around attempts to repair the Masquerade because of new or existing breaches, characters' questioning of the need of the Masquerade (and attracting unwelcome attention for doing so), or finding new and better ways to uphold the deception and trying to convince elders to accept the new-fangled notions.

• The Red List

Anyone on the legendary Red List is probably far, far out of the average coterie's league when it comes to combat. However, you can still use the rumor of a Red List vampire to stir up all sorts of plot-based trouble in your chronicle. And nothing says that the players' coterie can't get in on the action if other Kindred decide to join the hunt for a hated fugitive....

• The Traditions

The Traditions are the ironclad laws of the sect. Innumerable plots can come from attempts to circumvent, break or uphold them. Local variants on the Traditions can also be fun to play with, as newcomers to a city find themselves struggling to learn new laws before they get themselves killed over a misinterpretation....

• Conclaves

Conclaves are certainly Camarilla-specific; gatherings of all the sect's vampires (or at least as many as can travel) for a gathering that has the potential for all sorts of disasters. Putting that many Kindred in one place at one time has the potential for innumerable plots. Old enemies return, long lost lovers re-appear, ancient rivalries are renewed, political power plays are spawned — the possibilities are endless.

• Archons and Justicars

The heavy hitters of the sect can inspire story ideas just by the mere threat of their presence. Word that an archon is coming can produce all sorts of frenzied behavior on the parts of those who have something to hide. The actual arrival of an archon, or worse, her superior, can really shake the metaphorical tree. As for what comes down at that point, well, it's up to you.

• Elysium

Elysium means intrigue and the endless quest for social status. In a setting where use of Disciplines is prohibited, vampires must resort to more subtle means to achieve their ends, and that makes for more subtle plotlines.

CALAMITIES

To no one's surprise, pre-planned plots have a lemming-like habit of going astray. Characters don't open the doors they're supposed to or kill key witnesses accidentally; inter-coterie conflict diverts Kindred from vital clues. And so it goes as the players' characters go off on wild goose chases while your beautiful, meticulously constructed plot either falls to pieces or remains basically untouched.

In situations like that, the worst thing you can do as a Storyteller is to attempt to force your players to adhere to your plot. Such efforts are rarely subtle, often noticed and always resented. By telling the characters that they *have* to

do some things and *can't* do others, you disrupt the natural flow of the story.

Instead, think about where the characters are going with the storyline. See if there's any way you can direct them back toward the pre-planned plot gently. Introducing Storyteller characters who are tied strongly into the abandoned plot works well for this sort of thing.

Otherwise, the best thing you can do is take your pre-planned plot and shelve it temporarily, letting it slide until the characters are ready to give it another go. The vampires of the Camarilla are nothing if not patient. If they can hatch a plot that spans a hundred years, you can wait a few weeks to put it into action.

CONFLICT

Conflict is at the heart of all chronicle plotting. A city wherein all the Kindred dwell in perfect harmony, everyone is satisfied with his lot and the Masquerade is preserved perfectly may make for an wonderful place to live, but it honestly isn't a particularly exciting setting for Storytelling. Conflict, the opposition of forces and wills, is what makes for exciting Storytelling. Note that conflict is not automatically equivalent to combat. There are many, many ways in which the Kindred pit themselves against one another and their enemies, and most don't involve bloodshed — at least not immediately.

Deciding what the sources of conflict in your chronicle are and figuring out how the characters fit into those conflicts (A hint: If they don't figure at least peripherally in every conflict you've established, it's time to start looking for a different plot seed) should form the core of your plotting. Every area of contention you establish should somehow impact the characters' coterie, and should help to drive your plot toward its ultimate conclusion.

THE BASICS

The obvious and basic conflict in a Camarilla game pits the Camarilla itself against its enemies. Establishing an "us against them" conflict right off the bat helps to establish the characters as actively pro-Camarilla. By swinging into the fray against the Camarilla's enemies — and those enemies can be Sabbat, unaligned vampires, other supernatural beings or even

A SENSE OF AGE

Camarilla plots often have lineages stretching back centuries. If you involve older vampires in your storyline, you should make certain to see how far back their involvement in events goes, and why they got involved in the first place. Realizing that the characters' life-or-death struggle is just the latest, minor skirmish in a private war that's lasted since the Reformation does wonders for establishing a sense of perspective in your chronicle. If you're going to use old Kindred, make sure you use their age as well as their accumulated statistics as tools in telling your story.

vampire hunters — the characters clearly draw the line as to whom they are for, as well as whom they are against. A story with this sort of conflict at its heart doesn't necessarily have to be just a straight-up slugfest. A quest to find a Sabbat infiltrator or to stop a lone Ravnos from stealing the prince's symbols of office clearly sets the Camarilla, in the form of the players' coterie, up against its enemies. There's nothing wrong with a good old-fashioned brawl in the streets with a bloodthirsty pack of Sabbat neonates, but there's much more to lining the Camarilla up against its enemies than simply having everyone charge into a scrum, fangs bared and Uzis barking.

Conflict With the Sabbat

The Sabbat is the natural opponent for the Camarilla, and there are a wide variety of stories that can make use of this opposition. Whereas the Camarilla works through and around mortals, the Sabbat wants to ride roughshod over them. While the Camarilla is built on tradition and formality, the Sabbat was born in chaos and anarchy, and looks to mere custom for its guidelines. While the Camarilla putatively has laws to govern its members' dealings with both the world at large and one another, the Sabbat respects only brute strength and animal cunning. From these seeds of difference, massive conflicts can grow.

At a core level, conflict with the Sabbat can be seen as military. The Camarilla holds a city, the Sabbat wants it, and the two sides tussle bloodily. That sort of conflict is an excellent way to kick-start a plot with the Sabbat cast as the villains — throwing a fresh coterie into a combat situation does much to establish the vampires who are trying to kill them as antagonists — but it's not the only way to use the opposition of the Sabbat plot-wise. A strict diet of combat, combat and more combat gets dull rapidly, and a never-ending fight in the trenches to keep the Sabbat out of town can get murderously boring after the first half-dozen battles.

The Sabbat is smart, after all. It hasn't survived the past half-millennium by being repetitive in its tactics. So consider all of the ways conflict with the Sabbat can play itself out. Spies and recruiters from the Sabbat constantly attempt to cross Camarilla borders. Neonates and even more experienced Kindred succumb to Sabbat blandishments (or are kidnapped) and go over to the other side. Packs of *antitribu* constantly chip away at the Masquerade, forcing the Camarilla to expend resources to defend it. All of these instances — and by extension, all of the plots that can be spun from them — revolve around the conflict between the two great sects.

Conflict With Other Supernaturals

It's a truism that very few people in the World of Darkness like vampires. To Lupines they're corrupted targets, to be annihilated on sight. Mortal wizards have a track record of performing unpleasant experiments with vitae — *vide* the origins of Clan Tremere. Too many ghosts were created by sloppy or callous vampires for wraiths ever to be too friendly with their unliving counterparts. And there are even stranger monstrosities out there that hold no love for Caine's childer, even the supposedly civilized ones who dwell in the Masquerade's shadow.

So far, so good, but why conflict with the Camarilla in particular? The institution of the Masquerade provides much of the answer. By using mortals as tools, the Kindred trample other supernaturals' interests underfoot. A Ventrue with her fingers in the housing industry cares little that the three new developments she's putting up to gain economic advantage over a rival might be situated on top of territory sacred to the local Lupines. The city's sheriff doesn't know or care that there might have been a metaphysical connection between the cabdriver he just murdered as part of a cover-up and a vengeance-minded ghost. By involving or discarding others, the Kindred draw the ire of others as well.

Defending against the assaults of supernatural foes also presents a unique complication for Camarilla vampires. After all, theirs is still the responsibility to maintain the Masquerade, no matter what they might be confronted with. So after the walls stop dripping blood, summoned lightning stops streaking from a clear sky and assorted enraged werewolves have finished

Knowing Too Much

It cannot be overemphasized that when you cross over other supernatural creatures into your game ignorance is bliss. The line between player knowledge and character knowledge must be maintained vigilantly, otherwise familiarity breeds contempt. Remember, your coterie doesn't know anything about what werewolves, mages, etc. are really like — they're lucky if they've been taught the basics of being a vampire. So when a scruffy bum responds to a neonate's attempt at feeding by metamorphosing into a nine-foot-tall column of rage, fur and fangs, the characters should *not* respond with a shrug and, "Oh, it's a Bone Gnawer in Crinos form. Bob, flip me the book so I can see what Gifts he's likely to have." The players might know what a Bone Gnawer is, but the odds are very, very long against a given character knowing what one might be. Instead, the characters should react with the shock, fear and horror appropriate to seeing a puny mortal mutate into a hateful and terrifying killing machine.

If the characters survive, they will probably understand that they've just come face-to-snout with a Lupine. They may, if they decide they need to know more on the topic, uncover the fact that Lupines supposedly live in tribes and have some sort of magical powers, but little more unless they decide to devote their afterlives to the study of the beasts. Allowing your characters to know too much about their fellow travelers — or letting your players get away with sneaking out-of-game knowledge into in-play situations — can go a long way toward lessening the impact encounters with other supernatural beings should have.

Players who consistently metagame should be disciplined in some fashion, preferably by stripping experience from their characters. After all, characters who sound like they've just read the rulebook, and who can quote it chapter and verse, really don't sound like characters at all.

HUNTERS IN PACKS

While the fictional Van Helsing may have worked essentially by himself, there are dedicated and powerful organizations in the World of Darkness that view the eradication of the Kindred as their goal. The still-active Inquisition, using a combination of faith and technology, works tirelessly to rid the world of vampires and other monsters. Government agencies from the mysterious Project Twilight to more mundane branches like the CDC and FBI have all stumbled across vampire-related anomalies, and may be working toward an awareness of the Kindred presence. Occult groups such as the storied Arcanum work tirelessly to gather knowledge on vampires, and none know why they seek it. And then there are rumors — just rumors — of hunters blessed (or cursed) with supernatural powers themselves....

For more information on established groups of vampire-hunters in the World of Darkness, see **The Inquisition**.

tearing the place up, it's left to any vampires still standing to try to explain away the mess. Doing so takes valuable energy and resources that the Kindred could be using to defend themselves, thus making them easier targets for the next round of assaults, and so on. The need to maintain the Masquerade, even in the face of magick and claw, puts a uniquely Camarilla twist on what otherwise might be simply a dull monster mash.

CONFLICT WITH HUNTERS

Just because the Kindred see mortals as playthings and prey doesn't mean that mortals necessarily like it. From time immemorial mere humans have done their best to hunt the monsters who have plagued them. The names of the boldest of these hunters have been immortalized: Theseus, Beowulf, St. George and others. The modern era offers fewer heroic names, but that doesn't mean the urge to strike back has vanished. The conflict between Kindred and those humans who would turn the tables on them remains an energetic one, and one that holds not only lives, but also the Masquerade itself in the balance.

Conflict with vampire hunters usually takes two forms. The first is the cat-and-mouse game of hunter and prey, except that when it comes to would-be slayers of Kindred it's never quite sure who's the hunter and who's being hunted. Often such chases grow into closed loops, with the pursued Kindred desperately trying to rid themselves of their homicidal stalker even as their fellow vampires distance themselves for fear of becoming the next targets.

The other way to use conflict with hunters is more subtle, though perhaps more dangerous. While some modern-day Van Helsings think the best way to rid the world of vampires is with stake and shotgun, others see information as their ultimate weapon. These hunters seek to spread knowledge of vampires' very existence, to shatter the Masquerade irrevocably and to rouse all of humanity against all of the monsters in its midst. The battle between these mortals and the Kindred who seek to silence them is a constant one. Killing one such mortal merely makes others believe in her message; meanwhile the Kindred who tug on the strings of the media seek to have self-appointed supernatural investigators branded kooks, crackpots and worse. The battle for the hearts and minds of a city, and ultimately, the world, can make for a fascinating campaign as the Masquerade teeters on the brink.

Story Ideas

There are any number of stories that can come from setting up a conflict between the Camarilla and its enemies. The following are basic ideas, but they can serve as a basis for a more involved plot.

• The coterie notices the local Caitiff and anarchs are going missing. Investigating, they discover a Sabbat war party recruiting reinforcements for an assault on the city. Can the coterie make it out in one piece? What if they're ordered to go back and infiltrate the would-be invaders? And if all else fails, how can they help to stop the attack?

• A newcomer to the city turns out to be a Sabbat mole. He goes after the coterie one member at a time, recruiting them and turning them against one another. Can he be stopped, or will the Kindred turn *en masse* to the Sabbat? And what about the possibility of betrayal? An ambitious neonate can go far by selling out her friends to the sheriff as less-than-loyal citizens.

• There's a Sabbat infiltrator somewhere in the city, and it's the coterie's job to find her. Can they shake her loose before she weakens the local Camarilla too much? And how can the investigation proceed when all of the other Kindred of the city — guilty and innocent alike — have secrets they don't want the coterie uncovering?

• The vampires do something to anger a pack of Lupines who live on the outskirts of the city. Can they even figure out what they've done before the werewolves tear them to shreds, and is there any way to make amends? And if not, what can they do to have any chance at survival?

• A member of the coterie kills a mortal during feeding. Unfortunately, that's not the end of it, as the mortal returns from beyond the grave to haunt his murderer as a ghost. Now the unquiet soul is doing its best to ensure the vampire's destruction, and it doesn't care whom else it gets in the meanwhile. Is there anyway to free the besieged Kindred from these unwelcome attentions before they turn fatal for the entire coterie?

• The coterie gets sloppy and leaves behind evidence that a team of professional vampire-hunters picks up. Slowly but surely the hunters close the net on the coterie, even as the rest of the city's Kindred population abandons them to their fate. Can the vampires turn the tables on their pursuers, and even if they do, what about the inevitable next wave?

• A local professor goes to the media with astonishing news: Vampires really exist! In the confusion surrounding the attempts to suppress his information, the professor dies, possibly at the coterie's hands. Now his students and those who believed him are convinced of the truth of what he wrote — the man died for it, after all — and are seeking to spread their gospel as widely as possible. It's up to the coterie to contain and defuse the situation, but with each passing night more and more mortals join the crusade....

Internal Conflict: Kindred Versus Kindred

It has been stated, only half in jest, that if the Sabbat really wanted to destroy the Camarilla, all they really had to do was leave it alone. While this may be a slight exaggeration, there is no denying that the internal stresses of the sect keep things interesting for all concerned. Neonates struggle for survival against their peers, ancillae attempt to climb in power (often over the corpses of their predecessors), elders plot and scheme against one another, and even the clans themselves exist in only an uneasy peace. There is conflict a-plenty — and thus more than enough grist for a Storyteller's mill — within the Camarilla's borders. If you don't want to look out of the Camarilla for enemies for your players' characters, rest assured that there are plenty already inside the borders.

Looking Up: Neonates

There are numerous reasons for neonates to be hated. First of all, they are weak, and in a society of predators the strong always despise the weak. Even the most promising newcomer to the Blood is easy meat to the weakest ancilla, and rest assured that the ancillae take every opportunity to reinforce the truth of the notion.

Neonates are also only years, or on some cases hours, removed from their Humanity. They still act on occasion in very human fashion, making mistakes that will be repeated less and less often as they grow accustomed to their new status. Some Kindred loathe them for the incompetence thus displayed, others for the unwanted reminder these fledglings provide of earlier, more innocent times. Either way, the mere fact of a neonate's stumbling existence is enough to earn other Kindred's ire.

There's also the matter of politics. A neonate is far more than just another inexperienced vampire. She's a political statement, a favor fulfilled, a prize ghoul rewarded or snatched away from a rival. She's a potential successor to her sire — and competition to the rest of her sire's brood. She will eventually seek territory to govern and hunt in, and that territory can only come from the possessions of another Kindred. In the end, every vampire who is or who stands to be hurt by a neonate's Embrace has very good reason for hating, or seeking to destroy, her.

There's even the notion of rivalry between neonates. In a crowded city, when the numbers of vampires need to be culled, the culling's going to start at the bottom. It's neonates who are most likely to be sacrificed to the pressures of population. Getting ahead (or disposing) of one's peers is a more than just hyper-competitiveness; it's a question of survival. Multiple childer of a single sire may have especially intense sibling rivalries as a result, but the pressure comes from all sides. Besides, other neonates are generally the only other vampires

On Coterie Building

A coterie makes sense not only as a plot device to keep your players' characters together, but also as an in-game tool for keeping them alive. A solid and well-balanced coterie safeguards its individual members against bullying and random violence, while establishing a few built-in allies for each character. At the same time, coterie internal politics serve as good practice for the deadlier version that each neonate is going to encounter if he survives long enough. In addition, a coterie situation is a wonderful learning environment for new players, who get to work with more experienced players in a scenario where the stakes are not yet earthshattering.

With that in mind, you should encourage your players to build a stable and workable coterie for their characters. A strong coterie has a good central *raison d'être* (a common foe, princely fiat, acquaintance from before the Embrace, a shared blood bond, a mutual ambition) and a willingness to work together. No coterie lasts long if one of the characters is simply out to eliminate his fellows; the same holds if there are two characters locked in a bitter feud. The former scenario tends to devolve into cycles of vengeance; the latter often turns into a grandstand for the two rivals while everyone else sits around and takes notes. A good coterie has reasons for getting together and staying together, not flying apart. Those tend to arise on their own soon enough.

Once the reason for the coterie has been established, it makes sense to make certain that there's a level playing field within the group. If one member of the coterie can ride roughshod over the rest, it's not going to be much fun to play one of his doormats. Coteries are collections of peers, coteries of neonates especially so. So if one character appears overpowered or simply doesn't fit the concept of the group (a biker Gangrel who likes breaking things dropped among a flock of intriguing Toreador and Ventrue, for example), it can get disruptive. If you feel that a character simply doesn't work within the confines of your players' coterie, you can and should use coterie stability as a reason to get that player to think about modifying his persona to make the game run more smoothly.

that neonates stand a chance against; neonate-on-neonate conflict is a case of picking on someone your own size.

It is the external pressure from older and more experienced Kindred that forces coteries of neonates to form; it is the internal pressure from freshly budding rivalries that causes them to split apart in the end. A coterie of peers, all of similar experience and potential, is an excellent survival device. Within a stable coterie, there's always someone watching your back, and there's enough combined firepower present to encourage Kindred looking for someone to bully to look elsewhere.

Stories involving neonates always involve a high degree of paranoia. There's always someone gunning for the new kids on the vampiric block, and neonates who expect to survive know this. Furthermore, few neonates really know the ins and outs of their new status — sires often teach their childer enough to survive, but little more — and as such are constantly running into trouble spawned from myth, legend and ignorance. While most neonates can count on at least the cursory protection of their sires (the boon of creation is an expensive one, and few Kindred wish to throw it away lightly), the relentless Darwinian pressure of vampiric existence can take its toll. Any neonate worth his salt has earned the enmity of at least a half-dozen other Kindred, all of whom will take some form of steps to deal with the upstart.

Higher Ground: Ancillae

Neonates get picked on; ancillae get targeted. Those Kindred who survive their unliving adolescence don't have it any easier than the neonates do, they just have a slightly different range of rivals. For one thing, ancillae have been around long enough to recognize that the Camarilla equivalent of the glass ceiling is at least as permanent as the mortal one — there's no room at the top, and a great many immortal killing machines who'd like to keep it that way. The only way to ascend in power is to create an opening, and there are no easy targets waiting. Besides, any ancilla who looks like she's

Climbing the Ladder

By the time a vampire reaches ancilla status, the simple thrill of unliving existence is pretty much gone. After a few decades, immortality becomes less of a gift and more of a terrible, oppressive weight. Ennui sets in as cruising clubs and leaping across rooftops lose their charm. Simply existing is no longer enough; there has to be some sort of goal that can give an ancilla's nights meaning.

For many ancillae, the answer to this dilemma of boredom is politics. With a complex hierarchy of offices and titles already in place, the Camarilla offers any number of attainable and visible goals for the ambitious ancilla. Existence then becomes a grand strategy of maneuvering one's predecessor out of her office and oneself into it. Such intrigues can make for excellent low-combat, high-tension chronicles, as the characters attempt to destabilize their "superiors" while those Kindred seek to fend off the ancillae's challenges. Success can bring new challenges — how do the characters handle their new responsibilities, and how are the deposed Kindred's patrons responding to the loss of their catspaws — and new story ideas. On the other hand, even if the characters fail at their attempt at social climbing interesting plot developments can come out of it. Their former rivals might seek vengeance, and other Kindred could well see the defeated characters as easy targets. Kicking a coterie when it's down is a favorite habit among the Kindred, after all. And just because a coterie's down doesn't mean it's out — defeat (if the characters survive) is just an excuse to seek vengeance and start plotting anew.

competent to claw her way to a position of power is going to attract a great deal of attention from older, more established Kindred who may not fancy the status of potential victim.

Ancillae also have responsibilities, and with responsibilities come the consequences of failing to uphold those responsibilities. All competent vampires of this age have some form of domain or territory, perhaps even one as vital as keeping an eye on a newspaper or a freight yard. A failure to look after one's area properly will draw the ire of a great many other Kindred, and the attention of ambitious neonates who think they can handle the post better.

Neonates can also be a problem for the average ancilla. The newly made Kindred often travel in coteries that differ from Sabbat packs in precious few details, and such groups have an eye out for any lone ancilla who strays into its path. While a lone neonate is no great challenge for an ancilla, five bloodthirsty and well-armed ones can be, particularly if they've got their shotguns loaded and diablerie on their minds.

Of course, an ancilla's worst enemy can be his fellow ancillae. If there's a single office open — be it whip, keeper of Elysium or prince's dogcatcher — there will be any number of hungry ancillae who feel they can turn the post to their advantage. That perception inevitably leads to savage infighting, as the immortal equivalents of middle management tear out each others' throats for a shot at the corner office. While the fighting is rarely overt — a vampire who can't maneuver his rivals out of a posting isn't devious enough to hold it — it is vicious. The casualties can include allies, ghouls, property, reputations and precious mortals. Blackmail, seduction and the use of the mental Disciplines are all common tactics in this sort

THE OLD ONES

A single elder can be a terrifying antagonist for a coterie of neonates. It matters little how they first attract his enmity — perhaps rivals of his sired them, or he fears their ultimate ambitions — but his attentions can provide endless plot ideas. His stratagems to injure them can range from the blunt (sending his descendants, ghouls or mortal pawns to attack the coterie) to the subtle (intriguing against them and their patrons) to the monstrous (taking out his wrath on their mortal loved ones and allies). He should act through ever more powerful servants, raising the level of opposition every time the coterie proves equal to his challenge. He may even welcome the coterie's continued survival as an exciting game to leaven his otherwise dull existence. In the meantime the neonates slowly ascend the ladder of power, learning about politics and what it takes to maintain one's position in the ever-so-treacherous Camarilla. Should the characters achieve a reasonable level of success and power, a final confrontation with the inimical elder is not out of the question. In the meantime, however, the elder has served as the mover and shaker behind any number of chapters in your chronicle by merely staying true to his class and his fear.

of struggle, and any Kindred who goes in with a sense of fair play is liable to be eliminated from the running very early indeed.

THE VIEW FROM THE HILL: ELDERS

Elders of the Camarilla have achieved dizzying heights of power, and they are deathly afraid of falling. While unlife may not be sweet to the elders, it is precious, and they will go to any lengths to avoid risking their immortality. Elders have few friends, if any; they see other Kindred as rivals and potential usurpers. They know the temptations that younger Kindred feel, having experienced those same urges centuries ago. They also know the lengths to which ambitious vampires will go, and who the targets of those ambitions are.

A natural outgrowth of elders' unnatural paranoia is the way in which they treat their childer and other, less experienced vampires. The logic is simple: Younger Kindred who are off-balance and at each others' throats have neither the time nor the strength to assault their elders. As a result, elders spend endless hours setting pawns, childer and subordinates (theirs and other Kindred's) against one another. The endless dance is intended to sap the ability of neonates and ancillae to rebel against their sires and grandsires, while leaving them strong enough to remain useful tools. Maintaining such a delicate balance takes skill and centuries of practice; elders who don't acquire the knack often find themselves diablerized or alone in the face of well-prepared opposition.

Elders loathe ancillae and neonates for what they might become; their peers they hate because of what they are. The struggle between elders for status, dominion and power never ends, and each elder works ceaselessly to undermine her rivals. All fear the approach of Gehenna, and seek to fortify themselves against the true Final Nights. For many, such preparation includes setting up one's peers as easier targets for the ravening Antediluvians. Other elders prefer to concern themselves with the here and now, and see others of their kind as pressing threats to their existences. Still others play the game of the Jyhad to alleviate ennui, maneuvering against the same rivals for centuries in order to ensure having something to do every night.

For more information on using elders, see Chapter Eight of this book.

IN THE BLOOD: SIRES AND CHILDER

Some of the most bitter conflict the Camarilla has ever known has arisen between vampires and those who created them. Few Kindred ever asked for the Embrace; even those who did desire it often rationalize their longing away. In such a situation, it is only natural that a vampire's resentment arises against the one who sentenced him to unlife. "I didn't ask to be Embraced!" is the all-too-common cry of a neonate who is just discovering the downside to his new status. Meanwhile, sires see their childer grow in new and unexpected directions, and begin to fear them. "How long," many older Kindred wonder, "before he comes seeking my blood?" When the twisted influence of the blood bond is added into the equation, it is no surprise that too many Kindred share only a lineage and bitter hatred with their sires. Much can be done with the story of a vampire whose sire no longer trusts him, and who begins throwing increasingly deadly obstacles in his path.

Clan Versus Clan

Conflict is not limited to age or class. The uneasy balance between the clans of the Camarilla is difficult to maintain at the best of times, and these are hardly the best of times. The Ventrue look down on their peers, and make no secret of their disdain. The Toreador can't stand the presence of the Nosferatu, while the Sewer Rats revel in dragging the other clans into the muck. So it goes among the clans of the Camarilla, on both the grand scale and the immediate one as well.

It is extremely rare for two clans to go to war, even in so limited a scale as a single city. Fighting in the streets between the Brujah and the Ventrue is a clear invitation to the Sabbat, after all, and as much as a city's assorted vampire populations may hate one another, they recognize that if the *antitribu* march in, everyone loses. Instead, the clans (when not engaged in internecine strife of their own) seek to weaken one anothers' influences and relative strengths. If a city's Brujah benefit from local heavy industry, the Ventrue may act in concert to wreck the companies who own the plants. Why? Because doing so deprives the Brujah of both financial and human resources. When the heavy industry dries up, the workers are laid off, organized labor's influence decreases, and the Brujah's ability to marshal strength in the field diminishes. Once the Brujah have been deprived of their support, the Ventrue can force concessions from them, then import high-tech industry to revitalize the city's economic base and recoup their own resources lost in the maneuver.

Such plans can take decades or even centuries to come to fruition, but the clans are patient. The intention, after all, is not to wipe out the other clans — allies against the Sabbat are still needed, after all — but rather to weaken them and make them subordinate. How vicious the inter-clan conflict becomes depends on the city and the individual clan members involved, but it is never static. Just as individual Kindred jostle against one another for relative status, so too do the clans.

In many cases, conflict between clans in a single setting can be traced to the personality conflicts of individual members of the respective clans. As the elders' hatred grows, they draw their childer and their subordinates into the conflict, which then spirals out of control. Such petty origins in no way diminish the intensity of the hatred that the two sides can generate, but the scenario goes a long way toward explaining how the Nosferatu and Malkavians can have a grudging alliance in one city and be at each others' throats in the next.

Unholy Appetites: Diablerie

Power is one of the most basic sources of narrative conflict. Among the Kindred, power is defined by blood. It is little wonder, then, that some of the fiercest conflicts (and best stories) within the Camarilla are spawned by the lust for potent blood.

Technically, diablerie is condemned by the Camarilla except in certain unique circumstances (blood hunts, dealing with enemies of the sect, etc.). The use of the ability that Auspex grants to read auras is supposed to be sufficient to flush out diablerists, who are thus condemned by their own vital energies. Alas, vampires are no better than mortals at legislating morality. Elders spend sleepless days pondering who among their childer might be brave enough to attempt diablerie. Neonates dwell in terror of stories of elders who can only subsist on vampiric vitae. And so it goes, as the spectre of vampiric cannibalism infuses every Kindred with fear.

That's not to say the fear is unfounded. The lure of ascending generations is a powerful one, and more than one elder has been devoured by his ungrateful progeny. Such attempts can take years or longer to be completed, and the construction of such (whether your players' coterie is the hunter or prey is up to you) can provide an interesting thread to an ongoing chronicle. The situation grows even more fascinating if there is evidence that the proposed diablerie is tacitly supported by someone high in the city's power structure. Princes don't always like to do their own dirty work, and the unmistakable evidence of diablerie can be more than enough to condemn the prince's catspaws in this affair.

Story Ideas

Stories wherein the core conflict is contained entirely within the Camarilla are manifold. The trick is not creating such a conflict, but rather winnowing down the potential conflicts to a manageable number. For example:

Vlad and Juliet

Conflict between clans can do any number of intriguing things to a previously tight-knit coterie. When two of the group's members' clans go at it, odds are that someone on each side is going to call on the characters to do their clan duty. Things get even more problematic if one vampire is ordered to "do something" about his opposite number in the coterie. At that point, individual loyalty is placed against clan loyalty, and the consequences are dire no matter which choice the characters make. If the coterie's Kindred stay loyal to their coterie, their progenitors will most likely not be amused, and may take drastic measures to bring the errant vampires into line. On the other hand, if the characters bow to their duty, the coterie may well be rent asunder forever, a development that likely has dire consequences for the chronicle. Of course, the vampires can always try to fake carrying out their orders, but if the deception is discovered, the consequences will assuredly be extremely unpleasant.

Note that this sort of story idea doesn't hinge on romantic love between two characters. A simple respect and working relationship between two Kindred is more than enough to work from in such instances. Once a vampire has been told he needs to sabotage his working partner, he is a fool if he doesn't wonder if that partner has been ordered to do the same to him. Suspicion and fear inevitably replace trust. The bonds of the coterie are stretched, if not snapped. Can the coterie ever recover? It seems unlikely….

• The coterie earns the enmity of a slightly older gang of Kindred, who see the characters as unwelcome competition. The older vampires have more skills, more standing in the city and a better grasp on their Disciplines. How can the neonates survive?

• The prince's sheriff has decided that it's open season on neonates, and does his level best to goad the coterie into committing actions that will allow him to lower the boom. Can the neonates avoid the traps being laid for them, and what happens if they don't?

• One of the city's elders decides that the coterie reminds her of her first coterie. This isn't necessarily a good thing, as she eventually killed the rest of her companions off, but in the meanwhile she takes an unhealthy interest in the neonates' doings, going to far as to arrange "situations" to see how they might react. Will the younger Kindred figure out what's going on before the elder ups the stakes, or throws her toys away?

• A member of the coterie has a rival — a jealous ghoul who thinks that he should have received the Embrace instead of the character. The ghoul is now doing everything in his power to rectify the "mistake," up to and including making attempts on the character's life. Unfortunately, the character's sire values the ghoul's services too highly for him to be killed out of hand. So how does the character protect herself, and what does the rest of her coterie do about it?

• The city's keeper of Elysium is removed from her post by the primogen council for gross incompetence. Every ambitious ancilla in the city immediately begins positioning himself to be the next to take the job. How might a coterie of ancillae react to this opportunity? Would they throw their weight behind one candidate, or would it become every Kindred for himself?

• A coterie member's sire becomes obsessed with a neonate, leading him essentially to abandon his other childer. His enemies sense weakness and move in, plucking his supporters one by one. Can the coterie convince the elder to return his attention to where it belongs, and can they possibly survive long enough to do so?

• There are new neonates in town — in other words, easy pickings. The coterie moves quickly to show these whippersnappers where they fit into the pecking order, but get a surprise when it turns out the neonates have a powerful patron. Can the ancillae avoid offending the neonates' supporter, or is it already too late? Who will end up teaching a lesson to whom?

• The coterie is a collection of relatively experienced Kindred, perhaps even the city's primogen council. The local prince, unfortunately, is an incompetent buffoon. How can the coterie manage his removal without exposing the city to attack? Will a member of the coterie be chosen to replace the prince, and if so, what does that do to the fragile bonds holding the characters together?

• The characters are dispossessed elders searching for a new city to claim. They think they stumble across a lucky break

when they find a metropolis that has recently been cleansed by a justicar, but other elders have the same idea. The struggle for power becomes even deadlier than usual, as neither side has its usual machinery of ghouls and childer in place to fight their battles for them. Final Death is a very real possibility.

• An incident at Elysium leads to the city's Brujah being disgraced. As there's a Brujah in the coterie, the other members have to decide what to do about their erstwhile companion. Do they ignore the matter, hide her until the situation blows over or turn on her? And what happens when the crisis ends — if it ever does?

• Two elders get into a vicious squabble and draw the rest of their respective clans into the fray. While neither clan is represented in the characters' coterie, they are alternately recruited, bribed and threatened to pick a side as the battle lines are drawn. Which way does the coterie go, or can it stay neutral? Can it even afford to do so?

OTHER FORMS OF CONFLICT

There's more to conflict as a storytelling tool than just bloody constraint. Emotional conflict is just as powerful a device, and can make for a more intense roleplaying experience than the wildest battle in the streets. The struggle to break an unwanted blood bond can be as gripping as the struggle to cleanse the Sabbat from the city. The fight to remain calm long enough to plot vengeance on the Kindred who diablerized a character's sire or lover can be as terrifying as facing an angry elder in her haven.

Vampires are no longer human, but they remember being human, to a greater or lesser degree. Some neonates might not even recognize the difference, and therein lies fertile ground for tragedy. Consider the case of a neonate torn from a relatively happy existence. He has loved ones he must abandon, but he can't tear himself away from returning to them. Perhaps he breaks the Masquerade, confessing all in an

So Who's the Villain?

The term "villain" is a relative one when it comes to **Vampire**. After all, the protagonists of the game are blood-drinking, unliving corpses raised from the dead to feed on the pulsating vitae of the living — not exactly your textbook role models. The antagonists you line up for your chronicle may not be "bad guys" in the traditional sense, because the "heroes" can be pretty damn bad on their own. In fact, the "villains" of the chronicle may be mortal hunters out to stop the bloodsucking fiends' rein of unholy terror, something that the majority of people would probably regard as an admirable goal.

So bear in mind when you're creating your **Vampire** villains that they may not be all that villainous. Yes, rabid Sabbat packs may be far, far worse then your players' characters ever dreamed of being, but antagonists for the Kindred come from both ends of the spectrum.

attempt to earn their sympathy; perhaps he seeks to Embrace one or all of them in violation of the Traditions, just so he can be with them forever. Stories like this can provide plenty of tension and strong roleplaying without necessitating that your players reach for their dice every third minute.

NEMESES AND ANTAGONISTS

Behind every nefarious plot stands a nefarious plotter. While your characters may be the center of your story, they need an opposite number, someone against whom they can strive and compete. Without an opponent against whom the coterie can react, there's little tension in your chronicle. Instead of a foe to overcome, there's just a series of small skirmishes that devolves quickly into boredom. On the other hand, if it turns out that the anarchs who trashed the coterie's communal haven is actually a disguised Sabbat pack looking to soften up the city, suddenly all of those one-off gunfights and back-alley ambushes become part of a pattern. Your chronicle becomes more focused. And, by setting up an ultimate enemy, perhaps the bishop or cardinal behind the assault on the city, you set up the characters' confrontation with that enemy as the natural climax for your chronicle.

Villains don't just happen, though. You need to construct the ultimate nemesis of your chronicle carefully. After all, most of your plot developments must flow from him and his choices, especially those dealing with the characters. With that in mind, you need to start thinking about *who* your characters' enemy as much, if not more, than *what* he is.

It is a fact that no villain worth his salt does things simply to be villainous. Even the most sadistic Tzimisce or bad-ass Baali has a goal, something he's trying to accomplish. He has a plan, an overriding goal that he wants to achieve, and the coterie is merely a minor obstacle in his path to his eventual goal. Any actions he takes are not predicated on stopping the chronicle's central characters; they are directed taking care of his own business. If the coterie interferes, too bad for them.

GROUNDWORK

The first step is to figure out what the prime antagonist wants. A host of related questions spring from that one. What is he after, and why? What will he do to obtain that goal, and how soon must he accomplish it? Does he serve a greater power (a higher-up in the Sabbat, or a superior in the Inquisition) to whom he must report, and if so, what happens if he doesn't make fast enough progress? Will he bargain? The answers to these and other, similar questions provide an operational framework for your prime antagonist's actions. If you know how far he's willing to go and what he's striving for, you'll at least have a handle on how he'll react to setbacks and triumphs — and what his next move is likely to be.

You'll also want to figure out what your nemesis is — his species, sect, beliefs, powers, authority and so on. A good rule of thumb is to take the most prominent features of the players' characters and invert them for the nemesis. If your troupe plays a coterie of high-Humanity neonates seeking to restore their lost Humanity, an aged and amoral Tzimisce with a pack of hungry ghouls works well as an antagonist. This approach works on a general level as well — if the characters are sneaky, devious sorts, setting them up against a brute who relies on sheer force to achieve his ends provides both contrast and a challenge. After all, if the characters' usual bag of tricks is suddenly rendered ineffective, the coterie will need to try something new — fast — or else risk ending up as ash on the wind.

Also bear in mind that the villain doesn't necessarily see himself as a villain. Perhaps he has idealistic motivations for his actions. There is always the possibility that your villain is in it just for personal gain or power, but there's also every chance that he's serving what he perceives to be a higher purpose. Allowing your nemesis character to believe, honestly and moralistically, in what he's doing can add a fine moral shading to your game. Doing so also cuts down on the amount of moustachio-twirling scenery chewing your villain is likely to do — if he honestly believes that killing off the coterie is the best thing for the world, he's not likely to indulge in maniacal cackling, insane gloating or any of the other stereotypical "villain" behaviors that limit his effectiveness and turn him into a cartoon.

Playing the Part

It is imperative to remember that your prime antagonist has a personality. He does things for a reason. So when the characters thwart one aspect of his plot, don't just strike back with everything at his disposal. Instead, roleplay him. Get inside his head and consider how he's going to react naturally. Is this setback a minor annoyance? Or is it time for the hammer to come down? If your villain behaves believably, your plot becomes more believable as a result. If he reacts As The Plot Demands, he'll seem contrived, and, eventually, so will your chronicle. Let the story follow character, rather than the other way around.

You might even want to consider the archvillain to be your character in all of this, unless doing so means that the coterie is irrevocably doomed as a result. Otherwise, climb inside his head the way your players hop inside their characters, and play him to the hilt.

Henchmen, Henchwomen and Others

No good archvillain ever works alone. Even the most maniacal madman needs henchmen to run errands, do the dirty work, take the fall for plans gone awry, obtain victims and so on. More to the point, it doesn't make sense for you to spend hours creating an interesting and well-drawn villain only to throw him into a deathmatch with the coterie immediately. In a situation like that there's no sense of dramatic tension, and no time for the characters' dislike of the villain to grow to the point where defeating him means something to them. If your archvillain appears on the stage too soon, he's an obstacle, not an object of hatred. You need to take time to stoke the characters' loathing of their nemesis, and that means holding him back until the moment is right.

In the meanting, though, there needs to be someone onstage. Someone needs to be confronting the coterie each session, keeping them busy and stoking the flame of their dislike. That's where henchmen come in (or ghouls, as the case may be).

This approach, which works best when you throw ever-more powerful subordinate nemeses at the coterie, draws out the characters' road to the final confrontation. The best way to stretch the time between introduction and climax, in many cases, is with encounters with the servants and henchmen of your villain. After all, it's highly unlikely your main antagonist is going to be doing all of his legwork himself, so grant him some hired help. Think about what sort of person he is, and what sort of servants he's likely to have. A Sabbat archbishop has packs and other subordinates to turn loose, while a hunter with True Faith likely has a flock of true believers who just might be willing to die for him.

The next thing to consider is how the henchmen come in contact with the coterie. Odds are low that they'll wander up, introduce themselves as The Villain's Servants, and then proceed to whip out the TEC-9s in best Hong Kong cinematic fashion. Rather, it makes more sense to have the characters come across the henchmen busy running an un-palatable errand for their boss (say, staking a friend of the coterie) and put a stop to it, and then discover a connection to a "higher" power. Of course, that sets the players up in opposition to your archvillain nicely, and he now has an excuse to send servitors of increasing power and importance after them. They thwarted his will once, after all, which means that they need to be disposed of before they become a real threat. The closer the characters get to their main antagonist, of course, the greater the power and resources of the henchmen that said nemesis throws in their way, and the greater the challenge that must be overcome each time.

Don't make the mistake of having your villain only employ one sort of subordninate. This is the modern era, after all, and diversification is the name of the game. Give your villain more credit than that — and give your players more of a challenge. Vary tactics and approaches. A street gang, a ghouled police precinct, a crazed (but Dominated) arsonist, blood bound childer — all of these can be part of your villain's arsenal. If the characters never know what to expect next, they can't plan too far ahead — and can't get complacent.

You might want to consider henchmen as personalities with a relationship to your archvillain as well. Are they just hired thugs and bound ghouls, or is there something more? Did the villain send someone he cared about to work evil on the coterie? And if so, how will he react to his subordinate's failure — or death? Making your henchmen more well-rounded means that you can spin more complete plots off from their failures — and their successes.

Foes for the Sect

Some villains are more appropriate than others for a Camarilla chronicle. While the Sabbat is the obvious choice, it's not the only one. Consider the following:

- **Other Kindred**

A rival within the sect might be the ultimate enemy for the coterie. The struggle for advancement and power in the Camarilla can get deadly at the drop of a hat, and placing your villain inside the sect adds interesting complications to the coterie's attempts to strike back. Perhaps the villain is an elder who wants the coterie eliminated. Any move the characters make against him is going to look bad, and may well draw in the rest of the sect to defend the antagonists. On the other hand, perhaps the "villain" is a rival coterie or individual vampire gunning for power. The players' characters are rivals, and thus they must be eliminated.

- **Mortals**

Most humans who go vampire-hunting have the shelf life of a cold beer at a ballgame, which is to say practically none at all. Those few who survive, however, get very good indeed at what they do. Armed with faith, technology and just maybe a few supernatural powers of their own, top-flight mortal hunters should be sufficient to put the fear of God — literally, in some cases — into any coterie.

- **The Sabbat**

The default enemy for a Camarilla game is, of course, the Sabbat. Setting up your ultimate villain as a higher-up in the Sabbat allows you to throw endless waves of neonates and angry packs at the coterie, raising the stakes each time. If the coterie simply tries to fend off each attack, eventually they'll be overwhelmed. The only choices they have are to retreat, or to try to press forward and find their true enemy….

DEATH

While death may be the end of all things for an individual, it opens up new doorways and opportunities in a Camarilla chronicle. When one of the Kindred meets the Final Death, suddenly her ghouls are masterless, her holdings are up for grabs and her position in the city's hierarchy is wide open. All of these spell opportunity for a coterie of ambitious young vampires.

THE GREAT CHAIN OF FEEDING

One of the beauties of **Vampire: The Masquerade** is that no matter how powerful the characters get or their rivals might be, there's always someone more powerful squatting above them on the food chain. If your coterie gets rid of your hand-crafted villain too quickly, remember that someone had to sire him — and that sire may not be too happy about the way things turned out. You don't want to work your way up the ladder of generations too quickly, lest you end up seemingly forced to trump all-powerful player characters with Caine. (**Note**: If your chronicle gets to this point, scrap it and start over. Beings of such power are so far removed from human concerns that roleplaying them becomes a theoretical exercise, not a game.) but remember that you always have a bigger hammer at your disposal.

Then again, the coterie may not be the only ones vying for the deceased's property and titles. The creation of a sudden vacuum in the city's power structure can draw all those around it into conflict, if not open war. Just because one of your players' characters wants to take over for a recently deceased scourge or sheriff doesn't mean that he's going to pull it off — and the competition for the job can be deadly.

DEATH AS A STORYTELLING TOOL

Some storytellers shy away from using the Final Death in their chronicles. Killing a character off is rather permanent, after all; once you scatter someone's ashes on the wind, odds are she's gone forever. That sort of permanence can be scary, as few Storytellers want to lose the services of a favorite character *ad infinitum*.

Others see the death of a Storyteller character as something to be gotten over with quickly. The victim dies, his ashes are swept up, and the universe rolls along with one less vampire in it. Doing so avoids messy complications, but it robs the Storyteller of one of the most versatile tools in her arsenal — the power of life and death.

The ability and willingness to kill off characters, even important ones, is extremely useful to a good Storyteller. By sending a vampire (or even a familiar mortal or ghoul) into the hereafter, you establish that death is a real and potent part of your world. The death of a character, even a minor one, demonstrates that there are consequences to foolish actions, and that the price of failure is both very real and very high. Perhaps most importantly, once you demonstrate that you are willing to kill off any character, from mortal to primogen, the characters know that no one is safe — not even them.

KICKSTARTING PLOT

The death of a Storyteller character can get a story rolling in any number of ways. Any vampire, whether of high status or low, has a place in the Camarilla. Killing that vampire leaves a vacancy in that place, and starts all of the other Kindred of the city scurrying around it. If the vampire had holdings, ghouls or other possessions of value, the vultures immediately start to circle, seeking to profit from his death. Friends of the deceased tighten their defenses, in case they're next on the hit list. Enemies of the victim, fearful of being accused, ready their alibis and seek to discredit those who might accuse them. Rumors of diablerie or Sabbat infiltration might well fly.

From all this chaos, strong plots can arise. Consider:

- The coterie might be assigned by the prince or sheriff to uncover the murderer. If they do so, they can expect an impressive reward. If they fail, they just might become the next victims. Then again, what if someone — perhaps even the prince — doesn't really want them to succeed?

- The deceased held a position of some prominence in the city, and now that office is vacant. Does a member of the coterie think she can take over that role? What rivals does she have for the title, and how far will they go to seize it? What about the rest of the coterie, which may be linked to her ambition whether they want to be or not? And what challenges will the prince set her and her rival?

• The characters fall under suspicion of having murdered another Kindred. The prince gives them 48 hours to clear themselves, or else face a blood hunt. Can they find the real murderer, or at least prove themselves innocent? Why was the blame cast on them in the first place, and who is responsible for framing them? Worst of all, what if one of the characters did commit the murder, a possibility that can never be overlooked?

DEATH OF A CHARACTER

Few players enjoy seeing their characters reduced to ashes. The reaction is understandable; hours, if not months or years, have been poured into that character, and no one wants to lose that kind of investment cavalierly. On the other hand, if player's characters are rendered immune to the ultimate penalty, game balance can suffer. A Storyteller who refuses to make characters pay the price for foolish actions rapidly finds himself running a game wherein vampires regularly tempt fate because they know that, in the end, they are actually completely safe. That knowledge drains much of the tension from a good **Vampire** chronicle.

On the other hand, wiping out characters arbitrarily or to demonstrate who's really in charge can be just as damaging. Players will quickly learn to avoid a chronicle wherein their carefully crafted characters are liable to be exterminated at Storyteller whim. In the end, balance is necessary. Players should be aware of the fact that sometimes the metaphorical dragon wins, and Storytellers should make sure not to use the ultimate penalty unless the situation absolutely demands it.

CONSEQUENCES

For every action, there is an equal and opposite reaction. In similar fashion, for every action a vampire takes, there is a consequence. Nothing happens in the Camarilla without something else being affected. A mortal is killed in a feeding? Perhaps his loved ones start supporting hunters. Maybe he was targeted for the Embrace by an elder who, deprived of her childe, seeks vengeance. Then again, the killing might break the Masquerade, sending both mortal and immortal authorities after the unfortunate murderer.

The point is that everything in a Camarilla city is connected. Every action impacts the plans, plots and wishes of other Kindred, and they will react as a result. Vampires are not used to being thwarted or balked, and take steps to punish those who do so. Anything the characters do, from performing a favor for another Kindred to killing off a favorite childe, has immediate and profound consequences in the world of the Camarilla. Your players should be aware of this, and you should be, too.

PREVENTATIVE MEASURES

There are some steps you can take to make sure that the death of a character doesn't cause out-of-game hard feelings in your roleplaying group.

• Warn your players at the start of the chronicle that character death is a real possibility, and reiterate that warning periodically.

• When a character dies, make sure the killing doesn't look vengeful. If the character has at least a small chance of escape, the player usually feels better about things. On the other hand, pulling a dozen Brujah bruisers out of the woodwork to finish the job of the first 50 you sicced on the character reeks of a personal vendetta, and makes for a bad situation.

• If a character's death seems likely or nigh-inevitable, talk with the player about it and get her input. Perhaps the character can go out in spectacular or heroic fashion, sacrificing herself to save the city.

• Once a character dies, take some time to chat things over with the deceased's player. Let him know that you still want him in the group; it's just that his character is gone. On the other hand, don't use character death as a way of letting a player know you want him gone. The mutilating effect this sort of thing has on your plot thoroughly wrecks the game for your other players.

• If one player's character kills another, don't allow a vendetta to start. Make sure that there are no hard feelings between the players, and make sure that the new character that gets brought in isn't gunning for the old one's murderer "just as a coincidence."

GETTING AWAY WITH IT

In truth, letting your characters know that there are repercussions to their actions is one of the most important things you can do as a Storyteller. If the coterie breaks the Masquerade with abandon and nothing happens to them, then they're not going to worry about the Masquerade. At that point, one of the tentpegs of your chronicle's tension gets uprooted. Instead, if the characters do something "wrong" or "foolish," make sure they pay for it. That doesn't mean that you should automatically waste every vampire who makes a minor misstep. Rather, it means that if the characters break the Masquerade, hunters or policemen should come sniffing around. They may not find the coterie, but they can make life interesting for a while. By the same token, breaking one of the Traditions should bring down the ire of the local prince. If the prince doesn't come down on characters who break his laws, then he stops being an authority figure and becomes a cartoon. By making certain to show your players that their characters will be held accountable for what they do, you work to maintain the integrity of both your characters and your chronicle.

Allies, Enemies and Others

> *If you do not raise your eyes, you will think you are the highest point.*
> — Antonio Porchia, *Voces*

The Camarilla is not a homogenous body. There are stratifications and classifications, ranks and hierarchies. And, most importantly, there are those who are on the inside, those who are on the outside, and those who straddle the boundary as best they can.

For the Camarilla does not have clearly defined boundaries. The shadowy elders who stalk the salons and Elysiums are officially of the sect, but what about the willfully rebelling anarchs (so many of whom secretly return to the fold)? How about the ghouls who serve the organization but still have not tasted death or the Embrace? And what of the silent, eternally watchful Inconnu? What relation do they have to the keepers of the Masquerade?

Good questions, all. Alas that the answers are as shadowy as those who hold them.

Unlife Among the Anarchs

From sunset on, I feel the troubles lining up to hit me. There's smoke on the evening wind and an extra-harsh tone to the sound of the car horns. Children's voices echo off concrete warm with the last sun of summer. The voices have the flat, empty sound of shouts in a cement tunnel; of words yelled into the angry green and yellow of a brewing summer storm. There's bad juju coming, no doubt.

I pull my jacket around me and keep my head down, hoping. Maybe if I keep a low profile, the troubles will just pass me by. I spend the evening doubling back and walking into the wind, trying to keep myself ahead of the bad karma, to slip the sad-luck trap I can feel closing around my leg. By nine o'clock I realize I could never be so lucky. I just pick a spot and let the bad luck catch up. It takes its own sweet time to do so.

They come for me in the restaurant, just four men in cheap, conservative suits they're not comfortable wearing. They come in and talk quietly to the maitre'd, who begins ignoring me with a visible determination. One of them is Kindred; I can see he's got a snow-pale orange aura with streaks of blue. The other three are his ghouls, I guess. Their auras are both a tinge of violet that quavers like white heat. Of course they've come for me dressed as the police. Maybe the ghouls really are cops on their day job — who cares? The Lick and one of the ghouls stay at the door, the other two come out to the table to collect me.

Halfway to the table, they realize I know they're there. They start catching my eyes, then tossing ugly little strong-man's smiles back and forth. One pops his knuckles and smiles at me. My hand reaches for my steak knife almost on its own, and the bad mojo feelings circle like crows around my head, raucous laughter spiraling up into the night. Laughing at poor, failed, miserable me, dead and alone, brought to bay behind tempered glass and civility in the heart of the asphalt jungle.

I can feel the Beast rising in me as my body tenses and the blood inside me ebbs and shrinks away. Like a burning train shooting down a tunnel toward some impossibly bright light, like an orgasm of anger and hunger, it is rising toward the light. I can't let that happen here.

I show them the knife, and they slow, become more serious. They spread out, their eyes on the knife. Watch the knife. Look at it. Pay attention to the knife. The other diners are beginning to notice. Keep watching the knife. My every hair is standing on end, and I strap down the Hunger with iron bands. I break for in, knife in hand, and one of them steps in front of me. He grabs the hand that holds the knife and tries to tackle me.

My claws are out. I swipe at his restraining wrist, and he yelps, grasping the mangled mess to his chest. Blood pours out from between his fingers (oh God blood oh God **not now**), and I wave the table knife in a convenient excuse. My hip sends a table spinning across the room as I sprint for the kitchen, for the fire door that a 20nothing dishwasher used to sneak through on break so she could smoke cigarettes she'll never need again. They trail behind me shouting, "Stop! Police! Stop or we'll shoot!" But I know they won't, not here, shooting would mean too many questions, and hitting me would mean even more; how can bullets stop the dead?

I tear blindly up the steps, scrabbling on all fours, sprawling to bark shins that never bruise. Then I'm smashing through the fire door and onto the roof. The blinding, perfect beauty of the night strikes me, and I let my purse drop to my side. The moon is a hairline crescent, a sickle on the horizon, and cerement-thin clouds are painted on the city's gray night sky. If I could breathe then this scene, seen from this perfect eyrie, would leave me breathless. I turn and bring the gun out of my purse.

I can hear them down there, on the steps, creeping up like thieves. Their breathing is harsh, and the leather of their shoes grinds against the concrete treads of the fire stairs. They're listening to me listen to them. Behind and beyond me, the sussuruss of the city gains dozens of identities — car doors, sirens, tires on pavement and breaking glass. A thousand smells, a thousand sounds, and thousand shades of black and sodium-arc orange.

And then I let it all slip away, and fire the revolver into the fire stairs. One of the ghouls shrieks, and half a minute later, a voice comes up from below. "He isn't angry with you, Sarah. That's why he sent us — to tell you it was okay. He knew you'd come back. He wants you to know he loves you."

He's an emissary from my sire, then. Or maybe just the local scourge trying words to slow me down long enough for him to grab me. The Kindred's voice is honey, as deep as still water, a lover's caress. A lying lover. An adulterous, conniving lover, but one with hands that make you come back even though you know what going back will mean. Like biting into a warm, ripe plum — warm and sweet like blood on the tongue. Like blood on the tongue, a voice you could just sit and listen to for hours. I shake my head and blink. Will I go back? No — I remember.

The hours of his snuffling professions of eternal amour had I listened to. How many pleas to share blood had there been; first romantic, then demanding, then violent? I didn't ask for him to stalk me for six months and murder me in the name of his love. When he killed me, he didn't even know my name. Let him find some other victim to be his edelweiss, some more willing actress to conscript as the leading lady in his perpetual tragedy. Whatever he paid this emissary, it was wasted. I know I'll never go back. I take the first few crunching steps on the roof and shut the wreck of the fire door behind me. Distantly, I can hear the ghouls start to move again.

I turn to the edge of the building and the perfection of the city night. I hear them walking up the stairs now, calm and unworried. I run, and the Beast surges to run with me, invincible. I leap, a black arrow against the gray night sky. The Beast springs with me, full of the joy at the night and the black glee of the hunt.

The change comes over me as I plummet through the night — my corpse a frigid falling star from the black expanses of the grave. My arms and fingers stretch, an ecstatic agony, while the world grows huge around me. The colors fade to grays, and I stretch my wings to the embrace the city, with her great black vistas and soaring towers of heat from the gritty concrete below. Dead muscles tense, driving me through the darkness that is my home.

I will never love him for this. Ever.

But one day, I think that I may learn to love myself.

WHO ARE THE ANARCHS?

Vampiric society is stifling in a way that mortals cannot even imagine — the deck is loaded a dozen different ways against change. Increasing age doesn't bring encroaching senility to the Kindred, but increasing power. Barring Amaranth, the average vampire will never surpass her sire, because the Curse of Caine diminishes in potence with every generation. From generations-removed sires come orders to perform tasks the elders cannot be bothered to dirty their hands with. Inevitably, the most arduous and repulsive tasks pass down the generations to the youngest progeny. To many neonates, the gift of immortality seems to be little more than slavery at an eternity of menial labor.

In early nights, rebellious childer generally fled their sires' clutches to some remote location where they immediately set up shop perpetuating the cycle they had so recently escaped. Thus did the Children of Caine come to cover the world to its remotest corners. In modern times, however, every corner of the globe is spoken for. As the world gets smaller, the options for runaway Kindred grow fewer and fewer.

It was after the fall of the Western Roman Empire that Kindred overpopulation first became a serious issue in Europe and Asia Minor. For the first time, vampires who didn't like where they were living were unable to drift away and find a new home (or die trying — usually at the claws of a passing Lupine). Unwilling to eschew the cities, with their easy feeding and diversions from the potentially deadly ennui of centuries, Kindred were forced to form a real society. Inevitably, that society was based on the coercive power of elders over their progeny.

Just as inevitably, this coercion bred resentment, hate and rebellion among the ancillae. After centuries of simmering discontent, the dam broke in what came to be known as the Anarch Revolt. For decades, vampiric society was awash in bloodshed and chaos, as the young set upon the old in search of freedom and potent vitae. For good or for ill, there are few records of the revolt. Most Kindred who survived the era are unwilling to talk about the chaos that culminated in the Inquisition and the formation of the sects; most of those who survived lost friends and paramours.

But those who don't know history are doomed to repeat it, and with few survivors of the Anarch Revolt willing to teach their lessons, an entire generation of Kindred is stalking the nights, ignorant of what has gone before. The anarchs of today are the distant descendants of those long-ago rebels, ignorant of their heritage even as they rush blindly down their forefathers' path.

The Making of an Anarch

While worried elders and uninformed neonates talk about the "the Anarch Movement," anarchs are mostly just anarchic. There are as many different kinds of anarch as there are Kindred sick of being used as pawns, catspaws and menial laborers by their elders. Even so, the modern anarch is a far cry from the revolutionary firebrands who shattered the world of the Kindred during the Revolt. Today, the anarchs are almost an institution in the Camarilla.

While it's hardly a universal occurrence, running away from one's vampire's city of Embrace is a fairly common event in the lives of young Kindred. The flight usually occurs between 10 and 30 years after the Embrace, often after an extended (two- to five-year) depression. This sort of lengthy funk is jokingly referred to as the "Terrible Twenties" by ancillae who have seen it all before, but there's nothing funny about it to a neonate who's just suffered through as many years of servitude as she lived before the Embrace.

Most sires hold a neonate *sub stragulum* for between five and 10 years after the Embrace. When her sire isn't using her as a menial servant or ignoring her, a neonate is taught about life among the Kindred, usually via methods old enough to include 'reciting their lessons'. After a decade or two of this, the one thing that a neonate usually wants is *out*.

The average Kindred who "goes anarch" usually flees Kindred society for the open road, the unspoiled wilderness or some other imagined utopia between six months and two years after presentation. Some sires go to great lengths to prevent their progeny from escaping, but even the most closely supervised progeny can find a chance to escape if he works at it. After presentation, the neonate is considered responsible for his own actions and capable of upholding the Masquerade on his own, so there is no reason for anyone but

a sire and his ghouls to pursue an escapee. Experience has proven that chaining one's progeny up in the basement is generally a counterproductive strategy for dealing with radical impulses. Exposure to fire, mutilation and excruciating torture, while used extensively, have also proven ineffective. All of these methods of coercion result in progeny who are not only unproductive, but who are resentful as well.

Given that the average city's politics are a hothouse of Byzantine intrigue, bloodthirsty and vengeful offspring can be a serious liability. Progeny with unpopular sires may acquire their master's enemies' assistance in escaping. Even blood bound progeny can eventually break free of their regnants. While there are a few reactionaries and control addicts who just don't get the idea, sires who see their progeny slipping away usually just let them go; a childe is not worth suffering the Final Death over, and in the end, most of them come back anyway.

The Anarch Subculture

Who Are They?

Many of the neonates who take to their heels find themselves part of the anarch subculture — a nomadic society of Kindred who range far and wide across the highways and byways of America. The major strongholds of this mobile society run up and down the East and West Coasts, along the Boston-Atlanta and San Diego-Seattle metropolitan axes.

The anarch subculture is composed of vampires who have fled the influence of their sires. These rebels are often called Lost Boys, either in reference to Peter Pan's band of runaways or the movie of the same name. While some flee before their presentation (or are never educated in the ways of the Kindred at all), most anarchs usually run after having been presented to their prince and released by their sires. Those unfamiliar with Kindred society usually don't have enough contact with other Kindred to find the anarchs, however some Caitiff fall into the anarch lifestyle by coincidence, fortuitous or otherwise.

While the stereotypical member of the anarch subculture is a Camarilla Brujah sired after 1900, there is an immense variety of Kindred involved with the anarchs. Ancient vampires in mufti trying to adapt to modern culture rub elbows with young vampires from non-Camarilla bloodlines seeking to escape their own insular little hells. Joining the anarchs is attractive to any vampire seeking to break out of the restrictions of his sect without the shovel parties, fire dancing and pack life implicit to Sabbat membership.

Anarch culture also makes an excellent place for vampires interested in establishing new lives for less legitimate reasons; Inconnu Monitors and Sabbat scouts mingle with Assamite hitmen and renegade Setites on the lam. Using the anarchs as an underground railroad isn't entirely risk-free — many archons also run with the anarchs part-time, looking for just such undesirables. Also, just because the anarchs ride motorcycles and eschew Armani suits doesn't make them stupid. The sort of rough self-policing that occurs among the anarchs is just as effective as the formal sentences of a prince, and (as ways to die go) much less dignified.

How Do They Survive?

...all Agents defect, and all Resisters sell out....
— William S. Burroughs, *Naked Lunch*

The young Kindred of the anarch subculture are like the frontiersmen of old or the bikers of the modern era — ranging far and wide across the land, and occasionally gathering together for celebrations that would be legend if word of them ever reached the mortal world. Anarchs that fall in with these modern nomads usually take up their wandering lifestyle, keeping a few regular havens (usually maintained by ghouls) but otherwise following an irregular "circuit" of territory with no set schedule. The amount of ground that a young anarch pack covers in the modern era can be astonishing.

Anarchs become more territorial as they grow older. The risk-takers die off, and the territorial nature of the Kindred begins to set in by the end of the first century of unlife. Anarch ancillae usually cut back the territory they "claim" to avoid threats too large to deal with and areas difficult to traverse without serious risk. As the size of their territory decreases, the anarchs naturally begin to take its protection more and more seriously, and that means interacting with the neighborhood power structures. Even if the anarchs claim their territory by burning out the havens of the local Sabbat packs, they still need allies against the inevitable retaliation. Eventually, there is a point that the anarchs reach where they

Shovel Parties Waiting To Happen

A shovel party is slang for the Sabbat initiation, where's the initiate is buried and left to dig his way out of the grave. A lot of anarchs, whether they know it or not, are ripe for Sabbat recruiting teams. Many of the anarchs who end up in the Sabbat are actually looking to join, whether they know it or not. Most of these willing victims are on the run from unbearable blood bonds and looking for a way out, and either ignorant of Sabbat initiation rituals or beyond caring. Others are just of the mindset that makes the Sabbat seem attractive. The anarch subculture, by and large, is "responsible," at least by Camarilla standards. Its members seek to enjoy their immortality and their freedom; they reject Kindred society to enjoy their *situation*. A shovel party waiting to happen rejects Kindred society in order to enjoy his *state*. He wants to feed when he wants, use his Disciplines when he pleases, and generally assert his supernatural superiority over the humans he once stood among. If he meets a Sabbat pack that's taking recruits first, he gets to join the Sabbat. If he meets an archon or an angry prince first, he gets to be a dead anarch.

are no longer on the outside of the tent pissing in, but on the inside pissing out. In the end, many even return to the city of their Embrace, where their sires have been patiently awaiting their return; after all, what is a century, really?

Just as not every anarch becomes a motorcycle-riding nomad, not every nomad socializes into Camarilla society — a lot of anarchs just *die*. The "live hard, die young" ethos of the subculture means that by definition a lot of anarchs don't make it out as anything but ash. An anarch who gets a serious rip in her body bag and doesn't realize it in time will be just another burned-out car along the roadside. No amount of attitude can help a neonate who walks into the wrong place at the wrong time and meets a Sabbat pack coming in the opposite direction, or whose encounter with a Lupine gas station attendant results in an oil change straight to oblivion. Other anarchs end up adapting to the traveling life and become as static the Kindred society they oppose — trapped on the cutting edge of night, they ride the highways, too old to rock and roll, and too young to die *forever*. These Flying Dutchmen in black leather and chrome are both the heart of the anarch subculture and the exceptions to its rules. Most wandering anarchs have usually either returned to Kindred society or met the Final Death by the end of their first century of unlife.

Fashion And Manners

The anarchs are generally envisioned as rude, unwashed brutes, roving the countryside on motorcycles and flagrantly disregarding the Masquerade. This is far from the truth. Anarchs are very fashion-conscious. Like any Kindred, your average anarch would like to spend the rest of eternity looking good, if at all possible. Even more than that, the typical anarch owns little more than what she can carry on a bike or in the trunk of a car — her personal possessions are one of the few ways she can demonstrate her individual identity and display status. While the basics of anarch style are often rooted in motorcycle fashion, its expression differs considerably between the coasts. Also, like all nomad cultures, anarchs are very conscious of their manners and behavior. Far from possessing the stratospheric wealth of some Camarilla Kindred, most anarchs are hard-pressed to make ends meet. Often hard up and isolated with no allies other than their fellow rebels, the anarchs are remarkably careful about hospitality.

East Coast Fashion

East Coast anarch styles are very elaborate. The typical Eastern anarch wears jeans, sometimes bloused into combat boots. Shirts are button-down, and while anarchs claim that silk is where it's at, most simply can't afford it. (The material doesn't take the rigors of the road well, either, and so much of "standard anarch fashion" is honored more in the breach than in the observance.) A cowboy hat (usually black) and standard short motorcycle jackets are the rule, with each jacket painstakingly worked into an original pattern of paint and studs. The jacket, boots, blue jeans, and stud-and-paint work is the real core of

Eastern style — most style-conscious anarchs have the three key components custom-made for each individual outfit.

Eastern hair is often worn in elaborate beaded dreadlocks, or else shaved off entirely. In the case of beaded dreadlocks, the thinner the braid the better. If the anarch's head is shaved, it is generally decorated with elaborate patterns drawn in permanent marker (a technique which works much better on vampires than on mortals). Each night, after he wakes up, a bald anarch clips and shaves his head, then has a friend touch up any faded spots in the design. Tattoos applied *post mortem* have a nasty habit of spitting the ink out of the vampire's unliving flesh, but those the Kindred got while alive he's stuck with forever. (And no, laser surgery doesn't work on the unliving — somehow, the design regenerates.)

Piercing is uncommon in the East, and seen as a very "mortal" thing to do. Sunglasses, on those rare occasions when they are worn (usually to hide the effects of one too many frenzies on a Gangrel), are always mirrored.

Pistols are often chrome, at least among very young anarchs, and are usually short-barreled large-caliber revolvers. Cleavers and axes are cool, knives and clubs are not. Most anarchs carry one or more hoglegs (double-barreled sawed-off shotguns with a pistol grip) in addition to their pistols. The "pig knuckles" are intended for dealing with Lupines, and the shells are generally hand-loaded with cut-up bits of silver jewelry.

Traditional American and European bikes are favored over Japanese models — Goldwings, Nortons and Harley-Davidsons (stolen, of course) predominate. Most of the bikes are modified for touring, with outsized fuel tanks, improved suspensions, stowage and more comfortable seats. Cars (particularly sedans) are common, but uncool — they just don't have the carefree mystique of cycles. Well-heeled packs of anarchs often have a number of bikes and an RV (usually driven by a ghoul — the poor bastard driving the RV is in for a great deal of verbal abuse if he's Kindred) for more comfortable sleeping accommodations.

West Coast Fashion

West Coast style is distinctly different than the East Coast. Where East Coast style is elaborate, individualistic and almost elegant, West Coast style is uniform, hard-edged and flamboyant of the wearer's unearthly endurance. West Coast Kindred use the word *ausgezeichnet* (German for "outstanding!" or "great!") to describe someone who is apotheotic of their fashion tastes, and being *ausgezeichnet* is a way of life as much as a way of dress.

A West Coast anarch starts from the ground up, and armored motorcycle boots are a must. The more chrome armor the better, and boots are traditionally decorated with chains, spurs, rowles, tap cleats and whatever else the Kindred can find that's chrome and displays *ausgezeichnet* attitude. Pants are either leather or leather-faced jeans, and a stern black belt and chain wallet are *de rigeur* — even a vampire doesn't want to lose his ready cash or all the skin on his ass if he wipes out at 80 mph. Shirts are usually thick, also for protection in case of crashes. Vests are also common, sometimes with a long-fobbed silver pocketwatch in the watch pocket.

West Coast anarchs who like to advertise their status favor winter-wear leather dusters in all seasons, usually either in brown suede or black leather; more subtle ones tend to shy away from stereotype. Anything above the mid-calf is far too short, and ankle-length is best. Matching piercings with chrome and hematite hardware is a mark of distinction. Hair, however short, is brushed back and sprayed into immobility. Those with long hair generally either let the result fall down their back in waves or else wear a single ponytail. Those with long, kinky hair wear it back in a ponytail of thin, undecorated braids. Hats are *never* worn, nor are motorcycle helmets.

Stylish pistols are either blued or matte finished; automatics predominate, and handguns are carried and used in pairs by those who can afford them. Because of the quality of rigs available, under-the-shoulder carries are the rule. .40 S&W, .45 ACP and .44 magnum are the preferred pistol calibers. Carbines of matching caliber are usually carried in sheaths on the anarch's bike. Blades and chains are cool, imprecise or unwieldy weapons are not — *ausgezeichnet* is fast and fluid, not slow or brutal.

Bikes must be two things — fast and black. Japanese bikes, particularly Kawasaki and Yamaha, are the machines of choice for Western anarchs. Racing bikes don't modify well for touring, and so there are a number of "Lupine Alleys" on the northern end of the San Diego-Seattle metropolitan axis where fuel issues make it easy for werewolves to ambush traveling anarchs. Most anarchs rely on speed, balls and plain old luck to get through these areas safely.

The Anarch Free State

On December 21, 1944, Jeremy MacNeil and his fellow members of the Revolutionary Council began their campaign to overthrow Don Sebastian, the prince of Los Angeles. Their revolution was triggered by a long series of suppressions and attacks against anarchs and other young Kindred, culminating in an episode where MacNeil was seized and beaten by Kindred loyal to the Don in front of a number of other Brujah. By the morning of December 23, the issue had been decided, and the prince and primogen of the city of Los Angeles were no more. A manifesto known as the *Status Perfectus* was issued by the revolutionary council, essentially proclaiming every Kindred's right to freedom and independence, and affirming the Kindred of the newborn anarch free state's devotion to the goals of Kindred liberty. The revolutionary council then disbanded.

The Camarilla braced itself, waiting for the outbreak of a Terror in the fashion of the French Revolution, or another episode of the Anarch Revolt. Anarchs around the world cheered, hoping that at least there would be a land of freedom and equality for them as well. Both groups were disappointed.

Today, Los Angeles is an overpopulated hive of anarch gangs vying for turf. Until recently, the entire city was plagued by the depredations of the late Justicar Petrodon's archons. Even now, the only truly safe area of the town is the so-called Barony of Angels (mortal downtown Los Angeles), which Jeremy MacNeil protects as his own personal demesne. Those unable to survive in the gangland communities congregate in the Barony, where MacNeil allows any Kindred to feed, so long as they keep the Masquerade.

Even these areas are no longer safe. Recently, a number of Cathayans have become active in the city. A group of Chinese *kuei-jin* who call themselves the Flatbush and Stockton Posse have begun to tussle with the Crypt's Sons over the Los Angeles wholesale heroin market. So far, MacNeil has recognized the sovereignty of the Chinese tong, but the peace is fragile. Sooner or later, the location of Chinatown will force MacNeil to take a stand on the warfare between the Posse and the Crypt's Sons. In the meantime, MacNeil has recommended that all Kindred in the Barony of Angels strictly avoid Little Tokyo. It seems, however, as if more Chinese *kuei-jin* and their Triad soldiers arrive each night, and the anarchs of the Free State are beginning to wonder if perhaps these new arrivals are not the outriders of a foreign invasion.

Anarch Manners

While anarch fashion changes from location to location, there is a certain code of behavior an anarch anywhere is expected to follow. Just as every fledgling is taught the Traditions, each anarch is taught the rules of the road. Anarchs are a lot less forgiving about breaches of the rules than princes are — the line between undeath and Final Death is too thin for much in the way of politics when you're living on the open road. The rules of the road carry from place to place, but can be summarized as follows.

• Don't Rub Another Man's Rhubarb

Also called "Don't Shit Where You Eat." What little an anarch has is his, and his fellows should treat it with the respect it deserves. Don't feed around a fellow anarch's crash pads. Be polite to other anarchs' sucks. If you by some chance run into someone's mortal relatives, be cool and act like a gentleman (or lady, as the case may be). Don't be an inconsiderate guest — help out around a crash pad as much as you can, and leave quietly in the night if you think you're being a burden. In general, follow the Golden Rule. City Licks can fuck each other over, but out of the highway, everyone needs to be able to depend on one another.

• We're All In This Together

If you see an anarch in trouble, it's your solemn duty to help him out. Even if it's your worst enemy and you'd like nothing better that to see him fry, kill him *after* you save him from the Sabbat or the scourge. If you can cover up for someone, even if you've never met him, cover up for him. If you have to take the fall for your buddies, do it. Setting the precedent is the best way to ensure that when you're in need, someone's going to be there to catch *you.*

Anarchs are by no means restricted to the North American continent; it's just that the current focus and strength of the quote-unquote movement is there. There are still anarchs who remember the 15th century skulking around Europe — not to mention their more modern spiritual heirs — while in Australia, one can hardly tell the anarchs from the elders without a scorecard. It's just that in North America, as nowhere else on the globe, the anarchs have established a distinct place and identity for themselves. When the Camarilla thinks of anarchs, it thinks first of North America's lost souls.

For more information on what anarchs from around the globe are likely to be like, see **A World of Darkness: Second Edition.**

• Don't Eat Pork

Don't fuck with cops; run away or use Social Disciplines instead. Beat them up if you have no other choice, but don't *ever* kill them. They're all controlled by an elder somewhere, and killing them gets both their fellow cops *and* the elders pulling the strings pissed off.

• Settle Problems Out of Sight

Elders might be assholes, but that doesn't make the Masquerade any less of a good idea. Anarchs are on display 24/7 — if there's ever another Inquisition, you can bet they'll be the first to go up against the wall. Even if you're seriously *ausgezeichnet* on a hot night and wearing enough leather that would drive a mortal to his knees, don't wave it in the face of the Canaille. Mortals dress in eccentric fashions and do odd things in public all the time. Mortals do not publicly display fangs, one-inch claws and superhuman speed. Anarchs shouldn't either.

• No Killing

You'd think it wouldn't need to be stated, but it does. Killing other Kindred breeds blood-feuds, and that's bad enough to head off the need for explanation. Killing mortals feeds the Beast, risks the Masquerade, pisses off elders who have to cover up the murders and is generally impolite. How would you feel if you found someone had killed your mortal friends and relatives? Everyone has to feed, but killing mortals without need is dumb.

Autarkis

The other major group of anarchs are the Autarkis. Somewhere between anarch, Caitiff and Inconnu, Autarks are vampires who become disgusted with the politics of Kindred society and simply drop out.

The world is a big place, and a vampire who conscientiously avoids contact with other Kindred can spend a very long time alone. Precisely when a vampire has become an Autarkis is hard to say — most vampires drop out of society from time to time, either to contemplate their condition in solitude or (as they grow older) to enter torpor and drown their unlife in the dreams of the dead. Sometimes these episodes end in suicide or Wassail, but they are usually just periods of self-exploration. As a result, it's easy for even a relatively young member of the Camarilla to vanish; by the time anyone thinks to look for her, she's long gone.

The motivations behind a vampire dropping out of Camarilla society depend entirely on the vampire in question. Some leave the maddening crowd to seek Golconda. The line between these Autarkis and the Inconnu is a thin one, and many of the Monitors are recruited from Autarkis ranks. Other Kindred simply sicken of the incestuous politics and turn away to seek their own existence free of the Machiavellian *danse macabre* of Kindred society — this motivation is particularly common among the Gangrel.

Some defectors have less admirable reasons for leaving. The Masquerade may seem repressive, but it prevents the sorts of outrages that would without a doubt otherwise occur. For example, many Autarkis slip away from the bright light of social scrutiny to pursue careers as infernalists. Others fall in love with the Beast and flee to the seclusion of the wilderness, where they can give themselves to their inner monsters fully. And then there are those who hie off to play dark prince, embracing whole towns to raise legions of vampiric minions and take over the world. Most of these refugees from vampiric social mores don't last very long, but they're more than enough to keep the both the justicars of the Camarilla and the Sabbat paladins busy.

The existence of the Autarkis has some significant disadvantages over the life of the average anarch. The Auktarks have none of the community that the anarch subculture provides. The only support that an Autarkis can count on are his ghouls and any fellow Kindred who went with into exile with him. Neonate and ancillae Autarkis often have difficulty evading hunters and maintaining the Masquerade on their own.

Even more than from mortal hunters, Autarks are at risk from supernatural foes. Marauding Lupine packs put a lone Autarkis at risk. Even more serious is the threat presented by other members of Caine's brood. Diablerists who find out about an Autarkis are likely to consider him easy pickings, as are Sabbat vampires looking for Kindred to act as scouts in Camarilla cities.

Even the Camarilla is a threat. Undeclared Kindred are fair game for the depredations of the scourge, and declaring oneself before the local prince generally defeats the idea of escaping Kindred society. Even if a lone vampire is declared, justicars and their archons tend to assume that a vampire who has retreated from Camarilla society has something to hide. Given that infernalists, diablerists and newly inducted Sabbat members coming to grips with their path are all solitary creatures, they have good reason for thinking that way. If the justicar or archon in question is liberal, the Autarkis may only be forced to submit to an incredibly intrusive examination of her life. Less generous or less liberally minded enforcers of the social order may just eliminate the Autarkis out of hand and decide which crime she was committing from inspection the effects of the deceased.

WHO MAKES UP
THE ANARCHS?

THE CAMARILLA CLANS

Brujah: The youngest members of this clan debatably form the largest single subgroup of anarchs. The anarch subculture has certainly adopted all the trappings of modern Iconoclast Brujah culture — the motorcycles, the urban warrior ethic and the idealization of a nomadic existence that brings the vampire into contact with the freshest and youngest of both mortal and Kindred society. Even if most of the membership isn't actually descended from the blood of Troile, they act as if they were. Many Iconoclast Brujah Rants are better attended by pretenders to the clan than by actual Brujah — such are the benefits of image. While most anarchs grow out of the Iconoclast mindset as they socialize into Kindred society, the angry youth of the Camarilla are at the command of Brujah's blood, and most princes do not forget it easily.

How many of the anarchs are actually of Brujah's bloodline is open to debate. Some members of the clan claim that they makes up over 75 percent of the full-time anarchs; this is probably a serious exaggeration. Kindred on the run from strictly organized clans tend to claim descent from Brujah's line, rather than their actual clan. Even if directly confronted with evidence of a false progeny, most Brujah either say it is entirely possible they are the sire, or else lie and claim the childe simply to tweak the nose of another clan.

Toreador, Tremere and Ventrue: These three clans are the most conservative and taken together are probably the second-largest single source of anarchs. The pressure to perform, be it in art, magic or finance, gives the neonates of these clans excellent reason to rebel against their situation. Anarchs from these clans tend to fit one of two molds. The first stereotype are the rebels on the run from a brutal, controlling sire and grabbing their new freedom with both hands. They are the anarchs most likely to claim descent from Clan Brujah. They are also the anarchs most likely to have a reason to conceal their identity, be it a murdered sire, a burned-out haven or simply a lot of empty bank accounts.

The other, much more common stereotype is that of the weekend anarch. These are the dabblers who toe the line and work diligently for their clan and sire, and then "rebel" during their holidays, only to return meekly to the winepress when the allotted period of freedom has ended. Some weekend anarchs do it for the sake of rebellion, and some do it in an attempt to manipulate the real anarchs into their political games. How well the posers do depends on how tolerant the real anarchs present are and how good the act is. Skilled and personable weekend anarchs in tolerant company can be accepted as almost (but never quite) equals. Inept ones look like a Slayer fan at a Coolio show, and are treated accordingly. Tying the poser up securely, dropping him headfirst down a manhole, then putting the lid back on is something like the standard punishment for failing to make the grade as a weekend anarch. If the ghoul rats, alligators and sewer critters don't get him, the victim has a fair chance of survival.

Gangrel: A great many Gangrel fall in with the anarchs at some point, and the clan's departure from the Camarilla hasn't changed this situation. Gangrel and the anarchs share a similar existence, and anarch revels and escapades make damn good stories. Some Gangrels even end up as full-time members of the subculture, but most eventually wave their good-byes and depart for their beloved solitude. The Gangrel who do become fully involved in the anarch lifestyle almost inevitably end up there because of a paramour, friendship or some other personal reason, not because of any ideological commitment.

Malkavian: Not every Malkavian adapts to the support network for the insane that is the blood of Malkav. Some never become attuned to the divine madness of the Curse, and end up as people with derangements that don't really belong to them. A lot of these unfortunates end up in the anarch subculture, if they can cope well enough to function at all. Other Malkavians seeking to learn about the anarchs for pranking purposes make the same claims. Both types are prone to disappearance whenever it becomes time for the white-hot worms to eat their brains again, so it's hard to tell which Malkavians are the real rejects and which are just faking. Of course, since they're crazy, sometimes they're both sincere and faking at the same time. Malkavian anarchs are generally treated as whatever they act like, and not trusted with anything that would cause a major pain in the ass if it walked away or got screwed up.

Nosferatu: Like the Gangrel, the Nosferatu have a culture very much separate from "mainstream" Camarilla society. Unlike the Gangrel, the insular, sewer-dwelling families of the Nosferatu have little in common with the anarch lifestyle. Also, the Nosferatu are bottom-of-the-boot ugly, which creates a multitude of problems in the style-heavy anarch subculture. Life on the open highway presents certain problems to a vampire with a head like a rotting rat. Young Licks are often just as disgusted as mortals are by the Sewer Rats, and as a result, Nosferatu make up a very small number of the anarchs, possibly an even smaller percentage than the Malkavians.

Those Nosferatu who do become involved with the anarch subculture have invariably mastered Mask of a Thousand Faces, if only for ease of relations with the rest of the world. As a rule, Nosferatu anarchs have personalities that make them unsuited to life in the sewers. This may mean they're too deranged to fit in even with the Leatherfaces, or that they're Cleopatras who remain outgoing and vivacious despite their changed state. Some make it, and some go back to the sewers head-first.

Those Outside the Camarilla

Sabbat *Antitribu*: The Lasombra and Tzimisce both make only tiny contributions to the anarchs, though there are possibly more of both in the flotsam of the anarchs than in the recognized ranks of the Camarilla. Prejudices within the Camarilla and the Sabbat, the Viniculum and the determination of both the clans and the Black Hand to prevent defection makes *antitribu* even more infrequent than defectors from the Assamites, Setites and Giovanni family.

Miscellaneous Others: The seemingly endless minor clans, bloodlines and other miscellaneous offshoots of the curse of Caine also find homes among the anarchs. Cathayan agents often use the anarchs as an underground railroad, since most anarchs are unlikely to have ever *heard* of them. The children of Baron Samedi likewise find the anarchs willing companions, though the ones with Mask of a Thousand Faces are definitely better off than the less gifted members of their bloodline. The anarchs have for centuries served as the last home for survivors of other bloodlines thought long extinct. Many of the oldest anarchs actually have no ideological connection to the subculture, but instead simply use it as a cover, exchanging blood-feuds and ancient enmities for social prejudice and a traveling life.

As for the non-affiliated clans, they either do not spawn anarchs at all (a Giovanni who went rogue would last a matter of hours after incurring the wrath of his family) or fit in so neatly with the anarch subculture that there's no need for a differentiation.

Anarch Attitudes Toward the Camarilla

Anarchs are best known for their variety, and there are at least as many attitudes toward conventional Camarilla society as there are anarchs. While obviously none of them love the Camarilla and its associated trappings, attitudes range from careful respect to dismissive and hateful. The attitudes below are the opinions of individuals, not as those of anarchs as a whole.

The Clans

You've got to be kidding, right? They're just another way for the elders to puppeteer you. Why am I supposed to feel obligated to my sire? He didn't bring me back from the dead because he loved me, he Embraced me to be his tax accountant. Fuck that — I don't owe him or any of my other "ancestors" a goddamn thing.

— Reese Briggs, Clan Toreador

I owe my sire a great debt. When he Embraced me, I was dying of cancer, and I had never really had the guts to live at all. From him, I learned how to laugh, how to fight, how to dare without fear of failure. I feel the same way about my clan — from sire to sire, the gift of life has been passed down, and I owe each and every step on the ladder between myself and Caine a debt I can never repay. But as much as I love him, and as much as I owe my clan, I have my own existence. I survive for myself now, and I refuse to become a pawn in war over ideas that are long dead and cities that are long dust. If they have to ask me to repay the Embrace with service, then my elders have forgotten the magnitude of the gift they've been given.

— Melissa Benson, Clan Brujah

Princes and Elders

Most princes is jes' chaindogs — dey get der spot by toadyin' up to the primogeniture. Dey really don't got shit to say about how t'ings go on in der domain. Dat makes dem double-bad news for us, 'cause dey take out der frustrations on us with us wit' no politics to get in de way. Jus' like I said — dey's chaindogs. De primogen ain't as bad, dey got what dey want. Dey jus' try to drag ya into deir feudin' at every opportunity. Now if you can keep out from

CAMARILLA ATTITUDES TOWARD ANARCHS

It might seem strange that with all of the other, terrifying threats to its existence, the Camarilla devotes so much time to stamping out the anarchs. The reader must understand that the majority of those adopting a hardline stance in the modern Camarilla remember the terror and chaos of the Anarch Revolt so many centuries ago, and the Inquisition that followed it. Everyone who survived that time knew someone who wasn't so lucky. The conditions that led to the revolt — overpopulation, discontented youth, internecine strife — are being repeated on the modern stage. Many elders see the destruction of the anarchs as a prophylactic measure, like cauterizing an infected wound. Other elders are generally willing to make concessions to those with anti-anarch agendas in exchange for advancing their own plans. After all, it's not as if the destruction of a few neonates on motorcycles is an impediment to *their* plans.

Some elders, however, fear the anarchs for reasons other than anxiety over past experience. Some elders believe that when Gehenna arrives, the risen Antediluvians will move among the anarchs for a time, sating their hunger and marking the locations of their chosen victims. By destroying the anarchs, these elders hope to destroy the sea the Antediluvians will swim in, thus forcing them to reveal their hands when they are still hungry and disoriented from their long sleeps. Many close to the justicars believe that watching for signs of the Antediluvians is a major part of the job of those archons who run with the anarchs, though the archons themselves may not know it.

between dem, and remember to scrap the shit offa yer boots before you walk on der rugs, and otherwise act like you's a civil creature, dey ain't so bad. Just don' ever trust one, or you might as well bend over and grab yer ankles in advance.

— Emil Wenkel, Clan Gangrel

Elders and princes are monsters. For all they talk about civility and culture, you know what they're really doing? They're sitting down in their basements, behind their walls of influence and servants. They grow their portfolios, they go to Elysium every week or month or year, and they nurse their ancient little grudges and wait to see who Wassails and gets put down next. What a way to spend eternity. Not that riding your motorcycle from city to city and partying is much of an improvement, but at least the scenery changes. There has to be more to our unlife than this, or else we really are Damned.

— Ellen Porter, Clan Tremere

I think you can do it without turning into a monster. My friends and I have settled into this choady little suburb-city, outside of Chicago. Laugh all you want — I mean, I never thought I'd want to live in a place with so many damn strip malls. But we run things, keep the place clean. Suburban urbanization might suck to

look at, but it's giving younger Kindred a place to live outside the domains of the old bloods. We've seen how things are for them, and we won't make the same mistakes. Just you watch.

— William Van Meter, Clan Malkavian

JUSTICARS AND ARCHONS

Me and Wacky Jack, we capped one of the motherfuckers up in Seattle a couple months ago. He was one of that Nossie, what's his name — Pterodactyl or whatever — one of his bully-boys. Bloodbanker with a pattern. Crypt's Sons hooked us up with some laudanum, we Dominated the guy on the night shift and tuned the blood up good. Stupid-ass Gangrel didn't even make it through the first pint. Passed out right in his car. A couple gallons of gas and WHOOM! Just like the Fourth of July! One less cop to whack when the time comes.

—Charles "Chuck-E" Baines, Clan Brujah

It depends on the justicar and archon, really. Petrodon was a serious nutjob, and his archons weren't much better. Some of them are pretty decent people, though. Just don't forget they're cops. No matter how well you know one, or think you know one, you can never really trust them; they're cops first, and people second. It's just like that with archons, even the decent ones. The stupid ones, they're a pain in the ass. The smart ones are mainly looking for infernalists, Sabbat scouts, Setites — people you probably wouldn't mind seeing go away yourself. If you don't dick around with them, they'll usually just go play Mountie, get their man, and that's that. Be careful who you boo-yah. Offing the smart ones just makes the stupid ones look good, and killing any of them at all if you don't have to just makes life hard for anarchs everywhere.

— Melissa Benson, Clan Brujah

ATTITUDES TOWARD OTHER GROUPS

By and large, anarchs as a group have the same prejudices toward vampires outside the Camarilla and other Awakened creatures that their sires taught them as childer. Anarchs come into contact with sorcerers, changelings and the Creature from the Black Lagoon about as often as any other Kindred, and so they're no more likely to change their preconceptions that a vampire from any other sect. Certain attitudes *are* common among the anarchs, however, because they interact with the object in question in different way or more frequently than the average member of the Camarilla. If the following list doesn't cover a topic, assume that an anarch is fairly likely to have the same preconceptions as a more conformist member of her clan when it comes to that particular specimen of supernatural fauna.

MORTALS

You just can't party without them. What else need be said?

— Reese Briggs, Clan Toreador

We come into contact with mortals a lot. That makes it doubly important that we maintain the Masquerade — just because we're defying the authority of our sires doesn't mean we're not responsible for our actions. Not only do we have the most influence on the perceptions of the mortals, but we're always on trial. If we can show that we're responsible enough to be an asset to the Camarilla on our own, things will get a lot easier for us.

There's also a moral aspect — we're the people most likely to abuse mortals. We need ghouls to take care of our crash pads and havens. If we want to party, we need ghouls to do that too. It's simple to say to yourself, "Oh, well, I'm not doing anything wrong." But think about how easy it is for a ghoul blood bound to you to decide they want to smoke crystal methamphetamine for you. It's not just a matter of self-interest; they love you with the passion of the blood. Your central nervous system will be fine afterward — you're dead. Your ghoul may not come out so well. Sure, you can turn a couple of ghouls into clapped-out junkies, and the blood will keep them going until they're older than William S. Burroughs. But really, how much different does that make you from your sire, in the end?

— Melissa Benson, Clan Brujah

THE SABBAT

Oh, yeah — dey's crazy. Poison religion, jus' like de snake-handlin' and the speakin' in tongues dat used to go on at de backwoods churches my daddy took me to. Eatin' fire, sharin' blood like dey's heathens, buryin' demselves and livin' in grave-yards. Dey's jus' like backwoods people, 'cept dey's dead and knows it. Give any smart one de frissons. For now, I think I'm doin' jus' fine without 'em, t'ank you.

— Emil Wenkel, Clan Gangrel

The Sabbat are rough customers. They stick together like brothers, and if you kill one, they're worse than cops. They're also usually poor as piss. They hate ghouls with a passion, have no fear of fire and they frenzy constantly. That means you want to make them chase you into ambushes, burn 'em out during the day, and kill them off one at a time like a cat with mice so that the ones left get dumber and dumber as they get hotter and hotter for your ass. Oh, and be ready to run like hell if it all goes wrong, because they are some crazy motherfuckers. If you fuck with them wrong, they will turn around and bite you in the ass so fast you'll be calling for animal control. As if it needed said, don't ever take anything from one, don't ever believe anything one says, don't ever tell one your name or any information about you — even if you don't think they could possibly use it against you. Trust me, they will find a way. Whatever you do, don't ever go anywhere with one, no matter what.

—William Van Meter, Clan Malkavian

THE INCONNU

I think they're just the same as the elders of the Camarilla and the Sabbat. Another sect with their own agendas and their own axes to grind and their own internal politics that make a mess of everything. I mean, it's great that they're all into Golconda and everything. Of course, the Camarilla's into peaceful coexistence between Kindred and mortals, and staying away from getting too involved with the mortal world. I'm sure the Inconnu enjoy just the same astonishing success as the Camarilla in their relentless pursuit of their goals.

— Ellen Porter, Clan Tremere

Where I come from, a man who takes hisself out into de backwoods and lives all alone in a little cabin is eatin' hikers, doin' somethin' bad t' little boys or thinkin' Jesus is his new bes' friend.

I don't see no reason why bein' dead changes t'ings. You trust one of de Inconnu, he probl'y gonna fuck you, eat you or tell how God loves you so much he's jus' gotta fuck you and eat you.

— Emil Wenkel, Clan Gangrel

LUPINES

I hear they have a sophisticated culture and a religion that has stayed true to its animistic and totemic roots since prehistoric times. I heard their whole culture is a devoted to the defense of Earth from evil spirits. They probably also help little old ladies across the street. I'd appreciate their nature-loving culture of peace a little more if the furry little fuckers didn't get a big kick out of the ritual murder and dismemberment of people like me.

— William Van Meter, Clan Malkavian

Hoo boy, I see'd a loup-garou go through a bunch of hunters out for coon like it was a fox and they was enjoyin' dat henhouse livin'. I kilt two in my time, and one of de bastards bit my arm clean off. It took damn near took a month to grow back. I say we nuke 'em till dey glow, den shoot the hairy bastards in de dark.

— Emil Wenkel, Clan Gangrel

It's really hard to maintain an objective view of a people whose whole purpose in life focuses on terminating your existence. I understand that some sects of the Lupines are genuinely likable people. Unfortunately, most of them are walking Cuisinarts, and you're the salad-to-be. Waste them first, wonder if they remind you of a childhood pet later.

— Melissa Benson, Clan Brujah

PLAYING AN ANARCH GAME

Anarch games have an immense potential, but they are also some of the most neglected. Often ignored as being too simplistic or uninteresting, anarchs contain some of **Vampire: the Masquerade**'s most potent symbology. They are rebellious youth personified, neglected talent and determination boiling up from the streets to challenge established power structures. The Anarch Movement is not be as direct in its appeal as the struggle between the Kindred and the Lupines or the Camarilla and the Sabbat, but it offers a degree of emotional tension between the protagonists and antagonists that can easily vanish from a game built around a simple "us versus them" conflict. Below are some ideas to help a novice player or Storyteller "get their head around" an anarch character for a campaign. These suggestions are by no means the entire range of possibilities for an anarch game, but an assortment of possibilities. Storytellers should embroider upon them or add their own material, as they see fit. It is *your* game, after all.

PLAYING AN ANARCH

On the surface, anarchs are the angry youth of Kindred society. They are like mortal youths, but more so. From their point of view, their ideas and opinions are ignored by their elders, they're expected to do menial tasks below their dignity, and they're treated like the children they most certainly are not. Given that most Kindred are Embraced because of their expertise and life experiences, the fact that anyone *fails* to rebel is a tribute to the human propensities for honoring hierarchical systems and social controls.

Most anarchs fall into one of two categories. The first are those who have had all they're willing to take, ever, from their sires and other elders, and who are not going back under any circumstances. All have been psychologically abused and manipulated, and most have also been physically abused. Many have been treated badly enough for blood bonds to weaken or even break entirely. Whether they live as virtual hermits or take part in the nomadic lifestyles of the anarch subculture, these angry young Kindred make up the die-hard core of the anarchs. Though they range in age from a few years to a few centuries under the Embrace, most of these anarchs choose to die on their feet rather than live on their knees again. They give the subculture its reputation, its sense of tradition and its legends, living and otherwise.

To be honest, these ageless rebels are the exceptions.

The vast majority of anarchs are temporary exiles from the Camarilla, as noted above. Such Kindred are essentially blowing off steam and frustration with the norms of vampiric society, though from a mortal perspective, the period of rebellion can last lifetimes. Whether these vampires are anarchs on weekends only or spend a few decades learning to appreciate existence, they are still different than the die-hard ideologues. Hatred of the elders' authority hasn't ossified them and become the defining characteristic of their sense of identity. Most anarch characters are probably this latter sort of vampire — hardened firebrands are as one-sided and difficult to play as low-Humanity elders.

Below are a number of questions that a player creating an anarch should answer during the process of character creation. Answering these helps to flesh out and define the character in her role as an anarch. Obviously, the regular questions of the Concept stage of character creation still apply — these questions are to help define the character as an anarch, not as a vampire or a person.

• Why is the character with the coterie?

This is an extremely important question. In many games of **Vampire: the Masquerade**, the "coterie" is likely to have internal stresses, but stay together because of the limited geographic scope of their unlives and the social pressures on them either to cooperate or at least to form an alliance against manipulative elders. In an anarch game, this isn't the case. Anarchs are highly mobile individuals, and they exist outside the law. A lack of common interests leaves the group no reason to stay together, and serious internal tensions in the group usually mean that someone's going to meet the Final Death.

The Storyteller and the group as a whole should probably decide on the common interest(s) of the group *before* character generation, though this is not a mandate to make stereotypical characters for the sake of party unity. Common interests can bring all sorts of disparate people together. Also, be creative. Anyone can think of a rock band or motorcycle gang membership as common ground for characters. But what about an anarch pack composed of serious golfers, a jazz quartet or (for the particularly daring) a gaming group?

Compatible personalities are also a plus. While the characters don't have to get along like bestest buddies, there shouldn't be any really violently dissimilar personalities. It's the responsibility of the players to get together and compromise on issues of conflict that threaten the chronicle, though the Storyteller should probably be prepared to step in and mediate if a consensus doesn't develop easily.

• Why is the character rebelling?

The situation of the character prior to his "going anarch" deserves some thought. People who spend a lot of time being pushed around, mistreated and otherwise abused, especially by people they love, develop a lot of quirks relating to their situations. While the responses are different from person to person, they are usually closely related to the situation that caused them to develop. It's worth thinking about what it is that made the character into the person he is.

Try to keep in mind that sexual abuse is far too serious a topic to be used flippantly as a source of characterization, though the twisting of vampiric sexuality is still relatively unexplored terrain. Characterization is most likely to be affected by the psychological nature of the relationship between the character and his sire. The sire's personal habits, favorite method and environment for abuse, the anarch's regular tasks, the character of the abuse and the triggers that set off abusive episodes are the ones most likely to make an impression on the young vampire, as well as the ones which will help best define the sire from the character's point of view.

• How devoted is the character to his ideals? Is he a wanted criminal?

This is another important point. Some characters are just on the run from their own personal demons, while others have a commitment to changing things on a scale larger than their own personal concerns. Making a decision about the depth of the character's feelings is an important step in character creation, as is making sure that all the characters share generally the same feelings to generally the same degrees. The bomb-chucking revolutionary is going to be out of place in a band of Kindred who just want to forget about their collective past and make a new life. Likewise, an anarch is going to be a fifth wheel in a group that feels vampires need more and not less social control. Making sure this sort of consensus comes about during character generation is a matter for the group as a whole to decide on, with moderation and suggestions from the Storyteller.

THE ELDERS OF THE CAMARILLA

I sit in an empty chamber, surrounded by the treasures of centuries. Vases crafted in the day of the Peloponnesian league adorn my shelves; unknown sketches by Da Vinci are framed (poorly, I think) on the wall. The floor is of the whitest marble, the walls of smooth and luminous mahogany. From the ceiling comes the soft hum of the circulating air, its temperature and humidity calculated precisely to preserve the relics within.

I sit in the middle of all of this splendor and am bored out of my mind. I have been sitting in this room, night after night, for the past seven years. Before that, I sat in a different, but similar room in another city two thousand miles distant. And centuries before that, I sat in another chamber much like this one as the mobs raced through the streets of Paris overhead.

I am bored, burdened with an ennui so crushing that its weight would drive a lesser man mad. Every night my mind reaches out and caresses the wills of my servants, here and in a dozen nations, and gives them their instructions. One is to pull all of my assets out of a particular bank, precipitating that institution's collapse and damaging the retinue of a rival whose ghouls control that august savings and loan. Another hunts a renegade great-grandchilde of mine through the streets of Macao, my displeasure made manifest yet all unknowing.

I sit here, and watch my plans unfold. I sit here and watch my rivals do the same. Ghouls and childer come to me, bearing messages and tidbits of information. Sometimes they bring me food, humans or neonates no one will miss. One childe in particular has gotten clever, Embracing derelicts, cleaning them up, and bringing them to me to devour.

He's a trifle too clever, I think. How long before he gets the idea of lacing those meals with some modern chemical or other to disorient me, so he can dine on something rarefied himself? Not long, I think — he's ambitious. It's time for him to take an extended vacation, I think, or perhaps I'll simply grant him the fate he reserved for me. Soon, I think — I recognize that hungry gleam in his eye.

There's a rapping at the door. I call my assent to entry, and watch one of my favorite ghouls — what is the woman's name? I find myself forgetting — dragging a groggy neonate of some flavor or other. She explains that her baggage was apparently part of an assassination attempt, and had actually breached my haven.

I rise, and give orders for everything to be packed up and moved immediately. If this one piece of riffraff (whose unlife I take a second to end) can find his way in here, a dozen of his friends know about it. This place is no longer safe.

I am bored of existence, yes. Bored of endless nights retracing the same dance steps. Bored of the same challenges and lies. But I am not so bored as to abandon even so arid an existence as this. Life is still sweet, even to the unliving. And even as my ghouls and childer bustle around me, preparing for my departure from my home of seven years, I feel once again the familiar thrill of fear. Just a tiny taste of it, really — this neonate and a hundred of his allies could not harm me. But they might try, and they might have allies or powerful patrons, and thus the spider is coaxed from his lair.

Pity those who have been waiting for me to do so.

BEING AN ELDER

A vampire, unlike a fine wine or an exquisite cheese, does not become better with age. More cunning, certainly. More influential, more deadly, more feared and hated and resented, and more and more powerful — all of these things. But never better. Even in his own labyrinthine thoughts, the elder realizes this. He realizes that as his blood congeals and his skin slowly turns to parchment, what began as a fate worse than death becomes only more appalling with time. This knowledge, of the bitter rot at the heart of his own identity, drives the elder to further luxurious escapes of cruelty and deception. If he must live for millennia with his own excesses, so must everyone else.

Commonalities of the Elders

As wind and water erode once-distinct boulders down to a common smoothness, time and trial reduce the elder vampires to similarity. Although they are by no means identical, the elders increasingly have more in common with each other than they do with their childer. Together they shrink from a hateful age of machines and equality, together they scrabble to buttress the crumbling Camarilla and keep the fraying veil of the Masquerade intact. Elders remember the bonfires of the Inquisition and see the flames of the Sabbat in the distance, and grow cold together. Their ways become familiar to each other, and though familiarity breeds contempt, it remains a thing to be prized as change howls through the world of the Kindred.

Fear

The elders are fear incarnate. No lesser Kindred can contemplate the elders' vile machinations, casual brutalities and wealth of hidden powers without feeling an icy chill as thin, young vitae turns to water. But just as the elders' psychic corruption taints their physical actions, so too does the fear they create in others reflect the fear that grips them all. One might imagine that lordly immortal monsters, possessed of unbelievable abilities and commanding Disciplines of awesome might, would fear nothing. Unfortunately, the long unlives of the elders have taught them well that the World of Darkness contains fears that defy imagination. Rather than facing challenges and risking the loss of everything, those who survive for centuries in the upper ranks of the Camarilla have learned to make discretion indeed the soul of wisdom. Unchecked, conservatism breeds cowardice; immortality breeds enemies; betrayal breeds paranoia. This trap can be only too seductive for an elder with the all-too real enemies of Inquisition and Sabbat howling at her haven door. The deadly logic of the elders' unlives demonstrates time and again that only the fearful survive. Vampire elders have sacrificed much for immortality; the sacrifice of courage is trivial by comparison.

Fear of the Modern

Already inclined by their role and by their very natures to a conservative distrust of the new, elders seem insensate with fury at the speed with which the modern world destroys and casts aside the treasured ways of the past. Virtually all of the elders came of age in a world that changed only minutely; a new rigging for a sailing ship or a new sword design might come once in a century. The logic of tradition kept humanity close to the soil; when the old ways were forgotten, starvation was the inevitable result. The oldest elders remember the glories of Rome, Carthage and even Ur, and for millennia they rested secure in the knowledge that humanity could only rise so far before destroying itself in a wave of barbarism. The elders held the whip hand; loosely or tightly as suited their whim, but held it they did.

This smug certainty shivered with the end of the Dark Ages and shattered with the coming of the Machine Age. Suddenly the kine had the powers of speed, steel and wealth that the vampiric nobility had so jealously guarded. Worse than that, these new things freed the mortals from the soil; the old cycles were broken as humanity flowed into the greedy cities and left the Lupines in command of the desolate countryside. Kings lost their heads, humanity lost its respect for tradition, and the elders lost their last tenuous connection to the human world.

The Computer Age now grinds the fragments of the elders' world to powder before their horrified eyes. Every new decade seems to pile enormity and obscenity onto the ones before. The kine slaughter each other endlessly, constructing weapons that could scour the Earth clean of life — and of unlife. Information, once jealously guarded by secretive clerks, is flung about the globe faster than the speed of thought, leaving the sluggish elders gaping at its passage. Telegraph, telephone, television, satellites, Internet connections — somehow these empty shibboleths have become words of power that the elders find it difficult to even speak.

Fear of the Younger

The elders might think the whirlwind of changes survivable, or even desirable, if it caused the other Kindred to look to the Camarilla for guidance. Unfortunately for the elders, this madhouse is the world where the odious ancillae (and mayfly neonates) grew up. Somehow these impudent whelps have convinced themselves that they have mastered the unmasterable; they share the human delusion that technology and change make useful servants rather than dangerous enemies.

This weakness of mind and character shows in the increasing tendency of the younger Kindred to adopt anarch ways even when giving surface homage to their betters. The rot that has destroyed human churches and kingdoms now infests the Camarilla. The worms of equality, liberty and fraternity gnaw at vampiric society, although the elders respond with force undreamed of by mortal monarchs. The younger vampires gleefully accept this human prattle into their veins along with the contemptible narcotics, discordant music and proletarian fashions of the Canaille from whence they spring and upon whom they feed.

Seldom better than the rabble of humanity, the younger vampires resent the just and time-tested guidance of their elders. The elders compound this situation, of course, by setting childer against childer in endless games of manipulation, deception and intrigue. To the elders, this only amounts to sensible self-defense. After all, the only sure route to power for an ambitious childe lies over the diablerized husk of an elder. Normally, the young and thin of blood would be no danger — but the world changes too fast these days. The kine have trampled upon the virgin moon and discovered the seeds of human conception; it is hardly impossible that they may stumble upon some grave threat to the Kindred with their computers, DNA scanners and atomic metallurgies. If such a thing occurs, it is the elders' nightmare that only the weak and contemptible neonates will understand its potential — and that their ludicrous demands for independence and equality will tempt them to use it.

FEAR OF THE OLDER

As opposed to the half-formed nightmare of a changing world and rebellious youth, the elders' fear of the Methuselahs (and those who came before them) is real and rational. The Methuselahs certainly exist, and they purposefully hide themselves from the elders' best attempts at scrutiny. From these indubitable premises comes one conclusion only: The Methuselahs play deep games indeed, using the elders as their pawns in some covert struggle.

Elder vampires know that were they in the Methuselahs' position, they would show no mercy and give no hint to their unfortunate minions. The elders' fear of the Methuselahs is a fear of their own reflection. Whispers that the Methuselahs have increasingly gone Inconnu or even achieved Golconda give scant comfort. Both these fates are unknown, and the unknown is an undiscovered country to be walled out. The Inconnu, especially, unnerve the elders. Simultaneously a rebuke for elder cowardice and avarice and a threat to elder power, they can only be placated — or avoided.

Even more hateful to the elders' precarious sense of self is the memory of the Antediluvians, the powerful fathers of each clan who can unmake nations and roil the surface of the world even from deep in concealed torpor. With prophecy after prophecy from the *Book of Nod* manifesting in these end times, the elders see the Antediluvians slowly rising to the surface of Kindred affairs like great and aged sharks drawn to the blood spilled on the face of the deep. When the last red night falls, the elders fear they will fall too, indistinguishable from the most contemptible neonates in their sires' final blood frenzy.

The elders find themselves trapped in a cleft stick, desperately wishing that the rumors of the Antediluvians' demise (or ascension to Golconda) were true, while unable to give such rumors open support for fear of undermining the traditions of lineage and clan that hold the Camarilla together under the elders' tutelage. The attempt to square the circle of their forbidden wishes and the foundation of their power leaves the elders ever more dissociated from truth, and from the clarity of decision that truth brings.

FEAR OF EACH OTHER

Even greater than the potential threat of the young and the shadowy threat of the old is the actual and ongoing threat of an elder's fellows. Other elders jockey for power within cities and Camarilla; a cutting remark before the Inner Council, a brood of ghouls, or a trivial cash payment to a human arsonist can serve as daggers held by allies and enemies alike.

Every elder who falters inspires the others to new bouts of greed and envy, scrambling for the spoils. These struggles create new rivalries and inflame old ones. No allegiance is as permanent as any division seems to be. Each elder understands in the core of her polluted being that she must triumph or die under the talons of her fellows. That triumph may come

millennia from now or tomorrow night, but come it must or unlife has no meaning and the blasphemies committed to stave off Final Death will prove empty ones. Every elder plots against every other and justifiably fears the others' plots against him. The 500 years of the Camarilla are an eyeblink in the elders' potential lifespans; the oldest of them remember a time when the Lextalionis was the law of all against all. Cooperation comes hard, and always with caveats and fine print.

FEAR OF THE SABBAT

The elders' individual unease with each others' machinations still remains secondary to their terror of the Black Hand and the vile heresy that is the Sabbat. And for good reason; the plots and intrigues of their colleagues spring from roots all members of the Camarilla share, but the Sabbat blossoms in different soil. It cries openly for the destruction of the elders of the Camarilla, the drowning of Kindred society in a tide of fire and blood and an end to tradition and respect. The Sabbat blasphemes against the laws of the Camarilla, and tools and strategies honed in weary years of struggle within those laws seem blunt and worthless in the firelight of the new anarchy. Even and especially for the elder vampires, fear of the unknown other transcends hatred and fear of self.

Of course, the fear of the Sabbat is also a fear of the Beast within the elder vampire herself. Every secret whim repressed as too risky, every forbidden fantasy rejected as unsafe, every remembered privilege of malign power from the Dark Ages returns in the night on the whispers of the Sabbat's seductive call: Reject the Masquerade and hunt freely. Reject the Traditions and flood the globe with Kindred. Turn your back on the strictures of clan and edicts of justicars. These are the siren songs the Sabbat uses to destroy the will and sap the resolve of the Camarilla. If even the elders know doubt and feel temptation deep within their leathery hearts, the lure of the Sabbat must call even more seductively to the feckless ancillae and empty-headed neonates.

The Sabbat knows this, and dares to urge the childer on to blasphemous diablerie. Exposure to the contagion runs the risk of epidemic, but quarantine fails with every night that falls. Hordes of neonates shrieking for a taste of vintage vitae, overwhelming the elders' havens in the embodiment of the mob — this would be the price of failure.

FEAR OF HUNTERS

Even if the Sabbat is somehow parried, should the Camarilla riposte break through the fading scrim of the Masquerade, the elders risk destruction. Five centuries ago, human fears leagued with human knowledge carved a cauterizing path through the ranks of the Kindred. Only desperation and the luck of Caine saved the unliving race then. Should the cry of Inquisition be raised again in this hateful modern age, when the kine have bred their numbers into the billions and increased their infernally clear-eyed science and horrific technology even more so, even the Antediluvians might fall.

To be forced to hide from cattle is shameful, but medieval pride has proven suicidal. Those who once were and by rights still should be lords of the world must skulk in the shadows, pulling the strings of ignorant humanity like a Venetian puppetmaster rather than ruling with naked fang and mailed fist. More galling still, it is the elders' hateful lot to preserve the plodding kine from vampiric rapacity, knowing that only by keeping the sword at their throat intact can they keep it from plunging home.

This fear, like the other fears of the elders, is born of contradiction and the nature of modern unlife. The path of circumspection, of hidden power and conspiracy, is the only path open to the Kindred. Their corrupt bargain forces them to accept it, to impose it upon their ungrateful progeny, to defend it against insanity and suicidal rage and to transform it into a virtue of necessity.

FRUITS OF THE CAMARILLA

Twisted as they are by these rational fears, the elders of the Camarilla are incapable of treating their peers with the respect that each feels is his rightful due. To show consideration, to repay trust with trust, to act in honest concert or from genuine feeling is to show weakness and to bare one's throat for the fang of a rival. Rather than a band of brothers, then, the society of the Camarilla is a den of vipers. It is a poisoned garden bearing corrupt fruit.

HATRED

Elders hate everything that they fear. Fear exposes raw and dripping wounds in the elders' psyches. Short of the possibly mythical Golconda, elders cannot heal these wounds or reconcile the conflicting pressures that force them open. The only recourse left is to submerge their pain in the blinding heat of hatred.

Millennia of practice have made the elders very good indeed at hatred. Elders know just how to keep grudges boiling, how to recall slights and how to show a bold front or a respectful countenance to enemies while cringing and raging within. Newcomers observing Elysium see only the gilt and glory and the calm exercise of power and control, but the fires of hatred create the lambent glow of vampiric civilization. Hatred serves as a balm for the injuries of fellows or of fears, and as an excuse for anything gone wrong or left undone. A new hate becomes something to savor, to encourage, to nurture and develop. Hate gives an elder something precious — something to give unlife meaning. After all, to creatures who saw full moons rise over Justinian's Constantinople, governing Cleveland presents little challenge. Carrying on a successful rivalry with a predator as canny and cunning as themselves — this is the ultimate challenge. Hate, ironically, strengthens the Camarilla. Competition weeds out the weak, and hate fires the competition. Friendship and loyalty, on the other hand, become liabilities, weak points for the assaults of rivals. Thus, even natural allies keep some distance behind a hedge of curt formalities or flowery insults.

Among the curses of the elders, their long memories rank among the worst. Not only are they unable to forget a slight, they know that no other elder will forget one either. Thus saving face becomes nearly impossible — even the tiniest loss of position is remembered for all time, marking the loser as a weakling to be further preyed upon. Elders never forget, and they never forgive. To forget is to surrender both surcease and leverage, while to forgive is simply to surrender.

JEALOUSY AND LIES

Vampiric society functions as a classic zero-sum game: For every winner, there is at least one loser. The only way for elders to advance in the ranks of the Camarilla is by removing rivals — politically if possible, physically if necessary. With new Kindred engendered all the time and ambitious ancillae shoving from beneath in a desperate Darwinian *guerre à mort*, elders cannot even stand still without making enemies.

This makes elders preternaturally aware of the status of every other elder, eternally jealous for every erg of leverage or ounce of influence shown by another. If an elder rises, it is over the backs of his fellows. Even elders safe on the sidelines may resent his success as a prize rightfully theirs. Few parties, factions or sects can long hold under the corrosive force of elder jealousy. Only the tightly knit Tremere function as a true party, and the other clans' fear and resentment of their *arriviste* success conspire to keep the balance. Clan jealousy, therefore, is virtually the only higher loyalty that any vampire feels. Some elders find the presence of like-minded blood kin their only respite from the ordeal of Camarilla intrigue, but others resent even their clanmates for hogging the few rewards or horning in on delicate intrigues.

The constant demand for information on other elders' status within the Camarilla leads to gossip and innuendo, spread by enemies, allies of convenience or any other elder who finds a willing ear and an offer of a juicy tidbit in return. With the supply of real insider information at a premium, counterfeits — artfully constructed lies, spur-of-the-moment guesses, desperate hoaxes — spread through elder society. Those Kindred without true knowledge offer up false coin in desperate hope of bringing in a pennyworth of fact or reliable interpretation.

The channels of gossip run in at least two directions. Falsehoods inevitably find their way back to the target and spawn yet more jealous lies. True knowledge, like honest self-knowledge, is yet another pleasure forbidden to the elders by the walls of thorns they have built around themselves. Thus any news or action is immediately interpreted in the worst possible light; no news is good news, but there is always news. The cycle of jealousy spins ever forward, then, as elders passed over attempt to undermine their fellows with scurrilous rumor and intrigues. Meanwhile, the elders on top resort to blackening the image and poisoning the reputation of any below them, hoping that their real enormities can remain undiscovered in the cloud of falsehood.

SPITE AND INTRIGUE

With the coin of information unalterably debased, the elders must turn to other methods to keep score. With no reliable reason to injure another, pretexts must be created. With personal survival at stake, but without the courage or capacity to

strike openly, elders allow subterfuge and slight to take the place of combat and exile. The atmosphere of the Camarilla becomes a hothouse of tiny offenses and subtle undercuttings.

As if immortality did not possess enough dangers, it also brings with it a debilitating ennui. The sameness of the old fears and the old hatreds, the banality of the forcible gentility of Elysium, and the steep price of decisive action against any actual threat blend in a deadly cocktail. The resulting heady decoction leads to elders feuding for the sake of feuding itself. Stirring up yet another tempest in the Camarilla's stuffy chambers may be dangerous, but it is nearly the only true danger that elders engage in. Elysium's code keeps the stakes small, so spiteful revenges and petty one-upmanship broil for decades without any result save momentary diversion from important (but terrifying) problems.

Power

If the elders are frozen in terror, stiff with hatred, isolated by jealousy and distracted by intrigue, how is it that they maintain their grip on the reins? First, of course, a weak elder rapidly falls to his fellows — ambitious ancillae and grasping contemporaries remove any elder from the equation who proves unable to keep an eye on his own interests. Only the strong survive, and survival increases their might as the spoils of the fallen are shared.

Second, immortal beings fearful for their lives work continuously to increase their personal power. True, paranoia and conservative age hold many elders back from sudden, risky moves and large windfall profits. But a hundred slow accretions build immense resources over enough time — and time is one thing that every elder has in abundance. Never forget that elders have had many, many mortal lives to learn the lessons of power and to harvest fortunes and favors many times over.

Wealth

One innovation of the modern era has met with the elders' unqualified approval — the interest-bearing account. Even the most conservative Tremere, the most secretive Nosferatu and the most claustrophobic Gangrel find security in the knowledge that wizened, gray humans in offices from the Cayman Islands to Zurich to Hong Kong are adding coin after coin to many lifetimes' hoards. The smooth Ventrue know this best. They move easily among the boardrooms of Wall Street, the front offices of Panama City and the ancestral hoards of European nobility. With wealth comes anything the mortal world can offer: security, political power, luxury, position, life or death. If coin has replaced church and crown in modern hearts, with its power comes a crucial weakness. Everything — relics, souls, nations — can now be bought with enough money, and elders always have enough money.

Money has its downsides, of course, and modern money even more so. Today, computer-assisted arbitrageurs commit legal frauds and thefts on one continent, invest the proceeds on another, and withdraw the profits on a third — all in the time it takes a Ventrue elder to select a banker. Computers, globalization, capital flight and derivatives create increasing problems for elders barely used to letters of credit and still reeling from the introduction of fiat currency. Clever human assistants take up the slack for now, but eventually even the dimmest kine realizes his opportunity. Some clans' neonates, used to ATMs and the NASDAQ, are trusted to watch the humans, while other elders trust to the age-old powers of the blood bond. Swiss accountant ghouls make even better financial assistants than they do status symbols in some circles.

STATUS

Unlike money, status only counts within the Kindred community. Status is the marker that the endless intrigues of the Camarilla must be paid in; all transactions are denominated in the perception of power and the favorable nod of the harpies. Using any other measure of power within the confines of Elysium is forbidden by the Traditions, so those who have status have the ultimate medium of exchange. With status among the invisible lords of the world comes access to the prince, and to more concrete forms of power. Great fortunes and the fates of armies in the mortal word can hang on the reception of a chance remark or a flattering couplet within the rarefied heights of a prince's court.

Unlike hoards of treasure secure in Cayman Island vaults, status rises and falls for every elder whether he spends it or not. By failing to side with a rising star, an elder risks a loss as serious as actively backing a loser. Chains of association, of favor and intrigue, bind every elder in the Camarilla together. But status can be a mirage; success can grant status or status can grant success. If an elder's initiative deals a well-aimed blow to the local Sabbat, he might lose status in many eyes despite his victory. He has shown up the prince, after all, a dreadful act of *lese majesty*. Conversely, an elder enjoying high status in the city might find that her blows against that same enemy land harder as the other Kindred hasten to assist and bask in her reflected glory. A suitably dramatic triumph (even a brilliantly staged party) may radically change the rankings, but the winners and losers are not always the obvious ones.

Bred to judge the intangibles of art and to value image over everything, the Toreador elders discern and award status most keenly of all the clans. Unfortunately, as generation after generation demands its share of status while adding layer upon layer of falsehood and venom to the memories of every elder, every elder's status decays. Thus, the Toreador find that they must expend ever-greater amounts of political capital to retain their status as fear and jealousy erode the gentilities upon which their power rests.

DISCIPLINES

As status is exclusive to Elysium, the secrets of Disciplines are exclusive to the Kindred. Hence, their use becomes the commodity of final resort; when all other contests are ruled out, the powers of Caine underpin showdowns political and physical. With the elder reverence for the power of blood, great gifts with the Disciplines mark their possessor as a superior being indeed. Younger vampires often feel that their Disciplines make them demigods: How much more godlike do the elders,

who can crush any upstart ancillae with barely a thought, feel? Some Disciplines explicitly render power relationships clear, Presence and Dominate in particular.

The latest masters of the Disciplines, Clan Tremere, may well feel that they are masters of the Camarilla. By way of confirmation, their unique facility with Thaumaturgy allows them to counter many other clans' strengths. The Tremere build discipline within their clan's rigid hierarchy, and argue that disciplined power breeds powerful Disciplines. Elders of other clans smile politely at the presumption of this new-fledged line. Centuries of practice spent honing the arts of murder and darkness makes any Discipline a weapon to fear in the hands of an elder. Even passive Fortitude becomes deadly if its user selects the ground of a contest well and wisely: a greenhouse on a summer's morning, for example.

INFLUENCE

The Camarilla exists to keep human society at a talon's length from the unlives of the Kindred. It stands to reason, therefore, that its elders spare little effort to bend human society to their corrupt will. Of course, with every elder's claw raised against the gathering strength of every other, such influence is hard to gather unnoticed and even more difficult to maintain. Proxy conflicts within human communities make excellent release valves for vampiric rivalries denied a proper outlet by the strictures of Masquerade and Elysium. Thus, indirect attacks on rivals are best mounted through human intermediaries, often manipulated through shells and false flags that keep the elder unsullied by the grime of streetfighting or low politics.

By a twisted but somehow comprehensible logic, such indirection has become the province of the Malkavian elders above all else. The thousand tiny interactions not even a vampire can watch somehow seem to turn out in the Malkavians' favor. Is it simply Obfuscate and Demenation working below the radar of the more exalted clans, as the Tremere and Ventrue claim? Is it the power of lunacy itself made manifest in the Malkavian Madness Network, as some Toreador claim to perceive and the few lucid Malkavians seem to hint at? Or is it simply that discerning the Malkavians' true motives is always an exercise in indirection, and so any action they take must necessarily travel a twisted path through the human world? This does not mean that the other clans lie helpless. The Brujah call jackbooted thugs or firebombers into the streets, the Ventrue freeze cargoes and bank accounts in place, the Tremere work indirectly from the fringes of humanity. True, influence does not necessarily replace the force of a sudden killing blow. However, elder influence can expertly orchestrate such attacks from any convenient warehouse or passing crowd, an invisible hand wielding a visible blade.

CONTACTS

The true currency underlying status, influence and even wealth is information. Knowledge is power, and knowing who knows what is the first step in a successful campaign against any enemy. Every elder tries to maintain a network of childer, retainers and even common mortals to gather, correlate, and pass on vital information for her. This network, of course, becomes a target of subversion or disruption by her rivals. Worse yet, she must either devote vast amounts of her time to sorting through this information and finding the wheat amongst the chaff. Delegating this task leaves juniors with access to information — access, therefore, to power. Worse yet, it means trusting subordinates with her own secrets. To know what facts seem important to an elder is to know what that elder wants, wishes for and fears. This information is powerful leverage, which few elders willingly give up.

Nosferatu elders certainly do not, but they have the advantage of time. While other elders dance in attendance above ground in courts and elaborate charades, the Nosferatu scour the sewers and the subterranean channels for information. While other elders can never trust their subordinates, the subordinates of the Nosferatu can never trust each other — the Nosferatu's favorite Discipline of Obfuscate allows elders to hear anything as anyone. Thus, the Nosferatu can afford to keep their information pristine. Not for them is the ruck of rumor and lies that the Toreador and other court popinjays must parrot to remain *au courant*. The Nosferatu can sift streams of sewage for treasures of fact and sell them to the highest bidder. Of course, those streams have gotten thicker, and fouler, as the Camarilla subliminates into pettiness and paranoia. The Nosferatu elders must now decide whether to restrict the supply of good information and risk being attacked for their power, or to debase the coin of fact with alloys of plausible lies. Even the question must remain a secret, of course, but Nosferatu are not the only clan with ears in low places.

ALLIES

As the careful balance of the Camarilla tilts alarmingly, the clans and elders scramble for allies both within and without the court. Allies must be treated as equals, a galling task for the proud and fearful elders. If offended or betrayed, a shrewd ally knows that his allegiance can always be taken elsewhere — such as to the betrayer's rival. Unfortunately, a lifetime as lords of creation and an unlifetime as paranoid manipulators renders most elders less than perfectly fit for the kind of diplomacy needed to make allies in an increasingly dangerous world.

FORCE

When all else fails, sheer naked force is sure to solve any problem, at least in the short run. The founders of Carthage discovered that timeless truth, and this lesson is one that the world never tires of delivering to any elder who trusts to a quick tongue or a bribed lackey alone. The elders of the Camarilla hold their positions, after all, because in the final analysis nobody is strong enough to dislodge them — yet. But for now the elders fight their wars with human sword fodder, and a force of humans willing to kill or die for a vampire's political goals is a hard thing to find and a harder one to keep.

The Brujah elders are well-aware of the use of violence from their younger days; humans will kill or die gleefully for the ideals that the Brujah can articulate convincingly. Radicals of all stripes, fanatics with grudges or crusades, and thugs looking for a reason to smash heads follow Brujah leaders (whether Iconoclast ancillae taking direction from their elders or the Idealist elders themselves), swayed by impassioned appeals to emotions that elders of other clans cannot even feign. Other Kindred must fall back on fear, money and the lust for power to raise their armies — although Brujah belief makes dedicated warriors, Ventrue gold raises very big battalions. Nosferatu use blackmail (or failing that, a pipe bomb in a gas main), Tremere use sorcerous might; each clan holds its own arsenal with which to fight its secret wars. The Camarilla tries to direct these energies outward to the Sabbat, much as the elders' royal pawns tried to divert their own vassals into Crusade when vampire lords held power openly. Such policies of distraction worked only indifferently then, but the Camarilla's survival depends on it working far better now.

SURVIVAL

Survival is the great goal of the elders singly and of the Camarilla collectively. A vampiric elder gladly sacrifices anything or anyone to prolong his existence. An elder meets threats to his survival with crushing, panicked counterblows, like the flailings of a man deathly afraid of spiders when confronted with a fiddleback on the windowsill. Slow, charitable, merciful or reluctant elders do not survive. Every elder knows this and has seen it proved time and again in mountain villages, urban tenements and everywhere in between. The only thing that will frighten an elder out of his fear is mortal danger. A cornered rat seems placid compared with an elder in terror for her unlife. No strategy is too risky, no threat too lurid, no punishment too obscene, no retribution too final for a vampiric elder faced with Final Death.

Although this desperate devotion to unlife drives the paranoia, malice, jealousy and contempt that threaten to destroy the elders' society and the courts of the Camarilla, it is also the only force that could impel them to maintain it. As long as the threats from outside the Camarilla seem greater than the threats within it, the elders will cling to its framework with iron tenacity. Whether they pull it apart in their frantic adherence to its structure, or let it fall by huddling within its inadequate shelter rather than sallying forth to defend it, is known to no man.

THE ELDERS BY CLAN

Although all elders share the traits of fear, Camarilla-spawned hate, and desperate drive to prolong their own cancerous existence, their blood has not grown too turgid to recall their heritage. Clan differences show up in elders as well as brash neonates, sometimes even more eccentrically as age and strain take their slow but certain toll. The Curse of Caine and the strictures of Camarilla drive all elders to disintegration. Only the blood of the founders links them together with themselves and each other.

BRUJAH

The Brujah elders know the tension between their position of traditional power and their youth's posture of rebellious contempt. To outsiders, they seem to exorcise it in street fighting and rabble-rousing, leading to Ventrue barbs about "marketing rebellion." Truly, there is nothing new under the sun, or under the moon either. After a few centuries of power, revolution for its own sake loses its charms. However, the elders remember the old glories of Carthage by night and the flickering fires of Moloch and Tanith. To these Kindred, whose very existence speaks of the persistence of dead things, Carthage might still rise again. The elder Idealists believe it must rise on the ruins of the world; most Brujah elders feel that it can be founded behind the Camarilla's sheltering walls. Younger Iconoclasts have little hope of seeing behind a Brujah elder's mask, but the rare neonate who touches a chord of memory within an elder may be caught up in reverie — and in millennia-old revolution. Very little has the power of an old dream, except perhaps a very ancient dreamer.

MALKAVIAN

Elder Malkavians, born close to Malkav's blood and traveled far from Malkav's time, see the two extremes fracturing into one, along with all the other extremes, of course. Somewhere in that interlacing filigree lies the pattern, the truth that lies open only to those brave enough to look unflinchingly. These elders gaze into the world with a sight honed by a hundred visions called hallucinations by the willfully blind. Portents overlay themselves on every activity; a car alarm sounds the symphony of creation while the road to Nod lies down a human intestine. Everything is provisional, nothing is temporary. When Malkavian elders turn their gaze upon others, anything can happen, but it usually doesn't. This is quite a disappointment to the elders, who more and more pay attention to the important things that only they have the eyes to see properly.

NOSFERATU

Elder Nosferatu see the roiling and reformation of the upper world as a reflection of their own physical evolution. Pessimistic or unkind elders of other clans often agree. This seeming remaking of the world in their image leads some Nosferatu elders to argue for holding back from the final confrontation. Just as Nosferatu neonates are often redeemed by their physical deformities, perhaps the Camarilla or the entire race of Caine will be redeemed by this time of trial. Other Nosferatu point out the unpleasant similarity between this view and the heresies of the Sabbat. Meanwhile, the scuttlings of the Nictuku grow louder as certain prophecies, arcane even to the vampiric lords of information, manifest themselves. Will the ancient brothers of the Nosferatu emerge to remold the clan into a dark redemption? Danger from above, danger from below. Used to getting along without others and to keeping counsel as a clan, the Nosferatu elders remain unsure of the true and proper course of action. With just a *little* more information, perhaps the tunnel to safety will reveal itself....

TOREADOR

Changes in the outside world have not left the arts alone; if anything, the opposite is true. Keats thought beauty lasted forever; now even Keats may not endure. Assaults on the canon of literature, the standards of poetry, the laws of perspective and the principles of musical harmony leave many Toreador elders unable to comprehend any art at all, much as other elders are baffled by fax machines or white phosphorus grenades. Ancient beauties remain fine, but Shakespeare to the contrary, age doth wither and custom stale *anything* given too much time. Where will new beauty come from, when art is sewage and the young mutilate themselves for fashion? Those few Toreador elders who throw themselves into modern art often find themselves sliding down the road of postmodernism to true anarchy and loss of meaning. Once all the idols are smashed, all the conventions are dead, what role can art-as-rebellion play? Both flight into conservative reaction and frantic embrace of the new lead to the same dead end for these elders. Do not pity the Toreador who finds that after centuries her beloved art has desiccated into nothing but empty imitation and banal posturing. Pity, rather, those in her power.

TREMERE

The Tremere elders have less to fear from their own childer thanks to their strict rules of initiation and discipline. Of course, they still must fear the jealousy and hatred of other elders, who still consider the Tremere jumped-up interlopers in the legacy of Caine. These elders often turn a blind eye to their childer's actions against Tremere interests; this leads the Tremere elders to tighten their hold on power and to withhold help from other clans. Until recently, Clan Tremere was uniquely confident among Camarilla sects that their mastery of the mystic arts meant that their survival was assured. Security, as older clans could have warned but preferred not to, is fleeting for any Kindred. With rich irony that Tremere's rivals appreciate, the wizard clan faces diablerie, the hour of their danger predicted by their birth. The cannibal Assamites return, free at last of Tremere's enchantments, and no Warlock wonders which clan will feel the Assassins' wrath first and most frequently.

VENTRUE

The Ventrue elders claim they must bear all the problems of the Camarilla on their shoulders. Where other clans' elders can afford the luxury of tending their own gardens and carrying on private vendettas, Ventrue must look outward to the Sabbat and Inquisition. Meanwhile, other clans hold back or actually obstruct needed defensive measures. The Ventrue elders find their resources and attention stretched ever thinner; of late a certain irritation with the other clans has entered their private councils. Ventrue lords have always cultivated a certain *noblesse oblige*; after five centuries of bearing the entire burden of keeping the Masquerade intact and shepherding the Children of Caine through crisis after crisis, that veneer of nobility wears thin. Even immortal patience has its limits, it seems. Pride slowly curdles into arrogance, and protectiveness becomes condescension and even resentment. Some Ventrue elders wish privately that some horrible disaster would befall the other clans so that the Blue Bloods could be appreciated properly again.

GANGREL

Some elder Gangrel pass their blood on to progeny and then voluntarily enter torpor or Final Death, either out of concern for the natural environment (as they claim) or out of cowardice and funk (as their enemies claim). Those elders who remain, however, increasingly hold themselves apart from other vampires and other elders. Some Gangrel elders no longer stop traveling at all, endlessly crossing the country or even circling the globe, torn between the distastefulness of involvement and the lingering call of Kindred loyalty. Alienation imprisons these elders just as surely as terror paralyzes those of other clans, however; the difference between motion and stillness is not as great as it might seem. When younger Gangrel meet these elders at Gather, they learn what drives them away from the lights of the Camarilla's cities. Young vampires of other clans seldom encounter Gangrel elders any more. When such meetings happen, however, they resemble storm fronts, bringing thunder and change to all in their path.

Dealing with Elders

He must have a long spoon that must eat with the Devil.
— William Shakespeare, *Comedy of Errors*

No vampire can ignore the elders. Even anarchs and Caitiff find their actions constrained and infringed upon by the machinations of the elders at the heart of the Camarilla. Few vampires have seen a Methuselah, but nearly every city holds an elder prince, and even neonates can address their lord in council. The elders serve as the visible embodiment of vampiric society. Even the Sabbat defines itself primarily through its opposition to the will of the elders and the Traditions they uphold. Although the Sabbat expresses open contempt for the elders' fossilized beliefs and sluggish hearts, they never underestimate the cunning of an elder's mind or the sheer physical power she can bring to bear.

Elders thus hold a linchpin role in vampiric society, the hub of a hundred conflicts and a thousand intrigues. Dealing with elders is often a common occurrence not only for other Kindred but for many other beings and even the common human herd of the World of Darkness. Of course, not every interaction with an elder happens in a ballroom or across a negotiating table. Not everyone knows these dealings for what they truly are, and of those who do, still fewer enjoy them. Elders do not grow old letting others set the meeting grounds, or even by granting importunate strangers audience. Transactions with elders sometimes come indirectly through financial and legal mazes — or more immediately through a car bomb planted by a human minion of a neonate blood bound to an ancilla who serves the elder's whims, all unknowing. Sometimes only the quality of the betrayal or the sheer artistry of the persecution announces elders' work.

Elders Among the Kindred

On their home ground, the elders retain a calm aloofness, moving with all due speed or not at all. The appearance of disorder within the councils of the Camarilla cannot be tolerated. The elders and the Traditions both make a virtue of stability; even Malkavian elders must restrict their spasms while in Elysiums or salons. To show distraction, haste or even open anger is to show weakness before the harpies and before one's enemies at court. The necessity for calm, for sang-froid and for vampiric courtesy in all its flavors is a charade that rivals the Masquerade in importance within the ranks of the Camarilla. Delivering insults or striking fear into others in such surroundings can take decades, or even centuries, to master.

Outside Elysium, of course, an elder is able to give free reign to her emotions, especially when dealing with progeny or with younger vampires in general. Of course, an elder runs the risk of appearing undignified when investing any emotion at all, even contempt, on a neonate. It is the ancillae who most often feel the wrath and spite of the elders. Elders seldom praise younger vampires, save to humiliate those not receiving such notice — or to appropriate a useful pawn from another elder's chessboard. Intelligent neonates fear elders' open friendship and interest far more than they do the cold disregard they might expect.

Within an elder's own clan, restraint can be looser still. Among the Nosferatu, for example, elders have been known to congratulate childer for success and even to commiserate at failure. Such commiseration takes the form of giving the unfortunate youngster a chance to repair his mistake, but no other clan gives more consideration. Tremere elders also commend success, in the interest of efficiency, but it is a cold and mechanical approbation indeed. In other clans, success by even a coterie of ancillae (or worse yet, neonates) stands a greater chance of marking the coterie as ambitious, and therefore dangerous, than it does of occasioning a reward. The best outcome for such a coterie shows as a glacial increase in status: a half-inch deeper nod, an extra minute of public conversation with a Toreador primogen, or the like. Wise childer take these crumbs gratefully. When large rewards come from an elder, they often come as indirect strikes at her rivals — like everything else in Kindred society, success has its dark side.

Prestation

A wise ancilla (or over-ambitious neonate) can only rise in status and power by entering the economy of favor and obligation that weaves the elders together. This system of prestation serves as the true currency of the Camarilla. The same hypersensitivity to slight and insult that fuels the flame of the elders' continuous jealousy also allows them to keep track of every small assistance or trifling service performed (for them, or for their rivals) by another Kindred. In order to advance in the estimation of their peers, vampires of the Camarilla curry favor by assisting those peers' goals and hampering the efforts of their enemies. Small services such as attendance at a salon or a tidbit of reliable gossip bring small services in return — delivery of a message or the loan of a talented ghoul for a night.

Some Kindred continuously give and receive favors, keeping themselves afloat through the sheer variety of their contacts. Others try to assist each major faction, trusting that any rising tide will lift their political boats. Still others accumulate numerous small obligations, asking only for rare but significant boons in return. In the hothouse air of the Camarilla, granting a favor is a sign of strength. Only Kindred with great power, the reasoning goes, can afford to disoblige themselves for others. Hence, asking for a boon is a sign of weakness.

A similar logic governs the repayment of favors. Although only the elders' honor actually enforces any obligation to a creditor, an elder who refuses to repay a boon not only appears churlish and vulgar (bad enough in Ventrue or Toreador circles), but seems a weakling desperately hoarding even scraps of influence. The sharks circle at such a sign of weakness. Thus, a clever Kindred often seeks out status and advancements by doing many favors, and weakens her foes by never seeking anything in return. Kindred society sees the bestower as powerful and genteel, while the harpies paint the borrower as desperate for favor and able to subsist only on the sour mercies of his betters.

CONSPIRACY

Behind the mirrored surface of salon and court, Kindred elders labor to undermine their enemies' positions by any means available. Indeed, some elders work harder at weakening other elders than at opposing the Sabbat or the Lupines. This ongoing conspiracy for power consumes the elders' attention by necessity. Even a theoretical elder concerned only for the good of the Camarilla at large would be undone by a hundred plots against her if she did not conspire on her own behalf.

Some of these intrigues remain solely confined to a single clan. In the hierarchical Tremere, internal alliances and covert attempts to rise in faction or chantry politics remain vital; only the Inner Council can promote Tremere vampires within the clan structure. For a vampire to elevate herself in Kindred society at large, however, she must depend not only on her own clan (which usually, though by no means always, supports her ambitions to strengthen the clan as a whole in the city's primogen) but on her contacts and supporters within other clans as well, or with the anarch community. Reputation gains value when it spreads far, and no Kindred can afford to neglect any opening, no matter how indirect, into the councils of the great. A disreputable anarch may hold the key to some strike against the Sabbat, or a vampire of a rival clan might agree to sell out her own archenemy within it. The coins of opportunity and betrayal remain good even outside the Camarilla. Some aspiring Kindred deal with the Lupines (especially Gangrel elders), and particularly rash aspirants may even enter into arrangements with the Sabbat. Many rumors connect certain powerful elders with factions within the Sabbat, and whisper of deals allowing both to prosper from the destruction of a particularly vulnerable lord of the Camarilla.

Controlling the flow of information holds the key to success for any conspiracy. The Nosferatu have a great advantage in this, but this advantage works against them when every other clan instantly suspects their hand in a rumor or in the gathering of forces for rebellion. Although the Nosferatu loudly proclaim their neutrality, other Kindred universally believe that the Nosferatu protest too much. No elder believes in neutrality, anyway, especially not when eternal servitude remains an all-too-real possibility. Elders traditionally trust their greatest secrets only to those ghouls

and retainers blood bound into their service. The blood bond does allow any elder to maintain a fairly extensive local power structure — the system only breaks down when another elder must be consulted or somehow involved.

The risk of betrayal is the corpse at any feast of intrigue. If elder snares and plans run deep, their treacheries run deeper still. Virtually every elder who survives to this day carries a lengthy reputation of conspiracies betrayed and deals broken behind him; treason greases the path to power. Thus, the eldest of the elders find few takers for offers of allegiance, and the most ambitious youngsters can often build factions based on their not-yet debased word. As a result, news of ancillae organization or alliance often causes the elders to strike hard and fast — and to reward generously any informers within the group. Of course, any ancillae factions working against each other become tools for elder rivalries; the best such a coterie can hope for is to be a communal tool of the Camarilla against the Sabbat for a time.

MANIPULATION

Rather than run the risk of open collusion, then, many elders resort to manipulation of one kind or another to advance themselves over the bodies of their fellows. From the perspective of these elders, nothing gives more satisfaction than a struggle between others. Manipulators enjoy creating rivalries where none exist, and fanning enmities into open conflict. Simply by trading favors, "accidentally" letting a piece of malicious gossip drop in a salon or hinting at alliances that never seem to materialize, a clever elder can bring two other Kindred to an escalating hostility, or even to actual blows.

This potential for manipulation adds another layer to the elders' mutual jealousy and distrust. Elders analyze every action, every favor, every word of other Kindred searching for the hidden trap or poison pill within. Even finding the trap does not mean that the target can avoid it. Vampiric honor, survival or court status can all force an unwilling victim to "play along" with her own manipulation. Harpies and other onlookers particularly admire those elders who can manipulate a knowing victim.

Some manipulators hide traps within traps; when the first is discovered, acting upon it sets off the second. Malkavian elders have gained grim reputations for the unpredictability of the snares they spring; some Malkavians seem to take actions solely to send the victims (or witnesses) into a frenzy of paranoid speculation and countermeasure against a nonexistent threat. One Malkavian elder made a habit of offering a different flower each day to random neonates. Elder after elder tried to decipher the "flower code" and the significance of the choice of neonates; the poor childer were hauled in for interrogation by increasingly distrustful sires, and conducting Elysium became nearly impossible as discussions stopped whenever anyone brought flowers into the room.

It is difficult to manipulate older vampires. Some particularly observant or skilled childer can play upon their elders' natural tendencies to paranoia and jealousy, or to their vanity and suspicion. Most elders can spot these ploys for what they are, however, and ancillae make themselves particularly vulnerable if they attempt such manipulations on a whim or without preparation. Elders manipulate younger vampires, especially, by maneuvering two dangerous coteries to open feuding and mutual self-destruction. Young Kindred seldom know enough of their ground to pose a genuine threat to elders in the political realm, and that's just how the elders like it.

The elders keep their progeny ignorant to make them pliable. Many of the most experienced manipulators can recognize the signs in the seemingly artificial and contrived rivalries between and within clans of the Camarilla. Of course, the most experienced manipulators are also generally the most paranoid and distrusting. These elders fear that they themselves are the targets for such manipulation by the reclusive Methuselahs, or even by the seemingly disinterested Inconnu. This fear becomes another factor in the Camarilla's impotence against the Sabbat and other crises. If the Sabbat, for example, serves the Methuselahs as a stalking horse to weaken and paralyze the otherwise-dangerous Camarilla, then acting against the Sabbat would be playing into the hands of the shadowy Fourth Generation.

MISDIRECTION AND INDIRECTION

A successful conspiracy resembles a magic trick. Distraction and misdirection allow it to go forward. No elder simply moves to do something for a plain and easily understood reason. The eldest of all strive never to show the real reason for their actions. The Kindred of one city tell the story of a Ventrue elder arriving on the scene in time to save the unlife of the city's prince from a Sabbat attack. The Ventrue shouted: "Fear not, sire, I am here to save thee!" The prince paused in his defense, and responded: "I see that, your lordship, but what is in it for me?" Since that Ventrue now rules the city, the question was a good one.

Misdirection often involves a diversion — an elder who plans to weaken a rival may throw a party, take up a new lover or even start an entirely different feud to cover her actions. Attacking on one front to progress on a second is another common type of misdirection. An assault on a rival's resources may actually be intended to goad the target into lowering his own status by requesting a boon from a seemingly disinterested party.

Indirection also helps such schemes go forward. No elder reveals to another every favor she possesses, the extent of her resources or the names of every contact and mortal tool in her retinue. It's rare that they share any information at all, in fact. An example on a small scale: An intriguer might use his influence in the city's police department to hamper a rival's business interests or even her nightly feedings. By successful misdirection in Elysium, he could convince her that her problems stem from an ambitious ancilla (also secretly part of his faction). When she appeals to him for help against the ancilla, he can arrange for the harassment to cease, thus increasing his status at her expense. If the ancilla's ambition has been causing problems as well, he might even solve the problem by arranging an unpleasant fate for his luckless pawn, thus killing two birds with one indirectly hurled stone.

Elders and Other Supernaturals

To their distaste, the elders of the Kindred must occasionally share the stage with other supernatural beings of one sort or another. Such necessities irritate elders for many reasons. First, the rules which an elder Kindred spends centuries learning and perfecting have no use outside vampiric existence. Second, most elders know little about other supernaturals, and fear what they do not understand. This fear and ignorance, of course, works to poison the atmosphere of any such dealings. Often, that poison works on both sides; dealings between Kindred and werewolves almost always end badly for someone. Even in situations when no overt rivalries exist, however, confusion and miscommunication takes its toll. Virtually every elder has heard of some unfortunate vampire hampered by the mysterious vagaries of magi or wraiths.

Werewolves

Vampires fear Lupines more, if possible, than humans fear vampires. Since so much of the elders' power rests, ultimately, on fear and force, they instinctively respect, and therefore instinctively resent, the terror and violence inherent in the existence of werewolves. Cautious paranoia thus drives the elders of the Kindred to avoid any contact with Lupines if at all possible. If they absolutely must encounter lycanthropes, the elders take every imaginable precaution to ensure themselves the whip hand. Elders will arrange overwhelming force, arm their ghouls with silver shot and set meeting places in city parks rather than deserted suburbs or wild forest preserves. Elders also take any opportunity to betray and ambush werewolves, considering it to be nothing more than intelligent self-defense. Elders may promise the Lupines anything they want, only to unleash hordes of Brujah ancillae on the Lupine packs the instant their furry backs are turned.

Only the elders of Clan Gangrel find it possible to work with the Lupines on any consistent basis other than enmity and combat — and even they are far from friendship with the Werewolf. For whatever reason, perhaps because the Gangrel's intense need for and near-worship of the wilderness touches some chord within the shapeshifters' being, Gangrel can sometimes make cautious and transitory agreements with the Lupine tribes. To keep faith with the Lupines requires the Gangrel elders to build relationships of mutual trust (or at least bare toleration) over decades, made as difficult as possible by the maniacal suspicion that the werewolves hold for any Kindred regardless of clan.

Magi

For creatures who thrive on rules and order, the presence of a human being capable of violating any law of nature at a whim is nerve-wracking indeed. Fortunately for the Camarilla, not only do the human magi themselves work behind the scenes of reality, but their work seems to have virtually nothing to do with the ways of the Kindred. The mystics seem to inhabit an entirely different world from vampires at some times, and frankly no elder troubles herself greatly about them.

The sorcerous Clan Tremere, however, occasionally manages to put aside its qualms to dabble in mortal magi affairs. The clan has never quite been able to leave behind its old associations with the Hermetic houses of its birth, although open consorting between the two would lead to fatal disapproval from the elders of both sides. Elder Tremere recall too well that wizardly quarrels led them to their current state, partly in an attempt to gain some advantage in the battles between the Hermetic houses; they have had centuries to contemplate the choice.

Wraiths

Wraiths' intangibility, and their lack of involvement in mortal affairs, complicates dealings with the Restless Dead. Most elders are satisfied to leave ghostly things at that; their own lives roil with too much threat and confusion to add still more. However, wraiths make excellent spies; invisible and oft-ignored, they can eavesdrop on the most secret conference. Many of these ghosts seem greatly attached, even tied, to an object or person within the corporeal world, and these so-called Fetters make the best leverage an elder can have over a wraith. Having such a hold on one of the Restless Dead gives an elder a powerful resource — and a dangerous one, should the ghost rebel. Elders on bad terms with the Nosferatu may have overwhelming need to take these risks for such an agent.

Changelings

The Kindred know little about the changelings, those few faeries left on Earth. During the Dark Ages, Kindred dealt with the fae more often, yet even then mystery, myth and confusion shrouded such transactions. To most elders, dealing with the Fair Folk invites a farrago of mystification and chaos. The traditional and orderly elders of the Camarilla dislike this as much as they dislike the potential lawlessness of the magi. Fortunately, the effect the Fair Folk can have on the Camarilla's conspiracies remains minimal. Any faerie with power left this world long ago for Arcadia; the powerless remnant aren't worth the time it would take to understand them.

Thus, only the occasional Malkavian elder works with the fae. When he does, it seems that insanity and Glamour can find a meeting place somewhere in the forest of illusions and hallucinations surrounding both. What those meetings portend, what occurs within them, and even whether they actually occur in reality at all is known only to the Malkavians — and to the changelings themselves.

Cathayans

Although the Cathayans seem to be fellow vampires, dealing with them is as fraught mystery as with any enigmatic mage — and potentially as dangerous as with a berserker Lupine. There are two great mistakes that elders can make with a Cathayan. First, some elders are prone to treat Cathayans as personages of no great account. Since Cathayans have no status within the Camarilla, and their Disciplines and codes are foreign and unfamiliar, foolish elders feel that the Cathayans can be ignored or viewed solely as exotic curiosities. Centuries of unlife spent ruthlessly cutting and crushing any Kindred who diverges from the minutiae of Camarilla salon etiquette build reflexes of condescension and underestimation that prove most unwise when practiced on the Kindred of the

East. The Camarilla Kindred of Hong Kong and elsewhere on the Pacific especially can speak to the folly of such a path.

The other mistake holds equal danger, even if it appears less severe. Many Western Kindred treat the Cathayans as they would any other Kindred, with surface respect and secret resentment. Unfortunately, the Cathayans see the world differently from the Camarilla. Even though both cultures value politeness, reputation and power, the weight they give to each varies widely. Misperceptions build upon each other, and restoring amity becomes ever more difficult. For this reason, many elders of the Camarilla often go out of their way to avoid any dealings at all with the Cathayans. Kindred elders avoid risk even under the best of circumstances; dealing with the Kindred of the East never happens under the best of circumstances.

ELDERS AND MORTALS

Elders almost always deal with humanity through networks of false fronts, cut-outs and hired (or ghouled) henchmen. Only the most important, most compromised human servitors ever see an elder face to face. Even then, the elders never reveal their identity, posing as rich businessmen, eccentric collectors or organized crime figures. Humans are almost always expendable — an elder's faintest doubt of a human's trustworthiness or a mortal's first hint of independence signs that mortal's death warrant. No elder thinks twice about murdering a human; he undoubtedly has done so tens of thousands of times over. Humans are more apt to concern themselves with the lives of cattle than Kindred elders are with kine.

Many times, this blindness causes the elder to misjudge a human's capacity for violence or to mistake desperation for tractability. Human breaking points vary, and often the kine fail to recognize when rebellion is instant suicide. Used to dealing with very risk-averse Kindred, elders can be taken by surprise by a human gamble against overwhelming odds. Ossified folly can potentially lead an elder to underestimate a human minion's capacity and send an insufficient force to dispose of an unwanted tool. Any human who gets away once, however, is hunted down by everything available — the Masquerade itself, and the elder's life, is potentially at stake.

ELDERS IN THE CHRONICLE

Elders and their machinations often serve as the meat of a **Vampire: the Masquerade** chronicle. Even if the game does not focus on the elders, or even on court and salon, the schemes and plots of the Camarilla greatly affect every other vampire's life and political situation. The elders lie at the center of the Camarilla like bloated spiders within their webs. They notice every quiver of the Kindred around them, and can move to destroy threats with terrifying speed, surgical cunning and paralyzing power.

Elders can be frightening enemies or overwhelming allies, or vice versa, for a coterie of ancillae or neonates. Unless the coterie is made up of determined Caitiff anarchs, it will have to deal with the elders at some point, whether of the city or of their respective clans. The elders dislike and distrust anyone who attempts to stay out of Kindred politics; they cannot do anything about the Inconnu, but they can make unlife on Earth hell for a powerless coterie without allies. Once the coterie makes allies, of course, then it is just as thoroughly ensnared within the labyrinth of elder politics — and the elders win again.

ELDERS AS THEME

The elders of the Camarilla embody the theme of **Vampire: the Masquerade**. Elders demonstrate what happens after tragedy. Drained of Humanity, they now fester in the womb of their shadowy existence. Elders serve as a warning: This is what you must not become. And yet, these beings must be defeated at their own game: To avoid them, you must become them. Manipulation and lies beget manipulation and lies, and he who would oppose the elders must use their tools.

The elders also batten upon their childer as their childer batten upon the kine; once an elder gets old enough, metaphor becomes truth and he must physically drain his progeny of vitae to continue his baneful unlife. It is not amiss for a Storyteller to draw parallels between the characters' dysfunctional fear and hatred of their elders and that of the characters' own retinues feelings for them.

Elders of the Camarilla live by the archaic and lifeless Traditions because such is the way of the vampire. Bloodsucking monsters cannot, should not, pretend to life. Such is a parody and a mockery of anything human. The Masquerade separates Kindred from the mortal world just as the scrims and screens of Elysian politics separate the elders from the real concerns of the Kindred. The authority of the elders shares symbolically in the taint of Caine; they are inherently corrupt and foul, representing the corruption of evil and the foulness of diseased blood. The actions of the elders cry out to Heaven for redress and for a cleansing; the players would do well to look for reflections of their characters' actions in the dark glass the elders hold up.

ELDERS AS MOOD

As well as incarnating the themes of **Vampire: the Masquerade**, using elders in a chronicle can go far to set the mood of the game. More than other Kindred, elders seem *wrong*. This sense of the uncanny goes far to build an atmosphere laden with menace and unspoken threat. Aside from the sheer unease caused by the blood-freezing power a sixth-generation Kindred commands, players should feel unnerved by the elder's appearance, by his casual inhumanities, and perhaps by the very real feeling that this elder is no longer even remotely human.

Storytellers can easily create the mood of blackest paranoia and jealous suspicion by thrusting the characters into the cream of vampiric high society. A few innuendoes, a hint of a conspiracy, a casual snub, and the players are suddenly mad with envious fear of every other Kindred they meet. When the Storyteller can convey the idea that elders treat everything and everyone with that level of manic fear and hatred, then the mood of the elder mentality snaps firmly into place.

Simple vileness and evil can go some distance to establish mood. Show elders at a divertissement salon playing a game of living chess or holding a grotesque *tableau vivant* with Dominated thralls. The sparkling imagery of Elysium becomes a whited sepulcher after one or two such events, and even the most light-hearted Toreador should feel the hateful brutality at the core of her existence.

ELDERS AS PLOT

The greatest service that elders perform in a chronicle, of course, is to drive the plot. With a fistful of factions and hundreds of intrigues bubbling away merrily in even a medium-sized city, the Storyteller can hang any number of plots and storylines on the interactions of various elders. Simply gaining an invitation to an important Toreador salon can be a roleplaying challenge that stretches for weeks as the characters jockey to be noticed by the Toreador's neonates (or by her rival's), to find some other Kindred with a precious favor to trade and to unwind skeins of rumor and overheard gossip to discern their own standing. On the other hand, if the Storyteller wishes to throw the players headlong into the mire of Kindred upper-crust life, the characters can be plucked from obscurity by an elder looking for easily-manipulated tools.

Within the complex economy of status, jealousy and prestation that governs the Camarilla, any action the characters take can have repercussions that echo for decades. If they help an elder, his enemies will mark them for recruitment (as spies) or destruction (as threats). This will involve them in plots spun by those enemies' rivals, or their allies. Once they have done other Kindred a favor, even inadvertently, the characters are well and truly hooked.

Larger questions of plot often hang on the action of the elders. Since elders always have some deeply hidden reason for their actions, and act as indirectly as possible, the Storyteller can always tie any loose end or red herring back into the main plot simply by revealing (or inventing) some elder's heretofore-hidden hand behind the mystery. Not everything in the chronicle needs to be the elders' fault, although the elders should certainly react to every major event involving the characters. These reactions can vary from conferring status (even involuntarily) on them, or mistakenly assuming that the coterie was working for some other elder when in fact the coincidence in interests was pure happenstance.

Although it is unusual for a coterie of neonates or ancillae to outmaneuver an elder or think of some angle he missed, it's rather less unusual for a troupe of players to outthink a Storyteller juggling five plotlines and a hundred non-player characters. The Storyteller can respond to such a surprise in three ways. The first, which is the most realistic but the least satisfying, is to save the elder's bacon somehow; bring in an extra squad of ghouls or give the elder some heretofore unheard-of Discipline or occult artifact that coincidentally foils the characters' plan. Elders certainly have such resources, but players reasonably object to seeing them only at the last minute.

The second possibility is simply to accept it. Part of the elders' weakness, after all, is their intense conservatism of outlook and fossilization of mind. It's not unheard of for ancillae or even neonates to develop some fresh new insight that happens to solve some crisis very much to the discomfiture of a slower,

more hidebound, elder. This is, after all, part of why elders hate and fear the young. Of course, any coterie that has demonstrated an ability to take down, or even seriously inconvenience, an elder becomes an immediate target for every paranoid elder in the court, which is to say, every elder in the court, period. This certainly makes the characters' existences interesting, and gives the Storyteller a reason to beef up all the elders' defenses from now on so that she won't be caught that way again.

The final option is to reveal that the characters were, unbeknownst to them, following the agenda of another elder. Every clue they found, every hint they followed up on, every mistake their target made was set up by his rival. The players still feel the pleasure of success, but their reward is a nicely mixed one. Furthermore, such a denouement serves to tie the characters even more into elder politics, and thus into further plotlines and story arcs.

ELDERS IN THE GAME

Unlimited power is apt to corrupt the minds of those who possess it.

— William Pitt, the Elder

Directly portraying vampiric elders can challenge both Storytellers and players. After all, very few roleplayers have centuries of experience at intrigue, murder and court etiquette. Use the central tenets of paranoia, spite, jealousy and the all-important surface calm as your touchstones. Elders are unfeeling, but only in a bad way. They embody corrupt power leashed in silk — predatory cats who gain far more satisfaction from playing with their victims than from the act of consuming them.

ELDERS AS STORYTELLER CHARACTERS

The most important factor in playing an elder as Storyteller is control. The elder always desires the appearance of control, even (especially) if he is actually in a blind panicked funk over some real or imaginary threat. Elders strive to keep control of themselves, the conversation, the flow of information and their networks of allies and retainers. If the elder is at court, interrupt discussions with the characters as messengers deliver mysterious tidings, or with brief greetings to some other characters of higher status than the characters. If by some mischance a character scores a hit on an elder in conversation or innuendo, respond cuttingly and end the conversation. Elders do not get drawn into lengthy catfights or playing the dozens with upstarts.

Keep your elders unfailingly courteous and polite, even when angry or vengeful. No elder will lose her sang-froid for a coterie of juvenile riffraff. Keep your diction elegant, your poise controlled and your phrasing exact. Save the full body of vampiric rage for climactic scenes. If the characters see an elder angry, they should remember it for the rest of their (most probably short) unlives.

While embodying cool, harnessed, sadistic power, however, it is important for the Storyteller to remember that the elder is onstage to increase player involvement in the chronicle. The elder's role in the story is to advance theme, mood or plot, not to give the Storyteller a cheap ego trip at his players' expense. Elders can easily be overused. If the players are bored or resentful during scenes with elders, heed their message. Keep

CREATING AN ELDER

Elders don't spring wholly formed like Athena from the minds of their creators. They are characters with more backstory and history than most. Simply tossing an elder into your game without context is a recipe for disaster — there's a great deal more to these creatures than just piles of Disciplines. When creating an elder, it pays to ask yourself the following questions about her:

• **How old is she?**

Is she an American elder, witness to a bare handful of centuries, or a relic from the days of Magna Graecia? The answer says a great deal about the character's perspective — and how she'll react toward younger Kindred.

• **Where is she from?**

An elder Embraced in Bavaria at the height of the Reformation is likely to have different values than one who began her unlife in pre-Great Fire London or Hannibal's Carthage. Don't forget to take culture and history into account when thinking about how the elder reacts instinctively — the first lessons learned are the last to be forgotten.

• **Where has she been?**

What has she experienced? Did she flee from the Inquisition personally, or did she spend the years of terror hidden in torpor? What other elders or famous figures has she met? That sort of thing tends to impress neonates, as well as providing handy reference points for in-character reminiscences.

There are other questions along these lines that can be useful as well. Plotting out the elder's enemies, putative allies, preferences, quirks, childer and whatnot help fill in the gaps, and provides you with hooks on which to hang future stories. In the end, what your elder's Disciplines are, how many dots she has in each Attribute and so on — all of these things pale in importance when compared to figuring out *who* the elder is.

the elders in the shadows or across the salon floor. Their actions should convey a sense of mysterious menace, not overfamiliarity or pointless dominance games held over the players' heads.

ELDERS AS PLAYER CHARACTERS

Players should pay attention to the roleplaying hints given above for Storytellers if called upon to portray elders in a chronicle. The central themes of control overlaying jealousy, of corruption eating away at tradition and of fear paralyzing power should be foremost in any player's mind as he adopts the role of an elder of the Camarilla.

A chronicle where one player plays an elder and the other characters are lower in status can create problems. The "central" player can wind up annoying the others, especially if he abuses his authority and acts petty and spiteful. Never mind that an actual elder would do exactly that, it's no fun to *play*. Consider troupe play, where the players take turns portraying the elder in the coterie, as a possible solution. Another solution is to allow all the players to take the role of

elders. An all-elder chronicle can be too high-powered for some Storytellers, but the key is to develop threats sufficiently calibrated to the characters' exalted status.

If the players are mature enough to handle great in-character power, and the Storyteller creative enough to develop enough games of politics and intrigue (the ban on violence and Disciplines in Elysium can redress the balance somewhat here, too) or high-tension threats involving major foes, however, an all-elder game can be an exciting change from the endless round of manipulation and shadow-boxing.

Let the players take the roles of the primogen of the city; the Storyteller can spend a few sessions letting them get a feel for their new domain, exercising authority, judging salons, having nosy reporters or FBI agents killed with a languid wave of the hand to thirsty ancillae. Then, of course, the dread beast of politics rears its head. Clan differences may impel the players into maneuvering amongst themselves. If the players don't take each other's betrayal and conspiracy personally, this nicely solves the Storyteller's problem of threat calibration. If the players prefer coterie unity, however, facing down the Sabbat presents more than enough challenge. For mystery, the Storyteller might send the elders after the Antediluvians; for a more spiritual campaign, she could spotlight the blissful temptations of the Inconnu. Every elder harbors centuries of stories — why not your chronicle, too?

THE INCONNU

There's a presence hovering over this city, watching. I can feel it when I walk the supposedly empty streets. I can sense it when I'm in the mob at Elysium. And I can almost hear its voice whispering to me in the early hours before dawn, just before I fall asleep.

I think the voice tells me things, too, when I'm sleeping. It's indescribably old and sad, and it tells me stories from this town's not particularly illustrious history. I wake up every night and there's another memory, another image of something that happened a hundred years ago, fading at the edges of my mind. There's no way I could possibly know what color tie His Majesty was wearing when he staked out his sire, back in the year 1874, but I have these visions, and ask around, and damned if I haven't seen the thing just as it happened.

It scares me, I think. It scares me that this presence, this power, has been watching the city for so long, and it scares me that now it's watching me. I'd like to think, in my more optimistic moments, that it's watching me because it's lonely, and wants to share some of what it's seen with someone. If you buy that argument, it's picked me because I'm small and insignificant in the grand vampiric scale of things, and it doesn't matter if I know these things because, frankly, no one cares about me.

The other possibility — that I'm being watched because I'm going to do something worth watching — is what really scares me.

Ask a hundred Kindred what the Inconnu are really up to, and you'll get two hundred different answers. The sect remains mysterious and omnipresent, in the background of every vampire's thoughts. The fact that the Inconnu don't seem to do anything is maddening to other vampires. Plot and counterplot, thrust,

parry and riposte — vampires are used to that sort of thing. In a strange way, the endless dance of intrigue and conflict is comforting; everyone knows what to expect, after all.

But the Inconnu don't play those sorts of games. They do, as far as the average Kindred can see, nothing. And that drives the rest of the vampiric community *insane* with curiosity — primarily because no one who's been Embraced for more than an hour can believe that beings so old and so potent could refrain from engaging in the same sorts of games that the rest of the vampires play.

Perhaps this perspective is a failure of vampiric perspective; younger vampires simply can't conceive of their wiser elders being like anything but themselves. Perhaps the Inconnu simply do sit, and watch, and in some cases seek Golconda endlessly. Perhaps….

But there's no one out there who believes it.

What Are They?

Technically speaking, the Inconnu are not so much a vampiric sect as they are a sort of community of mutual respect. So far as anyone knows, there is no Inner Circle of Inconnu, no grand and terrible gathering of grand and terrible vampires deciding the fate of the sect. Instead, the Inconnu — on those rare occasions when a vampire identifies himself as such — seem to be a loosely affiliated band of individuals, brought together by shared interest and experience but distanced by a healthy fear and respect of one another's power. Certainly Golconda *seems* to be on the agenda of many members of the sect, but "seems to be" isn't quite enough to ensure mutual safety when two incredibly powerful Kindred get a little too close.

Most often, an Inconnu is sensed simply as a presence, a feeling of ineffable power lurking in the background whenever a too-inquisitive trespasser comes near the vampire's dwelling. Even random passersby often get some fragment of this effect, which explains at least some of the supposedly "haunted" or "cursed" places in the world. Many members of the sect have gone to ground somewhere and stayed in that spot for centuries (See "Monitors," p. 225), though only a select few choose cities in which to dwell. The remainder prefer isolated and rural locations, often outside the purview of even other supernatural creatures. Inconnu retreat from society to be distinctly alone, and they take that notion seriously. What good is solitude for purposes of contemplating Golconda if ancillae are poking around the haven every other year or so?

In the end, then, the Inconnu are the Kindred's favorite homegrown mystery, always present to be debated, but never rousing themselves to act and thus disprove anyone's pet theories about them. In a strange sense the Inconnu are almost a comforting presence to their younger brethren, a slumbering volcano in the distance that the locals simultaneously respect and fear. No, the vampires of the Camarilla most assuredly do *not* want the Inconnu to start playing an active role in vampiric society, but their quiet presence is more pleasant to contemplate than, say, the possible machinations of the Antediluvians. The Inconnu are the figurative "devil you know," though that knowledge is ever so slight — and even among Kindred, the devil you know is better than the one you don't.

FEAR

Any sane Kindred (and any Malkavian as well) has a healthy fear for the Inconnu. Everyone knows they *can* act, and act decisively — it's just that they don't. Paranoid sires tell their childer stories of entire towns (or in more grandiose versions, cities) wiped clean of their vampiric populations for some slight, real or imagined, against the Inconnu. As to whether or not these stories are true, let it suffice to say that it's hard to find evidence against them — which makes the tales all the more terrifying to particularly imaginative Kindred.

The likelihood is that the Inconnu themselves started those rumors (and may even have backed one or two of them up, just to prove the point) to ensure that younger Kindred have and maintain a gut-wrenching fear of what the Inconnu just might do. While this tactic might seem to deprive the Inconnu of potential helpers or allies, the truth is that should assistance be required, the Inconnu can no doubt compel it. Furthermore, the terror that these ancient Kindred inspire is sufficient to deter any number of would-be diablerists intent on potent Inconnu vitae. While the odds are that very few, if any, of these seekers would survive their quests, it's easier for the Inconnu never have to deal with them at all. As for those latter-day Troiles whom the stories don't discourage, even they are sufficiently affected by the tales to be hindered in their hunts by the effects of raw fear. A hunter who is distracted by legends and jumping at shadows soon becomes easy prey himself.

HISTORY

The Inconnu as a sect only came to prominence during the centuries immediately preceding the formation of the Camarilla and Sabbat; some historians claim that the Inconnu "formalized" as a result of those events. Older Kindred remember the Inconnu in those days as being described as remnants of the Roman order, vampires who had flourished under the *Pax Romana et Vampirica* and who felt displaced in the subsequent chaos. Precisely how the sect has evolved since then — particularly as regards its members' total rejection of the Jyhad and all its works — is shrouded in mystery. Again, the moment of decision would seem to be the mid-15th century, but that is sheerest conjecture.

TIME AND THE INCONNU

Part of the mystery of the Inconnu is their sense of scale, one so grand that it is simply beyond the comprehension of younger Kindred. A decade or even a century is nothing to one of these ancients. Matters of ultimate urgency to neonates and ancillae are like mayflies to them, gone in a matter of moments. In a sense, the Inconnu are to younger vampires what those vampires are to mortals — just as an ancilla sees things from a much longer perspective than does a human, so does an Inconnu see things from a much longer perspective than a young vampire. The impending overthrow of a prince, anarch revolutions, Ravnos infestations — all those things that are matters of life and death to neonates and ancillae alike — are mere eyeblinks to the Inconnu, no more worthy of attention than a mortal mayoral election is to a Kindred Embraced a century ago. Indeed, it would not be too far-fetched to say that one of the great frustrations Kindred have in dealing with the Inconnu is that the sect treats younger vampires exactly as they are accustomed to treating others — and that even elders are a lot better at dishing out that sort of thing than receiving it.

INTERFERENCE

The question of whether or not the Inconnu interfere in Camarilla society is one that has plagued the Camarilla since its inception. The consensus among Camarilla vampires seems to be "Yes, they do interfere, but we don't know how — and that's what terrifies us." The perceived hand of the Inconnu is everywhere, causing neonates and elders alike to react to the supposed manipulations of the mysterious sect. Further actions are taken to prepare against the (theoretically inevitable) day when the Inconnu do wish to take an active role.

So, by dint of others' reactions, paranoid fantasies and plans, the Inconnu do indeed affect the Camarilla on a nightly basis. On the other hand, the question of whether the Inconnu themselves actually do anything in addition to inspiring frenzies of activity remains debatable. This, presumably, is exactly the way the Inconnu like it.

On an individual basis, meetings with members of the Inconnu are rare and portentous. No one walks away from meeting a Methuselah unchanged, though whether the change is for the better or the worse is debatable. Encounters with Inconnu have specific purposes: warnings, threats, the odd moment of congratulation and the occasional recruitment onto the path of Golconda. Such encounters are more like audiences than discussions; the power dynamic in a room always tilts precipitously toward the Methuselah. Regardless of a given meeting's purpose, the sense of awe and power than an Inconnu brings to the table inevitably has an impact. Few vampires ever willingly speak of their contact with Inconnu, though whether this reticence grows out of fear, respect or compulsion no one can say.

GOLCONDA

One of the most prevalent rumors about the Inconnu is that some/most/all of them have achieved the semi-mythical state known as Golconda. While official Camarilla policy on Golconda is that it is a pleasant myth, that same policy subtly discourages anyone from diverting his energies from the sect to seeking that myth out. As a result, the notion that the Inconnu seemingly have the key to whatever Golconda might be (and trying to get consensus on *that* matter is like collecting hen's teeth) makes them slightly suspect in a fashion completely unrelated to their monstrous power.

Basic theory on Golconda is that it is the state wherein a vampire masters and tames his Beast, rendering himself immune to its ravages and frenzies. The effects this mastery has on matters such as vampiric hunger, Rotschreck and so on are open to debate among vampiric theorists (Golconda studies being second only to Noddist lore as a popular field for unliving scholars). Thus, it is no surprise that knowledge of this mysterious philosophy is ascribed to this mysterious sect of vampires.

Everybody Knows

Very few — perhaps a dozen — Kindred actually know what Monitors are. A bare handful more are even aware of their existence, and all of those are predictably close-mouthed about the subject. It's not that Monitors go door to door advising other vampires not to speak about them; rather, it's that Kindred who blather to others about mysterious Inconnu monitoring entire cities tend to be ignored, mocked or silenced. Whether the Inconnu themselves are behind this uniformly negative reaction is a matter of quiet debate among those "in the know," but no one's willing to risk his immortal neck to test the hypothesis.

On the other hand, a great many younger Kindred, particularly those with Auspex, report uncanny, undirected feelings of being watched, particularly in cities where a Monitor is present. There's also a prevalence of unquiet or nightmarish dreaming among these vampires, presumably a result of their fragile minds being touched by the Monitor's roving will. Unsolicited bits of memory and conjecture accidentally dropped into a neonate's mind in this fashion can give the young vampire remarkable insight — or set her up as a target because she knows too much.

On one level it makes sense that a majority of the Inconnu have in fact achieved Golconda; ultimate enlightenment would seem a better reason than most that the Methuselahs don't constantly interfere with or hunt their distant descendants. The isolation and desolation that the Inconnu demand of their havens also seem to lend themselves to contemplation, not distraction — a necessary prerequisite to Golconda, one would think. Furthermore, whispered conversations between those Kindred who have in fact met — knowingly or unawares — members of the Inconnu often agree on one point: the utter serenity and calm that seemingly radiated from the Methuselah.

It is commonly accepted rumor that members of the Inconnu who have attained enlightenment do in fact rouse themselves to seek disciples on the path to Golconda. The recruitment process can take years or centuries — some Kindred have reported being approached a half-dozen times over a half-dozen centuries. Other times, the target of the attempt is a freshly Embraced neonate of exceptional potential or lineage, as the Methuselah seeks to preempt centuries of torment and blood by starting the prize catch down the "right road" early. Coercion is never used in these matters. One cannot be forced onto the road to Golconda, only convinced to travel it for oneself.

Kindred who accept the Inconnu's blandishments on the matter make a point of setting their unliving affairs in order and then disappearing, presumably to join their new teachers in the wilderness. Such tidy disappearances are unsettling to the Kindred's "survivors," and since many students of Golconda never return home, a sinister air can sometimes shroud the whole process. Most of these disciples are never heard from again, though debate rages as to whether the vanished ones then take up positions among the Inconnu, change identities or simply are destroyed as part of the Inconnu's sinister, hidden plots.

Inconnu who hold the position of Monitor, it should be noted, never take students on the road to Golconda. They have other concerns and duties, and can offer none of what a true seeker after Golconda needs.

Monitors

If a younger Kindred comes in contact with a member of the Inconnu at all (a highly unlikely proposition at best), odds are that the one he meets is a city's Monitor. While the vast majority of Inconnu ensconce themselves in havens far from the hustle and bustle of the cities — not to mention the younger vampires therein — a few members of the sect pick for themselves a certain metropolis and become its Monitor. Birth, breeding and long habit have no bearing on a Monitor's choice of home — the Monitor of Chicago, for example, has spent only a tiny fraction of her unlife in the city. Instead, the selection seems dictated by factors invisible to less experienced observers; panicked rumors lay the blame at the feet of Noddist prophecies, patterns of ley lines, instructions from Caine himself and, most disturbingly, the notion that in places where the Methuselahs sleep, the Inconnu are bound to watch.

Be that as it may, once a Monitor chooses a city she is bound to it for, if not the remainder of her existence, then at least a considerable portion of it. It is her duty to observe all that goes on in that city, the overt as well as the hidden, and more importantly, to *understand* it. So far as anyone (other than the Inconnu know) there is no system whereby a Monitor turns in reports or makes presentations. It is simply the Monitor's duty to know — and somehow, the other Inconnu who need to know what she knows always seem to have that information as well. More than one recently relocated Kindred has found himself confronted with a mysterious stranger who seems to know entirely too much about his past….

In general, Monitors do not ever interfere with the course of events in their cities. There is no oath of noninterference taken, no geas against meddling, but it is understood that Monitors are in place to watch, not to act. Like most customs of the Kindred, this one is honored as much in the breach as in the observance, as many Monitors find themselves irresistibly drawn to interfere in the actions of a younger vampire who reminds them of a lover, a friend, a childe or perhaps even a long-ago version of themselves. Such dalliances are usually brief — no more than three or four decades in duration — and never of the sort to impact directly the greater flow of events in the city. A Monitor may bend her principles to protect a favorite from a random attack by a no-account Caitiff, but rarely will she so much as lift a finger to shelter him from a blood hunt.

INTERACTIONS AND LOCATIONS

Contrary to what one might expect, a Monitor usually has but a single haven from which to observe his charge. A Monitor's haven is usually central to the urban area he is responsible for, and more often than not located beneath some sort of public or historical building — one that is not likely to draw excessive visitors, but which has enough traffic to ensure its continued existence. Any vampire who wanders into a Monitor's home by accident is subtly compelled by a form of Presence (difficulty 10 to resist the suggestion) to exit as quickly as possible, satisfied as to the generally benign and empty nature of the place. That is not to say that Monitors' havens are undefended — most have effective, if not technologically sophisticated, traps and safeguards in serried ranks. Monitors don't, however, have obtrusive or extensive networks of vampiric, ghoul or mortal servants — the whole point of the position, after all, is to watch everyone. What ghouls a Monitor is likely to keep are animal in form, though these creatures are invariably centuries old, supernaturally intelligent and gifted with Disciplines. (See **Ghouls: Fatal Addiction** for more information on animal ghouls.)

Encounters with a Monitor follow only one rule: The Monitor never identifies himself as such. On those exceedingly rare occasions when a Monitor feels he absolutely must talk with a younger Kindred — or is caught socially outside his haven — he creates a false identity, usually that of an anarch or a traveler just passing through the city. The wise Monitor has a whole set

MONITORS OF NOTE

No one is sure precisely how many Monitors there actually are, as only a few have ever revealed themselves. Some of those who have been identified as such are:

• Rebekah, Monitor of Chicago — Rebekah is perhaps the most public of the Monitors, having dabbled repeatedly in Chicago's tumultuous affairs. She makes her haven at the city's aquarium, a locale entirely too accessible to make her sectmates happy.

• Mahatma, Monitor of Istanbul — Of all the Inconnu, Mahatma seems most closely interested in Saulot's many legacies. She speaks fondly of having known Saulot himself, at least in the company of her fellow Inconnu, and has acted on multiple occasions to assist his descendants.

• Maltheas the Ventrue — Maltheas was last seen in attendance at the Convention of Thorns. Since then his whereabouts and even his continued existence are matters of conjecture. The theory in vogue among survivors of that long-ago parley is that Maltheas, rather than Monitoring a single city, casts his unsleeping gaze over the Camarilla itself.

• Dondinni, Monitor of Genoa — Dondinni is among the most active of the Inconnu, fully convinced that Gehenna is imminent and zealously involved in searching for evidence to that effect. The Daughters of Cacophony in particular worry him, and members of that bloodline find his city to be an inhospitable place.

of additional auras (See Auspex, p.84) prepared for such situations, if not a set of new visages (See Obfuscate, p. 91). As it's highly unlikely that *anyone* in a given city is likely to have the power to pierce the powers an Inconnu brings to bear, it's not very hard for a Monitor to wrap himself in protective illusions.

A Monitor interacts with vampires outside of her sect on her terms only. That means she arranges the time and place of the meeting, and then nine times out of 10 sets things up so that the interaction appears coincidental. Most Monitors are plain-spoken; they have no patience for cryptic statements or convoluted riddles. The risk inherent in compromising her observer's position by interacting with the ones she is observing is too great; a Monitor has no interest in being Delphically obtuse. Centuries of observation have taught the Inconnu that plain information travels the best and with the least misinterpretation. No Monitor wants to risk coming out of hiding, only to have the ancilla she speaks to completely miss the point of what she was trying to say.

DISTRIBUTION

Not every city has a Monitor. Truth be told, precious few do, and those metropolitan areas blessed (or cursed) with such tend to be hotbeds of all sorts of vampiric activity. Once a Monitor chooses a locale to settle in, she stays there — forever. There are no vacations, no nights away; everything that goes on must be observed. There is also only one Monitor per city. While Monitors-in-place don't go out of their way to advertise their presence, they do subtly and psychically encourage other would-be observers to go elsewhere. No one, not even the Inconnu, know exactly which cities hold Monitors and how long those Kindred have

STORYTELLING WITH THE INCONNU

While it may be tempting to drop one or two Methuselahs into your chronicle, just to show uppity ancillae exactly how steep the World of Darkness' power curve really is, a wise Storyteller refrains from doing so. Familiarity breeds contempt, and the more times characters see a member of the Inconnu, the more the awe he should inspires diminishes. Once a band of neonates — or even ancillae or elders — gets chummy with a member of the Inconnu, there's no way to resurrect the impact this incredibly old, incredibly powerful and incredibly alien creature should have. Appearances by Inconnu should be rare, brief and telling — only matters of the gravest import should be able to coax one of these vampiric recluses out of hiding.

A better tack to take is to hint at Inconnu interest or interference — a shadowy observer here, an anonymous message there and above all an ominous sense of being observed. Above all, the sense of mystery the Inconnu project must be maintained, else they become just another set of powerful vampires/antagonists/mentors/whatever. Remember: The Inconnu have baffled the Camarilla for five centuries and more. They should be able to hold your players back from their secrets as well.

been in place; Mahatma of Istanbul is reasonably certain she has the longest tenure among current Monitors, but then reflects that in her youth she felt somehow discouraged from the idea of taking up residence in at least three other cities.

GHOULS

My master loves me.

I know this because he gives me his blood. He doles it out slowly, drop by drop, and he tells me to stand absolutely still while it drips on my tongue like liquid ecstasy. If I so much as move or make a sound he stops, and it's worse than torture having him take the blood away.

I know he loves me because if he didn't, he wouldn't spend the time to do that for me. He'd just leave a mason jar full of his vitae in the refrigerator, like he does for the other ghouls. I don't like them. They all think the master loves them as much as he loves me, and he doesn't. It makes me angry, their thinking they can come between me and him. I'm the one whom he trusts to spy on his enemies, I'm the one he feeds from when he can't risk going outside, I'm the one he trusts. They're just servants. I'm something more.

He loves me, you see. And that's why, in the end, he'll forgive me when he sees what I've done to make sure that no one comes between us.

Ever.

One of the fundamental differences between the Camarilla and the Sabbat is the former's policy of working, whenever possible, through mortals instead of running roughshod over them. A literal manifestation of that willingness to work with mortals is the Camarilla's reliance upon the half-human class of creatures called ghouls. Whereas the Sabbat (save the tradition-minded Tzimisce) shun and despise ghouls, the Camarilla regards them as vital cogs in the sect's machinery. Without the still-living ghouls, who would oversee the Masquerade in the daylight hours? Who would take care of the thousand dangling details that plague a vampire's existence? And who would move against the sect's enemies, external and internal, during those hours when all Kindred sleep, if not for the ghouls?

In truth, ghouls are integral to the Camarilla's existence and function. All of the grandiose plans laid by elders depend on a hundred small tasks being done properly — tasks that are inevitably entrusted to ghouls. Maintaining the Masquerade would also be impossible without ghoul assistance. The dozens of tiny tears that the fabric of the deception develops each year are best and most subtly stitched up from within the mortal community; a ghouled police captain or newspaper editor can repair a breach of the Masquerade reflexively, without fear of engendering further incidents. They *are* only human, after all.

WHAT IS A GHOUL?

In brief, a ghoul is a mortal being who has ingested Kindred vitae. While the term "ghoul" usually refers to a human being, animals of any sort can be ghouled (witness the horrific swarms of ghouled mosquitoes and flies hovering around the average Nosferatu). Odds are, however, that if someone uses the term "ghoul" she means a human being — more or less.

There are many benefits to becoming a ghoul — retarded aging; increased strength, speed and stamina; inhumanly fast healing and on occasion, the chance to learn some basic vampiric Disciplines. The deal does have its down side, however — part and parcel with a ghoul's abilities comes a slavering addiction to vitae, the likelihood of being blood bound and the fact that by becoming ghouled, a mortal takes an irrevocable half-step into the world of the Camarilla. There is no turning back once that first sip of vitae goes down; at that point the ghoul becomes a walking, talking violation of the Masquerade. The only two options are to go forward in hopes of the Embrace or to remain still, as a ghoul. To go back is to invite death in the name of protecting the Masquerade.

For more information on the powers, flaws and other foibles of ghouls, see **Ghouls: Fatal Addiction**.

SELECTING THE VICTIM

The Traditions prevent a Camarilla vampire from vigorously Embracing anyone she feels like, but that still leaves the question of how a law-abiding vampire can exert her influence on the mortal institutions that interest her. The best solution to this quandary is through judicious and appropriate ghouling. Camarilla vampires are prevented by custom, peer pressure and occasional princely fiat from creating too many ghouls — there are only so many worthwhile mortals to go around, after all — so they have to make the ones they pick count. Competition for prize humans has gotten so fierce in

TOO MANY GHOULS

While the limits on creating ghouls are not quite as strict for Camarilla vampires as are the limitations on bestowing the Embrace, there's still a common sense factor involved. Maintaining a ghoul takes blood. Maintaining a lot of ghouls takes a lot of blood. A vampire who surrenders a great deal of blood to ghouls every month needs to feed that much more to make up for the voluntary donations. Additional feedings leads to additional corpses, and more chances to break the Masquerade, and so on…. Most Kindred prefer to keep a few trusted ghouls. It's easier, safer and less wearing that way.

In addition, the wider a Kindred's network of ghouls is, the more suspicion she garners from her peers. A vampire with too many eyes on the street and too many hands to do her bidding is a danger to others of her kind, pure and simple. As a result, there are frequent "prunings" of ambitious Kindred's retainers and the like.

some places that "bag limits" have been imposed (See **A World of Darkness: Second Edition**, p. 16).

There are three factors that determine a mortal's potential for being ghouled: position, talent and availability. The first refers to what exactly the mortal does. Is he a judge who can squash cases that might expose vampiric shenanigans? What about a local sports figure who, by dint of his vitae-given advantages, can improve his team's fortunes and finances (not to mention all

those involved in industries ancillary to the team)? Perhaps a muckraking newspaper reporter can be convinced, after a taste of the vitae, to go dig up someone else's secrets. And so it goes, with the highest placed mortals attracting the most vampiric attention. Oftentimes, a particularly pivotal mortal is left alone by agreement among several vampires who previously competed for his allegiance, the idea being that it is better to have no one control him than to have a rival do so. Not all ghouls are selected for long-term cultivation, either — there are plenty of times when a particular mortal (say, an underdog prize fighter on whom a vampire has bet heavily) is useful *now*, but won't be in six months. Such mortals are ghouled, then thrown away — their position is only of concern for a brief and shining moment.

The second criterion is talent. The Toreador and Ventrue (and on an entirely different level, the Nosferatu) are past masters at spotting the potential in a mortal who has not yet made her name, and plucking that flower for themselves. There are also specific skills — accounting, computer literacy and the intricacies of modern law, just to name three — that many Kindred find beyond their experience, and as such they look to human beings with the skill sets they need to handle those affairs. Such ghouls are often left in place to pursue their normal lives, more or less, and are summoned by their masters only in need or to refresh the blood bond. It makes sense to do it that way, after all — why pay to support a ghoul full-time when he can be at your beck and call 24/7 while still paying his own way?

That being said, there are any number of Kindred who don't want their staff getting too far from them. Ventrue, for example, prefer to have certain ghouls with access to vital financial information kept on a very short leash. Such ghouls "disappear" from the mortal world (often with the able assistance of still other ghouls, who have performed this sort of extraction before) and become immersed in the world of the Camarilla.

The third, and least quantifiable, criterion for a Camarilla vampire ghouling someone is simply opportunity. A Toreador who sees a mortal too beautiful to pass up may ghoul her in lieu of Embracing her; a Nosferatu may ghoul a terminally ill vagrant out of pity and to create a debt of gratitude. Such ghouls rarely stick with their creators long, as the vampires tend to tire of their creations of the moment rather quickly. Even the supposedly civilized vampires of the Camarilla have no qualms about destroying their ghouls if the ghouls provide unsatisfactory service, grow too erratic, seek to escape servitude or simply catch a vampire in a bad mood.

A rare few ghouls are created as a sort of probationary status, to see if they're worthy of the Embrace. Most ghouls think this notion applies to them, that *they're* going to be next to ascend to immortality. The actual percentage of ghouls being groomed for Kindred status is tiny, but the Camarilla allows its servants to hope. It keeps them in line that much more efficiently.

USES AND ABUSES

The Camarilla uses ghouls for a wide variety of tasks, usually those too menial, repetitive or dangerous for the

GHOULS OF CONVENIENCE

Sometimes mortals receive the blood just because it's too annoying to do anything otherwise. The owner and bouncer of a Kindred's favorite club, for example, are prime targets for this sort of thing. The vampire is there five nights a week and has to go through the charade of pretending to be mortal each and every night. Sooner or later, it gets boring and tiresome, and there's always the possibility of a slip. It's much easier just to ghoul both the bouncer and the owner (and maybe a bartender as well, who can then be persuaded to stock suitable refreshment) and sidestep the whole process. Ditto for the human who comes to read the electric meter on the haven and other such routine mortal annoyances. The only hitch with this sort of thing is that there are probably six or seven other vampires who have exactly the same idea, and competition for ghouls, regardless of their utility, can get fatally vicious.

Kindred themselves to attend to. While ghouls of particular expertise or use are handled with kid gloves — no Toreador wants her pet sculptor having a fit of jealous pique with a blowtorch in hand — the ruck and run of the "half-bloods" are treated like the vampiric equivalent of the hired help.

MANUAL LABOR

Just because someone is dead doesn't mean that she doesn't have errands to run and minor details to tend to. While trips to the DMV and the grocery store might be replaced by a run to the hardware store for lightproofing supplies, the principle remains the same. There's too much to do, and only 12 hours a night to do it in. That means that Camarilla vampires need someone to take care of the necessaries, and that someone is inevitably a ghoul. Errand boy is actually a position of more trust than one might think; a ghoul who brings back faulty materials for rendering his mistress' haven lightproof is in a great deal of trouble — assuming his mistress survives the consequences of his mistake. Some particularly cautious Kindred even prefer to have systems of drop-offs and package pickups for their ghouls, thus lessening the chance that an unobservant delivery ghoul might be followed back home.

The Kindred also employ their ghouls for carpentry and construction projects, rather than trust outsiders. It is a far better thing to have your booby-traps and secret chambers constructed by those who love and trust you absolutely. After all, there is no such thing as a truly independent contractor in the World of Darkness.

PERSONAL ATTENDANCE

Toreador aren't the only vain vampires, and it isn't just the Degenerates who have gaggles of ghouls devoted to grooming them. The habit's been picked up by the Ventrue as well, particularly those looking to make a splash before the prince. Ghoulish personal attendants are much-loved, if they do their jobs well. A ghoul who can make a vampire look good and, more importantly, feel good about the way he looks, is an invaluable asset. Some Toreador spend literally hours gazing at their own reflections as their favorite ghouls pamper and preen them, lost in the ever-lovelier vision of themselves. Ghouls of this sort often travel with their regnants as well, tending to the slightest displaced tress or misplaced fold of cloth, and a vampire thus attended will make a tremendous production out of the fact that she is being tended so completely. Pity, then, the ghoul who doesn't quite measure up to her mistress' grooming standards….

Extra Eyes

No one can be two places at once, though some elders may give the idea their very best effort. Ghouls, on the other hand, can serve as a vampire's eyes-on-the-ground. A few loyal ghouls scattered throughout a city can pick up an awful lot of information during the course of a single day, then distill that knowledge for their regnant's benefit. Nosferatu and, surprisingly, Toreador love to set their ghouls up as living security cameras. Such ghouls can go weeks or even years before being called on to report, but in the meantime they are still out there, constantly watching.

Procurement

Many of the vampires of the Camarilla enjoy the very process of the Hunt — the chase, the subtlety, the sheer artistry of it and finally, the taste of vitae flavored with fear or arousal. Then there are those Kindred who, for whatever reason — a lack of skill at covering up, a nasty habit of frenzying or even just the press of the schedule — honestly don't have the inclination to go stalking the rain-slicked streets in search of sustenance. They'd rather order takeout, as it were. That's where the ghouls come in.

Doing procurement work for a Kindred is a dangerous and dirty job. It is no less than the kidnapping of human beings on a regular basis, and in all probability acting as the accessory to a great many murders as well. To be trusted to bring home supper for one's regnant means that a ghoul has nerves of steel and very little that is human left to him — in addition to whatever skills are required for the pickups. Ventrue in particular like to give this chore to their most trusted ghouls, saving them the trouble of having to hunt in accordance with their prey exclusion. A ghoul who's trained to bring home the right sort of bacon can save a busy Ventrue many precious hours, and may well be rewarded for such.

However, it is not lost on the Kindred that ghouls who go out hunting for them are honing the skills that might someday allow those ghouls to hunt the Kindred themselves. Any vampire who lets his ghouls hunt for him is constantly trapped between the necessity of having competent help and the danger that too-competent help represents.

Wetwork and Dirty Deeds

The vampires of the Camarilla don't like to risk their immortal necks, which means when there's a possibility that they'll get hurt, they try to send in the ghouls instead. The philosophy isn't quite as callous as it seems; a trained group of ghouls should be able to handle any mortal threat and a fair number of supernatural ones as well. A single ghoul may or may not be the equal of a vampire (though in a tussle between an experienced ghoul and a neonate, it pays to put your money on the mortal), but four heavily armed and practiced ghouls can extract a troublesome anarch from a crowded restaurant with a minimum of mess and bloodshed. Ghouls also make the perfect agents for more stereotypical intimidation techniques, as well as for taking out unsuspecting hunters. The average field Inquisitor isn't necessarily looking for an enemy who breathes, after all.

When wartime comes, however, things get more serious. The Sabbat's great advantage is in the sheer number of vampires they can bring to the fight; ghouls are the Camarilla's only hope of countering that weapon. Hopefully, the number of mortals the Camarilla throws into the line can stem the assault's tide, buying the Kindred the time they need to mount their other defenses. On a more macabre note, if the worst happens, dead ghouls in the street are much less of a threat to the Masquerade than dead neonates. Even in defeat, the Traditions must be observed.

Ghouls offer the Camarilla another, decided advantage on the attack: The ability to move and fight during daylight. When the Camarilla decides it's time for a counterstrike, it's ghouls who go in under the cover of sunlight. If the assault goes well, the ghouls catch their opponents at their sluggish worst, and an entire war party can be cleaned out in a matter of bare minutes.

For more on the Camarilla's strategies and tactics, see p. 118.

Holding To One's Place

Invaluable yet inferior — that dichotomy sums up ghouls' place in the Camarilla. The sect would crumble literally overnight were it to be deprived of its half-human servants, but the fact remains that they are servants — lesser beings by definition and by blood. Ghouls have no rights under the Camarilla save what their regnants choose to grant them, and the right of destruction can be invoked at any time.

Thus begins an intricate dance of status and favor. In theory, a ghoul has no place and no standing within the sect, but the trusted and ancient ghoul of an elder may well carry more weight in council than a blood-on-the-chin ranting neonate. Complicating matters is the fact that most ghouls are indeed blood bound to their masters, and get both enthusiastic and inventive in those masters' defense. Such zealotry often pits ghouls against other Kindred who pose a threat to their masters, and can lead to embarrassing moments for the vampires in question. The choice between setting the precedent of allowing a ghoul to attack a Kindred and get away with it, or sacrificing a favorite ghoul to appease a hated rival is a particularly unappealing one.

In the end, ghouls are held to a double standard — despised as a class but valued individually. No vampire — and no ghoul — should ever forget it. The consequences of a poor memory, on anyone's part, are invariably both fatal and brief.

INDEX